KEITH LAUMER

ODYSSEY

Edited and Compiled by Eric Flint
Introduction by David Weber

"Unrivalled, not only
in its class, but in a
class by itself."
—Gordon R. Dickson

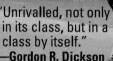

BAEN

$6.99 U.S.
$9.99 CAN.

ISBN 0-7434-3527-3

EAN

DÉJÀ VU ALL OVER AGAIN...

To the untrained eye, a Class-One Karg robot—the only kind ever used in Timesweep work—was undistinguishable from any other citizen. But my eye wasn't untrained. He was the same Karg I'd left in the hotel room back in 1936 with a soft-nosed slug in his head. Now here he was, with no hole in his head, climbing down onto the deck of the ship as neat and cool as if it had all been in fun. I hugged the deck and tried to look *hors de combat*.

I was just beginning to form a hopeless plan for creeping out of sight when the door I was lying against opened. Tried to open, that is. I was blocking it. Somebody inside gave it a hearty shove and started through.

The Karg's head had turned at the first sound. He whipped up a handsome pearl-mounted, wheel-lock pistol. The explosion was like a bomb. I heard the slug hit; a solid, meaty smack, like a well-hit ball hitting the fielder's glove. The fellow in the door plunged through and went down hard on his face.

The Karg turned back to his men and rapped out an order. The Karg was by the weather rail, calmly stripping the safety foil from a thermex bomb. He dropped it through the open hatch, then scrambled with commendable agility back to his ship. Quite suddenly I was alone, watching the attacking ship recede downwind under full sail.

Smoke billowed from the hatch, with tongues of pale flame in close pursuit. I got a pair of legs under me. A gun lay a yard from the empty hand of the man the Karg had shot. It was a .01 microjet of Nexx manufacture, with a grip that fitted my hand perfectly.

It ought to. It was my gun. I didn't like doing it, but I turned the body over and looked at the face.

It was my face.

(from *Dinosaur Beach*)

BAEN BOOKS by KEITH LAUMER

Retief!
Odyssey

KEITH LAUMER

ODYSSEY

edited & compiled by
ERIC FLINT

ODYSSEY

This is a work of fiction. All the characters and events portrayed in this book are fictional, and any resemblance to real people or incidents is purely coincidental.

Galactic Odyssey (aka *Spaceman!*) was first serialized in *IF* magazine (May–July, 1967) and first published in novel form by Berkley in 1967. "A Trip to the City" (aka "It Could Be Anything") was first published in *Amazing*, January 1963. "Hybrid" was first published in *The Magazine of F&SF* in November 1961. "Combat Unit" (aka "Dinochrome") was first published in *The Magazine of F&SF* in November 1960. "The King of the City" was first published in *Galaxy* in August 1961. "Once There Was a Giant" was first published in *The Magazine of F&SF* in November 1968. *Dinosaur Beach* was first published by Scribner's in 1971.

A Baen Books Original

Baen Publishing Enterprises
P.O. Box 1403
Riverdale, NY 10471
www.baen.com

ISBN: 0-7434-3527-3

Cover art by Richard Martin

First printing, March 2002

Distributed by Simon & Schuster
1230 Avenue of the Americas
New York, NY 10020

Production by Windhaven Press, Auburn, NH
Printed in the United States of America

Contents

PREFACE

Discerning people have always read Keith Laumer for a lot of reasons, and I am delighted that Baen Books is making his works available to be read yet again.

As David Drake pointed out in the preface to the first volume in this series, those with some knowledge of Laumer's life (and of history) can appreciate the telling accuracy of his trenchant, experience-based observations of the lunacies of real-world diplomacy in the Retief novels. Regarded by many, perhaps even most, of his readers as the crown jewels of his literary legacy, the Retief stories used frequently devastating humor to underscore the not particularly humorous dilemma of a tough-minded, principled pragmatist trapped on the far side of the Looking Glass. And as the best satire always is, they were teaching tools, as well.

Along with the humor, however, Retief communicated something else which was common to all of Laumer's

1

work. In addition to his highly capable pragmatism, his realism, or even his occasional cynicism, Retief, like Poul Anderson's Flandry, embodied the other qualities which Laumer obviously believed were the true measure of a human being: self-reliance, unswerving devotion to one's principles (however unfashionable those principles might be, or however uncomfortable one might be admitting that one held them), and gallantry. Always gallantry.

Something which is overlooked almost as often as the sheer scope of Laumer's work, is the spare, clean prose style and muscular storytelling technique which he shared with those other high prophets of human capability, H. Beam Piper and Robert Heinlein. There was a seeming simplicity to the way he wove his tales, coupled with a very real, often first-person colloquialism, which both moved events rapidly and deceived the eye into missing the complexity of what he had to tell us. Characterization in a Laumer story flows so simply and so naturally that its depths creep up upon us almost unnoticed. Yet it is the vibrancy of the characters which truly holds us, and when the final word is read, the reader comes away with both a sense of completion and a desire for the tale to go on . . . forever, if possible.

In my own opinion, that result stems not simply, or even primarily, from his undoubted skill as a literary craftsman so much as from his ability to touch the innermost chords of what makes all of us human. Whether it's Retief's biting wit, or Billy Danger's unwavering determination, or the unbreakable gallantry of his Bolos, Laumer's characters not only live and breathe but challenge. He was capable of bleakness and the recognition that triumph was not inevitable, however great one's determination might be, or that power could seduce even the most selfless, as in the case of Steve Dravek in "The Day Before Forever" or the protagonist of the chilling little gem "Test to Destruction" (which is one of my favorite Laumer pieces, despite its darkness). Yet in an era of cynicism and "enlightened" distrust of and even contempt for heroic virtues, Laumer's characters went about the day-to-day business of living up to those virtues with absolutely no sense that doing so made them special in any way. It was simply what responsible human beings did, and the profound simplicity of that concept made Laumer, like Piper, an author who was in many ways an uncomfortable fit in the America of the 1960s and 1970s. Perhaps that's one reason Retief tended to overshadow other works of his, like *Galactic Odyssey*, *A Plague of Demons*, "The Night of the Trolls," *Planet Run*, and other stories and novels too numerous to mention. Humor and satire were more acceptable techniques for sliding the author's sometimes discomforting precepts into the reader's consciousness, especially when they were wielded so deftly. Yet the very qualities which made Laumer's other characters misfits at the time he wrote are the same qualities which give them their classic timelessness.

At the end of the day, fate hit Keith Laumer with failing health that was a particularly savage blow to a man who had always celebrated human capability and the ability to triumph over seemingly unbeatable odds. It was a final battle which he did not win, yet in its own way, and for all the bitter irony it must have held for the teller of such tales, it could diminish neither the message nor the messenger, because the true essence of the tales Laumer told were actually less about triumph, in the end, than they were about an individual's ironclad responsibility to try. Like his Bolos, or the protagonist of *A Plague of Demons*, who chose to fight his hopeless battle to the death rather than permit his friend to die alone, Keith Laumer believed that the ability to confront challenges and adversities, however extreme and however remote the chance of final victory, were the ultimate measure of a human being. I suppose that's the reason I consider him to have been one of the three or four authors who had the greatest influence upon me throughout my life, as both a reader and a writer.

And it's also the reason that the title of one of the stories in this volume strikes me as a most fitting epitaph for him, because it's true.

"Once There Was a Giant."

David Weber
September, 2001

GALACTIC ODYSSEY

CHAPTER ONE

I remember hearing somewhere that freezing to death is an easy way to go; but the guy that said that never tried it. I'd found myself a little hollow where a falling-down stone wall met a dirt-bank, and hunkered down in it; but the wall wasn't high enough to keep the wind off or stop the sleet from hitting my neck like buckshot and running down cold under my collar. There were some moldy leaves drifted there, and I used the last of my lighter fluid trying to get a little blaze going, but that turned out like everything else I'd tried lately: a fizzle. One thing about it: My feet were so numb from the cold I couldn't feel the blisters from the eighteen miles I'd hiked since my last ride dumped me at a crossroads, just before dawn.

I had my collar turned up, for what good that might do, which wasn't much; the coat felt like wet newspaper. Both elbows were out of it, and two of the buttons were gone. Funny; three weeks ago it had been decent-looking enough to walk into a second-class restaurant in without attracting more than the usual quota of hostile stares. Three weeks: That's all it took to slide from a shaky toehold in the economic cycle all the way to the bottom. I'd heard of hitting the skids, but I never knew before just what it meant. Once you go over that invisible edge, it's downhill all the way.

It had been almost a year since I'd quit school, when Uncle Jason died. What money I had went for the cheapest funeral the little man with the sweet, sad smile could bear to talk about. After that, I'd held a couple of jobs that had wafted away like the morning mist as soon as the three months "tryout" was over and the question of regular wages came up. There'd been a few months of scrounging, then; mowing lawns, running errands, one-day stands as a carpenter's helper or assistant busboy while the regular man was off. I'd tried to keep up appearances, enough not to scare off any prospective employers, but the money barely stretched to cover food and what the sign said was a clean bed. Then one day I'd showed up looking just a little too thin, a little too hungry, the collar just a little too frayed.

And now I was here, with my stomach making whimpering sounds to remind me of all the meals it hadn't had lately, as far as ever from where I was headed—wherever that was. I didn't really have a destination. I just wanted to be where I wasn't.

And I couldn't stay here. The wall was worse than no protection at all, and the wind was blowing colder and wetter all the time. I crawled out and made it back up the slope to the road. There were no headlights in sight; it wouldn't have helped if there were. Nobody was going to stop in a sleetstorm in the middle of nowhere to give a lift to a hobo like me. I didn't have any little sign to hold up, stating that I was a hardship case, that comfortable middle-class conformity was my true vocation, that I was an honest young fellow with a year of college who'd had a little hard luck lately;

all I had were the clothes I stood in, a bad cough, and a deep conviction that if I didn't get out of the weather, fast, by morning I'd be one of those dead-of-exposure cases they're always finding in alleys back of cut-rate liquor stores.

I put my back to the wind and started off, hobbling on a couple of legs that ended somewhere below the knee. I didn't notice feeling tired anymore, or hungry; I was just a machine somebody had left running. All I could do was keep putting one foot in front of the other until I ran down.

2

I saw the light when I came up over a rise, just a weak little spark, glowing a long way off in the big dark beyond the trees. I turned and started off across the open field toward it.

Ten minutes later, I came up behind a big swaybacked barn with a new-looking silo beside it and a rambling two story house beyond. The light was shining from a ground-floor window. There was a pickup parked in the side yard near the barn, and a late-model Cadillac convertible, with the top down. Just looking at it made me ten degrees colder. I didn't have any idea of knocking on the door, introducing myself: "Billy Danger, sir. May I step inside and curl up in front of the fire?"—and being invited to belly up to a chicken dinner. But there was the barn; and where there were barns, there was hay; and where there was hay, a man could snuggle down and sleep, if not warm, at least not out in the freezing rain. It was worth a try.

The barn door looked easy enough: just warped boards hanging on big rusted-out hinges; but when I tried it, nothing budged. I looked closer, and saw that the hinges weren't rotted after all; they were just made to look that way. I picked at a flake of paint on the door; there was bright metal underneath. That was kind of strange, but all it meant to me then was that I wouldn't be crawling into that haystack after all.

The sleet was coming down thicker than ever now. I put my nose up and sniffed, caught a whiff of frying bacon and coffee that made my jaws ache. All of a sudden, my stomach remembered its complaint and tried to tie itself into a hard knot. I went back through tall weeds past some rusty iron that used to be farm machinery, and across a rutted drive toward the silo. I didn't know much about silos except that they were where you stored the corn, but at least it had walls and a roof. If I could get in there, I might find a dry spot to hide in. I reached a door set in the curved wall; it opened and I slid inside, into dim light and a flow of warm air.

Across the room, there was an inner door standing open, and I could see steps going up: glass steps on chrome-plated rails. The soft light and the warm air were coming from there. I went up, moving on instinct, like the first fish crawling out on land, reached the top and was in a room full of pipes and tubes and machinery and a smell like the inside of a TX set. Weary as I was, this didn't look like a place to curl up in.

I made it up another turn of the spiral stair, came out in a space where big shapes like cotton bales were stacked, with dark spaces between them. There was a smell like a fresh-tarred road here. I groped toward the deepest shadow I could find, and my hand touched something soft. In the faint light from the stairwell it looked like mink or sable, except that it was an electric-blue color. I didn't let that worry me. I crawled up on top of the stack and put my face down in the velvety fluff and let all the strings break at once.

3

In the dream, I was a burglar, holed up in somebody else's house, hiding in the closet, and in a minute they'd find me and haul me out and ride me into town in a police car to sit under the lights and answer questions about every unsolved chicken-stealing in the county in the past five years. The feet were coming up the stairs, coming closer. Somebody said something and a woman's voice answered in a foreign language. They went away and the dream faded. . . .

. . . And then the noise started.

It was a thin, high-pitched shrilling, like one of those whistles you call the dog with. It went right between my bones and pried at the joints. It got louder, and angrier, like bees boiling out of a hive, and I was awake now, and trying to get up; but a big hand came down and mashed me flat. I tried to get enough breath in to yell, but the air had turned to syrup. I just had time to remember the day back in Pineville when the Chevy rolled off the rack at Uncle Jason's gas station and pinned a man under the back bumper. Then it all went red and I was someplace else, going over Niagara Falls in a big rubber balloon, wearing a cement life jacket, while thousands cheered.

4

When I woke up, I heard voices.

". . . talking rot now. It's nothing to do with me." This was a man's voice, speaking with an English accent. He sounded as if he were a little amused by something.

"I mark well t'was thee I charged with the integrity

o' the vessel!" This one sounded big, and mad. He had a strange way of talking, but I could understand most of the words all right. Then a girl spoke, but in another language. She had a nice, clear, sweet voice. She sounded worried.

"No harm done, Desroy." The first man gave a soft laugh. "And it might be a spot of good luck, at that. Perhaps he'll make a replacement for Jongo."

"I don't omit thy ill-placed japery, Orfeo! Rid me this urchin, ere you vex me out of all humor!"

"A bit of a sticky wicket, that, old boy. He's still alive, you know. If I nurse him along—"

"How say you? What stuff is this! Art thou the parish comfort, to wax chirurgeonly o'er this whelp?"

"If he can be trained—"

"You o'ertax my patience, Orfeo! I'd make a chough of as deep chat!"

"He'll make a gun-boy, mark my words."

"Bah! You more invest the misadventure than a marketplace trinket chafferer! In any case, the imp's beyond recovery!"

Part of me wanted to just skip over this part of the dream and sink back down into the big, soft black that was waiting for me, but a little voice somewhere back behind my eyes was telling me to do something, fast, before bad things happened. I made a big effort and got one eyelid open. Everything looked red and hazy. The three of them were standing ten feet away, near the door. The one with the funny way of speaking was big, built solid as a line-backer, with slicked-back black hair and a little moustache. He wore a loose jacket covered with pockets; he looked like Clark Gable playing Frank Buck.

The other man was not much older than me; he had a rugged jawline, a short nose, curly reddish-brown hair, wide shoulders, slim hips in a form-fitting gray coverall. He was pretty enough to be a TV intern.

The girl . . . I had to stop and get the other eyelid up. No girl could be that pretty. She had jet black hair and smoky gray eyes big enough to go wading in; an oval face, mellow ivory-colored skin, features like one of those old statues. She was wearing a white cover-all, and the form it fit was enough to break your heart.

I made a move to sit up and pain broke over me like a wave. It seemed to be coming mostly from my left arm. I took hold of the wrist with my other hand and got up on one elbow with no more effort than it takes to swing a safe in your teeth.

Nobody seemed to notice; when the whirly lights settled down, they were still standing there, still arguing.

" . . . a spot of bother, Desroy, but it's worth a go."

"Methinks sloth instructs thee, naught else!" The big fellow turned and stamped off. The young fellow grinned at the girl.

"Just twisting the old boy's tail. Actually, he's right. You nip off and soothe him down a bit. I'll attend to this."

I slid over the edge of my nest and kind of fell to the floor. At the noise, they both whirled on me. I got hold of the floor and swung it around under me.

"I just came in to get out of the weather," I meant to say, but it came out as a sort of gargly sound. The man took a quick step toward me and over his shoulder said, "Pop off now, Milady." He had a hand on a thing clipped to his belt. I didn't need a set of technical specifications to tell me it was some kind of gun. The girl moved up quickly and put her hand on his arm.

"Orfeo—the poor creature suffers!" She spoke English with an accent that made it sound like music.

He moved her around behind him. "He might be dangerous. Now do be a good child and toddle off."

"I'm . . . not dangerous," I managed to get the words out. The smile was less successful. I felt sick. But I wasn't going to come unfed in front of *her*. I got my back against the pile of furs and tried to stand up straight.

"So you can talk," the man said. He was frowning at me. "Damn me if I know what to do with you." He seemed to be talking to himself.

"Just . . . let me rest a few minutes . . . and I'll be on my way . . ." I could hear my pulse thudding in my ears like bongo drums.

"Why did you come aboard?" The man snapped the question at me. "What did you think you'd find here?"

"I was cold," I said. "It was warm here—"

He snorted. "Letting yourself in for a devilish change of scene, weren't you?"

His first words were beginning to filter through. "What is this place?" I asked him.

"You're aboard Lord Desroy's yacht. He's not keen on contraband holed up in the aft lazaret—"

"A boat?" I felt I'd missed something somewhere. The last I remembered was a farmhouse, in the middle of nowhere. "You must be fooling me." I tried to show him a smile to let him know I got the joke. "I don't feel any waves."

"She's a converted ketch, stressed-field primaries, ion-pulse auxiliaries, fitted with full antiac and variable G gear, four years out of Zeridajh on a private expedition. Every square inch of her is allocated to items in specific support of her mission in life, which brings us back to you. What's your name?" He asked that last in a businesslike tone.

"Billy Danger. I don't understand all that about a catch . . ."

"Just think of her as a small spaceship." He sounded impatient. "Now, Billy Danger, it's up to me to—"

"Spaceship? You mean like they shoot astronauts off in?"

Orfeo laughed. "Astronauts, eh? Couple of natives paddling about the shallows in a dugout canoe. No, Billy Danger, this is a deep-space yacht, capable of cruising for many centuries at multiple-light velocities. At the moment, she's on course for a world very distant from your native Earth."

"Walt a minute," I said; I wanted everything to slow down for just a second while I got caught up with it. "I don't want to go to any star. I just want out of here." I tried a step and had to lean against the bale beside me. "Just let me off, and I'll disappear so quick you'll think you dreamed me——"

"I'm afraid that's not practical." Orfeo cut me off short. "Now you're here, the question is what to do with you. As you doubtless heard, Lord Desroy's in favor of putting you out the lock. As for myself, I have hopes of making use of you. Know anything about weapons? Hunted much?"

"Just let me off," I said. "Anywhere at all. I'll walk home."

"You must answer my questions promptly, Billy Danger! What becomes of you depends on how well you answer them."

"I never hunted," I said. My breath was short, as if I'd run a long way.

"That's all right. Nothing to unlearn. How old are you?"

"Nineteen, next April."

"Amazing. You look younger. Are you quick to learn, Billy Danger?"

"It's kidnaping," I said. "You can't just kidnap a man. There's laws——"

"Mind your tongue, Billy Danger! I'll tolerate no insolence, you'd best understand that at the outset! As for law, Lord Desroy makes the law here. This is his vessel; with the exception of the Lady Raire and myself, he owns every atom aboard her, including stowaways."

A sudden thought occurred to me, like an icepick through the heart. "You're not . . . Earthmen, are you?"

"Happily, no."

"But you look human; you speak English."

"Of course we're human; much older stock than your own unfortunate branch. We've spent a year on your drab little world, going after walrus, elephant, that sort of thing. Now, that's enough chatter, Billy Danger. Do you think you can learn to be a proper gunbearer?"

"How long—before we go back?"

"To Earth? Never, I trust. Now, see here! Don't fret about matters out of your control! Your job is to keep me happy with you. If you can do that, you'll stay alive and well. If not . . ." He let the rest hang. "But then, I'm sure you'll try your best, eh, Billy Danger?"

It was crazy, but the way he said it, I believed every word of it. The thing I had to do right now was stay alive. Then, later, I could worry about getting home.

"Sure," I said. "I'll try."

"Right. That's settled, then." Orfeo looked relieved, as if he'd just found an excuse to put off a mean chore. "You were lucky, you know. You took eight gravities, unprotected. A wonder you didn't break a few bones."

I was still holding my left arm by the wrist; I eased it around front, and felt the sharp point poking out through my sleeve.

"Who said I didn't?" I asked him, and felt myself folding like a windblown newspaper.

CHAPTER TWO

I woke up feeling different. At first, I couldn't quite dope out what it was; then I got it: I was clean, fresh-shaved, sweet-smelling, tucked in between sheets as crisp as new dollar bills. And I felt good; I tingled all over, as if I'd just had a needle shower and a rub-down.

The room I was in was a little low-ceilinged cubbyhole with nothing much in it but the pallet I was lying on. I remembered the arm then, and pulled back a loose yellow sleeve somebody had put on me. Outside of a little swelling and a bright pink scar under a clear plastic patch, it was as good as new.

Something clicked and a little door in the wall slid back. The man named Orfeo stuck his head in.

"Good; you're awake. About time. I'm about to field-strip the Z-guns. You'll watch."

I got up and discovered that my knees didn't wobble anymore. I felt strong enough to run up a wall. And hungry. Just thinking about ham and eggs made my jaws ache. Orfeo tossed me a set of yellow coveralls from a closet back of a sliding panel.

"Try these; I cut them down from Jongo's old cape."

I pulled them on. The cloth was tough and light and smooth as glove silk.

"How are you feeling?" Orfeo was looking me up and down.

"Fine," I said. "How long did I sleep?"

"Ninety-six hours. I doped you up a bit."

I ran a finger over my new scar. "I don't understand about the arm. I remember it as being broken; broken bad—"

"A hunter has to know a little field medicine," he said. "While I was about it, I gave you a good worming and balanced up your body chemistry." He shook his head. "Bloody wonder you could walk, the rot that boiled out of you. Bloody microbe culture. How's your vision?"

I blinked at the wall. If there'd been a fly there, I could have counted his whiskers. "Good," I said. "Better than it's ever been."

"Well, you're no good to me sick," he said, as if he had to apologize.

"Thanks," I said. "For the arm, and the bath and the pretty yellow pajamas, too."

"Don't thank me. The Lady Raire took care of that part."

"You mean . . . the girl?"

"She's the Lady Raire, Jongo! And I'm Sir Orfeo. As for the wash-up and the kit, someone had to do it. You stank to high heaven. Now come along. We've a great deal to cover if you're to be of any use to me on the hunt."

2

The armory was a small room lined with racks full of guns that weren't like any guns I'd ever seen before. There were handguns, rifles, rocket-throwers, some with short barrels, some with just a bundle of glass rods, some with fancy telescopic sights, one that looked like a flare pistol with a red glass thermometer on the side; and there were a few big elephant guns of Earth manufacture. The whole room glittered like Tiffany's front window. I ran a finger along a stock made of polished purple wood, with fittings that looked like solid gold. "It looks like Mister Desroy goes first class."

"Keep your hands off the weapons until you know how to service them." Sir Orfeo poked buttons and a table tilted up out of the floor and a section of ceiling over it glared up brighter than before. He flipped a switch and the lock-bar on a rack snapped up, and he lifted out a heavy-looking, black-stocked item with a drum magazine and three triggers and a flared shoulder plate, chrome-plated.

"This is a Z-gun," he said. "It's a handy all-round piece, packs 0.8 megaton/seconds of firepower, weight four pounds three ounces." He snapped a switch on the side back and forth a couple of times and handed the gun across to me.

"What's a megaton/second?" I asked him.

"Enough power to vaporize the yacht if it were released at one burst. At full gain the Z-gun will punch a three-millimeter hole through an inch of flint steel at a range of five miles with a five millisecond burst." He went on to tell me a lot more about Z-guns, crater-rifles, infinite repeaters, filament pistols.

At the end of it I didn't know much more about the weapons Lord Desroy would be using on his hunt, but I was feeling sorry for whatever it was he was after.

3

Sir Orfeo took me back to the little room I'd waked up in, showed me how to work a gadget that delivered a little can of pink oatmeal, steaming hot. I sniffed it; it smelled like seaweed. I tasted it. It was flat and insipid, like papier-mâché.

"Sir Orfeo, I hate to complain about a free gift," I said. "But are you sure this was meant for a man to eat?"

"Jongo wasn't a man."

I kind of goggled at him. "What was he?"

"A Lithian. Very good boy, Jongo. With me for a long time." He glanced around the room. "Damned if it doesn't give me a touch of something-or-other to see you in his kennel."

"Kennel?"

"Nest, pitch, call it cabin if you like." Sir Orfeo beetled a fine eyebrow at me. "Don't be putting on airs, Billy Danger. I've no patience with it."

He left me there to dine in solitude. Afterward, he gave me a tour of the ship. He was showing me a fancy leather-and-inlay lounge when Lord Desroy came in.

"Ah, there you are, Desroy," Orfeo said in a breezy way. "Just occurred to me you might like to have Jongo—ah, Billy Danger, that is—do a bit of a dust-up here in the lounge—"

"How now? Hast lost thy wits, Orfeo? Hie the mooncalf hence i' the instant!"

"Steady on, Desroy. Just thought I'd ask—"

"I've a whim to chide the varlet for his impertinence!" the big boss barked and took a step toward me. Orfeo pushed me behind him.

"Don't blame the boy. My doing, you know," he said in a nice cool tone.

"Thy role of advocate for this scurvy patch would want credit, an' I stood not witness on't!"

We went on down the stairs. Instead of looking mad, Sir Orfeo was smiling and humming between his teeth. He dropped the smile when he saw me looking at him.

"I advise you to stay out of Lord Desroy's way, Jongo. For now, he's willing to humor me along; I have a carefully nurtured reputation for temperament, you see. If I get upset, the game might turn out to be scarce. But if you ruffle his feathers by being underfoot, he might act hastily."

"He has a strange way of talking," I said. "What kind of accent is that?"

"Eh? Oh, it's a somewhat archaic dialect of English. Been some three hundred years since his lordship last visited Earth. Now, that's enough gossip, Jongo—"

"It's Billy Dan—"

"I'll call you Jongo. Shorter. Now let's get along to Hold F and you can earn your keep by polishing a spot of brightwork in Environmental."

The polishing turned out to be a job of scraping slimy deposits off the valves and piping. Sir Orfeo left me to it while he went back up and joined in whatever they were doing on the other side of the forbidden door.

4

One day Sir Orfeo showed me a star chart and pointed out the relative locations of Earth, Gar 28, the world we were headed for at the moment, and Zeridajh, far in toward the big gob of stars at the center of the Galaxy.

"We'll never get there," I said. "I read somewhere it takes light a hundred thousand years to cross the Galaxy; Gar 28 must be about ten light-years away; and Zeridajh is thousands!"

He laughed. "The limiting velocity of light is a myth, Jongo," he said. "Like the edge of the world your early sailors were afraid they'd fall over—or the sound barrier you used to worry about. This vessel could reach Zeridajh in eighteen months, if she stretched her legs."

I wanted to ask him why Lord Desroy picked such a distant part of the sky to go hunting in, but I'd learned not to be nosy. Whatever the reasons were, they were somebody's secret.

After my first few weeks away from all time indicators, I began to develop my own internal time-sense, independent of the three-hour cycles that were the Galactic shipboard standard. I could sense when an hour had passed, and looking back, I knew, without knowing how I knew, just about how long I'd been away from Earth. I might have been wrong—there was no way to check—but the sense was very definite, and always consistent.

I had been aboard just under six weeks when Sir Orfeo took me to the personal equipment room one day and fitted me out with thermal boots, leggings, gloves, a fancy pair of binocular sunglasses, breathing apparatus, a backpack, and a temperature suit. He spent an hour fussing over me, getting everything fitted just right. Then he told me to go and tie down in my digs. I did, and for the next hour the yacht shook and shrilled and thumped. When the noise stopped, Sir Orfeo came along and yelled to me to get into my kit and come down to F Hold. When I got there, walking pretty heavy with all the gear I was carrying or had strapped to my back, he was there, checking items off a list.

"A little more juldee next time, Jongo," he snapped at me. "Come along now; I'll want your help in getting the ground-car out shipshape."

It was a powerful-looking vehicle, wide, squatty, with tracks like a small tank, a plastic bubble dome over the top. There was a roomy compartment up front full of leather and inlaid wood and bright work, and a smaller space behind, with two hard seats. Lord Desroy showed up in his Frank Buck bush jacket and jodhpurs and a wide-brimmed hat; the Lady Raire wore her white coverall. Sir Orfeo was dressed in his usual tailored gray with a filament pistol strapped to his hip and a canteen and bush knife on the other side. We all wore temperature suits, which were like long-handled underwear, under the coveralls. "Keep your helmet closed, Jongo," Sir Orfeo told me. "Toxic atmosphere, you know."

He pushed a button and a door opened up in the side of the hold, and I was looking out at a plain of bluish grass. A wave of heat rolled in and the thermostat in my suit clicked, and right away it turned cool against my skin. Sir Orfeo started up and the car lifted a couple of inches from the floor, swung around, and slid out under the open sky of a new world.

For the next five hours I perched on my seat with my mouth open, taking in the sights: the high, blue-black sky, strange trees like overgrown parsley sprigs, the leathery grass that stretched to a horizon that was too far away—and the animals. The things we were after were big crab-armored monstrosities, pale purple and white, with mouths full of needle-pointed teeth and horns all over their faces. Lord Desroy shot two of them, stopping the car and going forward on foot. I guess it took courage, but I didn't see the point in it. Each time, he and Sir Orfeo made a big thing of hacking off one of the horns and taking a lot of pictures and congratulating each other. The Lady Raire just watched from the car. She didn't seem to smile much.

We loaded up and went on to another world then, and Milord shot a thing as big as a diesel locomotive. Sir Orfeo never talked about himself or the other members of the party, or the world they came from, but he explained the details of the hunt to me, gave me pointers on tracking and approaching, told me which gun to use for different kinds of quarry. Not much of it stuck. After the fourth or fifth hunt, it all got a little stale.

"This next world is called Gar 28," Sir Orfeo woke me up to tell me after a long stretch in space. "Doesn't look like much; dry, you know; but there'll be keen hunting. I found this one myself, running through tapes made by a survey team a few hundred years ago. The fellows we'll be going after they called dire-beast. You'll understand why when you see the beggars."

He was right about Gar 28. We started out across a rugged desert of dry-baked pink and tan and yellow clay, fissured and cracked by the sun, with points of purplish rock pushing up here and there, a line of jagged peaks for a horizon. It didn't look like game country to me, but then I wasn't the hunter.

The sun was high in the sky, too bright to look at, a little smaller than the one I was used to. It was cool and comfortable inside the car; it hummed along a couple of feet above the ground, laying a dust trail behind it from the air blast it was riding on. The tracks were for hills that were too steep for the air cushion to climb.

About a mile from the yacht, I looked back; it was just a tiny glint, like a lost needle, among all that desolation.

Up front, on the other side of the glass panel, Lord Desroy and Sir Orfeo and the Lady Raire chatted away in their odd language, and every now and then said something in that strange brand of English they spoke. I could hear them through a speaker hookup in the back of the car. If I'd had something to say, I don't know whether they could have heard it or not.

After two hours' run, we pulled up at the top of a high escarpment. Sir Orfeo opened the hatch, and we all got out. I remembered Sir Orfeo had told me always to stay close with his gun when we were out of the car so I got out one of the crater-rifles and came up behind them in time to see Sir Orfeo point.

"There—by the double peak at the far end of the fault-line!" He snapped his goggles up and whirled to start back and almost slammed into me. A very thin slice of an instant later I was lying on my back with my head swimming, looking into the operating end of his filament pistol.

"Never come up behind me with a weapon in your hand!"

I got up, with my head still whanging from the blow he'd hit me, and followed them to the car, and we went tearing back down the slope the way we'd come.

It was a fast fifteen-minute run out across the flats toward where Sir Orfeo had seen whatever it was he saw. I had my binocular goggles on and was looking hard, but all I saw was the dusty plain and the sharp rock spires, growing taller as we rushed toward them. Then Sir Orfeo swung the car to the left in a wide curve and pulled to a stop behind a low ridge.

"Everybody out!" he snapped, and popped the hatch up and was over the side.

"Don't sit there and brood, Jongo!" He was grinning, excited and happy now. "My crater-rifle; Z-guns for his lordship and Lady Raire!"

I handed the weapons down to him, stock-first, the way he'd told me.

"You'll carry the extra crater and a filament pistol," he said, and moved back up front to go into conference with the others. I strapped on the Z-gun and grabbed the rifle and hopped down just as Sir Orfeo and Lord Desroy started off. The Lady Raire followed about ten feet back, and I took up my post offside to the right about five yards. My job was to keep that relative position to Sir Orfeo, no matter what, until he yelled "Close!" Then I was to move in quick. That was about all I knew about a hunt. That, and don't come up behind Sir Orfeo with a gun.

The sun still seemed to be about where it had been when we started out. There was a little wind blowing from behind, keeping a light cloud of dust rolling along ahead. It seemed to me I'd heard somewhere that you were supposed to sneak up on game from downwind, but that wasn't for me to worry about. All I had to do was maintain my interval. We came to a slight rise of ground. The wind was picking up, driving a thick curtain of dust ahead. For a few seconds I couldn't see anything but that yellow fog swirling all around. I stopped and heard a sound, a deep *thoom! thoom! thoom!*

"Close! Damn your eyes, Jongo, close!" Sir Orfeo shouted. I ran toward the sound of his voice, tripped over a rock, and went flat. I could hear Lord Desroy shouting something and the *thoom-thoom*, louder than before. I scrambled up and ran on forward, and as suddenly as it had blown up, the gale died and the dust rolled away from us. Sir Orfeo was twenty feet off to my left, with Lord Desroy beside him. I changed direction and started toward them, and saw Sir Orfeo make a motion, and Lord Desroy brought his rifle up and I looked where he was aiming and out of the dust cloud a thing came galloping that was right out of a nightmare. It was big—twenty, thirty feet high, running on two legs that seemed to have too many knees. The feet were huge snowshoelike pads, and they rose and fell like something in a slow-motion movie, driving dust from under them in big spurts, and at each stride the ground shook. A second one came charging out of the dust cloud, and it was bigger than the first one. Their hides were a glistening greenish brown, except where they were coated with dust, and there was a sort of cape of ragged skin flapping from the narrow shoulders of one as he ran, and I thought he must be shedding. Thick necks rose from the shoulders, with wide flat heads that were all mouth, like the bucket of a drag-line. And then a third, smaller edition came scampering after the big fellows.

All this happened in maybe a second or two. I had skidded to a halt and was standing there, in a half crouch, literally paralyzed. I couldn't have moved if an express train had been coming straight at me. And these were worse than express trains.

They were about a hundred and fifty yards away when Lord Desroy fired. I heard the Z-gun make a sharp whickering noise and an electric-blue light flashed up and lit the rocks like lightning, and the lead monster broke stride and veered off to the left, running irregularly now. He leaned, losing his balance, but still driving on, his neck whipped back and up and the head flailed offside as he went down, hit, bounced half upright, his legs still pumping, then went into a tumble of flailing legs and neck and the dust closed over him and only then I heard the shuddering boom he made hitting the ground.

And the second one was still coming, closer now than number one had been when he was hit, and the little fellow—a baby, only fifteen feet high—sprinted up alongside him, tilted his head sideways, and snapped at his big brother's side. I saw a flash of white as the hide and muscle tore; then the little one was skidding to a halt on his haunches, his big jaws working hard over the bite he'd gotten, while the one that had supplied the snack came on, looming up as high as a two-story house, black blood streaming down his flank, coming straight at Lord Desroy. I saw the Lady Raire then, just beyond him, right in the path of the charge; and still I couldn't move. Lord Desroy had his gun up again and it flickered and flashed and made its slapping noise and the biped's head, that it had been carrying high on its long neck, drooped and the neck went slack and the head came down and hit the ground and the big haunches, with the big feet still kicking, went up and over high in the air in a somersault and slammed the ground with a smash like two semi's colliding, and flipped up and went over again with one leg swinging out at a crazy angle and the other still pumping, and then it was looping the loop on the ground, kicking up a dust cloud that hid everything beyond it.

"Watch for baby!" Sir Orfeo yelled, and I could barely hear his voice through the thudding and pounding. Then the little one stalked out of the dust, tossing his head to help him swallow down what he had in his mouth. Sir Orfeo brought his gun up and the cub was coming straight at me, and the gun tracked him and went off with a flat *crackkk!* that kicked a pit the size of a washtub in the rock beside him and the young one changed direction and trotted off and Sir Orfeo let him go.

The dust was blowing away now, except for what number two was still kicking up with one foot that was twitching, still trying to run. Lord Desroy and Sir Orfeo went over to it, and the hunter used his pistol to put it out of its misery. It went slack and a gush of fluid sluiced out of its mouth and it was quiet.

"In sooth, the beast raised a din to make the ground quake," Lord Desroy called in a light-hearted tone. He walked around the creature, and Sir Orfeo went over to the other one, and about then I got my joints unlocked and trotted after him. Sir Orfeo looked up as I came up and gave me a grin.

"I think perhaps you'll make a gun-boy yet, Jongo," he said. "You were a bit slow coming up, but you held steady as a rock during the charge."

And for some reason I felt kind of ashamed of myself, knowing how it had really been.

5

Lord Desroy spent a quarter of an hour taking movies of the dead animals; then we made the hike back to the car.

"We were lucky, Desroy," Sir Orfeo told him as we settled into our seats. "Takes a bit of doing to knock over a fine brace on the first stalk! I suggest we go back to the yacht now and call it a day—"

"What foolery's this?" Lord Desroy boomed out. "Wi' a foison o' quarry to hand, ye'd skulk back to thy comforts wi'out further sweat or endeavor?"

"No use pushing our luck—"

"Prithee, spare! Ye spoke but now of bull-devil, lurking in the crags yonder—"

"Plenty of time to go after them later." Orfeo was still smiling, but there was an edge to his voice. He didn't like to have anyone argue with him about a hunt.

"A pox on't!" Lord Desroy slammed his fist down on the arm of his chair. "Dost dream I'd loiter in my chambers with game abounding? Drive on, I say, or I'll take the tiller self!"

Sir Orfeo slapped the drive lever in and the engines started up with a howl.

"I was thinking of the Lady Raire," he said. "If you're that dead-set on running us all ragged, very well! Though what the infernal rush is, I'm sure I don't know!"

As usual, the Lady Raire sat by quietly, looking cool and calm and too beautiful to be real. Lord Desroy got out a silver flask and poured out yellow wine for her and himself, then lolled back in his chair and gazed out at the landscape rushing past.

An hour brought us to the foothills of the range that had been visible from the yacht. The going was rougher here; we switched over to tracks for the climb. Lord Orfeo had quit humming to himself and was beginning to frown, as if maybe he was thinking about how nice it would be to be back in his apartment aboard the yacht, having a bath and a nice dinner, instead of being in for another four hours, minimum, in the car.

We came out on a high plateau, and Sir Orfeo pulled the car in under a steep escarpment and opened up and climbed down without a word to anybody. I had his crater-rifle ready for him; I took the other guns and got out and Lord Desroy looked around and said something I didn't catch.

"They're here, right enough," Sir Orfeo answered him, sounding mad. He walked off and Lord Desroy and the girl trailed. I had to scramble up on rough ground to get to my proper position off to Sir Orfeo's right. He was headed into a narrow cut that curved up and away in deep shadow. The sun still seemed to be in the same spot, directly overhead. My suit kept me comfortable enough, but the heat reflecting back from the stone scalded my face.

Sir Orfeo noticed me working my way along up above him and snarled something about where the devil did I think I was going; I didn't try to answer that. I'd gotten myself onto a ledge that ran along twenty feet above the trail, with no way down. I stayed abreast of Sir Orfeo and looked for my chance to rejoin the party.

We kept going this way, nobody talking, the happy look long gone from Lord Desroy's face now, the Lady Raire walking just to his left, Sir Orfeo out in front twenty paces. The trail did a sharp jog to the left, and I had to scramble to catch up; as I did, I saw something move on the rocks up ahead.

Being above the rest of them, I had a view past the next outcropping that hung out over the trail; the movement I saw was just a flicker of something in the shadows, spread but flat on the rock like a giant leech. I felt my heart take a jump and jam itself up in my throat and I tried to yell and choked and tried again:

"Sir Orfeo! Up ahead! On the right!"

He stopped dead, swung his gun around and up, at the same time motioned to the others to halt. Lord Desroy checked for just a moment; then he started on up toward Sir Orfeo. The animal—creature—thing—whatever it was—moved again. Now I could see what looked like an eye near the front, surrounded by a fringe of stiff reddish hairs. I got just the one quick look before I heard the whisper of a Z-gun from below, and the thing jerked back violently and disappeared into black shadow. Down below, Lord Desroy was lowering his gun.

"Well, that tears it!" Sir Orfeo said in a too loud voice. "Nice bit of shooting, Desroy! You failed to keep to your position, fired without my permission, and then succeeded in wounding the beggar! Anything else you'd care to try before we go into that cranny after him?"

"Methinks you skirt insolence, Orfeo," Lord Desroy started.

"Not intentionally, as I'm damned!" Orfeo's face was

red; I could see the flush from where I was perched, twenty feet above him. "I'll remind you *I'm* master of the hunt, *I'm* responsible for the safety of the party—"

"I'm out of patience wi' cautious counsel!" Lord Desroy roared. "Shall I be merely cheated o' my sport whilst I attend your swoons?"

Sir Orfeo stared to answer that, then caught himself and laughed.

"'Pon my word, you have a way about you, Milord! Now, I suggest we give over this tomfoolery and give a thought to how we're going to get him out of there!" He turned and squinted up toward the place where the thing had disappeared.

"I warrant ye make mockery of me," Lord Desroy growled. He jerked his head in my direction. "Despatch yon natural to draw forth the beast!" Sir Orfeo looked up, too, then back at his boss.

"The boy's new, untrained," he said. "That's a risky bit of business—"

"D'ye aver thy gun-boy lacks spirit, then?"

Sir Orfeo gave me a sharp look. "By no means," he said. "He's steady enough. Jongo!" His voice changed tone. "Press on a few yards, see if you can rout the blighter out."

I didn't move. I just squatted where I was and stared down at him. The next instant, something smashed against the wall beside my head and knocked me sprawling. I came up spitting dust, with my head ringing, and Lord Desroy's second shot crashed close enough to drive stone chips into my cheek.

"Sir Orfeo!" I got the yell out. "He's shooting at *me!*"

I heard Sir Orfeo shout and I rolled over and looked for a hole to dive into and in that instant saw the wounded leech-thing flow down across the rock, disappear for a second behind a spur, come into view

again just above the trail, about thirty feet above Lord
Desroy, between him and the Lady Raire. It must have
made some sound I couldn't hear; before I could shout,
Lord Desroy whirled and brought his gun up and it
crackled and vivid shadows winked on the rocks and
the animal leaped out and down, broad as a blanket,
leathery dark, right into the gun. Lord Desroy stood
his ground, firing steadily into the leech-thing until the
instant it struck full on him, covering him completely.
It gathered itself together and lurched toward the Lady
Raire, standing all alone in the trail, sixty feet behind
where I was. As it moved, it left a trail of what was
left of Lord Desroy.

Sir Orfeo had fired once, while the thing was in the
air. He ran toward it, stopped and took aim and fired
again. I saw a movement off to the right, up the trail,
and a second leech-thing was there, coming up fast
behind Sir Orfeo, big as a hippopotamus, wide and flat
and with its one eye gleaming green.

I yelled. He didn't look up, just stood where he was,
his back to the leech, firing, and firing again. The
wounded leech was close to the Lady Raire now, and
I saw then that she had no gun, and I remembered
that Lord Desroy had taken it and had been carrying
it for her. She stood there, facing the thing, while Sir
Orfeo poured the fire into it. At each shot, a chunk
flew from its back, but it never slowed—and behind
Sir Orfeo the other one was closing the gap. Sir Orfeo
could have turned his fire on it and saved himself; but
he never budged. I realized I was yelling at the top
of my lungs, and then I remembered I had a gun, too,
slung across my back to free my hands for climbing.
I grabbed for it, wasted a second or more fumbling
with it, got it around and to my shoulder and aimed
and couldn't find the firing stud and had to lower it
and look and brought it up again and centered it on

the thing only yards from Sir Orfeo's exposed back and squeezed—

The recoil almost knocked me off my feet, not that it was bad, but I wasn't expecting it. I got back on target and fired again, and again; and it kept coming. Six feet from Sir Orfeo the thing reared up, tall as a grizzly, and I got a glimpse of a yellow underside covered with shredding hooks, and I fired into it and then it was dropping down on Sir Orfeo and at the last possible second he moved, but not far enough, and the thing struck him and knocked him rolling, and then he and it lay still. I traversed the gun across to the other beast and saw that it was down, ten feet from Milady Raire, bucking and writhing, coiling back on itself. It flopped up against the side wall and rolled back down, half on its back, and lay still and the echoes of its struggle went racketing away up the ravine. I heard Sir Orfeo make a moaning sound where he lay all bloody and the Lady Raire looked up and her eyes met mine and we looked at each other across the terrible silence.

CHAPTER THREE

Sir Orfeo was still alive, with all the flesh torn off the back of his thighs and the glistening white bone showing.

He caught at my arm when I bent over him.

"Jongo—your job now—the Lady Raire . . ."

I was shaking and tears were running down my face. I tried not to look at his horrible wounds.

"Buck up, man," Sir Orfeo's voice was a groan of agony. "I'm depending on you . . . keep her safe . . . your responsibility, now. . . ."

"Yes," I said. "I'll take care of her, Sir Orfeo."

"Good . . . now . . . water. Fetch water . . . from the car . . . ."

I ran off to follow his orders. When I came back the Lady Raire met me, looking pale and with dust sticking to the perspiration on her forehead. She told me that he'd sent her to investigate a sound and then dragged himself to where his filament pistol had fallen and blown his head off.

2

I used a crater-rifle to blast shallow pockets under the overhanging rock beside the trail; she helped me drag the bodies to them. Then we went back down to the car. We carried our guns at the ready, but nothing moved in all that jumble of broken rock. Sir Orfeo had been lucky about finding game, all right.

The Lady Raire got into the driver's seat and headed back down the way we'd come. When we reached level ground, she stopped and looked around as if she didn't know which way to go. I tapped on the glass and her head jerked around. I think she had forgotten I was there. Poor Lady Raire, so all-alone.

"That direction, Milady," I said, and pointed toward where the yacht was, out of sight over the horizon.

She followed my directions; three hours later we came up over a low ridge and there was the yacht, glittering far away across the desert. Another forty-five minutes and we pulled up in front of the big cargo door.

She jumped down and went to it and twinkled her fingers on a polished metal disc set in the hull beside it. Nothing happened. She went around to the smaller personnel door and the same thing happened. Then she looked at me. Having her look at me was an event even then.

"We cannot enter," she said in a whisper. "I mind well 'twas Sir Orfeo's custom to reset the entry code 'ere each planetfall lest the yacht be rifled by aborigines."

"There's got to be a way," I said. I went up and hammered on the panel and on the control disc and walked all the way around the yacht and back to the door that I had sneaked in by, that first night, and tried again, but with no luck. A terrible, hollow feeling was growing inside me.

"I can shoot a hole in it, maybe," I said. My voice sounded weak in the big silence. I unslung the crater-rifle and asked her to step back, and then took aim from ten feet and fired. The blast knocked me down, but the metal wasn't even scorched.

I got to my feet and brushed dust off my shins, feeling the full impact of the situation sinking in like the sun that was beating down on my back. The Lady Raire looked at me, not seeing me.

"We must . . . take stock of what supplies may be in the car," she said after a long pause. "Then can'st thou make for thyself a pallet here in the shadow of the boat."

"You mean—we're just going to sit here?"

"If any rescue comes, we must be close by the yacht, else they'll not spy us in this endless waste."

I took a deep breath and swallowed hard. "Milady, we can't stay here."

"Indeed? Why can we not?" She stood there, a slim, aristocratic little girl, giving me a level look from those cool gray eyes.

"I don't know much about the odds against anybody finding us, but we've got a long wait, at best. The supplies in the car won't last long. And the heat will wear us down. We have to try to find a better spot, now, while we're still strong." I tried to sound confident, as if I knew what I was doing. But my voice shook. I was scared; scared sick. But I knew I was right about moving on.

"'Tis a better thing to perish here than to live on in the wilderness, without hope."

"We're not dead yet, Milady. But we will be if we don't do something about it, now."

"I'll tarry here," she said. "Flee if thou wilt, Jongo."

"Sir Orfeo told me to take care of you, Milady. I'm going to do my best to follow his order."

She looked at me coolly. "Wouldst force me, then?"

"I'm afraid so, Milady."

She walked to the car stiffly; I got into my usual seat in back and she started up and we headed out across the desert.

3

We drove until the sun set and a huge, pock-marked moon rose, looking a lot like the old one back home, except that it was almost close enough to touch. We slept then, and went on, still in the dark. Day came again, and I asked the Lady Raire to show me how to drive so I could relieve her at the wheel. After that, we drove shift on, shift off, holding course steady to the northwest. On what I estimated was the third day, Earth-style, we reached a belt of scrub-land. Half an hour later the engine made a gargly sound and died, and wouldn't go again.

I went forward on foot to a rise and looked over the landscape. The scrub-dotted waste went on, as far as I could see. When I got back to the car, the Lady Raire was standing beside it with a filament pistol in her hand.

"Now indeed is our strait hopeless," she held the gun out to me. "Do thy final duty to me, Jongo." Her voice was a breathless whisper.

I took the gun; then I whirled and threw it as far as I could. When I faced her, my hands were shaking.

"Don't ever say anything like that again!" I said. "Not ever!"

"Would you then have me linger on, to wither in this heat, shrivel under the sun—"

I grabbed her arm. It was cool, as smooth as satin. "I'm going to take care of you, Milady," I said. "I'll get you home again safe, you'll see!"

She shook her head. "I have no home, Jongo; my loyal friends are dead—"

"I'm still alive. And my name's not Jongo. It's Billy Danger. I'm human, too. I'll be your friend."

She looked straight at me. It was the first time she ever really looked at me. I looked back, straight into her eyes. Then she smiled.

"Thou art valiant, Billy Danger," she said. "How can I then shrink from duty? Lead on, and I'll follow while my strength lasts."

4

The car was stocked with food concentrates, plus a freezer full of delicacies that would have to be eaten first, before they spoiled. The problem was water. The tanks held about thirty gallons, but with the distiller out of action, there'd be no refilling them. There were the weapons and plenty of ammunition, first-aid supplies, some spare communicators, goggles, boots. It wasn't much to set up housekeeping on.

For the next week, I quartered the landscape over a radius of about five miles, looking for a spring or water hole, with no luck. By that time, the fresh food was gone—eaten or spoiled, and the water was down to two ten-gallon jugs full.

"We'll have to try a longer hike," I told the Lady Raire. "There may be an oasis just one ridge farther than I've gone."

"As you wish, Billy Danger," she said, and gave me that smile, like sunrise after a long night.

We packed up the food and water and a few extras. I slung a Z-gun over my shoulder, and started off at twilight, after the worst of the day's heat.

It was monotonous country, just hilly enough to give us a long pull up to one low crest after another and an ankle-turning slog down the far side. I steered due west, not because the prospects looked any better in that direction, but just because it was easier to steer straight toward the setting sun.

We did about twenty miles before dark, another forty in two marches before the sun rose. I worried about the Lady Raire, but there was nothing I could do that I wasn't already doing. We slogged on toward the next ridge, hoping for a miracle on the other side. And always the next side looked the same.

We rested in the heat of the long day, then marched on, into the glare of the sun. And about an hour before sunset, we saw the cat.

5

He was standing on a rock on the crest of a rise, whipping his tail from side to side in a slow, graceful motion. He made a graceful leap to a lower rock and was just a dark shadow moving against the slope ahead. I unlimbered my rifle and watched him close. At thirty feet, he paused and sat down on his haunches and wrinkled his face and began licking his chest. He finished and stuck out a long tongue and yawned, and then rose and went loping off into the dusk, the way he'd come.

All the while, we stood there and watched him, not saying a word. As soon as he was gone, I went to where he'd been sitting. His paw-prints were plain in the powdery dust. I started believing in him, then. I might see imaginary cats, but never imaginary cat tracks. We set off following them as fast as we could in the failing light.

6

The water hole was in a hollow in the rock, hidden behind a wall of black-green foliage growing on the brink of a ravine. The Lady Raire stopped to gaze at it, but I stumbled down the slope and fell full-length in the water and drank in big gulps and luckily choked and had a coughing fit before I could drink myself to death.

There was a steep jumble of rock rising behind the pool, with the dark mouths of caves showing. I picked my way around the pond in the near-dark with my gun ready in my hand. There was a smell of cat in the air. I was grateful to tabby for leading me to water, but I didn't want him jumping on our backs now that it looked like we might live another few days.

The caves weren't much, just holes about ten feet deep, not quite high enough to stand up in, with enough dirt drifted in them to make a more or less level floor.

The Lady Raire picked out one for herself, and I helped her clean out the dead leaves and cat droppings and fix up a stone that could be rolled into the opening to block it, in case anything bigger than a woodchuck wanted in. Then she picked out another one and told me it was mine and started in on it. It was dark when we finished. I saw her to her den, then sat down outside it with the pistol in my hand and went to sleep. . . .

—and woke hungry, clear-headed, and wondering how a cat happened to be here, in this super-Mojave. I thought about the dire-beasts and the meat-shredding leeches that had killed Lord Desroy and Sir Orfeo. The cat was no relative of theirs. He had been a regulation-type, black and gray and tan striped feline, complete with vertical-slitted pupils and retractable claws. He looked like anybody's house-cat, except that he was the size of a collie dog. I'd heard about parallel evolution, and I hadn't been too surprised when Sir Orfeo had told me about how many four-legged, one-headed creatures there were in the Universe—but a copy this perfect wasn't possible.

That meant one of two things: Either I had dreamed the whole thing—which was kind of unlikely, inasmuch as when I looked down I saw two more cats, just like the other one, in the bright moonlight down by the water—or our yacht wasn't the first human-owned ship to land on Gar 28.

7

In the morning light, the water looked clear and inviting. The Lady Raire studied it for a while, then called to me. "Billy Danger, watch thee well the while I lave me. Methinks t'will be safe enow . . ." She glanced my way, and I realized she was talking about going for a swim. I just stared at her.

"How now, art stricken dumb?" she called.

"The pond may be full of poison snakes, crocodiles, quicksand and undertows," I said.

"I'd as lief be devoured as go longer unwashed." She proceeded to unzip the front of the tunic she'd changed into from the temperature suit, and stepped out of it. And for the second time in one minute, I was struck dumb. She stood there in front of me, as naked as a goddess, and as beautiful, and said, "I charge thee, Billy Danger, take not thine eyes from me," and turned and waded down into the water. It was the easiest order to follow I ever heard of.

She stayed in for half an hour, stroking up and down as unconcerned as if she were in the pool at some high-priced resort at Miami Beach. Once or twice she ducked under and stayed so long I found myself wading in to look for her. After the second time I complained and she laughed and promised to stay on top.

"Verily, hast thou found a garden in the wilderness, Billy Danger," she said after she had her clothes back on. "'Tis so peaceful—and in its rude way, so fair."

"Not much like home, though, I guess, Milady," I said; but she changed the subject, as she always did when the conversation brought back too many memories.

In the next few days, I made two trips back to the car, brought in everything that looked as if it might be useful; then we settled down to what I might describe as a very quiet routine. She strolled around, climbed the rocks, brought home small green shrubs and flowers that she planted around the caves and along the path and watered constantly, using a pot made of clay from the poolside cooked by a Z-gun on wide-beam. I spent my time exploring to the west and north, and trying to make friends with the cats.

There were plenty of them; at certain times of the day, there'd be as many as ten in sight at one time, around the water hole. They didn't pay much attention to us; just watched us when we came toward them and at about fifteen feet, rose casually and moved off into the thick growth along the ravine. They were well fed and lazy, just nice hearthside tabbies, a little larger than usual.

There was one with a few streaks of orange in among the black and tan that I concentrated on, mainly because I could identify him easily. Every time I saw him I'd go out and move up as close as I could without spooking him, sit down, and start to play with a ball of string from the car. He sat and watched. I'd roll it toward him, then pull it back. He moved in closer. I let him get a paw on it, then jerked it. He went after it and cuffed it, and I pulled it in and tossed it out again.

In a week, the game was a regular routine. In two, he had a name—Eureka—and was letting me scratch him between the ears. In three, he had taken to lying across the mouth of my cave, not even moving when I stepped over him going out.

The Lady Raire watched all this with a sort of indulgent smile. According to her, cats were pets on most of the human-inhabited world she knew of. She wasn't sure where they had originated, but she smiled when I said they were a native of Earth.

"In sooth, Billy Danger, 'tis a truism that each unschooled mind fancies itself the center of the Universe. But the stars were seeded by Man long ago, and by his chattels with him."

At first, the Lady Raire didn't pay much attention to my pet, but one day he showed up limping, and she spent half an hour carefully removing a splinter from his foot. The next day she gave him a bath, and brushed his fur to a high gloss. After that, he took to following her on her walks. And it wasn't long before he took to sleeping at the mouth of her cubbyhole. He got more petting that way.

I watched the cats, trying to see what it was they fed on, on the theory that whatever they ate, we could eat, too. Our concentrates wouldn't last forever. But

I never saw them pounce on anything. They came to the water hole to drink and lie around in the shade; then they wandered off again into the undergrowth. One day I decided to follow Eureka.

"As thou wilt," the Lady Raire said, smiling at me. "'Tho' I trow thy cat o' mountain lives on naught but moonbeams."

"Baked moonbeam for dinner coming up," I said.

The cat led me up the rocks and through the screen of alien foliage at the north side of the hollow, then struck out along the edge of the ravine, which was filled from edge to edge by a mass of deep-green vines.

The chasm was about three hundred yards long, fifty yards wide; I couldn't see the bottom under the tangle of green, but I could make out the big stems, as thick as my leg, snaking down into the deep shadows for at least a hundred feet. And I could see the cats. They lay in crotches of the big vine, walked delicately along the thick stems, peered out of shadows with green eyes. There were a few up on the rim, sitting on their haunches, watching me watching them. Eureka yawned and switched his tail against my thigh, then made a sudden leap, and disappeared into the green gloom. By getting down on all fours and shading my eyes, I could see the broad branch he'd jumped to. I could have followed, but the idea of going down into that maze full of cats lacked appeal. I got up and started off along the rim. I noticed that it was scattered with what looked like chips of thick eggshell.

8

The ravine shallowed out to nothing at the far end. The vines were less dense here, and I could see rock

strata slanting down into the depths. There were
strange knobs and shafts of blackish rock embedded
in the lighter stone. I found one protruding near the
surface and saw that it was a fossilized bone. The rock
was full of them. That would be a matter of deep
interest to a paleontologist specializing in the fauna of
Gar 28, but it was no help to me. I needed live meat.
If there was any around—excepting the cats, and I
didn't like the idea of eating them, for six or eight
reasons I could think of offhand—it had to be down
below, in the shade of the greenery. The descent looked
pretty easy, here at the end of the cut. I hitched my
gun around front for quick access, and started down.

The rock slanted off under me at an angle of about
thirty degrees. The big vines bending up over my head
were tough, woody, scaled with dead-looking bark. Only
a few green tendrils curled up here, reaching for
sunlight. The air was fresh and cool in the shade of
the big leaves; there was a sharp, pungent odor of
green life, mixed with the rank smell of cat. Fifty feet
down the broken slope the growth got too thick to be
ignored; it was switch over to limb-climbing or go back.
I went on.

It was easy going at first. The stems weren't too
close together to push between, and there was still
plenty of light to see by. I could hear the cats moving
around, back deeper in the growth. I reached a major
stem, as big as my torso, and started down it. There
were plenty of handholds here. Big seedpods hung
in clusters near me. A lot of them had been gnawed,
either by the cats or by what the cats ate. So far I
hadn't seen any signs of the latter. I broke off one
of the pods. It was about a foot long, knobby and
pale green. It broke open easily and half a dozen
beans as big as egg yolks rolled out. I took a nibble
of one. It tasted like raw beans. After a couple of

weeks on concentrates, even that was good—if it didn't kill me.

I went down. The light was deep green now; a luminous dusk filtered through a hundred feet of foliage. The trunk I was following curved sharply, and I worked my way around to the up side, descended another ten feet, and my feet thunked solidly against something hard. I had to get down on all fours to see that I was on a smooth, curving surface of tarnished metal.

9

Something thumped beside me like a dropped blanket; it was Eureka, coming over to check on me. He sat and washed his face while I rooted around the base of the big vine, saw that it was growing out through a fracture in the metal. The wood had bulged and spread and shaped itself to conform to the opening. I had the impression that it was the vine that had burst the metal.

By crawling, I was able to explore an oval area about fifteen feet long by ten wide before the vines slanted in too close to let me move. All of it was the same iodine-colored metal, with no seams, no variations in contour, with the exception of the bulge around the break. If I wanted to see more, I'd have to do a little land-clearance. I got out the pistol and set it on needle-beam, cut enough wood away to get a look into a room the size of a walk-in freezer, almost filled with an impacted growth of wood.

I backed out then, wormed my way over to the big trunk, and climbed back to the surface. There was a lot more to see, but what I wanted to do now was get back in a hurry and tell the Lady Raire that under the vines in the ravine, I'd found a full-sized spaceship.

CHAPTER FOUR

Fifteen minutes later, she stood on the rim of the ravine with me. I could dimly make out the whole three-hundred-foot length of the ship, now that I knew what to look for. It was lying at an angle of about fifteen degrees from the horizontal, the high end to the south.

"It must have been caught by an earthquake," I said. "Or a Garquake."

"I ween full likely she toppled thither," the Lady Raire said. "During a tempest, mayhap. Look thee, where a great fragment has fallen from the rim of the abyss—and see yon broken stones, crushed as she fell."

We found an access route near the south end, well worn by cats, and made an easier approach than my first climb. I led her to the hatch and we spent the next hour burning the wood away from it, climbed through onto a floor that slanted down under a tangle of vine stem to a drift of broken objects half buried in black dirt at the low end. The air was cool and damp, and there was a sour smell of rotted vegetation and stagnant water. We waded knee-deep in foul-smelling muck to a railed stair lying on its side, crawled along it to another open door. I stepped through into a narrow corridor, and a faint, greenish light sprang up. I felt the hair stand up on the back of my neck.

"I misdoubt me not 'tis but an automatic system," Milady said calmly.

"Still working, after all this time?"

"Why not? 'Twas built to endure." She pointed to a dark opening in a wall. "Yon shaft should lead us to the upper decks." She went past me, and I followed, feeling like a very small kid in a very large haunted castle.

2

The shaft led us to a grim-looking place full of broken piping and big dark shapes the size of moving vans that Milady said were primitive ion-pulse engines. There was plenty of breakage visible, but only a few dead tendrils of vine. We climbed on forward, found a storeroom, a plotting room full of still-shiny equipment, and a lounge where built-in furniture stuck out from what was now the wall. The living quarters were on the other side of the lounge and beyond there was a room with a ring of dark TV screens arching up overhead around a central podium that had snapped off at the base and was hanging by a snarl of conduits. Beyond that point, the nose of the ship was too badly crushed to get into. There were no signs of the original owners, with the possible exception of a few scraps that might have been human bone.

"What do you think, Milady?" I asked her. "Is there anything here we can use?"

"If so, 'twere wonderful, Billy Danger; yet would I see more ere I abandon hope."

Back in the hold, she spent some time crawling over the big vines that came coiling up from somewhere down below.

"'Tis passing strange," she said. "These stems rise not from soil, but rather burgeon from the bowels of the vessel. And meseemeth they want likeness to the other flora of this world."

I pulled one of the big, leathery leaves over to me. It was heart-shaped, about eight inches wide, strongly ribbed.

"It looks like an ordinary pea to me," I said. "Just overgrown—like the cats."

"We'll trace these to their beginnings, their mystery to resolve." The Lady Raire pointed. "An' mine eyes deceive me not, they rise through yonder hatch."

There was just room to squeeze through between the thigh-thick trunks, into a narrow service shaft. I flashed my light along it, and saw bones.

"Just a cat," I said, more to reassure me than Milady. We went on, ducking under festoons of thick vine. We passed another cat skeleton, well scattered. There was a strange smell, something like crushed almonds with an under-taint of decay. The vines led fifty feet along the passage, then in through a door that had been forced outward off its hinges. The room beyond was a dark mass of coiled white roots. On its far side, faint twilight shone in through a break in the hull. There was a soft clink, like water dripping into a still pond, a faint rustling. I flashed my light down. The floor of the big room slanted off sharply. Down among the snarled roots, a million tiny points of amber light glowed. The Lady Raire took a step back.

"Come, Billy Danger! I like this not—" That was as far as she got before the mass of vine roots in front of me trembled and bulged and all the devils in Hell came swarming out.

3

Something dirty white, the size of a football, jittering on six spindly legs rushed at me, clicking a pair of jaws that opened sideways in a face like an imp in one of those medieval paintings. I jumped back and swung a kick and its biters clamped onto my boot toe like a steel trap. Another one bounced high enough to rip at my knee; the tough coverall held, but the hide under it tore. Something *zapp*'ed from behind my right ear and a flash of blue fire winked and two of the things skittered away and a stink of burnt horn hit me in the face. All this in the first half-second. I had my pistol up then, squeezing the firing lever, playing it over them like a hose. They curled and jumped and died and more came swarming over the dead ones.

"We're losing," I yelled. "We've got to bottle them up!" The big vine stem was on fire, and sap was bubbling out and spitting in the flames. I ducked down and grabbed up a dead one and threw him into the opening, and beamed another one that poked his snout through and took a step and tripped and went flat on my face. I threw my hands up to protect my head and heard a yowl and something dark bounded across me and there was a snap and a thud and I sat up and saw Eureka, whirling and pouncing, batting with both paws. Behind him the Lady Raire, splashed to the knee with brown, a smear of blood on her cheek, was aiming and firing as steadily as if she were shooting at clay pipes at the county fair. And then Eureka was sitting on his haunches, making a face at me, and the Lady Raire was turning toward me, and there was a last awkward scuffling sound and then silence.

"Well, that answers one question," I said. "Now we know what the cats eat."

4

It was a hard climb back down along the lift shaft, out through the hold, and up to the last of the sunlight. She got out her belt medikit and started dabbing liquid fire into the cuts on my legs, back, arms and thighs. While she doctored, I talked.

"That was the hydroponics room. When the ship crashed, or fell in the ravine, or got caught in an earthquake, the hull was opened there—or near enough that the plants could sense sunlight. They went for it. Either the equipment that watered them and provided the chemicals they needed was still working, or they found water and soil at the bottom of the ravine; or maybe both. They liked it here; plenty of sunshine, anyway. They adapted and grew and with no competition from other plant life, they developed into what we found."

"There may be truth in thy imaginings, Billy Danger," Milady said. "The vessel's of a very ancient type; 'tis like to those in use on Zeridajh some seven thousand years since."

"That might be long enough for a plant to evolve giant size," I said. "Especially if the local sun puts out a lot of hard radiation. Same for the cats. I guess there were a couple of them aboard—or maybe just one pregnant female. She survived the crash and found water and food—"

"Nay, Billy Danger. Thy Eureka may sup on such

dainties as those he slew in thy defense—but they'd
make two snaps of any house-born puss."

"I didn't mean that; a cat can live on beans, if it has
to. Anyway, the critters weren't as big, then."

"How now? Knowest thou the history of Gar's creatures as well as of more familiar kinds?"

"They aren't natives, any more than the cats and the
peas. They came along on the ship; to be specific, on
the cat."

"Dost rave? Art feverish?"

"I'm ashamed to admit it," I said. "But I know a flea
when I see one."

5

We waited until daylight to go into the ship again.
The location of the cat bones gave us a pretty good
idea of where the boundaries of flea territory were.
Apparently they kept to their dark hold and lived long,
happy lives sucking juice from the vines, or an occasional lone cat who meandered over the line. Population pressure drove enough of them upstairs to keep
the cats supplied; and the cat droppings and their
bodies when they died wound up at the bottom of the
ravine, to keep the cycle going.

The Lady Raire had the idea of trying to locate the
ship's communication section; she finally did—in the
smashed nose section.

I crawled in beside her to look at the ruins of what
had once been a message center that could bounce
words and music across interstellar distances at a speed
that was a complicated multiple of the speed of light.
Now it looked like a junkman's nightmare.

"Alack, I deemed I might find here a signaler, intact.
'Twere folly—and yet . . ."

She sounded so downhearted that I had to say something to cheer her up.

"There's an awful lot of gear lying around in there," I said. "Maybe we could salvage something. . . ."

"Dost know aught of these matters, Billy Danger?" she asked in a lofty tone.

"Not much," I said. "I know my way around the inside of an ordinary radio. I'm not talking about sending three-D pictures in glorious color; but maybe a simple signal. . . ."

She wanted to know more. I explained all I'd learned from ICS one summer when I had the idea of Getting Into Radio Now. I felt like an unspoiled native of Borneo explaining flint-chipping techniques to a designer of H-bombs.

It took us a week to assemble a transmitter capable of putting out a simple signal that Milady Raire assured me would show up as a burst of static on any screen within a couple of light-years. We led a big cable from the energy cells that powered the standby lighting system, rigged it so that what juice was in them would drain in one final burst. The ship itself would act as an antenna, once we'd wired our rig to the hull. We climbed out of her, dragging a length of coaxial cable, got back a couple of hundred yards in case of miscalculation with the power core, and touched her off. For a couple of seconds, nothing happened; then I felt a tremor run through the ground and a moment later a dull *ka-whoom!* rumbled up from the chasm, followed by a rapid exodus of cats. For the next hour, there was a lot of activity: cats chasing fleas, fleas bouncing around looking for cover, and the Lady Raire and me trying to stay out of the way of both parties. Then the smoke faded away, the fleas scuttled for cover, the cats went back down to lie under the leaves or wandered off in the direction of the water hole, and Milady and I settled down to wait.

6

I made the discovery that by cutting into a vine just below a leaf, I could get a trickle of cool water. The Lady Raire had the idea of hauling a stem out and getting it growing in the direction of the caves; we did, and it grew enthusiastically. By the time we'd been in residence for another month, we had shade and running water on tap right outside the door.

I asked the Lady Raire to teach me her language, and along with the new words I learned a lot about her home world, Zeridajh. It was old—fifty thousand years of written history—but the men there were still men. It was no classless Utopia where people strolled in misty gardens spouting philosophy; there was plenty of strife and unhappiness, and although the Lady Raire never talked about herself, I got the impression she had her share of the latter. I wondered how it happened that she was off wandering the far end of the Galaxy in the company of two unlikely types like Lord Desroy and Sir Orfeo, but I didn't ask her; if she wanted to tell me, she could. But one day I said something that made her laugh.

"I thought—Sir Orfeo said Lord Desroy had been on Earth three hundred years ago. And you speak the same old-fashioned English—"

She laughed. "Billy Danger, didst deem me so ancient?"

"No—but—"

"I learned my English speech from Lord Desroy, somewhat altered, mayhap, by Sir Orfeo. But 'twas late;

indeed, I have but eighteen years, Earth reckoning."

"And you've been away from home for four years? Isn't your family worried . . ." Then I shut up, at the look that crossed her face.

The weather had been gradually changing; the days grew shorter and cooler. The flowers Milady had brought in from the caves dropped their blossoms and turned brown. The cats got restless, and we'd hear them yowling and scrapping, down in their leafy den. And one day, there were kittens everywhere.

Our diet consisted of beans, fried, baked, sliced and eaten raw, chopped and roasted, mixed with food concentrates to make stews and soups. We used the scissors from the first-aid kit to trim our hair back. Fortunately, I had no beard to trim. The days got longer again, and for a while the ravine was a fairy-land of blossoms that filled the air with a perfume so sweet it was almost dizzying. At sunset, the Lady Raire would walk out across the desert and look at the purple towers in the west. I trailed her, with a gun ready, in case any of Sir Orfeo's dire-beasts wandered this way.

And one night the ship came.

7

I was sound asleep; the Lady Raire woke me and I rolled out grabbing for my gun and she pointed to a star that glared blue and got bigger as we watched it. It came down in absolute silence and ground in the desert a quarter of a mile from us in a pool of blue light that cast hard shadows across Milady's face. I was so excited I could hardly breathe, but she wasn't smiling.

"The lines of yon vessel are strange to me, Billy

Danger," she said. "'Tis of most archaic appearance. Seest thou the double hull, like unto the body of an insect?"

"All I can see is the glare from the business end." The blue glow was fading. Big floodlights came on and lit up the desert all around the ship like high noon.

"Mayhap . . ." she started, and a whistling, whooping noise boomed out across the flats. It stopped and the echoes bounced and faded and it was silent again.

"If 'twere speech, I know it not," Milady said.

"I guess we'd better go meet them," I said, but I had a powerful urge to run and hide among the pea vines.

"Billy Danger, I like this not." Her hand gripped my arm. "Let's flee to the shelter of the ravine—"

Her idea was a little too close to mine; I had to show her how silly her feminine intuition was.

"And miss the only chance we'll ever have to get off this dust-ball? Come on, Milady. You're going home—"

"Nay, Billy—" But I grabbed her arm and advanced. As we came closer, the ship looked as big as a wasp-waisted skyscraper. Three cars came around from the far side of it. Two of them fanned out to right and left; the third headed toward us, laying a dust trail behind it. It was squat, rounded, dark coppery-colored without windows. It stopped fifty feet away with its blunt snout aimed at us. A round panel about a foot in diameter swung open and a glittery assembly poked out and rotated half a turn and was still.

"It looks like it's smelling of us," I said, but the jolly note in my voice was a failure. Then a lid on top popped up like a jack-in-the-box and the most incredible creature I had ever seen climbed out.

He was about four feet high, and almost as wide, and my first impression was that he was a dwarf in

Roman armor; then I saw that the armor was part of him. He scrambled down the side of the car on four short, thick legs, then reared his torso up and I got a good look at the face set between a pair of seal flippers in the middle of his chest. It reminded me of a blown-up photo of a bat I'd seen once. There were two eyes, some orifices, lots of wrinkled gray-brown skin, a mouth like a fanged frog. An odd metallic odor came from him. He stared at us and we stared back. Then a patch of rough, pinkish skin centered in a tangle of worms below his face bulged out and a gluey voice came from it. I didn't understand the words, but somehow he sounded cautious.

The Lady Raire answered, speaking too fast for me to follow. I listened while they batted it back and forth. Once she glanced at me and I caught my name and the word "property." I wasn't sure just how she meant it. While they talked, the other two cars came rumbling in from offside, ringing us in.

More of the midgets trotted up, holding what looked like stacks of silver teacups, glued together, the open ends toward us. The spokesman took a step back and made a quick motion of his flippers.

"Throw down guns," he said in Zeridajhi. He didn't sound cautious anymore.

The Lady Raire's hand went toward her pistol. I grabbed her arm.

"I know these hagseed now," she said. "They mean naught but dire mischief to any of my race—"

"Those are gunports under the headlights on the cars," I said. "I think we'd better do what it says."

"If we draw and fire as one—"

"No use, Milady. They've got the drop on us."

She hesitated a moment longer, then unsnapped her gunbelt and let it fall. I did the same. Our new friend made a noise and batted his flippers against the sides, and his gun-boys moved in. He pointed at the Lady Raire.

"Fetter this one," he said. "And kill the other."

Two or three things happened at once then. One of the teacup-guns swung my way and the Lady Raire made a sound and threw herself at the gunner. He knocked her down and I charged at him and something exploded in my face and for a long time I floated in a river, shooting the rapids, and each time I slammed against a submerged rock, I heard myself groan, and then I opened my eyes and I was lying on my face with my cheek in a puddle of congealing blood, and the ship and the monsters and the Lady Raire were gone.

8

For the first few hours my consciousness kept blinking on and off like a defective table lamp. I'd come to and try to move and the next thing I knew I was coming to again. Then suddenly it was daylight, and Eureka was sitting beside me, yowling softly. This time I managed to roll over and raise my head far enough to see myself. I was a mess.

There was blood all over me. I hurt all over, too, so that was no clue. I explored with my hands and found a rip in my coverall along my side, and through that I could feel a furrow wide enough to lay two fingers in. Up higher, there was a hole in my right shoulder that seemed to come out in back; and the side of my neck felt like hamburger, medium rare. The pain wasn't really as bad as you'd expect. I must have been in shock. I flopped back and listened to all the voices around me. I heard Sir Orfeo: *She's your responsibility now, Jongo. Take care of her.*

"I tried," I said. "I really tried—"

It's all right, the Lady Raire was standing by me, looking scared, but smiling at me. *I trust you, Billy Danger.* The light from the open furnace door glowed in her black hair, and she turned and stepped into the flames and I yelled and reached after her, but the fires leaped up and I was awake again, sobbing.

"They've got her," I said aloud. "She was frightened of them, but I had to show off. I led her out to them like a lamb to the slaughter. . . ." I pictured her, dragged aboard the dwarfs' ship, locked away in a dark place, alone and terrified, and with no one to help her. And she'd trusted me. . . .

"My fault," I groaned. "My fault! But don't be afraid, Milady. I'll find you. They think I'm dead, but I'll trick them; I won't die. I'll stay alive, and find them and take you home. . . ."

9

The next time I was aware of what was going on, the cat was gone and the sun was directly overhead and I was dying of thirst. By turning my head, I could see the vines along the edge of the ravine. There was shade there, and water. I got myself turned over on my stomach and started crawling. It was a long trip—nearly a hundred yards—and I passed out so many times I lost count. But I reached the vines and got myself a drink and then it was dark. That meant it had been about seventy-two hours since the slug-people had done such a sloppy job of killing me. I must have slept for a long time, then. When I woke up, Eureka was back, with a nice fresh flea for me.

"Thanks, boy," I said when he dropped the gift on

my chest and nudged me with his nose. "It's nice to know somebody cares."

"You're not dead yet," he said, and his voice sounded like Orfeo's. I called to him, but he was gone, down into the darkness. I followed him, along a trail of twisted vines, but the light always glimmered just ahead, and I was cold and wet and then the fleas came swarming out on the empty eyes of a giant skull and swarmed over me and I felt them eating me alive and I woke up, and I was still there, under the vines, and my wounds were hurting now and Eureka was gone and the flea with him.

I got myself up on all fours to have another drink from the water vine, and noticed a young bean pod sprouting nearby. I was hungry and I tore it open and ate the beans. And the next time I woke up, I was stronger.

For five long Garish days I stayed under the vines; then I made the trek to the caves. After that, on a diet of concentrates, I gained strength faster. I spent my time exercising my wounds so they wouldn't stiffen up too much as they healed, and talking to the cat. He didn't answer me anymore, so I judged I was getting better. No infections set in; the delousing Sir Orfeo had given me probably had something to do with that, plus the absence of microbes on Gar 28.

Finally a day came when it was time to get out and start seeing the world again. I slung my crater-rifle, not without difficulty, since my right arm didn't want to cooperate, and made a hike around the far side of the ravine, with half a dozen rest stops. I was halfway back to the hut and the drink of water I'd promised myself as a reward, when the second ship came.

CHAPTER FIVE

This one was smaller, something like Lord Orfeo's yacht, but with less of a polish. I hid behind the vines with my gun aimed until I saw what were undoubtedly Men emerge. Then I went up to meet them.

They were small, yellow-skinned, with round, bald heads. The captain was named Ancu-Uriru and he spoke a little Zeridajhi. He frowned at my scars, which were pretty spectacular, and wanted to know where the rest of the ship's complement were. I told him there was just me. That made him frown worse than ever. It seemed he had picked up our signal and answered it in the hope of collecting a nice reward from somebody, along with a little salvage. I told him about the ship in the ravine, and he sent a couple of men down who came back shaking their heads. They showed every sign of being ready to leave then.

"What about me?" I asked Ancu-Uriru.

"We leave you in peace," he said in an offhand way.

"There's such a thing as too much peace," I told him. "I want to go with you. I'll work my way."

"I have no need of you; space is limited aboard my small vessel. And I fear your wounds render you somewhat less than capable to perform useful labor. Here you are more comfortable. Stay, with my blessing."

"Suppose I told you where there was another ship, a luxury model, in perfect shape—if you can get the doors open?"

That idea seemed to strike a spark. We dickered for a while, and there were hints that a little torture might squeeze the answers out of me with no need for favors in return. But in the end we struck a deal: My passage to a civilized port in return for Lord Desroy's yacht.

It took them most of a Garish day to tickle her locks open. Ancu-Uriru looked her over, then ordered his personal effects moved into the owner's suite. I was assigned to ride on his old tub along with a skeleton crew. Just before boarding time, Eureka came bounding across the flats toward me. One of the men had a gun in his hand, and I jumped in front of him just in time.

"This is my cat," I told him. "He saved my life. We used to have long talks, while I was sick."

The men all seemed to be cat-lovers; they gathered around and admired him.

"Bring the beast along," Ancu-Uriru said. We went aboard then, and an hour later the ship lifted off Gar 28, as nearly as I could calculate, one year after I had landed.

2

It wasn't a luxury cruise. The man Ancu-Uriru had assigned to captain the tub—In-Ruhic, by name— believed in every man's working his way, in spite of the generous fare I'd paid. Even aboard as sophisticated a machine as a spaceship, there was plenty of coolie labor, as I well remembered from my apprenticeship under Sir Orfeo. The standards he'd taught me carried over here; after my assigned chores were done, I spent long hours chipping and scraping and cleaning and polishing, trying single-handed to clear away grime that had been accumulating since the days of the Vikings—or longer. According to In-Ruhic, the old ship had been built on a world called Urhaz, an unknown number of millenia ago.

At first, my wounds caused me a lot of pain, until In-Ruhic stopped me one day and told me my groans were interfering with his inward peace. He had me stretch out on a table while he rubbed some vile-smelling grease into the scars.

"How you survived, untended, is a matter of wonder," he said. "I think you lost a pound of flesh and bone here, where the pellet tore through your shoulder. And you've broken ribs, healed crookedly. And your throat! Man, under the web of scar tissue, I can see the pulse in the great vein each time you lift your chin!" But his hands were as gentle as any girl's could have been; he gave me a treatment every day for a few weeks. The glop he used must have had some healing effect because the skin toughened up over the scars and the pain gradually faded.

I told In-Ruhic and the others about the wasp-waisted ship and the armored midgets that had taken the Lady Raire; but they'd never seen or heard of their kind. They wagged their heads and grunted in vicarious admiration when I described her to them.

"But these are matters best forgotten, Biridanju—" that was as close as In-Ruhic seemed to be able to get to my name. "I've heard of the world called Zeridajh; distant it is, and inhabited by men as rich as emperors.

Doubtless these evil-doers you tell of have long since sold her there for ransom."

By the time the world where Ancu-Uriru planned to drop me was visible in the view-screen on the bridge where I was pulling watches as a sort of assistant instrument reader, I was almost a full-fledged member of the crew. Just before we started our landing maneuvers, which were more complicated for an old tub like In-Ruhic's command than they had been for Lord Desroy's ultramodern yacht, In-Ruhic took me aside and asked me what my plans were.

"If there's a Zeridajhi Embassy, I'll go there and tell them about the Lady Raire. Or maybe I can send some kind of message through. If not . . . well, I'll figure out something."

He shook his head and looked sad and wise. "You nurture a hopeless passion for this high-born lady," he started.

"Nothing like that," I cut him off short. "She was in my care. I'm responsible."

He put a hand on my shoulder. "Biridanju, you've shown yourself a willing worker, and quick to learn. Stay on with me. I offer you a regular berth aboard this vessel."

"Thanks, In-Ruhic. But I have another job to do."

"Think well, Biridanju. For a foreigner, work is not easy to find; and to shore folk, who know not the cruel ways of space, your little decorations may prove unsightly, an added incubus."

I put a hand up and felt the lumps and ridges along the side of my throat and jaw. "I know; it looks like hell. But I'm not asking for any beauty prizes. I'll pay my way."

"I suppose you must make your try. But after, Biridanju—remember: We're based nearby, and call here at Inciro ever and anon. I'll welcome you as shipmate whenever you're ready."

We landed a few hours later on a windswept ramp between a gray sea and a town growing on a hillside. Captain Ancu-Uriru was there ahead of us. He talked earnestly with In-Ruhic for a while, then invited me to his quarters aboard the yacht. There he sat me down and offered me a drink and a double-barreled cigar, rolled from two different weeds which, when combined, produced a smoke worse than any three nickle stogies.

"Biridanju, I tell you freely, you've made me a rich man," he said. "I thought at first you were a shill who'd bring pirates down on me. Almost, I had you shot before you boarded." He made a face that might have been a smile. "Your cat saved you. It passed reason that a man with your wounds, *and* an animal-lover, could be but a decoy for corsairs. I ordered In-Ruhic to watch you closely, and for long I slept but little, watching these beautiful screens for signs of mischief. Now I know I did you an injury."

"You saved my life," I said. "No apologies needed."

He lifted a flat box from a drawer of the gorgeous inlaid desk. "I am a just man, Biridanju; or so I hope. I sold the special stores aboard this cutter for a sum greater than any year's profits I've known since I first captained a trader. The proceeds are yours, your fair share."

I lifted the lid and looked at an array of little colored sticks an eighth of an inch square and an inch long.

"There is enough there to keep you in comfort for many years," he said. "If you squander it not on follies, such as star-messages or passenger fares—not that there's enough to take you far." He gave me a sharp look that meant In-Ruhic had told him my plans.

I thanked him and assured him I'd make it go as far as I could.

It took me ten minutes to collect my personal belongings from the ship and buckle Eureka into the harness I'd made for him. Then Ancu-Uriru took me through the port formalities, which weren't much for anyone with a bankroll, and found me an inn in the town. In-Ruhic joined us for a final drink in my room, and then they left, and I sat on the side of the plain little bunk in the plain little room in the yellow twilight and scratched Eureka behind the ears and felt the loneliness close in.

3

The town was named Inciro, like the planet. It was one of half a dozen ports that had been built ages past to handle the long-vanished trade in minerals and hides and timber from the interior of the one big continent. The population of about ten thousand people, many of whom had six fingers on each hand for some reason, were tall, dark-eyed, pale-skinned, gloomy-looking, with a sort of Black Irish family resemblance, like Eskimos or Hottentots. I spent a few days wandering around the town, sampling the food in different chophouses and seafood dives—they were all good—and drinking a tasty red beer called "izm." The mixed dialect I'd learned from In-Ruhic and his men was good enough to carry on a basic conversation. I soon learned there was no Zeridajhi Embassy anywhere on the planet; the nearest thing to it was a consular agent representing the commercial interest of the half dozen worlds within five light-years of Inciro.

I called on him. He was a fattish, hairy man in a

stale-smelling office over a warehouse. He steepled his pudgy fingers and listened to what I had to say, then solemnly suggested I forget the whole thing. It seemed it was a big Galaxy, and the things that had maimed me and stolen Milady Raire could be anywhere in it—probably at the far side of it by now. No belligerent nonhuman had been seen in these parts for more centuries than I had years. He would have liked to have told me I'd imagined it all, but his eyes kept straying back to my scars.

Eureka went with me on my walks, attracting quite a bit of attention at first. The Incirinos had seen a few cats before, but none his size. He did more than keep me company; one evening a trio of roughnecks with too many bowls of izm inside them came over to get a closer look at my scars, and he came to his feet from where he'd been curled up under the table and made a sound like tearing canvas and showed a mouthful of teeth, and they backed away fast.

I found a little old man who hung around one of the bars who knew half a dozen useful dialects. For the price of enough drinks each evening to keep him in a talking mood, he gave me language lessons, plus the beginnings of an education on the state of this end of the Galaxy. He told me how the human race had developed a long time ago on a world near Galactic Center, had spread outward in all directions for what must have been a couple of hundred thousand years, settled every habitable planet they found and built a giant empire that collapsed peacefully after a while of its own weight. That had been over twenty thousand years earlier; and since then the many separate tribes of Man had gone their own ways.

"Now, take you," he poked a skinny finger at me. "From a planet you call 'Eart.' Thought you were the only people in the Universe. But all you were was a passed-over colony, or maybe what was left of a party marooned by an accident; or a downed battleship. Or maybe you were a penal colony. Or perhaps a few people wandered out there, just wanting to be alone. A few thousand years pass, and—there you are!" He looked triumphant, as if he'd just delivered a rigorous proof of the trisection of the angle.

"But we've dug up bones," I told him. "Ape-men, and missing links. They show practically the whole chain of evolution, from animals to men. And we've got gorillas and chimps and monkeys that look too much like us to just be coincidence."

"Who said anything about coincidence?" he came back. "Life adapts to conditions. Similar conditions, similar life. You ever look at the legs and feet on a plink-lizard? Swear they were human, except they're only so long. Look at flying creatures; birds, mammals, reptiles, goranos, or mikls; they all have wings, all flap 'em, all have hollow bones, use two legs for walking—"

"Even Eureka here is related to humanity," I pressed on. "We have more similarities than we have differences. As embryos of a few weeks, you can't tell us apart."

He nodded and grinned. "Uh-huh. And where'd you say you got him? Not on Eart."

It was like arguing religion. Talking about it just confirmed everyone in his original opinion. But the talking was good experience. By the time I'd been on Inciro for three months, Earth time, I was fluent in the lingua franca that the spacers used, and had a pretty good working vocabulary in a couple of other dialects. And I kept my Zeridajhi sharpened up with long imaginary conversations with the Lady Raire, in which I explained over and over again how we *should* have greeted the midgets.

I looked up a local surgeon who examined my

wounds and clucked and after a lot of lab studies and allergy tests, put me under an anesthetic and rebuilt my shoulder with metal and plastic to replace what was missing. When the synthetic skin had stitched itself in with the surrounding hide, he operated again, to straighten out my ribs. He wanted to reupholster the side of my neck and jaw next, but the synthetic hide was the same pale color as the locals; it wouldn't have improved my looks much. And by then, I was tired of the pain and boredom of plastic surgery. My arm worked all right now, and I could stand straight again instead of cradling my smashed side. And it was time to move on.

In-Ruhic's ship called about then, and I asked his advice.

"I don't want to sign on for just a local run," I told him. "I want to work my way toward Zeridajh, and ask questions along the way. Sooner or later I'll find a lead to the midgets."

"This is a long quest you set yourself, Biridanju," he said. "And a vain one." But he took me along to a local shipowner and got me a place as an apprentice power-section tender on a freighter bound inward toward a world called Topaz.

4

Eureka and I saw Topaz, and after that Greu and Poylon and Trie and Pandache's World and the Three Moons. Along the way, I learned the ins and outs of an ion-pulse drive and a stressed-field generator; and I served my time in vac suits, working outside under the big black sky that wrapped all the way around and seemed to pull at me like a magnet that would suck me away into its deepest blackest depths, every hour I spent out on a hull.

And I had my head pounded by a few forecastle strong-arm types, until an oak-tough old tube-man who'd almost been fleet champion once in his home-world's navy showed me a few simple tricks to keep from winding up on the short end of every bout. His method was effective: he pounded me harder than the bully-boys until I got fast enough to bloody his nose one night, and graduated.

I learned to pull duty three on, three off, to drink the concoctions that space-faring men seemed to always be able to produce no matter how far they were from the last port, and to play seventy-one different games with hundred-and-four card decks whose history was lost in antiquity. And at every world I asked, and got the same answer: No such animals as the midgets had been seen in five thousand years and probably not then.

On a world called Unriss, in a library that was a museum relic itself, I found a picture of a midget— or a reasonable facsimile. I couldn't read the text, but the librarian could make out a little of the old language. It said the thing was called a H'eeaq, that it was a denizen of a world of the same name, and that it was extinct. Where H'eeaq was located, it neglected to say.

My small bankroll, which would have kept me in modest circumstances on Inciro, didn't last long. I spent it carefully, item by item outfitted my ship chest, including a few luxuries like a dreamer and a supply of tapes, a good power gun, and shore clothes. I studied astrogation and power section maintenance whenever I was able to get hold of a tape I hadn't seen before. By the time two years had passed, I had been pro-moted to power chief, second class, meaning I was qualified to act as standby chief on vessels big enough to have a standby complement. That was a big step forward—like jumping from Chinese junks to tramp steamers. It meant I could ship on bigger, faster vessels, with longer range.

I reached a world called Lhiza after a six months' cruise on a converted battle cruiser, and spent three months on the beach there, spending my back pay on new training tapes and looking for a berth that would take me into the edge of the sector of the Galaxy known as the Bar. It wasn't easy; few of the older, slower hulls that worked the Eastern Arm had business there. But the Bar was where Zeridajh was, still thousands of light-years away, but getting closer.

The vessel I finally shipped on was a passenger liner, operating under a contract with the government of a world called Ahax, hauling immigrant labor. I didn't much like the idea; it was my first time nursemaiding a shipload of Flatlanders. But I was offered a slot as first powerman, and the tub *was* going a long way, and in the right direction. So I signed on.

She was an old ship, like most of the hulls operating in the Arm, but she had been a luxury job in her day. I had a suite to myself, with room for Eureka, so for the first time aboard ship the old cat got to sleep across my feet, the way he did ashore. The power section was a massive, old-fashioned stressed-field installation; but after the first few weeks of shakedown and impressing my ideas on my crew I had the engines running smoothly. Everything settled down then to the quiet, slightly dull, sometimes pleasant, always monotonous routine that all long cruises are.

My first shift chief, Ommu, was a big-muscled, square-faced fellow with the faint greenish cast to his skin that said he was from a high C1 world. He listened to my story of the midgets, and told me that once, many years before, he'd seen a similar ship, copper-colored. It had drifted into a cometary orbit around a world in

the Guree system, in the Bar. She was a navigational
hazard and he'd been one of the crew assigned to rendezvous with her and set vaporizing charges. Against
standing orders, he and another sapper had crawled in
through a hole in her side to take a look around. The
ship had been long dead, and there wasn't much left of
the crew; but he had picked up a souvenir. He got it
from his ship chest and laid it on the mess table in front
of me. It looked like a stack of demitasse cups, dull
silver, with a loop at the base and a short rod projecting from the open end.

"Yeah," I said, and felt my scalp prickle, just looking at it. It wasn't identical with the guns that had shot
me up, back on Gar 28, but it was a close enough
relative.

I had him tell me all about the ship, everything he
could remember. There wasn't much. We went up to
the ship's psychologist and after a lot of persuasion and
a bottle of crude stuff from the power-section still, he
agreed to run a recall on Ommu under hypnosis. I
checked with the purser and located a xenologist among
the passengers, and got him to sit in on the session.

In a light trance, Ornmu relived the approach to the
ship, described it in detail as he came up on it from
sun-side. We followed him inside, through the maze
of compartments; we were with him as he stirred the
remains of what must have been a H'eeaq and turned
up the gun.

The therapist ran him back through it three times,
and he and the xenologist took turns firing questions
at him. At the end of two hours, Ommu was soaking
wet and I had the spooky feeling I'd been aboard that
derelict with him.

The xenologist wanted to go back to his quarters and
pore over his findings, but I talked him into giving us
a spot analysis of what he'd gotten.

"The vessel itself appears a typical artifact of what we call the H'eeaq Group," he said. "They are an echinodermoid form, originating far out in Fringe Space, or, as some have theorized, representing an incursion from a neighboring stellar assemblage, presumably the Lesser Cloud. Their few fully documented contacts with Man, and with other advanced races of the Galaxy, reveal a cultural pattern of marked schizoid-accretional character—"

"Maybe you could make that a little plainer," Ommu suggested.

"These are traits reflecting a basic disintegration of the societal mechanism," he told us, and elaborated on that for a while. The simplified explanation was as bad as the regular one, as far as my vocabulary was concerned. I told him so.

"Look here," he snapped. He was a peppery little man. "You're asking me to extrapolate from very scanty data, to place my professional reputation in jeopardy—"

"Nothing like that, sir," I soothed him. "I'd just like to have a little edge the next time I meet those types."

"Ummm. There's their basic insecurity, of course. I'd judge their home-world has been cataclysmically destroyed, probably the bulk of their race along with it. What this might do to a species with a strong racial-survival drive is anyone's guess. If I were you, I'd look for a complex phobia system: Fear of heights or enclosed spaces, assorted fetish symbologies. And of course, the bully syndrome. Convince them you're stronger, and they're your slaves. Weaker, and they destroy you."

That was all I got from him. Ommu gave me the teacup gun. I disassembled it and examined its workings, but it didn't tell me much. The routine closed in again then. I fine-tuned the generators, and put the crew on polishing until the section gleamed from one end to the other. I won some money playing tikal, lost it again at revo. And then one offshift I was shocked up out of a deep sleep to find myself lying on the floor, with Eureka yowling over me and every alarm bell on the ship screaming disaster.

5

By the time I reached the power section, the buffeting was so bad that I had to grab a rail to stay on my feet.

"I've tried to get through to Command for orders," Ommu yelled over the racket, "but no contact!"

I tried the interdeck screen, raised a young plotman with blood on his face who told me the whole forward end of the ship had been carried away by a collision, with what, he didn't know. That was all he told me before the screen blanked in the middle of a word.

A new shock knocked both of us down. The deck heaved up under us and kept going, right on up and over.

"She's tumbling," I yelled to Ommu. "She'll break up, fast, under this! Order the men to lifeboat stations!" A tubeman named Rusi showed up then, pale as chalk, hugging internal injuries. I gave him a hand and we crawled on floors, walls and ceilings, made it to our boat station. The bay door was blown wide and the boat was hanging in its davits with the stern torn out, and there were pieces of a dead man scattered around. I ordered the men up to the next station and started to help my walking wounded, but he was dead.

The upper bay was chaos. I grabbed a gun from

a lanky grandpa who was waving it and yelling, and fired over the crowd. Nobody noticed. Ommu joined me, and with a few crewmen, we formed up a flying wedge. Ommu got the hatch open while the rest of us beat back the mob. All this time, Eureka had stayed close to me, with his ears flattened and his tail twitching.

"Take 'em in order," I told Ornmu. "Anybody tries to walk over somebody else, I'll shoot him!" Two seconds later I had to make that good when a beefy two-hundred-pounder charged me. I blew a hole through him and the rest of them scattered back. The boat had been designed for fifty passengers; we had eighty-seven aboard when a wall of fire came rolling down the corridor and Ommu grabbed me just in time and hauled me in across the laps of a fat woman and a middle-aged man who was crying, and Eureka bounded in past me. I got forward and threw in the big red lever and a big boot kicked us and then there was the sick, null-G feel that meant we'd cleared the launch tube and were on our own.

6

In the two-by-four Command compartment, I watched the small screen where five miles away the ship was rotating slowly, end-over-end, with debris trailing off from her in a lazy spiral. Flashes of light sparkled at points along the hull where smashed piping was spewing explosive mixtures. Her back broke and the aft third of the ship separated and a cloud of tiny objects, some of them human, scattered out into the void, exploding as they hit vacuum. The center section blew then, and when the smoke cleared, there was nothing left but a major fragment of the stern, glowing red-hot, and an expanding dust-cloud.

"Any other boats get away?" I asked.

"I didn't see any, Billy."

"There were five thousand people aboard that scow! We can't be the only survivors!" I yelled at him, as if convincing him would make it true.

A powerman named Lath stuck his head in. "We've got some casualties back here," he said. "Where in the Nine Hells are we, anyway?"

I checked the chart screen. The nearest world was a planet named Cyoc, blue-coded, which meant uninhabited and uninhabitable.

"Nothing there but a beacon," Ommu said. "An ice world."

We checked; found nothing within a year's range that was any better—or as good.

"Cyoc it is," I said. "Now let's take a look at what we've got to work with."

I led the way down the no-G central tube past the passenger cells that were arranged radially around it, like the kernels on a corncob. They were badly overcrowded. There seemed to be a lot of women and children. Maybe the mob had demonstrated some of the chivalric instincts, after all; or maybe Ommu had done some selecting I didn't notice. I wasn't sure he'd done the right thing.

A big man, wearing what had been expensive clothes before the mob got them, pushed out in the aisle up ahead of me, waited for me to come to him.

"I'm Till Ognath, member of the Ahacian Assembly," he stated. "As highest ranking individual aboard, I'm assuming command. I see you're crew; I want you men to run a scan of the nearby volume of space and give me a choice of five possible destinations within our cruise capability. Then—"

"This is Chief Danger, Power Section," Ommu butted into his spiel. "He's ranking crew."

Assemblyman Ognath looked me over. "Better give me the gun." He held out a broad, well-tended hand.

"I'll keep it," I said. "I'll be glad to have your help, Assemblyman."

"Maybe I didn't make myself clear," Ognath showed me a well-bred frown. "As a member of the World Assembly of Ahax, I—"

"Ranking crew member assumes command, Assemblyman," Ommu cut him off. "Better crawl back in your hole, Mister, before you qualify yourself for proceedings under space law."

"You'd quote law to me, you—" Ognath's vocabulary failed him.

"I'll let you know how you can best be of service, Assemblyman," I told him, and we moved on and left him still looking for a suitable word.

7

The boat was in good shape, fully equipped and supplied—for fifty people, all of whom were presumed to have had plenty of time to pack and file aboard like ladies and gentlemen. Assemblyman Ognath made a formal complaint about the presence of an animal aboard, but he was howled down. Everybody seemed to think a mascot was lucky. Anyway, Eureka ate very little and took up no useful space. Two of the injured died the first day, three more in the next week. We put them out the lock and closed ranks.

There wasn't much room for modesty aboard, for those with strong feelings about such matters. One man objected to another man's watching his wife taking a sponge bath—(ten other people were watching, too; they had no choice in the matter, unless they screwed their eyes shut) and knocked his front teeth out with a belt-buckle. Two days later, the jealous one turned up drifting in the no-G tube with his windpipe crushed. Nobody seemed to miss him much, not even the wife.

Two hundred and sixty-nine hours after we'd kicked free of the foundering ship, we were maneuvering for an approach to Cyoc. From five hundred miles up, it looked like one huge snowball.

It was my first try at landing an atmosphere boat. I'd run through plenty of drills, but the real thing was a little different. Even with fully automated controls that only needed a decision made for them here and there along the way, there were still plenty of things to do wrong. I did them all. After four hours of the roughest ride this side of a flatwheeled freight car, we slammed down hard in a mountain-rimmed icefield something over four hundred miles from the beacon station.

CHAPTER SIX

The rough landing had bloodied a few noses, one of them mine, broken an arm or two, and opened a ten-foot seam in the hull that let in a blast of refrigerated air; but that was incidental. The real damage was to the equipment compartment forward. The power plant had been knocked right through the side of the boat. That meant no heat, no light, and no communications. Assemblyman Ognath told me what he thought of my piloting ability. I felt pretty bad until Ommu got him to admit he knew even less about atmosphere flying than I did.

The outside temperature was ten below freezing; that made it a warm day, for Cyoc. The sun was small and a long way off, glaring in a dark, metallic sky. It shed a sort of gray, before-the-storm light over a hummocky spread of glacier that ended at blue peaks, miles away. Assemblyman Ognath told me that now we were on terra firma he was taking charge, and that we would waste no time taking steps for rescue. He didn't say what steps. I told him I'd retain command as long as the emergency lasted. He fumed and used some strong language, but I was still wearing the gun.

There were a lot of complaints from the passengers about the cold, the short rations, the recycled water, bruises, and other things. They'd been all right, in space, glad to be alive. Now that they were ashore they seemed to expect instant relief. I called some of the men aside for a conference.

"I'm taking a party to make the march to the beacon," I told them.

"Party?" Ognath bellied up to me. "We'll all go! Only by pulling together can we hope to survive!"

"I'm taking ten men," I said. "The rest stay here."

"You expect us to huddle here in this wreck, and slowly freeze to death?" Ognath wanted to know.

"Not you, Assemblyman," I said. "You're coming with me."

He didn't like that, either. He said his place was with the people.

"I want the strongest, best-fed men," I said. "We'll be traveling with heavy packs at first. I can't have stragglers."

"Why not just yourself, and this fellow?" Ognath jerked a thumb at Ommu.

"We're taking half the food with us. Somebody has to carry it."

"Half the food—for ten men? And you'd leave seventy-odd women and children to share what's left?"

"That's right. We'll leave now. There's still a few hours of daylight."

Half an hour later we were ready to go, the cat included. The cold didn't seem to bother him. The packs were too big by half, but they'd get lighter.

"Where's your pack, Danger?" Ognath wanted to know.

"I'm not carrying one," I told him. I left the boat in charge of a crewman with a sprained wrist; when

I looked back at the end of the first hour all I could see was ice.

2

We made fifteen miles before sunset. When we camped, several of the men complained about the small rations, and a couple mentioned the food I gave Eureka. Ognath made another try to gather support for himself as trail boss, but without much luck. We turned in and slept for five hours. It wasn't daylight yet when I rolled them out. One man complained that his suit-pack was down; he was shivering, and blue around the lips. I sent him back and distributed his pack among the others.

We went on, into rougher country, sprinkled with rock slabs that pushed up through the ice. The ground was rising, and footing was treacherous. When I called the noon halt, we had made another ten miles.

"At this rate, we'll cover the distance in ten days," Ognath informed me. "The rations could be doubled, easily! We're carrying enough for forty days!"

He had some support on that point. I said no. After a silent meal and a ten-minute rest, we went on. I watched the men. Ognath was a complainer but he held his position up front. Two men had a tendency to straggle. One of them seemed to be having trouble with his pack. I checked on him, found he had a bad bruise on his shoulder from a fall during the landing. I chewed him out and sent him back to the boat.

"If anybody else is endangering this party by being noble, speak up now," I told them. Nobody did. We went on, down to eight men already, and only twenty-four hours out.

The climbing was stiff for the rest of the day. Night caught us halfway to a high pass. Everybody was dog-tired. Ommu came over and told me the packs were too heavy.

"They'll get lighter," I told him.

"Maybe if you carried one you'd see it my way," he came back.

"Maybe that's why I'm not carrying one."

We spent a bad night in the lee of an ice-ridge. I ordered all suits set for minimum heat to conserve power. At dawn we had to dig ourselves out of drifted snow.

We made the pass by mid-afternoon, and were into a second line of hills by dark. Up until then, every-one had been getting by on his initial charge; now the strain was starting to show. When morning came, two men had trouble getting started. After the first hour, one of them passed out cold. I left him and the other fellow with a pack between them, to make it back to the boat. By dark, we'd put seventy-five miles behind us.

I began to lose track of days then. One man slipped on a tricky climb around a crevasse and we lost him, pack and all. That left five of us: myself, Ommu, Ognath, a passenger named Choom, and Lath, one of my power-section crew. Their faces were hollow and when they pulled their masks off their eyes looked like wild animals'; but we'd weeded out the weak ones now.

At a noonday break, Ognath watched me passing out the ration cans.

"I thought so," his fruity baritone was just a croak now. "Do you men see what he's doing?" He turned to the others, who had sprawled on their backs as usual as soon as I called the halt. "No wonder Danger's got more energy than the rest of us! He's giving himself double rations—for himself and the animal!"

They all sat up and stared my way.

"How about it?" Ommu asked. "Is he right?"

"Never mind me," I told them. "Just eat and get what rest you can. We've still got nearly three hundred miles to do."

Ommu got to his feet. "Time you doubled up on rations for all of us," he said. The other two men were sitting up, watching.

"I'll decide when it's time," I told him.

"Ognath, open a pack and hand out an extra ration all around," Ommu said.

"Touch a pack and I'll kill you," I said. "Lie down and get your rest, Ommu."

They stood there and looked at me.

"Better be careful how you sleep from now on, Danger," Ommu said. Nobody said anything while we finished eating and shouldered packs and started on. I marched at the rear now, watching them. I couldn't afford to let them fail. The Lady Raire was counting on me.

3

At the halfway point, I was still feeling fairly strong. Ognath and Choom had teamed up to help each other over the rough spots, and Ommu and Lath stuck together. None of them said anything to me unless they had to. Eureka had taken to ranging far offside, looking for game, maybe.

Each day's march was like the one before. We got on our feet at daylight, wolfed down the ration, and hit the trail. Our best speed was about two miles per hour now. The scenery never changed. When I estimated we'd done two hundred and fifty miles—about the fifteenth day—I increased the ration. We made better time that day, and the next. Then the pace began to drag again. The next day, there were a lot of falls. It wasn't just rougher ground; the men were reaching the end of their strength. We halted in mid-afternoon and I told them to turn their suit heaters up to medium range. I saw Ognath and Choom swap looks. I went over to the assemblyman and checked his suit; it was on full high. So was Choom's.

"Don't blame them, Danger," Ommu said. "On short rations they were freezing to death."

The next day Choom's heat-pack went out. He kept up for an hour; then he fell and couldn't get up. I checked his feet; they were frozen waxy-white, ice-hard, hallway to the knee.

We set up a tent for him, left fourteen days' rations, and went on. Assemblyman Ognath told me this would be one of the items I'd answer for at my trial.

"Not unless we reach the beacon," I reminded him.

Two days later, Ognath jumped me when he thought I was asleep. He didn't know I had scattered ice chips off my boots around me as a precaution. I woke up just in time to roll out of his way. He rounded and came for me again and Eureka knocked him down and stood over him, snarling in a way to chill your blood. Lath and Ommu heard him yell and I had to hold the gun on them to get them calmed down.

"Rations," Ognath said. "Divide them up now; four even shares!"

I turned him down. Ommu told me what he'd do to me as soon as he caught me without the gun. Lath asked me if I was willing to kill the cat, now that it had gone mad and was attacking people. I let them talk. When they had it out of their systems, we went on. That afternoon Ommu fell and couldn't get up. I took his pack and told Lath to help him. An hour later

Lath was down. I called a halt, issued a triple ration all around and made up what was left of the supplies into two packs. Ognath complained, but he took one and I took the other.

The next day was a hard one. We were into broken ground again, and Ognath was having trouble with his load, even though it was a lot lighter than the one he'd started with. Ommu and Lath took turns helping each other up. Sometimes it was hard to tell which one was helping which. We made eight miles and pitched camp. The next day we did six miles; the next five; the day after that, Ognath fell and sprained an ankle an hour after we'd started. By then we had covered three hundred and sixty miles.

"We'll make camp here," I said. "Ommu and Lath, lend a hand."

I used the filament gun on narrow-beam to cut half a dozen foot-cube blocks of snow. When I told Ommu to start stacking them in a circle, he just looked at me.

"He's gone crazy," he said. "Listen, Lath; you too, Ognath. We've got to rush him. He can't kill all three of us—"

"We're going to build a shelter," I told him. "You'll stay warm there until I get back."

"What are you talking about?" Lath was hobbling around offside, trying to get behind me. I waved him back.

"This is the end of the line for you. Ognath can't go anywhere; you two might make another few miles, but the three of you together will have a better chance."

"Where do you think you're going?" Ognath got himself up on one elbow to call out. "Are you abandoning us now?"

"He planned it this way all along," Lath whispered. His voice had gone a couple of days before. "Made us pack his food for him, used us as draft animals; and now that we're used up, he'll leave us here to die."

Ommu was the only one who didn't spend the next ten minutes swearing at me. He flopped down on the snow and watched me range the snow blocks in a ten-foot circle. I cut and carried up more and built the second course. When I had the third row in place, he got up and silently started chinking the gaps with snow.

It took two hours to finish the igloo, including a six-foot entrance tunnel and a sanitary trench a few feet away.

"We'll freeze inside that," Ognath was almost blubbering now. "When our suit-packs go, we'll freeze!"

I opened the packs and stacked part of the food, made up one light pack.

"Look," Ognath was staring at the small heap of ration cans. "He's leaving us with nothing! We'll starve, while he stuffs his stomach!"

"If you starve you won't freeze," I said. "Better get him inside," I told Ommu and Lath.

"He won't be stuffing his stomach much," Ommu said. "He's leaving us twice what he's taking for himself."

"But—where's all the food he's been hoarding?"

"We've been eating it for the past week," Ommu said. "Shut up, Ognath. You talk too much."

We put Ognath in the igloo. It was already warmer inside, from the yellowish light filtering through the snow walls. I left them then, and with Eureka pacing beside me, started off in what I hoped was the direction of the beacon.

My pack weighed about ten pounds; I had food enough for three days' half-rations. I was still in reasonable shape, reasonably well-fed. With luck, I expected to make the beacon in two days' march.

I didn't have luck. I made ten miles before dark,

slept cold and hungry, put in a full second day. By sundown I had covered the forty miles, but all I could see was flat plain and glare ice, all the way to the horizon. According to the chart, the beacon was built on a hundred-foot knoll that would be visible for at least twenty miles. That meant one more day, minimum.

I did the day, and another day. I rechecked my log, and edited all the figures downward; and I still should have been in sight of home base by now. That night Eureka disappeared.

The next day my legs started to go. I finished the last of my food and threw away the pack; I had a suspicion my suit heaters were about finished; I shivered all the time.

Late that day I saw Eureka, far away, crossing a slight ripple in the flat ice. Maybe he was on the trail of something to eat. I wished him luck. I had a bad fall near sunset, and had a hard time crawling into the lee of a rock to sleep.

The next day things got tough. I knew I was within a few miles of the beacon, but my suit instruments weren't good enough to pinpoint it. Any direction was as good as another. I walked east, toward the dull glare of the sun behind low clouds. When I couldn't walk anymore, I crawled. After a while I couldn't crawl anymore. I heard a buzzing from my suit pack that meant the charge was almost exhausted. It didn't seem important. I didn't hurt anymore, wasn't hungry or tired. It felt good, just floating where I was, in a warm, golden sea. Golden, the color of the Lady Raire's skin when she lay under the hot sun of Gar 28, slim and tawny. . . . Lady Raire, a prisoner, waiting for me to come for her.

I was on my feet, weaving, but upright. I picked out a rock ahead, and concentrated on reaching it. I made it and fell down and saw my own footprints there. That seemed funny. When I finished laughing, it was dark. I was cold now. I heard voices. . . .

The voices were louder, and then there was light and a man was standing over me and Eureka was sitting on his haunches beside me, washing his face.

4

Ommu and Ognath were all right; Lath had left the igloo and never came back; Choom was dead of gangrene. Of the four men I had sent back to the boat during the first few days, three reached it. All of the party at the boat survived. We later learned that our boat was the only one that got away from the ship. We never learned what it was we had collided with.

I was back on my feet in a day or two. The men at the beacon station were glad to have an interruption in their routine; they gave us the best of everything the station had to offer. A couple of days later a ship arrived to take us off.

At Ahax, I went before a board of inquiry and answered a lot of questions, most of which seemed to be designed to get me to confess that it had all been my fault. But in the end they gave me a clean bill and a trip bonus for my trouble.

Assemblyman Ognath was waiting when I left the hearing room.

"I understand the board dismissed you with a modest bonus and a hint that the less you said of the disaster the better," he said.

"That's about it."

"Danger, I've always considered myself to be a man

of character," he told me. "At Cyoc, I was in error. I owe you something. What are your plans?"

He gave me a sharp look when I told him. "I assume there's a story behind that—but I won't pry. . . . "

"No secret, Mister Assemblyman." I told him the story over dinner at an eating place that almost made up for thirty days on the ice. When I finished he shook his head.

"Danger, do you have any idea how long it will take you to work your passage to as distant a world as Zeridajh?"

"A long time."

"Longer than you're likely to live, at the wages you're earning."

"Maybe."

"Danger, as a politician I'm a practical man. I have no patience with romantic quests. However, you saved my life; I have a debt to discharge. I'm in a position to offer you the captaincy of your own vessel, to undertake a mission of considerable difficulty—but one which, if you're successful, will pay you more than you could earn in twenty years below decks!"

5

The details were explained to me that night at a meeting in a plush suite on the top floor of a building that must have been two hundred stories high. From the terrace where I was invited to take a chair with four well-tailored and manicured gentlemen, the city lights spread out for fifty miles. Assemblyman Ognath wasn't there. One of the men did most of the talking while the other three listened.

"The task we wish you to undertake," he said in a

husky whisper, "requires a man of sound judgment and intrepid character; a man without family ties or previous conflicting loyalties. I am assured you possess those qualities. The assignment also demands great determination, quick wits and high integrity. If you succeed, the rewards will be great. If you fail, you can expect a painful death, and we can do nothing to help you."

A silent-footed girl appeared with a tray of glasses. I took one and listened:

"Ahacian commercial interests have suffered badly during recent decades from the peculiarly insidious competition of a nonhuman race known as the Rish. The pattern of their activities has been such as to give rise to the conviction that more than mere mercantile ambitions are at work. We have, however, been singularly unsuccessful in our efforts to place observers among them."

"In other words, your spies haven't had any luck."

"None."

"What makes this time different?"

"You will enter Rish-controlled space openly, attended by adequate public notice. Your movements as a lone Ahacian vessel in alien-controlled space will be followed with interest by the popular screen. The Rish can hardly maintain their pretence of cordiality if they offer you open interference. Your visit to the capital, Hi-iliat, will appear no more than a casual commercial visit."

"I don't know anything about espionage," I said. "What would I do when I got there—if I got there?"

"Nothing. Your crew of four will consist of trained specialists."

"Why do you need me?"

"Precisely because you are not a specialist. Your training has been other than academic. You have faced disaster in space, and survived. Perhaps you will survive among the Rish."

It sounded simple enough: I'd be gone a year; when I got back, a small fortune would be waiting for me. The amount they mentioned made my head swim. Ognath had been wrong; it wasn't twenty years' earnings; it was forty.

"I'll take it," I said. "But I think you're wasting your money."

"We pay you nothing unless you return," the spokesman said. "In which case the outlay will not have been wasted."

6

The vessel they showed me in a maintenance dock at the port was a space-scarred five-thousand tonner, built twelve hundred years ago and used hard ever since. If the Rish had any agents snooping around her for hidden armor, multi-light communications gear, or superdrive auxiliaries, they didn't find them; there weren't any. Just the ancient stressed-field generators, standard navigation gear, a hold full of pre-coded computer tapes for light manufacturing operations. My crew of four were an unlikely-looking set of secret agents. Two were chinless lads with expressions of goggle-eyed innocence; one was a middle-aged man who gave the impression of having run away from a fat wife; and the last was a tall, big-handed, silent fellow with moist blue eyes.

I spent two weeks absorbing cephalotapes designed to fill in the gaps in my education. We lifted off before dawn one morning, with no more fanfare than any other tramp streamer leaving harbor. I left Eureka behind with one of the tech girls from the training center. Maybe that was a clue to the confidence I had in the mission.

For the first few weeks, I enjoyed captaining my own ship, even as ancient a scow as *Jongo*. My crew stared solemnly when I suited up and painted the letters on her prow myself; to them, the idea of anthropomorphizing an artifact with a pet name was pretty weird.

We made our first planetfall without incident. I contacted the importers ashore, quoted prices, bought replacement cargo in accordance with instructions, while my four happy-go-lucky men saw the town. I didn't ask them what they'd found out; as far as I was concerned, the less I knew about their activities the better.

We went on, calling at small, unpopulous worlds, working our way deeper into the Bar, then angling toward Galactic South, swinging out into less densely populated space, where Center was a blazing arch in the screens.

We touched down on Lon, Banoon, Ostrok and twenty other worlds, as alike as small towns in the midwestern United States. And then one day we arrived at a planet which looked no different than the rest of space, but was the target we'd been feeling our way toward for five months: The Rish capital, and the place where, if I made one tiny mistake, I'd leave my bones.

7

The port of Hi-iliat was a booming, bustling center where great shining hulls from all the great worlds of the Bar, and even a few from Center itself, stood ranged on the miles-wide ramp system, as proud and aloof as carved Assyrian kings. We rode a rampcar in from the remote boondocks where we'd been parked by Traffic Control to a mile-wide rotunda constructed of high arched ribs of white concrete with translucent filigree-work between them. I was so busy staring up at it that I didn't see the Rish official until one of my men prodded me. I turned and was looking at a leathery five-foot oyster all ready for a walk on the beach, spindly legs and all. He was making thin buzzes and clicks that seemed to come from a locket hanging on the front side of him. It dawned on me then that it was speaking a dialect I could understand:

"All right, chaps, just in from out-system, eh? Mind stepping this way? A few formalities, won't take a skwrth."

I didn't know how long a skwrth was, but I followed him, and my four beauties followed me. He led us into a room that was like a high, narrow corridor, too brightly lit for comfort, already crowded with Men and Rish and three or four other varieties of life, none of which I had ever seen before. We sat on small stools as directed and put our hands into slots and had lights flashed in our eyes and sharp tones beeped at our ears. Whatever the test was, we must have passed, because our guide led us out into a ceilingless circular passage like a cattle run and addressed us:

"Now, chaps, as guests of the Rish Hierarchy, you're welcome to our great city and to our fair world. You'll find hostelries catering to your metabolic requirements, and if at any time you are in need of assistance, you need merely repair to the nearest sanctuary station, marked by the white pole, and you will be helped. And I must also solemnly caution you: Any act unfriendly to the Rish Hierarchy will be dealt with instantly and with the full rigor of the law. I trust you'll have a pleasant stay. Mind the step, now." He pushed a hidden control and a panel slid back and he waved us through into the concourse.

An hour later, after an ion-bath and a drink at the hotel bar, I set out to take a look at Hi-iliat. It was a beautiful town, full of blinding white pavement, sheer towers, tiled plazas with hundred-foot fountains, and schools and shoals of Rish, zooming along on tiny one-wheeled motorbikes. There were a few Men in sight, and an equal number of other aliens. The locals paid no attention to them, except to ping their bike-bells at them when they stepped out in front of them.

I found a park where orange grass as soft as velvet grew under trees with polished silver trunks and golden yellow leaves. There were odd little butterfly-like birds there, and small leathery animals the size of squirrels. Beyond it was a lake, with pretty little buildings standing up on stilts above the water; I could hear twittery music coming from somewhere. I sat on a bench and watched the big, pale sun setting across the lake. It seemed that maybe the life of a spy wasn't so bad after all.

It was twilight when I started back to the hotel. I was halfway there when four Rish on green-painted scooters surrounded me. One of them was wearing a voice box.

"Captain Billy Danger," he said in a squeak like a bat. "You are under arrest for crimes against the peace and order of the Hierarch of Rish."

CHAPTER SEVEN

The prison they took me to was a brilliantly-lit rabbit warren of partitions, blind alleys, cubicles, passages, tiny rooms where inscrutable oyster-faces stared at me while carrying on inaudible conversations that made my eardrums itch. I asked questions, but got no answers. For all I know it was the same oyster I talked to each time; it might even have been the same office. I got very hungry and thirsty and sleepy, but nobody got out any rubber hoses. I could have done worse in any small town in Mississippi.

After about an hour of these silent examinations, I wound up in a room the size of a phone booth with a Rishian wearing a talk box. He told me his name was Humekoy and that he was Chief of Physical Interrogation and Punishment. I got the impression the two duties were hard to tell apart.

"You are in a most serious position," he told me in his mechanically translated squeak. "The Rish Hierarchy has no mercy for strangers seeking to do evil. However, I am aware that you yourself have merely been used—possibly even without your knowledge—as an agency for transporting criminals. By cooperating with me fully, you may save yourself from the more unpleasant consequences of your actions. Accordingly, you will now give me full particulars of the activities of your associates."

"I want to see the Ahacian consul," I said.

"Don't waste my time," he shrilled. "What were the specific missions of the four agents who accompanied you here?"

"If my crew are under arrest, I want to see them."

"You have an imperfect grasp of the situation, Captain Danger! It is *I* who make the demands!"

"I'm afraid I can't help you."

"Nonsense, I know you Men too well. Each of you would sell his own kind to save his person."

"Then why are you afraid to let me see the consul?"

"Afraid?" He made a sound which was probably a laugh, but it lost something in translation. "Very well, then. I grant your plea."

They took me to a bigger room with softer light and left me, and a minute later an egg-bald man in dandified clothes came in, looking worried and mad.

"I understand you demanded to see me," he said and handed me a gadget and looped a similar one around his neck, with an attachment to the left ear and the Adam's apple. I followed suit.

"Look here, Danger," his voice peeped in my ear. "There's nothing I can do for you! You knew that when you came here. Insistence on seeing me serves merely to implicate Ahax."

"Who are you kidding?" I sub-vocalized. "They know all about the mission. Something leaked. That wasn't part of the deal."

"That's neither here nor there. Your duty now is to avoid any appearance that yours is an official mission."

"You think they're dumb enough to believe I'm in the spy business for myself?"

"See here, Danger, don't meddle in affairs that are beyond your grasp! You were selected for this mission because of your total illiteracy in matters of policy."

"Let's quit kidding," I said. "Why do you think they let you see me?"

"*Let* me? They practically kidnaped me!"

"Sure; this is a test. They want to see what you'll do. Species loyalty is a big thing with them—I learned that much studying tapes, back on Ahax. Every time they capture and execute a Man with no reaction from his home world, they get a little bolder."

"This is nonsense, a desperate bid for rescue—"

"You made a mistake, seeing me, Mister Consul. You can't pretend you don't know me, now. Better get me out of this; if you don't, I'll spill the beans."

"What's that?" He looked shocked. "What can you tell them? You know nothing of the actual—" He cut himself off.

"I can tell them all about you, for a starter," I told him.

"Tell them what about me?"

"That you're the mastermind of the Ahacian espionage ring here on the Rish world," I said. "And everything else I can think of. Some of it might even be true."

He got his back stiffened up and gave me the old ice-blue glare. "You'd play the treacher to the Ahacian Assembly, which trusted you?"

"You bureaucrats have a curious confidence in the power of one-way loyalty. You'd sell me down the river just to maintain a polite diplomatic lie; and you expect me to go, singing glad hosannas."

He struggled some more, but I had him hooked in the eye. In the end he said he'd see what he could do and went away, mopping his forehead. The oysters hustled me into an elevator and took me down into what must have been a sub-sub-basement and made me crawl through a four-foot tunnel into a dim-lit room with a strange, unpleasant smell. I was still sniffing and trying to remember what it was about the odor that made my scalp crawl when something moved in the deep gloom of the far corner and an armored, four-foot midget rose up on a set of thick legs and two oversized eyes stared at me from the middle of its chest.

2

For the first five seconds I stood where I was, feeling the shock reaction slamming through my brain. Then, without any conscious decision on my part, I was diving for it. It tried to scuttle aside, but I landed on it, grabbed for what passed for its throat. Its body arced under me and the stubby legs beat against the floor, and it broke free and went for the exit tunnel, making a sound like water gurgling down a drain. I kicked it away from the opening and it curled up and rolled to a neutral corner and I stood over it, breathing hard and looking for a soft spot to attack.

"Peace!" the word sounded grotesque coming from what looked like an oversized armadillo. "I yield, Master! Have mercy on poor Srat!" Then it made sounds that were exactly like an Australian bush baby— or a crying child.

"That's right," I said, and my voice had a high, quavering note. I could feel the gooseflesh on my arms, just from being this close to the thing. "I'm not ready to kill you yet. First you're going to tell me things!"

"Yes, Master! Poor Srat will tell Master everything he knows! All, all!"

"There was a ship—wasp-waisted, copper-colored, big. It answered our distress call. Bugs like you came out of it. They shot me up, but I guess they didn't know much human anatomy. And they took the Lady Raire. Where did they take her? Where is she? What did they do to her?"

"Master, let poor Srat think!" it gurgled, and I realized I'd been kicking it with every question mark.

"Don't think—just give me the answers." I drew a deep breath and felt the rage draining away and my hands started to shake from the reaction.

"Master, poor Srat doesn't understand about the lady—" It *oof*ed in anticipation when I took a step toward it.

"The ship, yes," it babbled. "Long ago poor Srat remembers such a ship, all in the beauty of its mighty form, like a great mother. But that was long, long ago!"

"Three years," I said. "On a world out in the Arm."

"No, Master! Forty years have passed away since last poor Srat glimpsed the great mother-shape! And that was deep in Fringe Space—" It stopped suddenly, as if it had said too much, and I kicked it again.

"Poor Srat is in exile," it whined. "So far, so far from the heaving, oil-black bosom of the deeps of H'eeaq."

"Is that where they took her? To H'eeaq?"

It groaned. "Weep for great H'eeaq, Master. Weep for poor Srat's memories of that which was once, and can never be again...."

I listened to the blubbering and groaning, and piece by piece, got the story from it: H'eeaq, a lone world, a hundred lights out toward Galactic Zenith, where Center spread over the sky like a blazing roof; the discovery that the sun was on the verge of a nova explosion;

the flight into space, the years—centuries—of gypsy wandering. And a landing on a Rish-controlled world, a small brush with the Rish law—and forty years of slavery. By the time it was finished, I was sitting on the bench by the wall, feeling cold, washed out of all emotion, for the first time in three years. Kicking this poor waif wouldn't bring the Lady Raire back home. That left me with nothing at all.

"And Master?" poor Srat whimpered. "Has Master, too, aroused the cruel ire of these Others?"

"Yeah, I guess you could say that. They're using me for a test case—" I cut myself off. I wasn't ready to start gossiping with the thing.

"Master—poor Srat can tell Master many things about these Rishes. Things that will help him."

"It's a little late for that," I said. "I've already had my say. Humekoy wasn't impressed."

The H'eeaq crept closer to me. "No, Master, listen to poor Srat: Of mercy, the Rish-things know nothing. But in matters of business ethic . . ."

3

I was asleep when they came for me. Four guards with symbols painted on their backs herded me along to a circular room where a lone Rish who might have been Humekoy sat behind a desk under a spotlight. Other Rish came in, took seats along the walls behind me. My buddy, the Ahacian consul, was nowhere in sight.

"What will you offer for your freedom?" the presiding Rish asked bluntly.

I stood there remembering what poor Srat had told

me about the Rish and wondering whether to believe him.

"Nothing," I said.

"You offer nothing for your life?"

"It's already mine. If you kill me you'll be stealing."

"And if we imprison you?"

"Stealing is stealing. My life is mine, not yours."

I felt the silent buzzing that meant they were talking it over. Then Humekoy picked up two rods, a white one and a red one, from the desk. He held the white one out to me.

"You will depart the Rish world at once," he said. "Take this symbol of Rish magnanimity and go."

I shook my head, and felt the sweat start up. "I'll take my life and freedom because it's mine, not as a gift. I don't want *any* gifts from you; no gifts at all."

"You refuse the mercy of the Hierarch?" Humekoy's canned voice went up off the scale.

"All I want is what's mine."

More silent conversation. Humekoy put the rods back on the desk.

"Then go, Captain Danger. You have your freedom."

"What about my crew?"

"They are guilty. They will pay their debt."

"They're no good to you. I suppose you've already pumped them dry. Why not let them go?"

"Ah, you crave a gift after all?"

"No. I'll pay for them."

"So? What payment do you offer?"

Poor Srat had briefed me on this, too. I knew what I had to do, but my mouth felt dry and my stomach was quivering. We bargained for ten minutes before we agreed on a price.

My right eye.

4

They were skillful surgeons. They took the eye out without anesthetic, other than a stiff drink of what tasted like refrigerant fluid. Humekoy stood by and watched with every indication of deep interest. As for me, I had already learned about pain: the body is capable of registering only a certain amount of it; about what you'd get from laying your palm on a hot plate. After that, it's all the same. I yelled and screamed a little, and kicked around a bit, but it was over very quickly. They packed the empty socket with something cold and wet that numbed it in a few seconds. In half an hour I was back on my feet, feeling dizzy and with a sort of gauzy veil between my remaining eye and the world.

They took me to the port and my crew were there ahead of me, handcuffed and looking pale green around the ears. And the consul was there, too, with his hands clamped up as tight as the rest.

"It has been a fair exchange, Captain Danger," Humekoy told me after the others were aboard. "These paid cheats have garnered their petty harvest of data on industrial and port facilities, volume of shipping and sophistication of equipment, on which to base estimates of Rish assault capability. And in return, the Hierarch has gained valuable information for proper assessment of you humans. Had we acted on the basis of impressions gained by study of the persons so-cleverly trained to delude us heretofore, we might have made a serious blunder."

We parted on that note, not as pals, exactly, but with what might be described as a mutual wary respect. At the last minute a rampcar pulled up and a pair of Rish guards dumped poor Srat out.

"The creature aided, indirectly, in our rapprochement," Humekoy said. "His payment is his freedom. Perhaps you, too, may have an account to settle."

"Put him aboard," I said. "He and I will have a lot of things to talk over before I get back to Ahax."

5

By the time the fifty-seven-day voyage was over, I knew as much about H'eeaq as poor Srat could tell me.

"Why these mistaken kin of mine may have stolen a lady of Master's kind, I can't say," he insisted. But as to where—he had a few ideas on that.

"There are worlds, Master, where long ago H'eeaq established markets for the complex molecules so abundantly available to her in those days. Our vessels call there still, and out of regard for past ties perhaps, the in-dwellers supply our needs for stores. And in return, we give them what we can."

He gave me the details of a few of these old marketplaces—worlds far out in Fringe Space, where few questions were asked, and a human was a rare freak.

"We'll go take a look," I said. "As soon as I collect my pay."

At Ahax, Traffic Control allotted me a slot at the remotest corner of the port. We docked and my four cheery crewmen were gone in a rampcar before I finished securing the command deck. I told Srat to follow me, and started off to walk the two miles to the nearest power way. A rampcar went past in a hurry in the next lane over, headed out toward where my tub was parked. I thought about hailing it, but even with the chill wind blowing, walking felt good after the weeks in space.

Inside the long terminal building, a P.A. voice was droning something. Srat made a gobbling noise and said, "Master, they speak of you!" I looked where he pointed with one flipper and saw my face looking down from a public screen.

" . . . distinguishing scar on the right side of the neck and jaw," the voice was saying. "It is the duty of any person seeing this man to detain him and notify Central Authority at once!"

6

Nobody seemed to be looking my way. I was wearing a plain gray shipsuit and a light windbreaker with the collar turned up far enough to cover the scar; I didn't look much different than a lot of other space-burned crew types. Poor Srat was crouching and quivering; they hadn't put him on the air, but he would attract attention with his whimpering. We had to get to cover, fast. I turned and headed for the nearest ramp exit and as I reached the vestibule a woman's voice called my name. I spun and saw a familiar face: Nacy, the little tech operator I'd left Eureka with.

"I was in Ops Three when your clearance request came, four hours ago," she said in a fast whisper. She saw the patch over my eye and her voice faltered and went on: "I thought . . . after all, no one expected you to come back . . . it would be nice to come down and meet you.

"Then . . . I heard the announcement. . . ."

"What's it all about, Nacy?"

She shook her head. She was a pert little girl with a turned-up nose and very white, even teeth. "I don't know, Billy. Someone said you'd gone against your orders, turned back early—"

"Yeah. There's something in that. But you don't want to be seen talking to me—"

"Billy—maybe if you went to them voluntarily . . ."

"I have a funny feeling near the back of my neck that says that would be a wrong play."

Her face looked tight; she nodded. "I think I understand." She took a bite of her lip. "Come with me." She turned and started across the lobby. Srat plucked at my sleeve.

"You'll do better on your own," I said, and followed her.

She led me through a door marked for private use, along a plain corridor with lots of doors, out through a small personnel entry onto a parking lot full of ramp vehicles.

"Good thinking, girl," I said. "You'd better fade out fast now—"

"Just a minute." She ducked back inside. I went to a small mail-carrier, found the controls unlocked. I started it up and backed it around by the door as it swung open and a sleek pepper and salt and tan animal stalked through, looking relaxed, as always.

"Eureka!" I called, and the old boy stopped and looked my way, then reached the car in one bound and was in beside me. I looked up and Nacy was watching from the door.

"Thanks for everything," I said. "I don't know why you took the chance, but thanks."

"Maybe it's because you're what's known as a romantic figure," she said and whirled and was gone before I could ask her what that meant.

I pulled the car out and into a lane across the ramp, keeping it at an easy speed. There was a small click from over my head and a voice said, "Seven-eight-nine-o, where do you think you're going?"

"Fuel check," I mumbled.

"Little late, aren't you? You heard the clear ramp order."

"Yeah, what's it all about?"

"Pickup order out on some smuggler that gave Control the slip a few minutes ago. Now get off the ramp!" He clicked off. I angled right as if I were headed for the maintenance bay at the end of the line, but at the last second I veered left and headed out toward where I'd parked *Jongo.* I could see rampcars buzzing back and forth, off to my left; I passed two uniformed men, on foot. One of them stared at me and I kept my chin down in my collar and waved to him. A hundred yards from the tub, I saw the cordon of cars around it. So much for my chances of a slick takeoff under their noses. I pulled the car offside between a massive freighter that looked as if it hadn't been moved for a couple of hundred years, and a racy yacht that reminded me of Lord Desroy's, and tried to make my brain think. It didn't seem to want to. My eyes kept wandering back to the fancy enamel-inlaid trim around the entry lock of the yacht. The port was open and I could see the gleam of hand-rubbed finishes inside. . . .

I was out of the car and across to the yacht before I realized I'd made a decision. Eureka went in ahead of me, as if he owned the boat. Just as I got a foot on the carpeted four-step ladder, one of the pedestrian cops came into sight around the side of the old freighter. He saw me and broke into a run, fumbling with a holster at his side in a way that said he had orders to shoot. I unfroze and started up, knowing I wouldn't make it, and heard a scuffling sound and a heavy thud and a crash of fire that cracked and scorched the inlay by the door. I looked back and he was spread out on the pavement, out cold, and poor Srat was untangling himself from his legs. He scrambled in behind me and I tripped the port-

secure lever and ran for the flight deck. I slammed the
main drive lever to full emergency lift-off position and
felt my back teeth shake as the yacht screamed off the
ramp, splitting the atmosphere of Ahax like a meteor-
ite outward-bound.

7

The ship handled like a yachtsman's dream; for the
first few hours I ducked and bobbed in an evasion
pattern that took us out through the planetary patrols.
I kept the comm channels open and listened to a lot
of excited talk that told me I'd picked the personal
transportation of an Ahacian official whose title translated roughly as Assistant Dictator. After a while
Assemblyman Ognath came on, looking very red around
the ears, and showed me a big smile as phony as a UN
peace proposal.

"Captain Danger, there's been a misunderstanding,"
he warbled. "The police officers you may have seen
at the port were merely a guard of honor—"

"Somebody forgot to tell the gun-handlers about
that," I said in a breezy tone that I thought would have
the maximum irritant value. "I had an idea maybe you
fellows decided forty years' pay was too much to spend,
after all. But that's OK; I'll accept this bucket as payment in full."

"Look here, Danger," Ognath let the paper smile
drop. "Bring the vessel back, and I'll employ my influence to see that you're dealt with leniently."

"Thanks; I've had a sample of your influence. I don't
think I'd live through another."

"You're a fool! Every civilized world within ten
parsecs will be alerted; you'll be hunted down and
blasted without mercy—unless you turn back now!"

"I guess the previous owner is after somebody's scalp, eh, Ognath? Too bad."

I gave him, and a couple of naval types who followed him, some more funny answers and in the process managed to get a fair idea of the interference I could expect to run into. I had to dodge three patrols in the first twenty hours; by the thirtieth hour I was running directly toward Galactic Zenith with nothing ahead but the Big Black.

"Give me the coordinates of the nearest of the worlds where you H'eeaq used to trade," I ordered Srat.

"It is distant, Master. So far away, so lonely. The world called Drope."

"We'll try it anyway," I said. "Maybe somewhere out there we'll run into a little luck."

The yacht was fueled and supplied in a way that suggested that someone had been prepared for any sudden changes in the political climate back home. It carried food, wines, a library that was all the most self-indulgent dictator could want to while away those long, dull days in space.

I showed Srat how to handle the controls so that he could relieve me whenever I felt like taking a long nap or sampling the library. I asked him why he had stuck with me, but he just looked at me with those goggle-eyes, and for the first time in many weeks it struck me what a strange-looking thing he was. You can get used to anything, even a H'eeaq.

8

Eureka was better company than the alien, in spite of not being able to talk. He settled in in a cabin full of frills that conjured up pictures of a dance-hall floozie with the brains of a Pekinese and a voice to match. Fortunately, the dictator's taste in music and books was closer to mine than his choice of mistresses. There were tapes aboard on everything from ancient human history to the latest techniques in cell-surgery, thoroughly indexed. I sampled them all.

The Fringe worlds, I learned, were the Museum of the Galaxy. These lonely planets had once, long eons ago, been members of the tightly packed community of Center; their races had been the first in the young Galaxy to explore out through the Bar and Eastern Arm, where their remote descendants still thrived. Now the ancient Mother-worlds lingered on, living out the twilight of their long careers, circling dying suns, far out in the cool emptiness of the space between Galaxies. One of those old races, Srat assured me, was the ancestral form of Man—not that I'd recognize the relationship if I encountered a representative of the tribe.

One day I ran through a gazeteer of the Western Arm, found a listing of an obscure sun I was pretty sure was Sol and coded its reference into the index. The documentary that came onto the view-screen showed me a dull-steel ball bearing with a brilliant highlight that the voice track said was the system's tenth planet. Number nine looked about the same, only bigger. Eight and seven were big fuzz-balls flattened at the poles. I had just about decided I had the wrong star when Saturn swam into view. The sight of that old familiar ring made me feel homesick, as if I'd spent the long happy hours of childhood there. I recognized Big Jupe, too. The camera came in close on this one, and then there were surface scenes on the moons. They looked just like Luna.

Mars was a little different than the pictures I

remembered seeing; the ice caps were bigger, and in the close scan the camera moved in on what looked like the ruins of a camp; not a city, just a lash-up collection of metal huts and fallen antennas, such as a South Pole expedition might have left behind. And then I was looking at Earth, swimming there on the screen, cool and misty green and upside down, with Europe at the bottom and Africa at the top. I stared at it for half a minute before I noticed that the ice caps were wrong. The northern one covered most of Germany and the British Isles, and as the camera swung past, I could see that it spread down across North America as far as Kansas. And there wasn't any south polar cap. Antarctica was a crescent-shaped island, all by itself in the ocean, ice-free; and Australia was connected to Indochina. I knew then the pictures had been made a long time ago.

The camera moved in close, and I saw oceans and jungles, deserts and ice-fields, but nowhere any sign of Man. The apparent altitude at the closest approach was at least ten thousand feet, but even from that height I could make out herds of game. But whether they were mammoths and megatheria or something even older, I couldn't tell.

Then the scene shifted to Venus, which looked like Neptune, only smaller and brighter, and I switched the viewer off and made myself a long, strong drink and settled down for the long run ahead.

CHAPTER EIGHT

Drope was a lone world, circling a tired old star the color of sunset in Nevada. No hostile interceptors rose to meet me, but there was no welcoming committee either. We grounded at what Srat said was a port, but all I saw was a windblown wasteland with a few hillocks around it, under a purplish-black sky without a star in sight, Center being below the horizon. The air was cold, and the wind seemed to be whispering sad stories in the dusk. I went back aboard; I dined well and drank a bottle of old Ahacian wine and listened to music, but it seemed to be telling sad stories, too. Just before dawn Srat came back with a report that a H'eeaq ship had called—about a century ago, Earth time.

"That doesn't help us much," I pointed out.

"At least," Poor Srat got down and wriggled in the dust, but I sensed a certain insolence in his voice— "at least Master knows now I speak truly of the voyages of the H'eeaq."

"Either that or you're a consistent liar," I said, and

stopped. My tone of voice when I talked to the midget reminded me of something, but I couldn't say what it was.

Srat's informant had mentioned the name of the H'eeaq vessel's next port of call: a world known as E'el, ten lights farther out into intergalactic space, which meant a two weeks' run. I set ship time up on a cycle as close to Earth time as I could estimate, and for a while I tried to sleep eight hours at a stretch, eat three meals a day, and maintain some pretense of night and day; but the habit of nearly six years in space was too strong. I soon reverted to three on, three off, with meals every other off-period.

We picked up E'el on our screens at last, a small, dim star not even shown on the standard charts. I set the yacht down on a grassy plain near a town made of little mud-colored domes and went into the village with Srat. There was nothing there but dust and heat and a few shy natives who scuttled inside their huts as we passed. An hour of that was enough.

After that we called at a world that Srat called Zlinn, where a swarm of little atmosphere fliers about as sturdy as Spads came up and buzzed us like irate hornets. They refused us permission to disembark. If any H'eeaq vessel had been there in the last few decades, it was their secret.

We visited Lii, a swamp-world where vast batteries of floodlights burned all day under a dying sun, and Shoramnath, where everyone had died since Srat's last visit, and we walked around among the bones and the rusted machines and the fallen-in buildings, and wondered what had hit them; and we saw Far, and Z'reeth, and on Kish they let us land and then attacked us, just a few seconds prematurely, so that we made it back to the lock and lifted off in the middle of a barrage of HE fire that burned some of the shine off the hull. Suicide fliers threw themselves at us as we streaked for space; they must have been tough organisms, because some of them survived the collisions and clung to the hull and I heard them yammering and rat-tat-tatting there for minutes after we had left the last of the atmosphere behind.

On Tith, there were fallen towers that had once been two miles high, lying in rows pointing north, like a forest felled by a meteor strike. We talked to the descendants of the tower builders, and they told me that a H'eeaq ship had called; a year ago, a century ago, a thousand years—it was all the same to them.

We pushed on, hearing rumors, legends, hints that a vessel like the one I described had been seen once, long ago, or had visited the next world out-system, or that creatures like Srat had been found, dead, on an abandoned moon. Then even the rumors ran out; and Srat was fresh out of worlds.

"The trail's cold," I told him. "There's nothing out here but death and decay and legends. I'm turning back for Center."

"Only a little farther, Master," Poor Srat pleaded. "Master will find what he seeks, if only he presses on." He didn't have quite the whimpering tone now that he used to use. I wondered about poor Srat; what he had up his sleeve.

"One more try," I said. "Then I turn back and try for Center, even if every post office this side of Earth has my picture in it."

But the next sun that swam into range was one of a small cluster; eight small, long-lived suns, well past Sol on the evolutionary scale, but still in their prime. Srat almost tied himself into a knot.

"Well do I remember the Eight Suns, Master! These are rich worlds, and generous. After we filled our holds here with succulent lichens—"

"I don't want any succulent lichens," I cut off his rhapsody. "All I want is a hot line on a H'eeaq ship."

I picked the nearest of the suns, swung in on a navigation beam from Drath, the ninth planet, with Srat doing the talking to Control, and sat the ship down on a ramp that looked as though it had survived some heavy bombardments in its day. A driverless flatcar riding on an airstream came out to pick us up. We rode in it toward a big pinkish-gray structure across the field. Beyond it, a walled city sprawled up across a range of rounded hills. The sky was a pre-storm black, but the sun's heat baked down through the haze like a smelter.

There were rank, tropical trees and fleshy-looking flowers growing along the drive that ran the final hundred yards. Up close, I could see cracks in the building.

There were no immigration formalities to clear through, just a swarm of heavy-bodied, robed humanoids with skin like hard olive-green plastic and oversized faces—if you can call something that looks like a tangle of fish guts a face. Eureka stayed close to my side, rubbing against my leg as we pushed through the crowd inside the big arrival shed. Srat followed, making the *oof!*ing sounds that meant he didn't like it here. I told him to find someone he could talk to, and try for some information; he picked a non-Drathian, a frail little knob-kneed creature creeping along by a wall with the fringe of its dark blue cloak dragging in the mud. It directed him along to a stall at the far side of the lobby, which turned out to be a sort of combination labor exchange and lost-and-found. A three-hundred-pound Drathian in a dirty saffron toga listened to Srat, then rumbled an answer

"No vessel of H'eeaq has called here, says he, Master," Srat reported. "Drath trades with no world; the produce of Drath is the most magnificent in the

Universe; he demands why anyone would seek items made elsewhere. He says also that he can offer an attractive price on a thousand tons of glath."

"What's glath?"

"Mud, Master," he translated.

"Tell him thanks, but I've sworn off." We left him and pushed on through to take a look at the town.

The buildings were high, blank-fronted, stuccoed in drab shades of ochre and pink and mauve. There was an eerie feeling hanging over the place, as if everyone was away, attending a funeral. The click and clatter and pat-pat of our assorted styles of feet were jarringly loud. A hot rain started up, to add to the cheer. It struck me again how alike cities were, on worlds all across the Galaxy. Where creatures gather together to build dwellings, the system of arranging them in rows along open streets is almost universal. This one was like a Mexican village, with water; all poverty and mud. I saw nothing that would pass for a policeman, an information office, a city hall or government house. After an hour of walking I was wet to the skin, cold to the bone, and depressed to the soul.

I was ready to give it up and head back to the ship when the street widened out into a plaza crowded with stalls and carts under tattered awnings of various shades of gray. Compared to the empty streets, the place looked almost gay.

The nearest stall displayed an assortment of dull-colored balls, ranging from lemon to grapefruit size. Srat tried to find out what they were, but the answer was untranslatable. Another bin was filled with what seemed to be dead beetles. I gathered they were edible, if you liked that sort of thing. The next displayed baubles and gimcracks made of polished metal and stone, like jewelry in every time and clime. Most of the metal was dull yellow, lead-heavy gold, and I felt a faint stir of an impulse to fill my pockets. Up ahead, an enterprising merchant had draped the front of his stall with scraps of cloth. From the colors, I judged he was color-blind, at least in what I thought of as the visible spectrum. One piece of rag caught my eye; it was a soft, silvery gray. I fingered it and felt a shock go through me as if I'd grabbed a hot wire. But it wasn't electricity that made my muscles go rigid; it was the unmistakable feel of Zeridajhan cloth.

It was a piece about two feet long and a foot wide, raggedly cut. It might have been the back panel from a shipsuit. I started to lift it and the stall-keeper grabbed for it, and cracked something in the local language, a sound like hot fat sizzling. I didn't let go.

"Tell him I want to buy it," I told Srat

The stall-keeper tugged and made more hot-fat sounds.

"Master, he doesn't understand the trade tongue," Srat said.

The merchant was getting excited, now. He made an angry buzzing and yanked hard; I ripped the cloth out of his balled fists; then Srat was clutching at my arm and saying, "Beware, Master!"

2

I looked around. A large Drathian who could have been the same one who offered me the load of glath except for the white serape across his chitinous shoulder was pushing through the gathering crowd toward me. Something about him didn't look friendly. As he came up, he crackled at the merchant. The merchant crackled back. The big Drathian planted himself in front of me and spit words at me.

"Master," Srat gobbled, "the Rule-keeper demands to know why you seek to rob the merchant!"

"Tell him I'll pay well for the cloth." I took out a green trade chip that was worth six months' pay back on the Bar Worlds, and handed it over, but the Rule-keeper still didn't seem satisfied.

"Find out where he got the cloth, Srat," I said. There was more talk then; I couldn't tell whether the big Drathian was a policeman, a guild official, a racket boss, or an ambulance-chasing shyster, but he seemed to pull a lot of weight. The stall-keeper was scared to death of him.

"Master, the merchant swears he came by the rag honestly; yet if Master insists, he will make him a gift of it."

"I'm not accusing him of anything. I just want to know where the cloth came from."

This time the bully-boy did the talking, ended by pointing across the plaza.

"Master, a slave sold the cloth to the merchant."

"What kind of slave?"

"Master . . . a Man-slave."

"Like me?"

"He says—yes, Master."

I let my elbow touch the butt of my filament pistol. If the crowd that had gathered around to watch and listen decided to turn nasty, it wouldn't help much; but it was comforting anyway.

"Where did he see this Man-slave?"

"Here, Master; the slave is the property of the Least Triarch."

"Find out where the Triarch lives."

"There, Master." Srat pointed to a dusty blue facade rising behind the other buildings like a distant cliff-face. "That is the palace of His Least Greatness."

"Let's go." I started past the Rule-keeper and he jabbered at Srat.

"Master, he says you have forgotten his bribe."

"My mistake." I handed over another chip. "Tell him I'd like his assistance in getting an interview with the Triarch."

A price was agreed on and he led the way across the plaza and through the network of dark streets, along a complicated route that ended in a tiled courtyard with a yellow glass roof that made it look almost like a sunny day. There were trees and flowering shrubs around a reflecting pool, a shady cloister along the far side. Srat was nervous; he perched on a chair and mewed to himself. Eureka stretched out and stared across at a tall blue-legged bird wading in the pool.

A small Drathian came over and took orders. He asked Eureka three times what he'd have; he couldn't seem to get the idea that the old cat didn't speak the language. The drinks he brought were a thick, blue syrup with a taste of sulfur and honey. Srat sniffed his cup and said, "Master must not drink this," and proceeded to swallow his share in one gulp. I stared into the shadows under the arcade where my guide had disappeared, and pretended to nibble the drink. Rain drummed on the glass overhead. It was steamy hot, like a greenhouse. After half an hour, the Drathian came back, with a friend.

The newcomer was six feet tall, five feet wide, draped in dark blue velvet and hung with ribbons and tassels and fringes like a Victorian bonnet. He was introduced as Hruba. He was the Triarch's majordomo, and he spoke very bad, but understandable lingua.

"You may crave one boon of His Greatness," he stated. "In return, he will accept a gift."

"I understand the Triarch owns a human slave," I said. "I'd like to see him, if His Greatness has no objection."

The majordomo agreed, and gave orders to a servant; in ten minutes the servant was back, prodding a man along ahead of him.

He was a stocky, strong-looking fellow with close-cropped black hair, well-cut features, dressed in a plain dark blue kilt. There was an ugly, two-inch scar on his left side, just below the ribs. He saw me and stopped dead and his face worked.

"You're a human being!" he gasped—in Zeridajhi.

3

His name was Huvile, and he had been a prisoner for ten years. He'd been captured, he said, when his personal boat had developed drive control troubles and had carried him off course into Fringe Space.

"In the name of humanity, Milord," he begged, "buy my freedom." He looked as if he wanted to kneel, but the big Drathian servant was holding his arm in a two-handed grip.

"I'll do what I can," I said.

"Save me, Milord—and you'll never regret it! My family is wealthy—" That was as far as he got before Hruba waved an arm and the servant hustled him away.

I looked at the majordomo.

"How much?"

"He is yours."

I expressed gratification, and offered money in return. Hruba indicated that Bar money was hard to spend on Drath. I ran through a list of items from *Jongo II*'s well-stocked larders and storage hold; we finally agreed on a mixed consignment of drugs, wines, clothing and sense-tapes.

"His Greatness will be gratified," Hruba said

expansively, "at this opportunity to display his graciousness." He aimed a sense-organ at me. "Ah . . . you wouldn't by chance wish to accept a second slave?"

"Another Man?"

"As it happens."

"How many more humans have you got?"

"His Greatness owns many properties; but only the two humans." His voice got almost confidential: "Useful, of course, but a trifle, ah, intractable. But *you'll* have no trouble on that score, I'm sure."

We dickered for ten minutes and settled on a deal that would leave *Jongo II*'s larder practically stripped. It was lucky the Triarch didn't own three men; I couldn't have afforded any more.

"I will send porters and a car to fetch these trifles from your vessel," Hruba said, "which His Greatness accepts out of sentiment. You wish the slaves delivered there?"

"Never mind; I'll take them myself." I started to get up.

Hruba made a shocked noise. "You would omit the ceremonies of Agreement, of Honorable Dealing, of Mutual Satisfaction?"

I calmed him down and he sent his staff scurrying for the necessary celebratory paraphernalia.

"Srat, you go to the ship, hand over the goods we agreed on, and see that the men get aboard all right. Take Eureka with you."

"Master, Poor Srat is afraid to go alone—and he fears for Master—"

"Better get going or they'll be there ahead of you."

He made a sad sound and hurried away.

"Your other slave," the majordomo pointed. Across the court, a Drathian servant came out from a side entry leading a slim figure in a gray kilt like Huvile had worn.

"You said another man," I said stupidly.

"Eh? You doubt it is a Man?" he asked in a stiff voice. "It is not often that the probity of His Least Greatness is impugned in his own Place of Harmonious Accord!"

"My apologies," I tried to recover. "It was just a matter of terminology. I didn't expect to see a female."

"Very well, a female Man—but still a Man and a sturdy worker," the majordomo came back. "Not so large as the other, perhaps, but diligent, diligent. Still, His Greatness would not have you feel cheated. . . ." His voice faded off. He was watching me as I watched the servant leading the girl past, some twenty feet away. She had a scar on her side, exactly like Huvile's. Beside the horny, gray-green thorax of the Drathian beside her, her human breast looked incredibly vulnerable. Then she turned her head my way and I saw that it was the Lady Raire.

4

For a long, echoing instant, time stood still. Then she was past. She hadn't seen me, sitting in the deep shade of the canopy. I heard myself make some kind of sound and realized I had half risen from my chair.

"This slave is of some particular interest for you?" the majordomo inquired, and I could tell from the edge on his voice that his commercial instinct was telling him he had missed a bet somewhere.

I sat down. "No," I managed to croak. "I was wondering . . . about the scars. . . ."

"Have no fear; the cicatrice merely marks the point where the control drive is embedded. However, perhaps I should withdraw His Greatness's offer of this gift, since it is less than you expected, lest the generosity of the Triarch suffer reflection. . . ."

"My mistake," I said. "I'm perfectly satisfied." I could feel my heart slamming inside my chest. I felt as though the universe was balanced on a knife-edge. One wrong word from me and the whole fragile deal would collapse.

The liquor pots arrived then, and conversation was suspended while my host made a big thing of tasting half a dozen varieties of syrupy booze and organizing the arrangement of outsize drinking pots on the table. I sat tight and sweated bullets and wondered how it was going back at the ship.

The Drathian offered the local equivalent of a toast. While my host sucked his cup dry, I pretended to take a sip, but he noticed and writhed his face at me.

"You do not sup! Is your zeal for Honorable Dealing less than complete?"

This time I had to drink. The stuff had a sweet overflavor, but left an aftertaste of iron filings. I forced it down. After that, there was another toast. He watched to be sure I drank it. I tried not to think about what the stuff was doing to my stomach. I fixed my thoughts on a face I had just seen, looking no older than the day I had seen it last, nearly four years before; and the smooth, suntanned skin, and the hideous scar that marred it.

There was a lot of chanting and exchanging of cups, and I chewed another drink. Srat would be showing Milady Raire to a cabin now, and she'd be feeling the softness of a human-style bed, a rug under her bare feet, the tingle of the ion-bath for the first time in four years. . . .

"Another toast!" Hruba called; His command of lingua was slipping; the booze was having a powerful effect on him. It was working on me, too. My head was buzzing and there was a frying-egg feeling in my stomach. My arms felt almost too heavy to lift. The taste of the liquor was cloying in my mouth. When the next cup was passed my way I pushed it aside.

"I've had all I can take," I said, and felt my tongue slur the words. It was hard to push the chair back and stand. Hruba rose, too. He was swaying slightly—or maybe it was just my vision.

"I confess surprise, Man," he said. "Your zeal in the pledging of honor exceeded even my own. My brain swims in a sea of consecrated wine!" He turned to a servant standing by and accepted a small box from him.

"The control device governing your new acquisition," he said and handed the box over to me. I took it and my finger touched a hidden latch and the lid valved open. There was a small plastic ovoid inside, bedded in floss.

"Wha's . . . what's this?"

"Ah, you are unfamiliar with our Drathian devices!" He plucked the egg from its niche and waved it under my nose.

"This gnurled wheel; on the first setting, it administers sharp reminder; at the second position . . ." he pushed the control until it clicked, " . . . an attack of angina which doubles the object in torment. And at the third . . . but I must not demonstrate the third setting, eh? Or you will find yourself with a dead slave on your hands, his heart burned to charcoal by a magnesium element buried in the organ itself!" He tossed the control back into the box and sat down heavily. "That pertaining to the female is in the possession of her tender; he will leave it in the hands of your servant. You'll have no trouble with 'em. . . ." He made a sound that resembled a hiccup. "Best return to zero setting the one I handled; if its subject lacks stamina, he may be dead by now."

I tilted the box and dumped the ovoid on the ground and stamped on it; it crunched like a blown egg. Hruba came out of his chair in a rush. "Here—what are you doing!" He stared down at the smashed controller, then at me. "Have you lost your mind, Man?"

"I'm going now," I said, and went past him toward the passage I had entered by, a long time ago, it seemed. Behind me, Hruba was shouting in the local dialect. A servant jittered in front of me, and I yanked my pistol out and waved it and he jumped aside.

Out in the street, night had fallen, and the wet pavement glimmered under the yellow-green glare of lanterns set on the building fronts. I felt deathly ill. The street seemed to be rising up under my feet. I staggered, stayed on my feet by holding onto the wall. A pain like a knife-thrust stabbed into my stomach. I headed off in the direction of the port, made half a block before I had to lean against the wall and retch. When I straightened there were half a dozen Drathians standing by, watching me with their obscene faces. I yelled something at them, and they scattered back, and I went on.

I passed the plaza where I had found the Zeridajhi cloth, recognized the street along which Srat and Eureka and I had come. It seemed to be a steep hill, now. My legs felt like soft tallow. I fell and got up and fell again. I retched until my stomach was a dry knot of pain. It was harder getting to my feet this time. My lungs were on fire. The pain in my head was like a hammer swinging against my temples. My eyes were crossing, and I stumbled along between twinned walls, seeing the two-headed Drathians retreat before me.

Then I saw the port ahead, the translucent, glowing dome rising at the end of the narrow alleyway. Not much farther, now. Srat would be wondering what happened; maybe he would be waiting, just ahead. And at the ship, the Lady Raire. . . .

I was lying on my face, and the sky was spinning slowly over me, a pitch-black canopy with the great dim blur of Center sprawled across it, and the faint avenue that was the Bar reaching out to trail off into the dwindling spiral curve of the Eastern Arm. I found the pavement under me, and pushed against it, and got to my knees, then to my feet. I could see the ship across the ramp, tall and rakish, her high polish dimned by the years of hard use, her station lights glaring amber from high on her slim prow. I steadied myself and started across toward her, and as I did the rectangle of light that was the open port narrowed and winked out. The amber lights flicked out and the red and green pattern of her running lights sprang up. I stopped dead and felt a drumming start up, vibrating through the pavement under my feet.

I started to run then, and my legs were broken straws that collapsed and my head hit and the blow cleared it for a moment. I got my chin up off the pavement; and *Jongo II* lifted, standing up away from the surface on a tenuous pillar of blue flame that lengthened as she rose. Then she was climbing swiftly into the night, tilting away, dwindling above the licking tongue of pale fire that shrank, became a tiny point of twinkling yellow, and was gone.

5

They were all around me in a tight circle. I stared at their horny shins, their sandaled feet, as alien as an alligator's, and felt the icy sweat clammy on my face. Deathly sickness rose inside me in a wave that knotted my stomach and left me quivering like a beached jellyfish.

The legs around me stirred and gave way to a tall Drathian in the white serape of a Rule-keeper. Hard hands clamped on me, dragged me to my feet. A light glared in my face.

"Man, the Rule-keeper demands you produce the two slaves given as a gift to you by His least Greatness!"

"Gone," I gargled the words. "Trusted Srat. Filthy midget . . ."

"Man, you are guilty of a crime of the first category! Illegal manumission of slaves! To redress these crimes, the Rule-keeper demands a fine of twice the value of the slaves, plus triple bribes for himself and his attendants!"

"You're out of luck," I said. "No money . . . no ship . . . all gone. . . ."

I felt myself blacking out then. I was dimly aware of being carried, of lights glaring on me, later of a pain that seemed to tear me open, like a rotten fruit; but it was all remote, far away, happening to someone else. . . .

6

I came to myself lying on a hard pallet on a stone floor, still sick, but clear-headed now. For a while, I looked at the lone glare-bulb in the ceiling and tried to remember what had happened, but it was all a confused fog. I sat up and a red-hot hook grabbed at my side. I pulled back the short, coarse-weave jacket I was wearing, and saw a livid, six-inch cut under my ribs, neatly stitched with tough thread. It was the kind of wound that would heal in a few weeks and leave a welted scar; a scar like I'd seen recently, in the sides of Huvile and the Lady Raire. A scar that meant I was a slave.

CHAPTER NINE

The controller made a small lump under the skin. It wasn't painful—not unless you got too close to your overseer. At ten feet, it began to feel like a slight case of indigestion. At five, it was a stone knife being twisted in your chest. Once, in an experimental mood, I pushed in to four feet from him before he noticed and waved me back. It was like a fire in my chest. That was just the mild form of its action, of course. If he had pushed the little lever on the egg-shape strapped to his arm— or died, while the thing was tuned to his body inductance—the fire in my chest would be real. Once, months later, I saw three slaves whose keeper had been accidentally killed; the holes burned in their chests from the inside were as big as dinner plates.

As a rule, though, the Lesser Triarch believed in treating his slaves well, as valuable property deserved. Hruba dropped by twice a day for the first few days to be sure that my alien flesh was healing properly. I spent my time lying on the bed or hobbling up and down the small, windowless room, talking to myself:

"You're a smart boy, Billy Danger. You learned a lot, these last four years. Enough to get yourself a ship of your own, and bring it here, against all the odds there are, to find her. And then you handed her and the ship to the midget on a silver platter—for the second time. He must have had a good laugh. For a year he followed you like a sick pup, and wagged his tail every time you looked his way. But he was waiting. And you made it easy. While you sat there poisoning yourself, he strolled back to the ship, told Huvile you weren't coming, and lifted off. The Lady Raire might have interfered, but she never knew; she didn't see you. And now Srat has her right back where she started. . . ."

It wasn't a line of thought that made me feel better, but it served the purpose of keeping me on my feet, pacing. With those ideas chewing at me, I wasn't in a mood for long, restful naps.

When the wound had stitched up, a Drathian overseer took me out of my private cell and herded me along to a big room that looked like a nineteenth century sweatshop. There were other slaves there, forty or fifty of them, all shapes, all sizes, even a few Drathians who'd run foul of the Rule-keepers. I was assigned to a stool beside a big, broad-backed animal with a face like a Halloween mask snipped out of an old inner tube and fringed with feathery red gills. The overseer talked to him in the local buzz-buzz, and went away. He looked at me with big yellow eyes like a twin-yolked egg, and said, "Welcome to the club, friend," in perfect, unaccented lingua, in a voice that seemed to come from under a tin washtub.

He told me that his name was Fsha-fsha, that he had been left behind seventeen years before when the freighter he was shipping on had been condemned here on Drath after her linings went out, and that he had been a slave since his money ran out, three months after that.

"It's not a bad life," he said. "Plenty of food, a place to sleep, and the work's not arduous, after you've learned the routine."

The routine, he went on to explain, was Sorting. "It's a high-level job," Fsha-fsha assured me. "Only the top-category workers get this slot. And let me tell you, friend, it's better than duty in the mines, or on the pelagic harvesting rafts!"

He explained the work; it consisted of watching an endless line of glowing spheres as they came toward us along a conveyor belt, and sorting them into one of eight categories. He told me what the types were, and demonstrated; all the while he talked, the bulbs kept coming, and his big hands flicked the keys in front of him, shunting them their separate ways. But as far as I could tell, all the bulbs were exactly alike.

"You'll learn," he said blandly, and flipped a switch that stopped the line. He fetched a lightweight assembly of straps from a wall locker.

"Training harness," he explained. "It helps you catch on in a hurry." He fitted it to me with the straps and wires crisscrossing my back and chest, along my arms, cinched up tight on each finger. When he finished, he climbed back on his stool, and switched on the line.

"Watch," he said. The glowing bulbs came toward him and his fingers played over the keys.

"Now you follow through on your console," he said. I put my hands on the buttons and he reached across to attach a snap that held them there. A bulb came toward me and a sensation like a hot needle stabbed the middle finger on my right hand. I punched the key under it and the pain stopped, but there was another bulb coming, and the needle stabbed my little finger this time, and I jabbed with it, and there was another bulb coming. . . .

"It's a surefire teaching system," Fsha-fsha said in

his cheery, sub-cellar voice. "Your hands learn to sort without even bringing the forebrain into it. You can't beat pain-association for fast results."

For the rest of the shift, I watched glorm-bulbs sail at me, trying to second-guess the pain circuits that were activated by Fsha-fsha's selections. All I had to do was recognize a left-forefinger or right ring-finger bulb before he did, and punch the key first. By the end of the first hour my hands ached like unlanced boils. By the second hour, my arms were numb to the elbow. At the end of three hours I was throbbing all over.

"You did fine," Fsha-fsha told me when the gong rang that meant the shift was ended. "Old Hruba knew what he was doing when he assigned you here. You're a quick study. You were coding ten percent above random the last few minutes."

He took me along a damp-looking tunnel to a gloomy barracks where he and twenty-six other slaves lived. He showed me an empty alcove, got me a hammock and helped me sling it, then took me along to the mess. The cook was a warty creature with a ferocious set of ivory tusks, but he turned out to be a good-natured fellow. He cooked me up a sort of omelette that he assured me the other Man-slaves had liked. It wasn't a gourmet's delight, but it was better than the gruel I'd had in the hospital cell.

I slept then, until my new tutor shook me awake and led me back to the Sorting line.

The training sessions got worse for the next three shifts; then I started to catch on—or my eye and fingers did; I still couldn't consciously tell one glorm-bulb from another. By the time I'd been at it for six weeks, I was as good as Fsha-fsha. I was promoted to a bulb-line of my own, and the harness went back in the locker.

The Sorting training, as it turned out, didn't only

apply to glorm-bulbs. One day the line appeared with what looked like tangles of colored spaghetti riding on it.

"Watch," Fsha-fsha said, and I followed through as he sorted them into six categories. Then I tried it, without much luck.

"You have to key-in your response patterns," he said. "Tie this one . . ." he flipped his sorting key, " . . . to one of your learned circuits. And this one . . ." he coded another gob of wires, " . . . to another. . . ."

I didn't really understand all that, but I tried making analogies to my subliminal distinctions among apparently identical glorm-bulbs—and it worked. After that, I sorted all kinds of things, and found that after a single run-through, I could pick them out unerringly.

"You've trained a new section of your brain," Fsha-fsha said. "And it isn't just a Sorting line where this works; you can use it on any kind of categorical analysis."

During the off-shifts, we slaves were free to relax, talk, gamble with homemade cards and dice, commune with ourselves, or sleep. There was a small, walled court we could crowd into when the sun shone, to soak up a little vitamin D, and a cold, sulfury-smelling cave with a pool for swimming. Some of the slaves from watery worlds spent a lot of time there. I developed a habit of taking long walks—fifty laps up and down the barrack-room—with Fsha-fsha stumping along beside me, talking. He was a great storyteller. He'd spent a hundred and thirty years in space before he'd been marooned here; he'd seen things that took the curl out of my hair to listen to.

The weeks passed and I sorted, watched, and listened. The place I was in was an underground factory, located, according to Fsha-fsha, in the heart of the city. There was only one exit, along a tunnel and up a flight of stairs barred by a steel gate that was guarded day and night.

"How do they bring in supplies?" I asked my sidekick. "How do they ship the finished products out? They can't run everything up and down one little stairway."

Fsha-fsha gave me what I had learned to interpret as a shrug. "I don't know, Danger. I've seen the stairs, because I've been out that way quite a few times—"

I stopped him and asked for a little more detail on that point.

"Now and then it happens a slave is needed for labors above-ground," he explained. "As for me, I prefer the peacefulness of my familiar routine; still, so long as the finger of the Triarch rests here—" he tapped a welted purple scar along his side— "I follow all orders with no argument."

"Listen, Fsha-fsha," I said. "Tell me everything you remember about your trips out: the route you took, the number of guards. How long were you out? How close did they watch you? What kind of weapons did they carry? Any chains or handcuffs? Many people around? Was it day or night? Did you work inside or outside—"

"No, Danger!" Fsha-fsha waved a square purple-palmed hand at me. "I see the way your mind's working; but forget the idea! Escape is impossible—and if you did break away from a work detail, you'd still be alone in the middle of Drath, an alien, not knowing the language, with every Rule-keeper in the city ready to pounce on you—"

"I know all that. But if you think I'm going to settle down here for the rest of my life, you're dead wrong. Now start telling me: How many guards escorted you?"

"Just one. As long as he has my controller in his pocket, one is all that's needed, even if I were the most intractable slave in the pens."

"How can I get picked for an outside detail?"

"When you're needed, you'll be called."

"Meanwhile, I'll be getting ready. Now give."

Fsha-fsha's memory was good. I was surprised to hear that for as much as an hour at a time, he had worked unsupervised.

"It's no use creeping off and hiding out under an overturned cart or in an unused root-cellar," he said. "One touch of the controller, and you're mewling aloud for your keeper."

"That means we'll have to get our hands on the control devices before we break."

"They've thought of that; the thing is tuned to your neuronic carrier frequency. If you get within three feet of it, it's triggered automatically. If the holder dies, it's triggered. And if it's taken off of the overseer's body, the same thing."

"We can stand it long enough to smash them."

"If the controller's destroyed, you die," he said flatly. "It's covered any way you play it."

"That's where you're wrong, Fsha-fsha." I told him about crushing the controller the night I had been arrested. "Huvile didn't die. The Rule-keeper saw him board *Jongo II,* an hour afterward."

"Strange—it's common knowledge among the slaves that if your controller is damaged, it kills you."

"It's a useful story for the slave-owners to spread."

"Maybe that's why they grabbed you so fast. You might have given the game away. Hell's ice, if the slaves knew. . . ."

"How about it, Fsha-fsha? Are you with me?"

He stared at me in the gloom of the comer where we'd drifted to talk in private. "You're a strange, restless creature, Danger," he said. "For a being as frail as you are, with that soft skin and brittle bones, you've got an almighty urge to look for trouble. Why not take a tip from me and make the best of it—"

"I'll get out of here, Fsha-fsha—and get clear of the planet, too—or die trying. I'd as soon be dead as here, so I'm not risking much."

Fsha-fsha made the noise that served him as a sigh. "You know, we Rinths see the Universe differently from your Propagators," he said. "With us, it's the Great Parent that produces the spores. We workers have the mobility, the intelligence—but no future, except the Parent. We have the instinct to protect the Tree, fertilize it and water it, prune it, insure its survival; but we've got no personal stake in the future, the way you have. Your instincts tell you to stay alive and propagate. Your body knows this is a dead end as far as offspring go, so it tells you to get out or die." He sighed again. "When I left Rinth, it was hard; for a long time, I had a homesickness that you wouldn't be able to understand—any more than I can really understand the way you feel now. But I can remember how it was. And if it's anything like that with you—yes; I can see you've got to try."

"That's right; I've got to try. But not you, Fsha-fsha. If you're really content here, stay. I'll make it on my own."

"You wouldn't have a chance, Danger. I know the language, the routes around the town. You need me. Not that it'll do any good in the end. But knowing about the controllers will make a difference."

"Forget it. You can teach me the language, and tell me all you can about the town. But there's no point in your getting killed—"

"That's another advantage a Rinth has," Fsha-fsha cut me off. "No instinct for self-preservation. Now, let's get started planning the details."

2

The weeks went by. I sorted, slept, took my language lesson, and worked to memorize the map of the city I drew up from Fsha-fsha's descriptions. About two months after our decision to crash out, Fsha-fsha got a call for an outside detail. He vetoed my suggestion that I volunteer to go along.

"This is a lucky break," he said. "It will give me a chance to look over the ground again, in the light of our plans. Rest easy. We'll get our chance."

"We Propagators aren't as patient as you Tree-farmers," I told him. "It may be another six months before an outside detail comes up again."

"Better to propagate in your old age than not at all, eh?" he reminded me, and I had to bite my teeth and watch him go. I got one quick look at the passage as he left. It was narrow, dim-lit; the Drathians didn't like a high level of illumination. I wondered if there was a useful tip for me in that.

Fsha-fsha came back rippling his gill-flaps in a way that I knew meant he was excited. But it turned out not to be pleased anticipation.

"It's hopeless, Danger," he assured me. "The Worm-face in charge of the detail carries the controllers in a special rack, strapped to his chest for quick access. He keeps his distance; ten feet was as close as I could get before he warned me back."

"What weapons did he carry?" I asked him.

"What weapon does he need? He holds your life in his hand as it is!"

"Too bad," I said. "We'll have to get our armaments somewhere else then."

Fsha-fsha goggled at me. "You're an amazing crea-ture, Danger. If you were cornered by a Fangmaster,

I think you'd complain that his teeth weren't larger,
so as to provide you with a better dagger!"

The routine settled in again then. Every day was like
the one before; the glorm-bulbs rushed at me in a
stream that never ended, never changed. I ate omelettes,
played revo and tikal and a dozen other games, walked
my two miles a day, up and down the dark room; and
waited. And one day, I made a blunder that ended our
plans with total finality.

3

The work-shift had ended half an hour before. Fsha-
fsha and I had settled down in his alcove to play our
favorite game of telling each other what we'd do, once
we were clear of Drath. A big Drathian slave who'd been
assigned to the Sorting crew a few hours earlier came
lumbering over, breathing out fumes that reminded me
of a package of rotten broccoli I'd opened once by
mistake.

"I'll take this alcove," he said to Fsha-fsha. "Get out,
animal."

"Makes himself right at home, doesn't he?" I
pointed across the room to an empty alcove. "Try over
there, sport," I said to the broccoli-breather. "Lots of
room—" I got that far when he reached out with a
couple of arms like boa constrictors and ripped down
the hammock. He yanked again, and tore the other
end free. He tossed it aside and swung his own kit
down onto the floor. I stood up.

"Wait," Fsha-fsha said quickly. "The overseer will
deal with this one. Don't—"

The big Drathian took a quick step, threw a punch
at me. I ducked, came up with a three-foot length of

steel pipe the Rinth had tucked under the hammock for possible future use, and brought it down in a two-handed blow across the Drathian's shoulder. He gave a bleat like a branded steer and went down bucking and kicking. In his convulsion, he beat his head against the floor, whipped his body against the wall hard enough to give off a dull *boom!* like a whale slapping the water with his tail. Thick, yellowish blood spattered. Every slave in the barracks came crowding around to see what was going on, but in thirty seconds it was all over. The big Drathian was dead. The Rule-keepers got there a minute or two later and took me away, up the stairs I'd looked forward to seeing for so long.

My hearing didn't amount to much. I explained to Hruba that the dead slave had attacked me, that I didn't know Drathians kept their brains under their shoulder blades; but it was an open-and-shut case. I'd killed a fellow slave. My Sorting days were over.

"Transportation to the harvesting rafts," the major-domo intoned in Drathian and repeated it in lingua. "Too bad, Man," he added in his unofficial voice. "You were a valuable Sorter—but like your kind, you have a savage streak in you most unbecoming in a chattel."

They clamped my wrists in a steel ring and hustled me out into a courtyard where a big, tarry-smelling air-barge was waiting. I climbed aboard, and was kicked into a metal-walled broom-closet. They slammed the door on me, and I lay in the dark and felt the barge lift off.

4

The harvesting rafts were mile-square constructions of metal floats linked by woven-rope mats and carpeted with rotting vegetable husks and the refuse of the canning sheds, which worked night and day processing the marine life hoisted aboard by the seining derricks. A pair of husky Drathians threw me off the side of the barge into foul-odored ankle-deep muck, and another pair grabbed me, knocked me around a little just to keep in practice, and dragged me away to a long lean-to which served to keep the worst of the subtropical rains off any of the workers who were lucky enough to be on off-shift. They took off the wrist-irons and rigged a fine-gauge fiber loop around my neck, not tight enough to choke me, but plenty snug enough to wear the skin raw, until it toughened and formed a half-inch-wide scar that itched and burned day and night. There was a limp bladder attached to the rope, designed to inflate and keep my head above water if I happened to fall overboard; slaves weren't allowed to evade their labors by anything as easy as drowning, intentionally or otherwise. I learned all this later; the first night the only orientation I got was what I could deduce from being dragged to a line of workers who were shelling out big crustaceans, and yelled at to get to work. The command was emphasized with a kick, but I had been watching for that; I slid aside from it and smashed my fist into the short ribs of the Drathian and chopped him again as he scrambled back. My reward for this effort was a solid beating, administered by three Drathians, two holding and one swinging a rod as heavy and limber as a golf club. They finished after a while, threw water over me, and someone shoved a sea-lobster at me.

"Better look busy," the slave on my left tipped me off. He was a medium-sized Drathian with a badly scarred face; that made us pals on two counts. I followed his advice.

There wasn't anything complicated about the work;

you grabbed your chzik, held him by the blunt end, hooked a finger under his carapace, and stripped it off him. Then you captured his four flailing limbs, and with a neat twist of the wrist, removed them. The chziks were active creatures, and they showed their resentment of this treatment by writhing frantically during the operation. When you found yourself tackling a big fellow—weight ten pounds or more—it could sometimes be a little difficult to carry out the job as smoothly as the overseers desired. They usually let you know when this was the case by hitting you across the back with the golf club.

At first, my fingers had a tendency to bleed, since the carapaces were razor-sharp and as tough as plexiglass, and the barbs on the legs had a way of lodging in my palms. But the wounds healed cleanly; the microorganisms of Drath were too alien to my metabolism to give rise to infections. And after a while calluses formed.

I was lucky in timing my arrival near the end of a shift; I was able to look busy enough to keep the overseer away, and make it under my own power to the shed. There were no bunks, no assigned spaces. You just crowded in as far as possible from the weather side and dropped. There was no insomnia on the rafts. The scarred Drathian—the same one who had given me some good advice the first night—helped me out again the next shift, by showing me how to nip off a chunk of raw chzik and suck it for the water content. The meat itself was spongy and inedible as far as I was concerned; but the slop dipped up to us at the regular feeding time was specially designed to be assimilable by a wide variety of species. When an off-brand worker showed up who couldn't live on the stuff, he soon starved, thus solving the problem.

Instead of the regular cycle of alternating

work- and rest-shifts, we harvesters worked two shifts out of three, which effectively prevented any chance of boredom. For six hours at a stretch, we manned our places by the chute with the squirming heaps of chziks arriving just a little faster than we could shell them out. The slippery mat under foot rose and fell in its never-ending rhythm, and beyond its edge, the steel-gray sea stretched to the horizon. Sometimes the sun beat down in a dead calm, and the unbelievable stink rose around us like a foul tide. At night flood-lights glared from high on the derricks, and the insects swarmed in to fly into our mouths and eyes and be trampled underfoot to add to the carpet. Sometimes rain came, hot and torrential, but the line never slowed. And later, when gray sleet coated the rigging and decks with soft ice, and the wind cut at us like sabers, we worked on, those of us who could stand the cold; the others settled into the muck and were hauled away and put over the side. And some of us who were still alive envied them.

I remembered reading, years before, back on old Earth, of concentration camp prisoners, and I wondered what it was that kept men going under conditions that made life a torture that never ended. Now I knew; it wasn't a high-minded determination to endure, or a dauntless will to take a blood-curdling revenge. It was an instinct older than thought, older than hate, that said: "Survive!"

And I survived. My hands toughened, my muscles strengthened, my skin hardened against the cold and the rain. I learned to sleep in icy slush, without pro-tection, with horny feet stumbling over me in the dark; to swallow the watery gruel and hold out the cup for more; to take the routine club-blows of the overseers without hitting back; in the end, without really notic-ing. There were no friendships on the rafts, no recreations. There was no time or energy for anything not directly related to staying alive for one more day. The Drathian who had helped me on the first day died one wet night, and another took his place; I had never even learned his name.

During my years in space, I had developed an instinctive time-sense that told me when a week, or a month, Earth-style, had passed. I had been almost five years away, now. Sometimes I wondered what had happened during those years, back on that small planet. But it was so far away that it seemed more like a dream than a reality.

For hours at a stretch, sometimes for a whole double shift, my mind would wander far away from the pelagic rafts of Drath. My memories seemed to become more vivid with time, until they were almost realer than the meaningless life around me.

And then one night, the routine broke. A morose-looking Drathian boss-overseer caught me as I went toward the chzik chute, shoved me toward the boat wharf.

"You're assigned as a net-handler," he told me. Except for the heavy leather coat he was wearing, he looked as cold and filthy and miserable as the slaves. I climbed down into the twenty-foot, double-prowed dory that was pitching in the choppy water at the foot of the loading ladder, and we shoved off. In five minutes the high-sided raft was out of sight in the ragged fog.

I sat in the stern and stared at the oily gray surface of the water. It was the first new sight I'd seen in many months. The wake was a swirl of foam that drifted aft, forming a pattern like an ugly face that leered up at me through the murky water. The face grew clearer, and then it broke water, a devil-mask of rippling black leaves edged with feathery red gills. An arm swept up, dripping water; I saw the flash of a knife blade as it swept down toward me—and felt the rope fall from my neck. A wide hand clamped on my arm, tumbled me over the stern, and before I could draw a breath, had dragged me down into the cold and the dark.

5

I woke up lying on my back in a warm, dry place. From the motion and the sound, I could tell I was on a boat. The air that moved over my face carried the sweet, clean smell of the sea. Fsha-fsha was standing beside the bunk; in the soft glow from the deck lamp, his face looked almost benign.

"It's a good thing I recognized you," I said, and was surprised at the weakness of my voice. "I might have spoiled things by putting a thumb in your eye."

"Sorry about the rough treatment," he said. "It was the best we could work out. The tender-master wasn't in on it; just the boss-overseer."

"It worked," I said, and stopped to cough, and tasted the alien saltwater of Drath. "That's all that counts."

"We're not clear yet, but the trickiest part went all right. Maybe the rest will work out, too."

"Where are we headed?"

"There's an abandoned harbor not far from here; about four hours' run. A filer will meet us there." I started to ask another question, but my eye was too heavy to hold open. I closed it and the warm blanket of darkness folded in on me.

6

Voices woke me. For a moment, I was back aboard Lord Desroy's yacht, lying on a heap of uncured *Nith*-hides, and the illusion was so strong that I felt a ghostly pang from the arm, broken and mended so long ago. Then Fsha-fsha's voice cut through the dream.

" . . . up now, Danger, have to walk a little way. How do you feel?"

I sat up and put my legs over the side of the cot and stood. "Like a drowned sailor," I said. "Let's go."

Up on the deck of the little surface cutter, I could see lights across the water. Fsha-fsha had put a heavy mackinaw across my shoulders. For the first time in a year, I felt cold. The engines idled back and we swung in beside a jetty. A small, furtive-looking Drathian was waiting beside a battered cargo-car. We climbed up into the box and settled down under some stiff tarpaulins, and a moment later the truck started up and pulled out in a whine of worn turbos.

I slept again. The habit of almost a year on the rafts, to sleep whenever I wasn't on the line, was too strong to break in an hour; and breathing the salt seas of Drath isn't the best treatment for human lungs. When I woke up this time, the car had stopped. Fsha-fsha put a hand on my arm and I lay quiet. Then he tapped me and we crawled out and slid down the tailgate, and I saw we were parked at the edge of the spaceport at Drath City. The big dome loomed up under the black sky across the ramp, as faded and patched as ever; and between us and it, the clumsy bulk of an ancient cargo-carrier squatted on battered parking jacks.

Something moved in the shadows and a curiously shaped creature swathed in a long cloak came up to us. He flipped back the hood and I saw the leathery face of a Rishian.

"You're late," he said unhurriedly. "A couple of local gendarmes nosing about. Best we waste no time." He turned and moved off toward the freighter. Fsha-fsha and I followed. We had covered half the distance when an actinic-green floodlight speared out to etch us in light, and a rusty-hinge voice shouted the Drathian equivalent of "Halt or I'll shoot!"

7

I ran for it. The Rishian, ten feet in the lead, spun, planted himself, brought up his arm and a vivid orange light winked. The spotlight flared and died, and I was past him, sprinting for the open cargo-port, still a hundred yards away across open pavement. A gun stuttered from off to the right, where the searchlight had been, and in the crisp yellow flashes I saw Drathian Rule-keepers bounding out to intercept us.

I altered course and charged the nearest Rule-keeper, hit him fair and square. As he fell, my fingers, which had learned to strip the carapace from a twelve-pound chzik with one stroke, found his throat and cartilage crumpled and popped and he went limp and I was back on my feet in time to see the other Drathian lunge for Fsha-fsha. I took him from behind, broke his neck with my forearm, lifted him and threw him ten feet from me. And we were running again.

The open port was just ahead, a brilliant rectangle against the dark swell of the hulk. Something gleamed red there, and Fsha-fsha threw himself sideways and a ravening spout of green fire lanced out and I went flat and rolled and saw a giant Drathian, his white serape thrown back across his shoulder, swinging a flare-muzzled gun around to cover me. I came to my feet and dove straight at him, but I knew I wouldn't make it—

Something small and dark plunged from the open port, leaped to the Drathian's back. He twisted, struck down with the butt of the gun, and I heard it thud on flesh. He struck again, and bone crunched, and the small, dark thing fell away, twisting on the pavement; and then I was on the Rule-keeper. I caught the gun muzzle, ripped it out of his hands, threw it away into the dark. His face was coming around to me, and I swung with all the power that the months of mule-labor had given my arm, and felt the horny mask collapse, saw the ochre blood spatter; he went down and I stepped over him and the small, dark creature that had attacked him moved and the light from the entry fell across it and showed me the mangled body of a H'eeaq.

8

Up above, a shrill Rishian voice was shouting. Behind me, I heard the thud of Drathian feet, their sharp, buzzing commands.

"Srat," I said, and could say no more. Thick, blackish blood welled from ghastly wounds. Broken rib-ends projected from the warty hide of his chest. One great goggle-eye was knocked from its socket. The other held on me.

"Master," the ugly voice croaked. "Greatly . . . my people wronged you. Yet—if my wounds . . . may atone for yours . . . forego your vengeance . . . for they are lonely . . . and afraid. . . ."

"Srat . . . I thought . . ."

"I fought the Man, Master," he gasped out. "But he was stronger . . . than I. . . ."

"Huvile!" I said. "*He* took the ship!"

Srat made a convulsive movement. He tried to speak, but only a moan came from his crocodile mouth.

I leaned closer.

"I die, Master," he said, "obedient . . . to your . . . desires. . . ."

CHAPTER TEN

Fsha-fsha and a Rishian crewman hauled me aboard the ship; Srat's corpse was left on the ramp. Other species aren't as sentimental about such things as Man is. There were a few angry objections from Drath Traffic Control as we lifted, but the Drathians had long since given up Deep Space travel, and the loss of a couple of runaway slaves wasn't sufficient reason to alienate the Rishians. They were one of the few worlds that still sent tramps into Fringe Space.

Once away, Fsha-fsha told me all that had happened since I was sent to the rafts:

"Once you'd planted the idea of escape, I had to go ahead with it," he said. "The next chance was three months later, two of us this time, just one overseer. I had a fancy plan worked out for decoying him into a side alley, but I had a freak piece of luck. It was a loading job, and a net broke and scattered cargo all over the wharf. The other slave got the whole load on his head—and a nice-sized iron casting clipped the guard and laid him out cold. He had the controllers

149

strapped to his arm, in plain sight, but getting to them was the hardest thing I ever did in my life. I used a metal bar from the spilled cargo on them and fainted at the same time.

"I came out of it just in time. The Load-master and a couple of Rule-keepers were just arriving. I got up and ran for it. They wasted a little time discovering my controller was out of action, and by then I had a good start. I headed for a hideaway I'd staked out earlier, and laid up there until dark.

"That night I came out and took a chance on a drinking-house that was run by a non-Drathian. I thought maybe he'd have a little sympathy for a fellow alien. I was wrong, but I strapped him to the bed and filled both my stomachs with high-lipid food, enough to keep me going for two weeks, and took what cash he had in the place and got clear.

"With money to spend, things were a little easier. I found a dive where I could lie low, no questions asked, and sent out feelers for information on where you'd been sent. The next day the little guy showed up: Srat.

"He'd been hanging around, waiting for a chance to talk to someone from the Triarch's stable. I don't know what he'd been eating, but it wasn't much; and he slept in the street.

"I told him what I knew; between us, we got you located. Then the Rish ship showed up."

The Rishian captain was sitting with us, listening. He wrinkled his face at me.

"The H'eeaq, Srat, spoke to me in my own tongue, greatly to my astonishment. Long ago, at Rish, I'd heard the tale of the One-Eyed Man who'd bartered half of the light of his world for the lives of his fellows. The symmetry of the matter demanded that I give such a one the help he asked."

"The little guy didn't look like much," Fsha-fsha said. "But he had all the guts there were."

"You may take pleasure in the memory of that rarest of creatures," the Rishian said. "A loyal slave."

"He was something rarer than that," I said. "A friend."

2

Fsha-fsha and I stayed with the freighter for three months; we left her on a world called Gloy. We could have ridden her all the way to Rish, but my destination was in the opposite direction: Zeridajh. Fsha-fsha stayed with me. One world was like another to him, he said. As for the ancestral Tree, having cut the ties, like a man recovered from an infatuation, he wasn't eager to retie them. The Rish captain paid us off for our services aboard his vessel—we had rebuilt his standby power section, as well as pulling regular shifts with the crew. That gave us enough cash to re-outfit ourselves with respectable clothes and take rooms at a decent inn near the port, while we looked for a Center-bound berth.

We had a long wait, but it could have been worse. There were shops and taverns and apartments built among the towering ruins of a vast city ten thousand years dead; but the ruins were overgrown and softened by time, so that the town seemed to be built among forested hills, unless you saw it from the air and realized that the mountains were vine-grown structures.

There was work for us on Gloy; by living frugally and saving what we earned, we accumulated enough for passenger berths inward to Tanix, a crossroads world where the volume of in-Galaxy shipping was more encouraging. After a few days' wait, we signed on a mile-long super-liner. It was a four months' cruise; at the end of it we stepped off on the soil of a busy trading planet, and looked up at the blaze of sky that meant Center was close.

"It's still three thousand lights run to Zeridajh," the Second Officer for Power told me as he paid me off. "Why not sign on for another cruise? Good powermen are hard to find; I can offer you a nice bonus."

"It's useless, Second," Fsha-fsha answered for me. "Danger is searching for a magic flower that only grows in one special garden, at the hub of the Galaxy."

After a couple of weeks of job-hunting, we signed on as scrapers on a Center-bound tub crewed by small, damp dandies from the edge of Center. That was the only berth a highbrow Center skipper would consider handing a barbarian from what they called the Outworlds. It was a long cruise, and as far as I could tell, the jobs that fell to a scraper on a Center ship were just as dirty as on any Outworld tub.

On our next cruise, we found ourselves stranded on a backwater world by a broken-down guidance system on the rotting hulk we had shipped in on. We waited for a berth outbound for a month, then took service under a local constabulary boss as mercenaries. We did a lot of jumping around the planet, marching in ragged jungle and eating inedible rations, and in the end barely got clear with our hides intact when the constabulary turned out to be a dacoit force. I made one interesting discovery; my sorting skill came in handy in using the bill-hook machetes issued to the troops. After one or two small run-ins, I had keyed-in a whole set of reflex responses that made me as good as the battalion champion.

Usually, though, we didn't see much of the planets we visited. It was normal practice, all across the Galaxy, for a world to channel all its space-faring commerce and traffic through a single port, for economy of facilities and ease of control. The ports I saw were like ports in all times and climes: cities without personality, reduced to the lowest common denominator of the thousand breeds of being they served.

After that, we found another slot, and another after that, on a small, fast lugger from Thlinthor; and on that jump we had a change in luck.

3

I was sound asleep in the off-watch cubbyhole I rated as a scraper when the alarm sirens went off. It took me thirty seconds to roll out and get across the deck to the screens where Fsha-fsha and half a dozen other on-watch crewmen were gaping at a sight that you only see once in a lifetime in Deep Space: a derelict hulk, adrift among the stars. This one was vast—and you could tell at one glance that she was old. . . .

We were five hundred miles apart, closing on courses that were only slightly skew; that made two miracles. We hove-to ten miles from her and took a good look, while the power officer conferred with Command Deck. Then the word came through to resume course.

"Huh?" Both Fsha-fsha and I swiveled on him. From the instant I'd seen the hulk, visions of prize-money had been dancing in my head like sugarplums. "He's not going to salvage her?" Fsha-fsha came as close to yelling as his mild nature would let him.

The power officer gave him a fishy look from fishy eyes in a fishy face. Like the rest of the crew, he was an amphibian who slept in a tank of salty water for three hours at a stretch—and like all his tribe, he was an agoraphobe to the last feathery scale on his rudimentary rudder fin. "It ith not practical," he said coldly.

"That tub's fifty thousand years old if she's a day," Fsha-fsha protested. "And I'm a mud-puppy if she's not a Riv Surveyor! She'll be loaded with Pre-collapse star maps! There'll be data aboard her that's been lost since before Thlinthor lofted her first satellite!"

"How would you propoth that we actthelerate thuch a math as that to interthtellar velothity?" he put the question to us. "The hulk outweigth uth a million to one. Our engines were not dethigned for thuch threthes."

"She looks intact," I said. "Maybe her engines are still in working order."

"Tho?"

"We can put a prize crew aboard her and bring her in under her own power."

The Thlinthorian tucked his head down between his shoulder plates, his version of a shudder.

"We Thlinthorians have no tathte for thuch exthploiths," he said. "Our mithion is the thafe delivery of conthigned cargo—"

"You don't have to go out on the hull," Fsha-fsha said. "Danger and I will volunteer."

The power officer goggled his eyes at us and conferred with Command Deck. After a few minutes of talk word came through that his Excellency the Captain was agreeable.

"One stipulation," I said. "We'll do the dirty work; but we take a quarter-share between us."

The captain made a counter-offer of a twentieth share each. We compromised on a tenth.

"I don't like it," Fsha-fsha told me. "He gave in too easily."

We suited up and took a small boat across to the old ship. She was a glossy brown ovoid about half a mile in diameter. Matching up with her was like landing on a planetoid. We found a hatch and a set of outside controls that let us into a dusty, cavernous hold. From there we went on through passenger quarters, recreation areas, technical labs and program rooms. In what looked like an armory, Fsha-fsha and I looked over a treasure-house of sophisticated personal offense and defense devices. Everything was in perfect order; and nowhere, then or later, did we ever find a bone of her crew, or any hint of what had happened to her.

A call from the captain on the portable communicator reminded us sharply that we had a job to do.

We followed a passage big enough to drive a moving van through, found the engine room, about the size of Grand Central Station. The generators ranged down the center of it were as massive as four-story apartment buildings. I whistled when I saw them, but Fsha-fsha took it in stride.

"I've seen bigger," he said. "Let's check out the system."

It took us four hours to work out the meaning of the oversized controls ranged in a circular console around a swiveled chair the size of a bank vault. But the old power plant started up with as sweet a rumble as if it had been in use every day.

After a little experimental jockeying, I got the big hull aligned on course coordinates and fed the power to the generators. As soon as we were up to cruise velocity, His Excellency the Captain ordered us back aboard. "Who are you sending over to relieve us?" I asked him.

"You may leave that detail to my discrethion," he told me in a no-argument tone.

"I can't leave this power section unmanned," I said.

He bugged his eyes at me on the four-inch screen of the pocket communicator and repeated his order, louder, with quotations from the Universal Code.

"I don't like it," Fsha-fsha said. "But I'm afraid we haven't got much choice."

Back aboard the mother-ship, our reception was definitely cool. Word had gotten around that we'd pigged an extra share of the goodies. That suited me all right. The Thlinthorians weren't the kind who inspired much in the way of affection.

When we were well inside the Thlinthorian system the power officer called Fsha-fsha and me in and showed us what was probably a smile.

"I confeth I entertained a thertain thuthpithion of you both," he confided. "But now that we have arrived in the Home Thystem with our thuperb prize thafely in the thlave orbit, I thee that my cauthion was exthethive. Gentlemen, join me in a drink!"

We accepted the invitation, and he poured out nice-sized tumblers of wine. I was just reaching for mine when Fsha-fsha jostled the table and sloshed wine from the glasses. The power officer waved aside his apologies and turned to ring for a mess-boy to mop up the puddle. In the instant his back was turned, Fsha-fsha dropped a small pellet in our host's drink, where it dissolved instantly. We all sat smiling benignly at each other while the small Thlinthorian servant mopped up, then lifted our glasses and swallowed. Fsha-fsha gulped his down whole. I took a nice swallow of mine, nodded my appreciation and took another. Our host chugalugged and poured another round. We sipped this one; he watched us and we watched him. I saw his eyes wander to the time-scale on the wall. Fsha-fsha looked at it, too.

"How long does it take your stuff to work?" he inquired pleasantly of the Thlinthorian. The latter goggled his eyes, made small choking noises, then, in a strangled voice said: "A quarter of an hour."

Fsha-fsha nodded. "I can feel it, a little," he said.

"We both belted a couple of null-pills before we came up, just in case you had any funny stuff you wanted to try. How do you feel?"

"Not well," the fish-mouth swallowed air. "I cannot control my . . . thpeech!"

"Right. Now, tell us all about everything. Take your time. It'll be an hour or two before we hit Planetary Control. . . ."

4

Fsha-fsha and I reached the port less than ten minutes behind the boat we had trailed in from where our ship and the Riv vessel were parked, a hundred thousand miles out. We found the captain already at the mutual-congratulation stage with the portmaster. His already prominent eyes nearly rolled down his scaled cheeks when he saw us.

"Perhaps the captain forgot to mention that he owes Captain Danger and myself a tenth-share in the prize," Fsha-fsha said, after the introductions were over.

"That's a prepothterouth falthhood!" the officer started, but Fsha-fsha cut him off by producing a pocket recorder of a type allowable in every law court in the Bar. The scene that followed lacked that sense of close comradeship so desirable in captain-crew relationships, but there was nothing our former commander could do but go along.

Afterward, in the four-room suite we treated ourselves to to rest up in, Fsha-fsha said, "Ah, by the way, Danger, I happened to pick up a little souvenir aboard that Riv tub—" He did something complicated with the groont-hide valise he carried his personal gear in and took out a small packet which opened out into a crisscross of flat, black straps with a round pillbox in the center.

"I checked it out," he said, sounding like a kid with a new bike. "This baby is something. A personal body shield. Wear it under your tunic. Sets up a field nothing gets through!"

"Nifty," I agreed, and worked the slides on the bottom of my kit bag. "I took a fancy to *this* little jewel." I held up my memento. It was a very handsome jeweled wristlet, which just fit around my neck.

"Uh-huh, pretty," Fsha-fsha said. "This harness of mine is so light you don't know you're wearing it—"

"It's not only pretty, it's a sense-booster," I interrupted his paean. "It lowers the stimulus-response threshold for sight, hearing and touch."

"I guess we out-traded old Slinth-face after all," Fsha-fsha said, after we'd each checked out the other's keepsake. "This squares the little finesse he tried with the sleepy-pills."

The salvage authorities made us wait around for almost a month, but since they were keeping forty Thlinthorian crew members waiting, too, in the end they had to publish the valuation and pay off all hands. Between us, Fsha-fsha and I netted more cash than the lifetime earnings of a spacer.

We shipped out the same day, a short hop to Hrix, a human-occupied world in a big twenty-seven-planet system only half a light from Thlinthor. It seemed like a good idea not to linger around town after the pay-off. On Hrix, we shopped for a vessel of our own; something small, and superfast. We still had over two thousand lights to cover.

Hrix was a good place to ship hunt. It had been a major shipbuilding world for a hundred thousand years, since before the era known as the Collapse when the original Central Empire folded—and incidentally gave the upstart tribe called Man its chance to spread out over the Galaxy.

For two weeks we looked at brand-new ships, good-as-new second- and third- and tenth-hand jobs, crawled over hulls, poked into power sections, kicked figurative tires in every shipyard in town, and were no further along than the day we started. The last evening, Fsha-fsha and I were at a table under the lanterns swinging from the low branches of the Heo trees in the drinking garden attached to our inn, taking over the day's frustrations.

"These new hulls we've been looking at," Fsha-fsha said; "mass-produced junk; not like the good old days—"

"The old stuff isn't much, either," I countered. "They were built to last, and at those crawl-speeds, they had to."

"Anything we can afford, we don't want," Fsha-fsha summed it up. "And anything we want, costs too much."

The landlord who was refilling our wine jug spoke up. "If you gentlebeings are looking for something a little out of the usual line, I have an old grand-uncle—fine old chap, full of lore about the old times—he's over three hundred you know—who still dabbles in buying and selling. There's a hull in his yard that might be just what the sirs are looking for, with a little fixing up—"

We managed to break into the pitch long enough to find out where the ship was, and after emptying our jug, took a walk down there. It looked like every junkyard I've ever seen. The place was grown with weeds taller than I was, and the sales office was a salvaged escape blister, with flowers growing in little clay pots in the old jet orifices. There was a light on, though, and we pounded until an old crookbacked fellow with a few wisps of pink hair and a jaw like a snapping turtle poked his head out. We explained what we wanted, and who had sent us. He cackled and rubbed his hands and allowed as how we'd come to the right place. By this time we were both thinking we'd made a mistake. There was nothing here but junk so old that even the permalloy was beginning to corrode. But we followed him back between towering stacks of obsolete parts and assemblies, over heaps of warped hull-plates, through a maze of stacked atmosphere fittings to what looked like a thicket dense enough for Bre'r Rabbit to hide in.

"If you sirs'll just pull aside a few tendrils of that danged wire vine," the old boy suggested. Fsha-fsha had his mouth open to decline, but out of curiosity, I started stripping away a finger-thick creeper, and back in the green-black gloom I saw a curve of dull-polished metal. Fsha-fsha joined in, and in five minutes we had uncovered the stern of what had once been elegance personified.

"She was built by Sanjio," the oldster told us. "See there?" he pointed at an ornate emblem, still jewel-bright against the tarnished metal. Fsha-fsha ran his hand over curve of the boat's flank, peered along the slim-lined hull. Our eyes met.

"How much?" he asked.

"You'll put her in shape, restore her," the old man said. "You wouldn't cut her up for the heavy metal in her jump fields, or convert her for rock-prospecting." It was a question. We both yelled no loud enough to satisfy him.

The old man nodded. "I like you boys' looks," he said. "I wouldn't sell her to just anybody. She's yours."

5

It took us a day to cut the boat free of the growth that had been crawling over her for eighty years. The old man, whose name was Knoute, managed, with curses and pleas and some help from a half-witted lad named Dune, to start up a long-defunct yard-tug and move the boat into a cleared space big enough to give us access to her. Fsha-fsha and I went through her from stem to stern. She was complete, original right down to the old logbook still lying in the chart table. It gave us some data to do further research on. I spent an afternoon in the shipping archives in the city, and that evening at dinner read the boat's history to Fsha-fsha:

"*Gleerim*, fifty-five feet, one hundred and nine tons. Built by Sanjio, master builder to Prince Ahax, as color-bearer to the Great House, in the year Qon. . . ."

"That would be just over four thousand years ago," Knoute put in.

"In her maiden year, the Prince Ahax raced her at Poylon, and at Gael, and led a field of thirty-two to win at Fonteraine. In her fortieth year, with a long record of brilliant victories affixed to her crestplate, the boat was sold at auction by the hard-pressed and aged prince. Purchased by a Vidian dealer, she was passed on to the Solarch of Trie, whose chief of staff, recognizing the patrician lines of the vessel, refitted her as his personal scout. Captured nineteen years later in a surprise raid by the Alzethi, the boat was mounted on a wooden-wheeled platform and hauled by chained dire-beasts in a triumphal procession through the streets of Alz. Thereafter, for more than a century, the boat lay abandoned on her rotting cart at the edge of the noisome town.

"Greu of Balgreu found the forgotten boat, and set a crew to cutting her out of her bed of tangled wildwood. Fancying the vessel's classic lines, the invading chieftain removed her to a field depot, where his shipfitters hammered in vain at her locked port. Greu himself hacked in at her crestplate, desiring it as an ornament, but succeeded only in shattering his favorite dress short-sword. In his rage, he ordered flammable rubble to be heaped on the boat, soaked with volatiles, and fired. After he razed the city and departed with his troops, the boat again lay in neglect for two centuries. Found by the Imperial Survey Team of His Effulgent Majesty, Lleon the fortieth, she was returned to Ahax, where she was refitted and returned to service as color-bearer to the Imperial House."

"That was just her first days," Knoute said. "She's been many places since then, seen many sights. And the vessel doesn't exist to this day that can outrun her."

It took us three months to repair, refit, clean, polish, tune and equip the boat to suit ourselves and old Knoute. But in the end even he had to admit that the Prince Ahax himself couldn't have done her more proud. And when the time came to pay him, he waved the money aside.

"I won't live to spend it," he said. "And you boys have bled yourselves white, doing her up. You'll need what you've got left to cruise her as she should be cruised, wanting nothing. Take her, and see that the lines you add to her log don't shame her history."

6

Two thousand light-years is a goodly distance, even when you're riding the ravening stream of raw power that *Jongo III* ripped out of the fabric of the continuum and converted to acceleration that flung us inward at ten, a hundred, a thousand times the velocity of propagation of radiation. We covered the distance in jumps of a month or more, while the blaze of stars thickened across the skies ahead like clotting cream. We saw worlds where intelligent life had existed for thousands of centuries, planets that were the graveyards of cultures older than the dinosaurs of Earth. When our funds ran low, we made the discovery that even here at the heart of the Galaxy, there were people who would pay us a premium for fast delivery of passengers and freight.

Along the way we encountered life-forms that ranged from intelligent gnat-swarms to the titanic slumbering swamp-minds of Buroom. We found men on a hundred worlds, some rugged pioneers barely holding their own against hostile environments of ice or desert or competing flora and fauna, others the polished and refined products of millenia-old empires that had evolved cultural machinery as formal and complex as a lifelong ballet. There were worlds where we were welcomed to cities made of jade and crystal, and worlds where sharpers with faces like Neapolitan street-urchins plotted to rob and kill us; but our Riv souvenirs served us well, and a certain instinct for survival got us through.

And the day came when Zeridajh swam into our forward screens, a misty green world with two big moons.

7

The Port of Radaj was a multilevel composition of gardens, pools, trees, glass-smooth paving, sculpture-clean facades, with the transient shipping parked on dispersed pads like big toys set out for play. Fsha-fsha and I dressed up in our best shore-going clothes and rode a toy train in to a country-club style terminal.

The landing formalities were minimal; a gray-haired smoothie who reminded me of an older Sir Orfeo welcomed us to the planet, handed us illuminated handmaps that showed us our position as a moving point of green light, and asked how he could be of service.

"I'd like to get news of someone," I told him. "A Lady—the Lady Raire."

"Of what house?"

"I don't know; but she was traveling in the company of Lord Desroy."

He directed us to an information center that turned out to be manned by a computer. After a few minutes of close questioning and a display of triograms, the machine voice advised me that the lady I sought was of the House of Ancinet-Chanore, and that an interview with the head of the house would be my best bet for further information.

"But is she here?" I pressed the point. "Did she get back home safely?"

The computer repeated its advice and added that transportation was available outside gate twelve.

We crossed the wide floor of the terminal and came out on a platform where a gorgeous scarlet and silver inlaid porcelain car waited. We climbed in, and a discreet voice whispered an inquiry as to our destination.

"The Ancinet-Chanore estate," I told it, and it clicked and whooshed away along a curving, soaring avenue that lofted us high above wooded hills and rolling acres of lawn with glass-smooth towers in pastel colors pushing up among the crowns of multi-thousand-year-old Heo trees. After a fast half-hour run, the car swooped down an exit ramp and pulled up in front of an imposing gate. A gray-liveried man on duty there asked us a few questions, played with a console inside his glass-walled cubicle, and advised us that the Lord Pastaine was at leisure and would be happy to grant us an interview.

"Sounds like a real VIP," Fsha-fsha commented as the car tooled up the drive and deposited us at the edge of a terrace fronting a sculptured facade.

"Maybe it's just a civilized world," I suggested.

Another servitor in gray greeted us and ushered us inside, through a wide hall where sunlight slanting down through a faceted ceiling shed a rosy glow on luminous wood and brocaded hangings, winked from polished sculptures perched in shadowy recesses. And I thought of the Lady Raire, coming from this, living in a cave grubbed out of a dirt-bank, singing to herself as she planted wild flowers along the paths. . . .

We came out into a patio, crossed that and went along a colonnaded arcade, emerged at the edge of a stretch of blue-violet grass as smooth as a billiard table, running down across a wide slope to a line of trees with the sheen of water beyond them. We followed a tiled path beside flowering shrubs, rounded a shallow pool where a fountain jetted liquid sunshine into the air, arrived at a small covered terrace, where a vast, elderly man with a face like a clean-shaven Moses rested in an elaborately padded chair.

"The Lord Pastaine," the servant said casually and stepped to adjust the angle of the old gentleman's chair to a more conversational position. Its occupant looked us over impassively, said, "Thank you, Dos," and indicated a pair of benches next to him. I introduced myself and Fsha-fsha and we sat. Dos murmured an offer of refreshment and we asked for a light wine. He went away and Lord Pastaine gave me a keen glance.

"A Man from a very distant world," he said. "A Man who is no stranger to violence." His look turned to Fsha-fsha. "And a being equally far from his home-world, tested also in the crucible of adversity." He pushed his lips out and looked thoughtful. "And what brings such adventurers here, to ancient Zeridajh, a world in the twilight of its greatness, to call upon an aged idler, dozing away the long afternoon of his life?"

"I met a lady, once, Milord," I said. "She was a long way from home—as far as I am, now, from mine. I tried to help her get home, but . . . things went wrong." I took a deep breath. "I'd like to know, sir, if the Lady Raire is here, safe, on Zeridajh."

His face changed, turned to wood. "The Lady Raire?" His voice had a thin, strained quality. "What do you know of her?"

"I was hired by Sir Orfeo," I said. "To help on the hunt. There was an accident. . . ." I gave him a brief account of the rest of the story. "I tried to find a lead to the H'eeaq," I finished. "But with no luck." It was on the tip of my tongue to tell him the rest, about Huvile and the glimpse I'd gotten of her, three years before, on Drath; but for some reason I didn't say it. The old man watched me all the while I talked. Then he shook his head.

"I am sorry, sir," he said, "that I have no good tidings for you."

"She never came back, then?"

His mouth worked. He started to speak, twice, then said, "No! The devoted child whom I knew was spirited away by stealth, by those whom I trusted, and never returned!"

I let that sink in. The golden light across the wide lawn seemed to fade suddenly to a tawdry glare. The vision of the empty years rose up in front of me.

" . . . send out a search expedition," Fsha-fsha was saying. "It might be possible—"

"The Lady Raire is dead!" the old man raised his voice. "Dead! Let us speak of other matters!"

The servant brought the wine, and I tried to sip mine and make small talk, but it wasn't a success. Across the lawn a servant in neat gray livery was walking a leashed animal along a path that sparkled blood-red in the afternoon sun. The animal didn't seem to like the idea of a stroll. He planted all four feet and pulled backward. The man stopped and mopped at his forehead while the reluctant pet sat on his haunches and yawned. When he did that, I was sure. I hadn't seen a cat for almost three years, but I knew this one. His name was Eureka.

CHAPTER ELEVEN

Ten minutes later, as Fsha-fsha and I crossed the lawn toward the house, a broad-shouldered man with curled gray hair and an elegantly simple tunic emerged from a side path ahead.

"You spoke to His Lordship of Milady Raire?" he said in a low voice as we came up.

"That's right."

He jerked his head toward the house. "Come along to where we can talk quietly. Perhaps we can exchange information to our mutual advantage." He led us by back passages into the deep, cool gloom of a room fitted up like an office for a planetary president. He told us his name was Sir Tanis, and got out a flagon and glasses and poured a round.

"The girl reappeared three months ago," he said. "Unfortunately," he added solemnly, "she is quite insane. Her first act was to disavow all her most hallowed obligations to the House of Ancinet-Chanore. Now, I gather from the few scraps of advice that reached my ears—"

"Dos talks as well as listens, I take it," I said.

"A useful man," Sir Tanis agreed crisply. "As I was saying, I deduce that you know something of Milady's activities while away from home. Perhaps you can tell me something which might explain the sad disaffection that afflicts her."

"Why did Lord Pastaine lie to us?" I countered.

"The old man is in his dotage," he snapped. "Perhaps, in his mind, she *is* dead." His lips quirked in a mirthless smile. "He's unused to rebellion among the very young." The brief smile dropped. "But she didn't stop with asserting her contempt for His Lordship's doddering counsels; she spurned as well the advice of her most devoted friends!"

"Advice on what?"

"Family matters," Tanis said shortly. "But you were about to tell me what's behind her incomprehensible behavior."

"Was I?"

"I assumed as much—I confided in you!" Tanis looked thwarted. "See here, if it's a matter of, ah, compensation for services rendered . . ."

"Maybe you'd better give me a little more background."

He looked at me sternly. "As you're doubtless aware, the House of Ancinet-Chanore is one of the most distinguished on the planet," he said. "We trace our lineage back through eleven thousand years, to Lord Ancinet of Traval. Naturally, such a house enjoys a deserved preeminence among its peers. And the head of that house must be an individual of the very highest attainments. Why . . ." he looked indignant, "if the seat passed to anyone but myself, in a generation—less! we should deteriorate to the status of a mere fossil, lacking in all finesse in the arts that mark a truly superior seat!"

"What's the Lady Raire got to do with all that?"

"Surely you're aware. Why else are you here?"

"Pretend we're not."

"The girl is an orphan," Sir Tanis said shortly. "Of the primary line. In addition . . ." he sounded exasperated, " . . . all the collateral heirs—all! are either dead, exiled, or otherwise disqualified in the voting!"

"So?"

"She—a mere girl, utterly lacking in experience— other than whatever bizarre influences she may have come under during her absence—holds in her hands five ballots! Five, out of nine! *She*—ineligible herself, of course, on a number of counts—controls the selection of the next head of this house! Why else do you imagine she was kidnapped?"

"Kidnapped?"

He nodded vigorously. "And since her return, she's not only rebuffed my most cordial offers of association—but has alienated every other conceivable candidate as well. In fact . . ." he lowered his voice, "it's my personal belief the girl intends to lend her support to an Outsider!"

"Sir Tanis, I guess all this family politics business is pretty interesting to you, but it's over my head like a wild pitch. I came here to see Milady Raire, to find out if she was safe and well. First I'm told she's dead, then that she's lost her mind. I'd like to see for myself. If you could arrange—"

"No," he said flatly. "That is quite impossible."

"May I ask why?"

"Sir Revenat would never allow it. He closets her as closely as a prize breeding soumi."

"And who's Sir Revenat?"

He raised his eyebrows. "Her husband," he said. "Who else?"

2

"Tough," Fsha-fsha consoled me as we walked along the echoing corridor, following the servant Sir Tanis had assigned to lead us back into the outside world. "Not much joy there; but at least she's home, and alive."

We crossed an inner court where a fountain made soft music, and a door opened along the passage ahead. An elderly woman, thin, tight-corseted, dressed in a chiton of shimmering white, spoke to the servant, who faded away like smoke. She turned and looked at me with sharp eyes, studied Fsha-fsha's alien face.

"You've come to help her," she said to him in a dry, husky voice. "You know, and you've come to her aid."

"Ah . . . whose aid, Milady?" he asked her.

The old lady grimaced and said: "The Lady Raire. She's in mortal danger; that's why her father ordered her sent away, on his deathbed! But none of them will believe me."

"What kind of danger is she in?"

"I don't know—but it's there, thick in the air around her! Poor child, so all alone."

"Milady," I stepped forward. "I've come a long way. I want to see her before I go. Can you arrange it?"

"Of course, you fool, else why would I have lain here in wait like a mud-roach over a wine-arbor?" She returned her attention to Fsha-fsha. "Tonight—at the Gathering of the House. Milady will be present; even Sir Revenat wouldn't dare defy custom so far as to deny her; and you shall be there, too! Listen! This is what you must do. . . ."

3

Half an hour later, we were walking along a tiled street of craftsmen's shops that was worn to a pastel smoothness that blended with the soft-toned facades that lined it. There were flowers in beds and rows and urns and boxes and in hanging trays that filtered the early light over open doorways where merchants fussed over displays of goods. I could smell fresh-baked bread and roasting coffee, and leather and wood-smoke. It was an atmosphere that made the events inside the ancient House of Ancinet-Chanore seem like an afternoon with the Red Queen.

"If you ask me, the whole bunch of them is round the bend," Fsha-fsha said. "I think the old lady had an idea I was in touch with the spirit world."

On a bench in front of a carpenter's stall, a man sat tapping with a mallet and chisel at a slab of tangerine-colored wood. He looked up and grinned at me.

"As pretty a bit of emberwood as ever a man laid steel to, eh?" he said.

"Strange," Fsha-fsha said. "You only see hand labor on backward worlds and rich ones. On all the others, a machine would be squeezing a gob of plastic into whatever shape was wanted."

In another stall, an aged woman was looming a rug of rich-colored fibers. Across the way, a boy sat in an open doorway, polishing what looked like a second-hand silver chalice. Up ahead, I saw the tailor shop the old woman—Milady Bezaille her name was—had told us about. An old fellow with a face like an elf was rolling out a bolt of green cloth with a texture like hand-rubbed metal. He looked up and ducked his head as we came in. "Ah, the sirs desire a change of costume?"

Fsha-fsha was already feeling the green stuff. "How about an outfit made of this?"

"Ah, the being has an eye," the old fellow cackled. "Radiant, is it not? Loomed by Y'sallo, of course."

I picked out a black like a slice of midnight in the Fringe. The tailor flipped up the end of the material and whirled it around my shoulders, stepped back and studied the effect thoughtfully.

"I see the composition as an expression of experience," he nodded. "Yes, it's possible. Stark, unadorned—but for the handsome necklace—Riv work is it not? Yes, a statement of self-affirmation, an incitement to discipline."

He went to work measuring and clucking. When he started cutting, we crossed a small bridge to a park where there were tables on the lawn beside a small lemon-yellow dome. We sat and ate pastries and then went along to a shoemaker, who sliced into glossy hides and in an hour had fitted new boots to both of us. When we got back to the tailor shop, the new clothes were waiting. We asked directions to a refresher station, and, after an ion-bath and a little attention to my hair and Fsha-fsha's gill fringes, tried out our new costumes.

"You're an impressive figure," Fsha-fsha said admiringly. "In spite of your decorations, your size and muscular development give you a certain animal beauty; and I must say the little tailor set you off to best advantage."

"The high collar helps," I conceded. "But I'm afraid the eye-patch spoils the effect."

"Wrong; it enhances the impression of an elegant corsair."

"Well, if the old Tree could see you now, it would have to admit you're the fanciest nut that ever dropped off it," I said.

It was twilight in the parklike city. We still had an hour to kill, and decided to use it in a stroll around the Old Town—the ancient marketplace that was the original center of the city. It was a picturesque place, and we were just in time to see the merchants folding up their stalls, and streaming away to the drinking terraces under the strung lights among the trees. The sun set in a glory of painted clouds; the brilliant spread of stars that covered the sky like luminous clotted cream was obscured by the overcast. The empty streets dimmed into deep shadow, as we turned our steps toward the gates of the estate Ancinet-Chanore.

4

My sense-booster was set at 1.3 normal; any higher setting made ordinary sound and light levels painful. For the last hundred feet I had been listening to the gluey wheeze that was the sound of human lungs, coming from somewhere up ahead. I touched Fsha-fsha's arm. "In the alley," I said softly. "Just one man."

He stepped ahead of me, and in the same instant a small, lean figure sprang into view twenty feet ahead, stopped in a half-crouch facing us, with his feet planted wide and his gun hand up and aimed. I saw a lightning-wink and heard the soft *whap!* of a filament pistol. Fsha-fsha *oof*ed as he took the bolt square in the chest; a corona outlined his figure in vivid blue as the harness bled the energy off to the ground. Then he was on the assassin; his arm rose and fell with the sound of a hammer hitting a grapefruit, and the would-be killer tumbled backward and slid down the wall to sprawl on the pavement. I went flat against the wall, flipped the booster up to max, heard nothing but the normal night sounds of a city.

"Clear," I said. Fsha-fsha leaned over the little man.

"I hit him too hard," he said. "He's dead."

"Maybe the old lady was right," I said.

"Or maybe Sir Tanis wasn't as foolish as he sounded," Fsha-fsha grunted. "Or Milord Pastaine as senile as they claimed."

"A lot of maybes," I said. "Let's dump him out of sight and get out of here, in case a cleanup squad is following him up."

We lifted him and tossed him in the narrow passage he had picked as a hiding place.

"Which way?" Fsha-fsha asked.

"Straight ahead, to the main gates," I said.

"You're still going there—after this?"

"More than ever. Somebody made a mistake, sending a hit man out. They made a second not making it stick. We'll give them a chance to go for three."

5

The Lady Bezaille had given instructions to the gate-keeper; he bowed us through like visiting royalty into an atmosphere of lights and sounds and movement. The grand celebration known as the Gathering of the House seemed to be going on all over the grounds and throughout the house. We made our way through the throngs of beautiful people, looking for a familiar face. Sir Tanis popped up and gave a lifted-eyebrow look, but there wasn't enough surprise there to make him the man behind the assassination attempt.

"Captain Danger; Sir Fsha-fsha; I confess I didn't expect to see you here . . ." He was aching to ask by whose order we were included in the select gathering, but apparently his instinct for the oblique approach kept him from asking.

"It seemed the least I could do," I said in what I hoped was a cryptic tone. "By the way, has Milady Raire arrived yet?"

"Ha! She and Lord Revenat will make a dramatic entrance after the rest of us have been allowed to consume ourselves in restless patience for a time, you can be sure."

He led us to the nearest refreshment server, which dispensed foamy concoctions in big tulip glasses; we stood on the lawn and fenced with him verbally for a few minutes, parted with an implied understanding that whatever happened, our weight would go to the side of justice—whatever that meant.

Milady Bezaille appeared, looked us over and gave a sniff that seemed to mean approval of our new finery. I had a feeling she'd regretted her earlier rash impulse of inviting two space tramps to the grand soiree of the year.

"Look sharp, now," she cautioned me. "When Milord Revenat deigns to appear he'll be swamped at once with the attentions of certain unwholesome elements of the House; that will be your chance to catch a glimpse of Milady Raire. See if you read in her face other than pain and terror!"

A slender, dandified lad sauntered over after the beldame had whisked away.

"I see the noble lady is attempting to influence you," he said. "Beware of her, sirs. She is not of sound mind."

"She was just tipping us off that the punch in number three bowl is spiked with hand-blaster pellets," I assured him. He gave me a quick, sideways look.

"What, ah, did she say to you about Sir Fane?"

"Ah-hah!" I nodded.

"Don't believe it!" he snapped. "Lies! Damnable lies!"

I edged closer to him. "What about Sir Tanis?" I muttered.

He shifted his eyes. "Watch him. All his talk about unilateral revisionism and ancillary line vigor—pure superstition."

"And Lord Revenat?"

He looked startled. "You don't mean—" he turned and scuttled away without finishing the sentence.

"Danger—are you sure this is the right place we're in?" Fsha-fsha whispered. "If the Lady Raire is anything like the rest of this menagerie. . . ."

"She isn't," I said. "She—"

I stopped talking as a stir ran through the little conversational groups around us. Across the lawn a servant in crimson livery was towing a floating floodlight along above the heads of a couple just descending a wide, shallow flight of steps from a landing terrace above. I hadn't seen the heli arrive. The man was tall, wide-shouldered, trim, like all Zeridajhans, dressed in a form-fitting wine-colored outfit with an elaborate pectoral ornament suspended around his neck on a chain. The woman beside him was slim, elegantly gowned in silvery gauze, with her black hair piled high, intricately entwined in a jeweled coronet. I'd never seen her in jewels before but that perfect face, set in an expression that was the absence of all expression, was that of Milady Raire.

6

The crowd had moved in their direction as if by a common impulse to rush up and greet the newcomers;

but the movement halted and the restless murmur of chatter resumed, but with a new, nervous note that was evident in the shrill cackle of laughter and the over-hearty waving of arms. I made my way across through the crowd, watching the circle of impressively clad males collecting around the newcomers. They moved off in a body, with a great deal of exuberant joking that sounded about as sincere as a losing politician's con-gratulatory telegram to the winner.

I trailed along at a distance of ten yards, while the group swirled around a drink dispenser and broke up into a central group and half a dozen squeezed-out satellites. The lucky winners steered their prize on an evasion course, dropping a few members along the way when clumsy footwork involved them in exchanges of amenities with other, less favored groups. In five minutes, the tall man in the burgundy tights was fenced into a corner by half a dozen hardy victors, while the lady in silver stood for the moment alone at a few yards distance.

I looked at her pale, aloof face, still as youthful and unlined as it had been seven years ago, when we last talked together under the white sun of Gar 28. I took a deep breath and started across the lawn toward her.

She didn't notice me until I was ten feet from her; then she turned slowly and her eyes went across me as coolly as the first breath of winter. They came back again, and this time flickered—and held on me. Sud-denly I was conscious of the scar, two-thirds concealed by the high collar of my jacket, that marked the cor-ner of my jaw—and of the black patch over my right eye. Her eyes moved over me, back to my face. They widened; her lips parted, then I was standing before her.

"Milady Raire," I said, and heard the hoarse note in my voice.

"Can . . . can it be . . . *you?*" Her voice was the faintest of whispers.

A hard hand took my arm, spun me around.

"I do not believe, sir," a furious voice snarled, "that you have the privilege of approach to Her Ladyship—" He got that far before his eyes took in what they were looking at; his voice trailed off. His mouth hung open. He dropped my arm and took a step back. It was the man named Huvile.

7

"Sir Revenat," someone started, and let it drop. I could almost hear his mind racing, looking for the right line to take. But nobody, even someone who had only talked to me for five minutes three years before, could pretend to have forgotten my face: black-skinned, scarred, one-eyed.

"It . . . it . . . I . . ."

"Sir Revenat," I said as smoothly as I could under the circumstances, and gave him a stiff little half-bow. That passed the ball to him. He could play it any way he liked from there.

"Why, why . . ." He took my arm, in a gentler grip this time. "My dear fellow! What an extraordinary pleasure. . . ." His eyes went to Milady Raire. She returned a look as impersonal as the carved face of a statue. She didn't look at me.

"If you will excuse us, Milady," Huvile/Revenat ducked his head and hustled me past her, and the silent crowd parted to let us through.

8

Inside a white damask room with a wall of glass through which the lights of the garden cast a soft polychrome glow, Huvile faced me. He looked a little different than he had the last time I had seen him, wearing the coarse kilt of a slave in the household of the Triarch of Drath. He had lost the gaunt look and was trimmed, manicured and polished like a prize-winning boar.

"You've . . . changed," he said. "For a moment, I almost failed to recognize you." His voice was hearty enough, but his eyes were as alert as a coiled rattler's.

I nodded. "A year on the Triarch's rafts have that effect."

"The rafts?" He looked shocked. "But . . . but . . ."

"The penalty for freeing slaves," I said. "And not being able to pay the fines."

"But . . . I assumed . . ."

"Everything I owned was on my boat," I said.

His face was turning darker, as if pressure was building up behind it. "Your boat . . . I . . . ah . . ." he made an effort to get hold of himself. "See here, didn't you direct, ah, the young woman to lift ship at once?" His look told me he was waiting to see if I'd pick up the impersonal reference to the Lady Raire. I shook my head and waited.

"But—she arrived a moment or two after I reached the port. You *did* send her?"

"Yes—"

"Of course," he hurried on, "She seemed most distraught, poor creature. I explained to her that a kindly stranger—yourself—had purchased my freedom—and presumably hers as well—and while we spoke, a creature appeared; a ghastly-looking little beggar. The unfortunate girl was terrified by the sight of him; I drove the thing off, and then . . . and then she insisted that we lift at once!" Huvile shook his head, looking grieved. "I understand now; in her frenzy to make good her escape, she abandoned you, her unknown savior. . . ." A thought hit him, sharpened his eyes. "You hadn't, ah, personally known the poor child?"

"I saw her for a moment at the Triarch's palace— from a distance."

He sighed. His look got more comfortable. "A tragedy that your kindness was rewarded by such ingratitude. Believe me, sir, I am eternally in your debt! I acknowledge it freely. . . ." He lowered his voice. "But let us keep the details in confidence, between us. It would not be desirable, at this moment, to introduce a new factor, however extraneous, into the somewhat complex equations of House affairs." He was getting expansive now. "We shouldn't like my ability to reward you as you deserve suffer through any fallacious construction that might be put on matters, eh?"

"I take it you took the female slave under your wing," I said.

He gave me a sharp look. He would have liked her left out of the conversation.

"She would have needed help to get home," I amplified.

"Ah, yes, I think I see now," he smiled a sad, sweet smile. "You were taken with her beauty. But alas . . ." his eyes held on mine, "she died."

"That's very sad," I said. "How did it happen?"

"My friend, wouldn't it be better to forget her? Who knows what terrible pressures might not have influenced her to the despicable course she chose? Poor waif; she suffered greatly. Her death gave her surcease." His expression became brisk. "And now, in what way

can I serve you, sir? Tell me how I can make amends
for the injustice done you."

He talked some more, offered me the hospitality of
the estate, a meal, even, delicately, money. His relief
when I turned them down was obvious. Now that he
saw I wasn't going to be nasty about the little misunderstanding, his confidence was coming back. I let him
ramble on. When he ran down, I said:

"How about an introduction to the lady in silver?
The Lady Raire, I understand her name is?'

His face went hard. "That is impossible. The lady
is not well. Strange faces upset her."

"Too bad," I said. "In that case, I guess there's not
much for me to stay around for."

"Must you go? But of course if you have business
matters requiring your attention, I mustn't keep you."
He went across to an archway leading toward the front
of the house; he was so eager to get rid of me the easy
way that he almost fell down getting there. He didn't
realize I'd turned the opposite way and stepped back
out onto the terrace, until I was already across it and
heading across the lawn to where Milady Raire still
stood alone, like a pale statue in the winking light of
an illuminated fountain.

9

She watched me come across the lawn to her. I could
hear the hurrying footsteps of Sir Revenat behind me,
not quite running, heard someone intercept him, the
babble of self-important voices. I walked up to her and
my eyes held on her face; it was as rigid as a death mask.
"Milady, what happened after you left Drath?" I
asked her without preamble.

"I—" she started and her eyes showed shock. "Then—on Drath—it was you—"

"You're scared, Milady. They're all scared of Huvile, but you most of all. Tell me why."

"Billy Danger," she said, and for an instant the iron discipline of her face broke, but she caught herself. "Fly, Billy Danger," she whispered in English. "Fly hence in the instant, ere thou, too, art lost, for nothing can rescue me!"

I heard feet coming up fast behind me and turned to see Sir Revenat, his face white with fury, masked by a ghastly grin.

"You are elusive, my friend," he grated. His fingers were playing with the heavy ornament dangling on his chest, an ovoid with a half-familiar look. . . . "I fear you've lost your way. The gate lies at the opposite end of the gardens." His hand reached for me as if to guide me back to the path, but I leaned aside from it, turned to Milady Raire. I put out my hand as if to offer it to her, instead reached farther, ran my fingers down her silken side—and felt the slight, telltale lump there. She gasped and drew back. Huvile let out a roar and caught at my arm savagely. A concerted gasp had gone up from every mouth within gasping range.

"Barbarian wretch!" Huvile howled. "You'd lay hands on the person of a lady of the House of Ancinet Chanore . . ." the rest was just an inarticulate bellow backed up by a chorus of the same from the assembled spectators.

"Enough!" Huvile yelled. "This adventurer comes among us to mock the dignity and honor of this house, openly offers insult to a noble lady of the ancient line!" He whirled to face the crowd. "Then I'll oblige him with a taste of the just fury of that line! Milords! Bring me my sword box!" He turned back to me, and there was red fury enough in his eyes for ten houses. He stepped close, put his face close to mine. His fingers played with the slave controller at his neck. I judged the distance for a jump, but he was ready with his finger on the control. And we both knew that a touch by anyone but himself would activate it.

"You saw," he hissed. "You know her life is in my hands. If you expose me, she dies!"

CHAPTER TWELVE

The lords and ladies of the House of Ancinet-Chanore may have been out of touch with reality in some ways, but when it came to setting up the stage for a blood-duel on their fancy lawn under the gay lights, they were the soul of efficiency. While a ring of armed servants stood obtrusively around me, others hurried away and came back with a fancy inlaid box of darkly polished wood. Huvile lifted the lid with a flourish and took out a straight-bladed saber heavy enough to behead a peasant with. There was a lot of gold thread and jewel-work around the hilt, but it was a butcher's weapon. Another one, just like it but without the jelly beans was trotted out for me.

Sir Tanis made the formal speech; he cited all the hallowed customs that surrounded the curious custom that allowed an irate Lord of the House to take a cleaver to anyone who annoyed him sufficiently, and then in a less pompous tone explained the rules to me. They weren't much: we'd hack at each other until Sir Revenat was satisfied or dead.

"Man to man," Sir Tanis finished his spiel. "The House of Ancinet-Chanore defends its honor with the ancient right of its strong arm! Let her detractors beware!"

Then the crowd backed off and the servants formed up a loose ring, fifty feet across. Huvile brandished his sword and his eyes ate me alive. Fsha-fsha took my jacket and leaned close to give me a last word of advice.

"Remember your Sorting training, Billy Danger! Key-in your response patterns to his attack modes! Play him until you read him like a glorm-bulb line! Then strike!"

"If I don't make it," I said, "find a way to tell them."

"You'll make it," he said. "But—yeah—I'll do my best."

He withdrew at a curt command from Tanis, and Huvile moved out to meet me. He held the sword lightly, as if his wrist was used to handling it. I had an idea the upstart sir had spent a lot of hours practicing the elevating art of throwing his weight around. He moved in with the blade held low, pointed straight at me. I imitated his stance. He made a small feint and I slapped his blade with mine and moved back as he dropped his point and lunged and missed my thigh by an inch. I tried to blank my mind, key in his approach-feint-attack gambit to a side-jump-and-counter cut syndrome. It was hard to bring the pattern I wanted into clear focus without running through it, physically. I backed, made Huvile blink by doing the jump and cut in pantomime, two sword-lengths from contact distance. A nervous titter ran through the audience, but that was all right. I was pretty sure I'd set the response pattern I wanted to at least one of his approaches. But he had others.

He came after me, cautious now, checking me out. He tried a high thrust, a low cut, a one-two lunge past

my guard. I backed shamelessly, for each attack tried
to key-in an appropriate response—

I felt myself whip to one side, slash in an automatic
reaction to a repetition of his opening gambit. My point
caught his sleeve and ripped through the wine-red
cloth. So far so good. Huvile back-pedaled, then tried
a furious frontal attack; I gave ground, my arm coun-
tering him with no conscious thought on my part. He
realized the tactic was getting him nowhere and
dropped his point, whipped it up suddenly as he dived
forward. I caught it barely in time, deflected the blade
over my right shoulder, and was chest to chest with
him, our hilts locked together.

"It's necessary for me to kill you," he whispered.
"You understand that it's impossible for me to let you
live." His eyes looked mad; his free hand still gripped
the controller. "If I die—she dies. And if I suspect you
may be gaining—I plunge the lever home. Your only
choice is to sacrifice yourself." He pushed me away and
jabbed a vicious cut at me and then we were circling
again. My brain seemed to be set in concrete. Huvile
was nuts—no doubt about that. He had brazened his
way into the midst of the House of Ancinet-Chanore
on the strength of the invisible knife he held at Milady's
heart; and if he saw the game was up—the fragile game
he'd nursed along for months now—he'd kill her with
utter finality and in the most incredible agony, as the
magnesium flare set in her heart burned its way
through her ribs.

There was just one possibility. The Drathians had
gone to a lot of trouble to link the life of the slave
to the well-being of the master; but there was one
inevitable weak spot. Even the most sophisticated circuitry couldn't do its job after it was destroyed. I'd
proven that; I had crushed Huvile's controller under
my foot—and he was still alive.

But on the other hand, maybe that had been a freak, a defective controller. Huvile had been two miles away at the time. And it was no special trick to rig an electronic device so that the cut-off of a carrier signal actuated a response in a receiver. . . .

There was sweat on my face, not all of it from the exercise. My only chance was to smash the controller and kill Huvile with the same stroke—and hope for the best. Because, win or lose, the Lady Raire was better dead than slave to this madman.

While these merry thoughts were racing through my mind, I was backing, feinting and parrying automatically. And suddenly Huvile's blade dropped, flickered in at me and out again and I felt my right leg sag and go out from under me. I caught myself in time to counter an over-eager swing and strike back from one knee, but it was only a moment's delay of the inevitable. I saw his arm swing back for the finishing stroke—

There was swirl of silver, and the Lady Raire was at his side, clutching his sword arm—and then she crumpled, white-faced, as the controller's automatic angina circuit clamped iron fingers on her heart. But it was enough. While Huvile staggered, off-balance, his free hand groping, I came up in a one-legged lunge. He saw me, brought his sword up and back, at the same time snatched for the controller. He was a fraction of a second late. My point struck it, burst it into chips, slammed on through bone and muscle and lodged in his spine. He fell slowly, with an amazed look on his face. I saw him hit; then I went over sideways and grabbed for the gaping wound in my thigh and felt darkness close in.

2

The House of Ancinet-Chanore was very manly about acknowledging its mistake. I sat across from old Lord Pastaine under the canopy on his favorite sun terrace, telling him for the sixth or seventh time how it had happened that I had bought freedom for two slaves and then sent them off together in my boat while I went to the rafts. He wagged his Mosaic head and looked grave.

"A serious misjudgment of character on your part," he said. "Yet were we not all guilty of misjudgment? When the Lady Raire returned, so unexpectedly, I wished to open my heart to her—supposed—savior. I granted the interloper—Huvile, you say his name was?" He shook his head. "An upstart, of no family—I granted him, I say, every freedom, every honor in the gift of Ancinet-Chanore. As for Milady—if she chose to closet herself in solitary withdrawal from the comfort of her family—could I say nay? And then I saw the beginnings of the wretched maneuverings that would make this stranger Head after my death. I called for Milady Raire to attend me—and she refused! Me! It was unheard of! Can you blame me for striking her from my memory, as one dead? And as for the others—venal, grasping, foolish—to what depths has the House not fallen since the days of my youth, a thousand years agone. . . ."

I listened to him ramble on. I had been hearing the same story from a variety of directions during the past three days, while my leg healed under the miracle-medicines of old Zeridajh. If any one of the Lady Raire's doting relations had cared enough about her to take just one, good, searching look into her eyes, they'd have seen that something was seriously amiss. But all they saw was a pawn on the board of House politics, and her silent appeals had gone unanswered. As for why she hadn't defied Huvile, faced death before submitting to enslavement to his ambitions—I could guess that half an hour of sub-fatal angina might be a persuasion that would convince a victim who could laugh at the threat of mere death.

"If you'd arrange for me to see the Lady Raire for a few minutes," I butted in Milord's rumbling assessment of the former Sir Revenat's character, "I'd be most appreciative."

He looked grave. "I believe we all agree that it would be best not to reawaken the unhappy emotions of these past months by any references thereto," he said. "We are grateful to you, Captain Danger—the House will be forever in your debt. I'm sure Milady will understand if you slip quietly away, leaving her to the ministrations of her family, those who know where her interests lie."

I got the idea. It had been explained to me in slightly varying terms by no less than twelve solemn pillars of the House of Ancinet-Chanore. The Lady Raire, having had one close brush with an interloper, would not be exposed to the questionable influences of another. They were glad I'd happened along in time to break the spell—but now the lady would return to her own kind, her own life.

And they were right, of course. I didn't know just what it was that Jongo would have to say to Milady Raire of the ancient House of Ancinet-Chanore; I'd had my share of wild fancies, but none of them were wild enough to include offering her boudoir space aboard my boat as an alternative to the estates of Ancinet-Chanore.

On the way out, Sir Tanis offered me a crack at a lot of fancy trade opportunities, letters of recommendation to any house I might name, and assorted other vague rewards, and ended with a hint, none too closely veiled, that any further attempt to see the lady would end unhappily for me. I told him I got the idea and walked out into the twilight through the high gates of the house with no more than a slight limp to remind me of my visit.

3

Fsha-fsha was waiting for me at the boat. I told him about my parting interviews with the House of Ancinet-Chanore. He listened.

"You never learn, do you, Billy?" he wagged his head sadly.

"I've learned that there's no place for me in fancy company," I said. "Give me the honest solitude of space, and a trail of new worlds waiting ahead. That's my style."

"You saved the lady's life on Gar 28, you know," Fsha-fsha said, talking to himself. "If you hadn't done what you did—when you did—she'd never have lived out the first week. It was too bad you didn't look and listen a bit before you handed her over to the H'eeaq— but then, who would have known, eh?"

"Let's forget all that," I suggested. "The ship's trimmed to lift—"

"Then at Drath, you picked her out from under the Triarch's nose in as smooth a counter-swindle as I've ever heard of. He had no idea of letting them go, you know. They'd have been arrested at the port—except that the Rule-keepers were caught short when the tub lifted without you. Your only mistake was in trusting Huvile—"

"Trusting Huvile!"

"You trusted him. You sent him along to an unguarded ship. If you'd worked just one angle a little more subtly— gone out yourself to see the lady aboard and then lifted, leaving Huvile behind—but this is neither here nor there. For the second time, you saved her—and handed her over to her enemy."

"I know that," I snapped. "I've kicked myself for it—"

"And now—here you are, repeating the pattern," he bored on. "Three times and out."

"What?"

"You saved the lady again, Billy. Plucked her out of the wicked hands of her tormentor—"

"And . . .?"

"And handed her over to her enemies."

"Her family has her—"

"That's what I said."

"Then. . . ." wheels were beginning to whirl in front of my eyes.

"Maybe," I said, "you'd better tell me exactly what you're talking about. . . ."

4

. . . She opened her eyes, startled, when I leaned over her sleeping couch.

"Billy Danger," she breathed. "Is it thee? Why came you not to me ere now?"

"An acute attack of stupidity, Milady," I whispered.

She smiled a dazzling smile. "My name is Raire, Billy. I am no one's lady."

"You're mine," I said.

"Always, my Billy." She reached and drew my face down to hers. Her lips were softer even than I had dreamed.

"Come," I said.

She rose silently and Eureka rubbed himself across her knees. They followed me across the wide room, along a still corridor. In the great hall below, I asked her to show me the shortest route to the grounds. She led the way along a cloistered arcade, through a walled garden, onto a wide terrace above the dark sweep of sky-lit lawn.

"Billy—when I pass this door, the house alarms will be set off. . . ."

"I know. That's why I dropped in on the roof in a one-man heli. Too bad we couldn't leave the same way. There's no help for it. Let's go. . . ."

We started out at a run toward the trees. We had gone fifty feet when lights sprang up across the back of the house. I turned and took aim with my filament gun and knocked out the two biggest polyarcs, and we sprinted for cover, Eureka loping in the lead. A new light sprang up, just too late, swept the stretch of grass we had just crossed. We reached the trees, went flat. Men were coming through the rear doors of the house. There was a lot of yelling. I looked up. Against the swirls and clots of stars, nothing was visible. I checked my watch again; Fsha-fsha was two minutes late. The line of men was moving down across the lawn. In half a minute, they'd reach the trees.

There was a wink of light from above, followed by a dull *baroom!* as of distant thunder. A high, whistling screech became audible, descended to a full-throated roar; something flashed overhead—a long shape ablaze with lights. A second gunboat slammed across in the wake of the first.

"That cuts it," I said. "Fsha-fsha's been picked off—"

A terrific detonation boomed, drawling itself out into a bellow of power. I saw a dark shape flash past against the clotted stars. The men on the lawn saw it, too. They halted their advance, looking up at the dark boat that had shot past on an opposite course to the security cutters.

"Look!" The Lady Raire pointed. Something big and dark was drifting toward our position across the lake. It was *Jongo III,* barely a yard above the surface of the water, concealed from the house by the trees. We jumped up and ran for it. Her bow lights came on, dazzling as suns, traversed over us, lanced out to blind the men beyond the trees. I could see the soft glow from her open entry-port. We splashed out into knee-deep water; I tossed Eureka in, then jumped, caught the rail, pulled myself in, reached back for the Lady Raire as men burst through the screen of trees. Then we were inside, pressed flat against the floor by the surge of acceleration as the old racer lifted and screamed away at treetop level at a velocity that would have boiled the surface off any lesser hull.

5

From a distance of half a million miles, Zeridajh was a misty emerald crescent, dwindling on our screens.

"It was a pretty world, Milady," I said. "You're going to miss it."

"Dost know what place I truly dreamed of, my Billy, when the gray years of Drath lengthened before me?"

"The gardens," I suggested. "They're very beautiful, with the sun on them."

"I dreamt of the caves, and the green shade of the giant peas, and the simple loyalty of our good Eureka. . . ." She stroked the grizzled head resting on her knee.

"Never," Fsha-fsha said from the depths of the big command chair, "will I understand the motivations of you Propagators. Still, life in your company promises to be diverting, I'll say that for it." He showed us that ghastly expression he used for a smile. "But tell me, Milady—if the question isn't impertinent: what were you doing out there, at the far end of the Eastern Arm, where Billy first saw you?"

"Haven't you guessed?" she smiled at him. "Until Lord Desroy caught me, I was running away."

"I knew it!" Fsha-fsha boomed. "And now that the great quest is finished—where to?"

"Anywhere," I said. I put my arm around Raire's flower-slim waist and drew her to me. "Anywhere at all."

The sweet hum of the mighty and ancient engines drummed softly through the deck. Together, we watched the blaze of Center move to fill the screens.

A TRIP TO THE CITY

1

"She'll be pulling out in a minute, Brett," Mr. Phillips said. He tucked his railroader's watch back in his vest pocket. "You better get aboard—if you're still set on going."

"It was reading all them books done it," Aunt Haicey said. "Thick books, and no pictures in them. I knew it'd make trouble." She plucked at the faded hand-crocheted shawl over her thin shoulders, a tiny bird-like woman with bright anxious eyes.

"Don't worry about me," Brett said. "I'll be back."

"The place'll be yours when I'm gone," Aunt Haicey said. "Lord knows it won't be long."

"Why don't you change your mind and stay on, boy?" Mr. Phillips said, blinking up at the young man. "If I talk to Mr. J.D., I think he can find a job for you at the plant."

"So many young people leave Casperton," Aunt Haicey said. "They never come back."

Mr. Phillips clicked his teeth. "They write, at first," he said. "Then they gradually lose touch."

"All your people are here, Brett," Aunt Haicey said. "Haven't you been happy here?"

"Why can't you young folks be content with Casperton?" Mr. Phillips said. "There's everything you need here."

"It's that Pretty-Lee done it," Aunt Haicey said. "If it wasn't for that girl—"

A clatter ran down the line of cars. Brett kissed Aunt Haicey's dry cheek, shook Mr. Phillips's hand, and swung aboard. His suitcase was on one of the seats. He put it up above in the rack and sat down, then turned to wave back at the two old people.

It was a summer morning. Brett leaned back and watched the country slide by. It was nice country, Brett thought, mostly in corn, some cattle, and away in the distance the hazy blue hills. Now he would see what was on the other side of them: the cities, the mountains, and the ocean: strange things. Up until now all he knew about anything outside of Casperton was what he'd read or seen pictures of. As far as he was concerned, chopping wood and milking cows back in Casperton, they might as well not have existed. They were just words and pictures printed on paper. But he didn't want to just read about them. He wanted to see for himself.

Pretty-Lee hadn't come to see him off. She was probably still mad about yesterday. She had been sitting at the counter at the Club Rexall, drinking a soda and reading a movie magazine with a big picture of an impossibly pretty face on the cover—the kind you never see just walking down the street. He had taken the next stool and ordered a Coke.

"Why don't you read something good, instead of that pap?" he asked her.

"Something good? You mean something dry, I guess. And don't call it . . . that word. It doesn't sound polite."

"What does it say? That somebody named Doll Starr is fed up with glamor and longs for a simple home in the country and lots of kids? Then why doesn't she move to Casperton?"

"You wouldn't understand," said Pretty-Lee.

He took the magazine, leafed through it. "Look at this: all about people who give parties that cost thousands of dollars, and fly all over the world having affairs with each other and committing suicide and getting divorced. It's like reading about Martians."

"I just like to read about the stars. There's nothing wrong with it."

"Reading all that junk just makes you dissatisfied. You want to do your hair up crazy like the pictures in the magazines and wear weird-looking clothes—"

Pretty-Lee bent her straw double. She stood up and took her shopping bag. "I'm glad to know you think my clothes are weird—"

"You're taking everything I say personally," Brett objected. "Look." He showed her a full-color advertisement on the back cover of the magazine. "Look at this. Here's a man supposed to be cooking steaks on some kind of back-yard grill. He looks like a movie star; he's dressed up like he was going to get married; there's not a wrinkle anywhere. There's not a spot on that apron. There isn't even a grease spot on the frying pan. The lawn is as smooth as a billiard table. There's his son; he looks just like his pop, except that he's not grey at the temples. Did you ever really see a man that handsome, or hair that was just silver over the ears and the rest glossy black? The daughter looks like a movie starlet, and her mom is exactly the same, except that she has that grey streak in front to match her husband. You can see the car in the drive; the treads of the tires must have just been scrubbed; they're not even dusty. There's not a pebble out of place. All the flowers are in full bloom; no dead ones. No leaves on the lawn; no dry twigs showing on the tree. That other house in the background looks like a palace, and the man with the rake, looking over the fence: he looks like this one's twin brother, and he's out raking leaves in brand-new clothes—"

Pretty-Lee grabbed her magazine. "You just seem to hate everything that's nicer than this messy town—"

"I don't think it's nicer. I like you; your hair isn't always perfectly smooth, and you've got a mended place on your dress, and you feel human, you smell human—"

"Oh!" Pretty-Lee turned and flounced out of the drug store.

Brett shifted in the dusty plush seat and looked around. There were a few other people in the car. An old man was reading a newspaper; two old ladies whispered together. There was a woman of about thirty with a mean-looking kid; and some others. They didn't look like magazine pictures, any of them. He tried to picture them doing the things you read in newspapers: the old ladies putting poison in somebody's tea; the old man giving orders to start a war. He thought about babies in houses in cities, and airplanes flying over, and bombs falling down: huge explosive bombs. *Blam!* Buildings fall in, pieces of glass and stone fly through the air. The babies are blown up along with everything else—

But the kind of people he knew couldn't do anything like that. They liked to loaf and eat and talk and drink beer and buy a new tractor or refrigerator and go fishing. And if they ever got mad and hit somebody—afterwards they were embarrassed and wanted to shake hands. . . .

The train slowed, came to a shuddery stop. Through

the window he saw a cardboardy-looking building with the words BAXTER'S JUNCTION painted across it. There were a few faded posters on a bulletin board. An old man was sitting on a bench, waiting. The two old ladies got off and a boy in blue jeans got on. The train started up. Brett folded his jacket and tucked it under his head and tried to doze off. . . .

Brett awoke, yawned, sat up. The train was slowing. He remembered you couldn't use the toilets while the train was stopped. He got up and went to the end of the car. The door was jammed. He got it open and went inside and closed the door behind him. The train was going slower, clack clack . . . clack-clack . . . clack; clack . . . cuh-lack . . .

He washed his hands, then pulled on the door. It was stuck. He pulled harder. The handle was too small; it was hard to get hold of. The train came to a halt. Brett braced himself and strained against the door. It didn't budge.

He looked out the grimy window. The sun was getting lower. It was about three-thirty, he guessed. He couldn't see anything but some dry-looking fields.

Outside in the corridor there were footsteps. He started to call, but then didn't. It would be too embarrassing, pounding on the door and yelling, "Let me out! I'm stuck in the toilet. . . ."

He tried to rattle the door. It didn't rattle. Somebody was dragging something heavy past the door. Mail bags, maybe. He'd better yell. But dammit, the door couldn't be all that hard to open. He studied the latch. All he had to do was turn it. He got a good grip and twisted. Nothing.

He heard the mail bag bump-bump, and then another one. To heck with it; he'd yell. He'd wait until he heard the footsteps outside the door again and then he'd make some noise.

Brett waited. It was quiet now. He rapped on the door anyway. No answer. Maybe there was nobody left in the car. In a minute the train would start up and he'd be stuck here until the next stop. He banged on the door. "Hey! The door is stuck!"

It sounded foolish. He listened. It was very quiet. He pounded again. Still just silence. The car creaked once. He put his ear to the door. He couldn't hear anything. He turned back to the window. There was no one in sight. He put his cheek flat against it, looked along the car. All he saw was the dry fields.

He turned around and gave the door a good kick. If he damaged it, that was too bad; the railroad shouldn't have defective locks on the doors. If they tried to make him pay for it, he'd tell them they were lucky he didn't sue the railroad. . . .

He braced himself against the opposite wall, drew his foot back, and kicked hard at the lock. Something broke. He pulled the door open.

He was looking out the open door and through the window beyond. There was no platform, just the same dry fields he could see on the other side. He came out and went along to his seat. The car was empty now.

He looked out the window. Why had the train stopped here? Maybe there was some kind of trouble with the engine. It had been sitting here for ten minutes or so now. Brett got up and went along to the door, stepped down onto the iron step. Leaning out, he could see the train stretching along ahead, one car, two cars—

There was no engine.

Maybe he was turned around. He looked the other way. There were three cars. No engine there either. He must be on some kind of siding. . . .

Brett stepped back inside, and pushed through into the next car. It was empty. He walked along the length of it, into the next car. It was empty too. He went back through the two cars and his own car and on, all the way to the end of the train. All the cars were empty. He stood on the platform at the end of the last car, and looked back along the rails. They ran straight through the dry fields, right to the horizon. He stepped down to the ground, went along the cindery bed to the front of the train, stepping on the ends of the wooden ties. The coupling stood open. The tall, dusty coach stood silently on its iron wheels, waiting. Ahead the tracks went on—

And stopped.

2

Maybe all train trips were like this, Brett thought. After all, this was his first. If he'd been asleep, say, he'd never have noticed the train stopping and all the rest of it. Probably his best bet was to get back aboard and wait. Yet he didn't. He started walking.

He walked along the ties, following the iron rails, shiny on top, and brown with rust on the sides. A hundred feet from the train they ended. The cinders went on another ten feet and petered out. Beyond, the fields closed in. Brett looked up at the sun. It was lower now in the west, its light getting yellow and late-afternoonish. He turned and looked back at the train. The cars stood high and prim, empty, silent. Then he thought of his suitcase, still in the rack, and his new jacket on the seat. He walked back, climbed in, got his bag down from the rack, pulled on his jacket. He jumped down to the cinders, followed them to where they ended. He hesitated a moment, then pushed between the knee-high stalks. Eastward across the field he could see what looked like a smudge on the far horizon.

He walked until dark, then made himself a scratchy nest in the dead stalks and went to sleep.

He slept for what seemed like a long time; then he woke, lay on his back, looking up at pink dawn clouds. Around him, dry stalks rustled in a faint stir of air. He felt crumbly earth under his fingers. He sat up, reached out and broke off a stalk. It crumbled into fragile chips. He wondered what it was. It wasn't any crop he'd ever seen before.

He stood, looked around. The field went on and on, dead flat. A locust came whirring toward him, plumped to earth at his feet. He picked it up. Long, elbowed legs groped at his fingers aimlessly. He tossed the insect in the air. It fluttered away. To the east the smudge was clearer now; it seemed to be a grey wall, far away. The city? He picked up his bag and started on.

He was getting hungry. He hadn't eaten since the previous morning. He was thirsty too. The city couldn't be more than three hours' walk. He tramped along, the dry plants crackling under his feet, little puffs of dust rising from the dry ground. He thought about the rails, running across the empty fields, ending . . .

He tried to remember just when the strangeness had begun: he had heard the locomotive groaning up ahead as the train slowed. And there had been feet in the corridor. Where had they gone?

He thought of the train, Casperton, Aunt Haicey, Mr. Phillips. They seemed very far away, something remembered from long ago. Up above the sun was hot. That was real. The other things, from the past, seemed unimportant. Ahead there was a city. He would walk until he came to it. He tried to think of other things: television, crowds of people, money; the tattered paper and worn silver—

Only the sun and the dusty plain and the dead plants were real now. He could see them, feel them. And the suitcase. It was heavy; he shifted hands, kept going.

There was something white on the ground ahead, a small shiny surface protruding from the earth. Brett put the suitcase down, went down on one knee, dug into the dry soil, and pulled out a china teacup, the handle missing. Caked dirt crumbled away under his thumb, leaving the surface clean. He looked at the bottom of the cup. It was unmarked. Why just one teacup, he wondered, here in the middle of nowhere? He dropped it, took up his suitcase, and went on.

After that he watched the ground more closely. He found a shoe; it was badly weathered, but the sole was good. It was a high-topped work shoe, size 10½C. Who had dropped it here? He thought of other lone shoes he had seen, lying at the roadside or in alleys. How did they get there . . . ?

Half an hour later he detoured around a rusted front fender from an old-fashioned car. He looked around for the rest of the car but saw nothing. The wall was closer now; perhaps two miles more.

A scrap of white paper fluttered across the field in a stir of air. He saw another, more, blowing along in the fitful gusts. He ran a few steps, caught one, smoothed it out.

BUY NOW—PAY LATER!

He picked up another.

PREPARE TO MEET GOD

A third said:

WIN WITH WILKIE

3

He plodded on, his eyes on the indifferent wall ahead
as it came closer. At last he reached it. Nothing changed.
He was still tired and hungry. Now the wall loomed
above him, smooth and grey. He was uncomfortably
aware of the dust caked on his skin and clothes. He
decided to follow the wall, maybe find a gate. As he
walked he brushed at himself absently. Aunt Haicey
would scold him if she knew how dirty he had gotten
his new clothes. Swell impression *he'd* make! The suitcase dragged at his arm, thumped against his shin. He
was very hungry and thirsty. He sniffed the air, instinc-
tively searching for the odors of food. He had been
following the wall for a long time, searching for an
opening. It curved away from him, rising vertically from
the level earth. Its surface was porous, unadorned, too
smooth to climb. It was, Brett estimated, twenty feet
high. If there were anything to make a ladder from—

Ahead he saw a wide gate, flanked by grey columns.
He came up to it, put the suitcase down, and wiped
at his forehead with his handkerchief. It came away
muddy. Through the opening in the wall a brick-paved
street was visible, and the facades of buildings. Those
on the street before him were low, not more than one
or two stories, but behind them taller towers reared
up. There were no people in sight; no sounds stirred
the hot late-afternoon air. Brett picked up his bag and
passed through the gate.

4

For the next hour he walked empty pavements, listening to the echoes of his footsteps against brownstone

fronts, empty shop windows, curtained glass doors, and here and there a vacant lot, weed-grown and desolate. He paused at cross streets, looked down long vacant ways. Now and then a distant sound came to him: the lonely honk of a horn, a faintly tolling bell, a clatter of hooves. He didn't think they had horses any more in cities.

He came to a narrow alley that cut like a dark canyon between blank walls. He stood at its mouth, listening to a distant murmur, like a crowd at a funeral. He turned down the narrow way.

It went straight for a few yards, then twisted. As he followed its turnings the crowd noise gradually grew louder. He could make out individual voices now, an occasional word above the hubbub. He started to hurry, eager to find someone to talk to.

Abruptly the voices—hundreds of voices, he thought—rose in a roar, a long-drawn *Yaaayyyyy . . . !* Brett thought of a stadium crowd as the home team trotted onto the field. He could hear a band now, a shrilling of brass, the clatter and thump of percussion instruments. Now he could see the mouth of the alley ahead, a sunny street hung with bunting, the backs of people, and over their heads the rhythmic bobbing of a passing procession, tall shakos and guidons in almost even rows. Two tall poles with a streamer between them swung into view. He caught a glimpse of tall red letters:

. . . FOR OUR SIDE!

He moved closer, edged up behind the grey-backed crowd. A phalanx of yellow-tunicked men approached, walking stiffly, fez tassels swinging. A small boy darted out into the street, loped along at their side. The music screeched and wheezed. Brett tapped the man before him.

"What's it all about . . . ?"

He couldn't hear his own voice. The man ignored him. Brett moved along behind the crowd, looking for a vantage point or a thinning in the ranks. There seemed to be fewer people ahead. He came to the end of the crowd, moved on a few yards, stood at the curb. The yellow-jackets had passed now, and a group of round-thighed girls in satin blouses and black boots and white fur caps glided into view, silent, expressionless. As they reached a point fifty feet from Brett they broke abruptly into a strutting prance, knees high, hips flirting, tossing shining batons high, catching them, twirling them, and up again. . . .

Brett craned his neck, looking for TV cameras. The crowd lining the opposite side of the street stood in solid ranks, drably clad, eyes following the procession, mouths working. A fat man in a rumpled suit and a panama hat squeezed to the front, stood picking his teeth. Somehow, he seemed out of place among the others. Behind the spectators, the store fronts looked normal, dowdy brick and mismatched glass and corroding aluminum, dusty windows and cluttered displays of cardboard, a faded sign that read TODAY ONLY, PRICES SLASHED. There were a few cars in sight, all parked at the curb, none in motion, no one in them. They were all dusty and faded, even the late models. To Brett's left the sidewalk stretched, empty. To his right the crowd was packed close, the shout rising and falling. Now a rank of blue-suited policemen followed the majorettes, swinging along silently. Behind them, over them, a piece of paper blew along the street. Brett turned to the man on his right.

"Pardon me. Can you tell me the name of this town?"

The man ignored him. Brett tapped the back of the man's shoulder. "Hey! What town is this?"

The man took off his hat, whirled it overhead, then threw it up. It sailed away over the crowd, lost. Brett wondered briefly how people who threw their hats ever recovered them. But then, nobody he knew would throw his hat. . . .

"You mind telling me the name of this place?" Brett said, as he took the man's arm, pulled. The man rotated toward Brett, leaning heavily against him. Brett stepped back. The man fell, lay stiffly, his arms moving, his eyes and mouth open.

"Ahhhhh," he said. "Whum-whum-whum. Awww, jawww . . ."

Brett stooped quickly. "I'm sorry," he cried. He looked around. "Help! This man . . ."

Nobody was watching. The next man, a few feet away, stood close against his neighbor, hatless, his jaw moving.

"This man's sick," said Brett, tugging at the man's arm. "He fell."

The man's eyes moved reluctantly to Brett. "None of my business," he muttered.

"Won't anybody give me a hand?"

"Probably a drunk."

Behind Brett a voice called in a penetrating whisper: "Quick! You! Get into the alley . . . !"

He turned. A gaunt man in his thirties with sparse reddish hair, perspiration glistening on his upper lip, stood at the mouth of a narrow way like the one Brett had come through. He looked like some kind of an actor; he wore a grimy pale yellow shirt with a wide-flaring collar, limp and sweat-stained, dark green knee-breeches, soft leather boots, scuffed and dirty, with limp tops that drooped over his ankles. He gestured, drew back into the alley. "In here!"

Brett went toward him. "This man . . ."

"Come on, you fool!" The man took Brett's arm,

pulled him deeper into the dark passage. Brett resisted. "Wait a minute. That fellow . . ." He tried to point.

"Don't you know yet?" The redhead spoke with a strange accent. "Golems . . . You got to get out of sight before the—"

The man froze, flattened himself against the wall. Automatically Brett moved to a place beside him. The man's head was twisted toward the alley mouth. The tendons in his weathered neck stood out. He had a three-day stubble of beard. Brett could smell him, standing this close. He edged away. "What—"

"Don't make a sound! Don't move, you idiot!" His voice was a thin hiss.

Brett followed the other's eyes toward the sunny street. The fallen man lay on the pavement, moving feebly, eyes open. Something moved up to him, a translucent brownish shape, like muddy water. It hovered for a moment, then dropped on the man, like a breaking wave, flowed around him. The stiff body shifted, rotating stiffly, then tilted upright. The sun struck through the fluid shape that flowed down now, amber highlights twinkling, to form itself into the crested wave, flow away.

"What the hell . . . !" Brett burst out.

"Come on!" the redhead ordered and turned, trotted silently toward the shadowy bend under the high grey walls. He looked back, beckoned impatiently, passed out of sight around the turn—

Brett came up behind him, saw a wide avenue, tall trees with chartreuse springtime leaves, a wrought-iron fence, and beyond it, rolling green lawns. There were no people in sight.

"Wait a minute! What is this place?!"

His companion turned red-rimmed eyes on Brett. "How long have you been here?" he asked. "How did you get in?"

"I came through a gate. Just about an hour ago."

"I knew you were a man as soon as I saw you talking to the golem," said the redhead. "I've been here two months; maybe more. We've got to get out of sight. You want food? There's a place . . ." He jerked his thumb. "Come on. Time to talk later."

Brett followed him. They turned down a side street, pushed through the door of a dingy cafe. It banged behind them. There were tables, stools at a bar, a dusty juke box. They took seats at a table. The redhead groped under the table, pulled off a shoe, hammered it against the wall. He cocked his head, listening. The silence was absolute. He hammered again. There was a clash of crockery from beyond the kitchen door. "Now don't say anything," the redhead said. He eyed the door behind the counter expectantly. It flew open. A girl with red cheeks and untidy hair, dressed in a green waitress's uniform appeared, marched up to the table, pad and pencil in hand.

"Coffee and a ham sandwich," said the redhead. Brett said nothing. The girl glanced at him briefly, jotted hastily, whisked away.

"I saw them here the first day," the redhead said. "It was a piece of luck. I saw how the Gels started it up. They were big ones—not like the tidiers-up. As soon as they were finished, I came in and tried the same thing. It worked. I used the golem's lines—"

"I don't know what you're talking about," Brett said. "I'm going to ask that girl—"

"Don't say anything to her; it might spoil everything. The whole sequence might collapse; or it might call the Gels. I'm not sure. You can have the food when it comes back with it."

"Why do you say 'when "it" comes back'?"

"Ah." He looked at Brett strangely. "I'll show you."

Brett could smell food now. His mouth watered. He hadn't eaten for more than twenty-four hours.

"Care, that's the thing," the redhead said. "Move quiet, and stay out of sight, and you can live like a County Duke. Food's the hardest, but with this place—"

The red-cheeked girl reappeared, a tray balanced on one arm, a heavy cup and saucer in the other hand. She clattered them down on the table.

"Took you long enough," the redhead said. The girl sniffed, opened her mouth to speak—and the redhead darted out a stiff finger, jabbed her under the ribs. Instead of the yell Brett expected, she stood, mouth open, frozen.

Brett half rose. "He's crazy, miss," he said. "Please accept—"

"Don't waste your breath." Brett's host was looking at him triumphantly. "Why do I call it 'it'?" He stood up, reached out and undid the top buttons of the green uniform. The waitress stood, leaning slightly forward, unmoving. The blouse fell open, exposing round white breasts—unadorned, blind.

"A doll," said the redhead. "A puppet; a golem."

Brett stared at her, the damp curls at her temple, the tip of her tongue behind her teeth, the tiny red veins in her round cheeks, the white skin curving . . .

"That's a quick way to tell 'em," said the redhead. "The teat is smooth." He buttoned the uniform back in place, then jabbed again at the girl's ribs. She straightened, patted her hair.

"No doubt a gentleman like you is used to better," she said carelessly. She went away.

"I'm Awalawon Dhuva," the redhead said.

"My name's Brett Hale." Brett took a bite of the sandwich. It wasn't bad.

"Those clothes," Dhuva said. "And you have a strange way of talking. What county are you from?"

"Jefferson."

"Never heard of it. I'm from Wavly. What brought you here?"

"I was on a train. The tracks came to an end out in the middle of nowhere. I walked . . . and here I am. What is this place?"

"Don't know." Dhuva shook his head. "I knew they were lying about the Fire River, though. Never did believe all that stuff. Religious hokum, to keep the masses quiet. Don't know what to believe now. Take the roof. They say a hundred kharfads up; but how do we know? Maybe it's a thousand—or only ten. By Grat, I'd like to go up in a balloon, see for myself."

"What are you talking about?" Brett said. "Go where in a balloon? See what?"

"Oh, I've seen one at the Tourney. Big hot-air bag, with a basket under it. Tied down with a rope. But if you cut the rope . . . ! But you can bet the priests will never let that happen, no, sir." Dhuva looked at Brett speculatively. "What about your county? Fesseron, or whatever you called it. How high do they tell you it is there?"

"You mean the sky? Well, the air ends after a few hundred miles and space just goes on—millions of miles—"

Dhuva slapped the table and laughed. "The people in Fesseron must be some yokels! Just goes on up; now who'd swallow that tale?" He chuckled.

"Only a child thinks the sky is some kind of tent," said Brett. "Haven't you ever heard of the Solar System, the other planets?"

"What are those?"

"Other worlds. They all circle around the sun, like the Earth."

"Other worlds, eh? Sailing around up under the roof? Funny; I never saw them." Dhuva snickered.

"Wake up, Brett. Forget all those stories. Just believe what you see."

"What about that brown thing?"

"The Gels? They run this place. Look out for them, Brett. Stay alert. Don't let them see you."

"What do they do?"

"I don't know—and I don't want to find out. This is a great place—I like it here. I have all I want to eat, plenty of nice rooms for sleeping. There's the parades and the scenes. It's a good life—as long as you keep out of sight."

"How do you get out of here?" Brett said. He drank the last of his coffee.

"Don't know how to get out; over the wall, I suppose. I don't plan to leave, though. I left home in a hurry. The Duke—never mind. I'm not going back."

"Are all the people here . . . golems?" Brett said. "Aren't there any more real people?"

"You're the first I've seen. I spotted you as soon as I saw you. A live man moves different than a golem. You see golems doing things like knitting their brows, starting back in alarm, looking askance, and standing arms akimbo. And they have things like pursed lips and knowing glances and mirthless laughter. You know: all the things you read about, that real people never do. But now that you're here, I've got somebody to talk to. I did get lonesome, I admit. I'll show you where I stay and fix you up with a bed."

"I won't be around that long."

"What can you get outside that you can't get here? There's everything you need here in the city. We can have a great time."

"You sound like my Aunt Haicey," Brett said. "She said I had everything I needed back in Casperton. How does she know what I need? How do *you* know? How do I know myself? I can tell you I need more than food and a place to sleep—"

"What more?"

"Everything. Things to think about and something worth doing. Why, even in the movies—"

"What's a movie?"

"You know, a play, on film. A moving picture."

"A picture that moves?"

"That's right."

"This is something the priests told you about?" Dhuva seemed to be holding in his mirth.

"Everybody's seen movies."

"Have you now? What else have you got in Fesseron?"

"Jefferson," Brett said. "Well, we've got records, and stock car races, and the radio and TV, and—"

"Stockar?"

"You know: automobiles; they race."

"An animal?"

"No, a machine; made of metal."

"Made of metal? And yet alive?"

"No, it's—"

"Dead and yet it moves." Dhuva burst out laughing. "Those priests," he said. "They're the same everywhere, I see, Brett. The stories they tell, and people believe them. What else?"

"Priests have nothing to do with it!"

Dhuva composed his features. "What do they tell you about Grat, and the Wheel?"

"Grat? What's that?"

"The Over-Being. The Four-eyed One." Dhuva made a sign, caught himself. "Just habit," he said. "I don't believe that rubbish. Never did."

"I suppose you're talking about God," Brett said.

"I don't know about God. Tell me about it."

"He's the creator of the world. He's . . . well, super-human. He knows everything that happens, and when you die, if you've led a good life, you meet God in Heaven."

"Where's that?"

"It's . . ." Brett waved a hand vaguely. "Up above."

"But you said there was just emptiness up above," Dhuva recalled. "And some other worlds spinning around, like islands adrift in the sea."

"Well—"

"Never mind, Brett." Dhuva held up his hands. *"Our* priests are liars too. All that balderdash about the Wheel and the River of Fire. It's just as bad as your Hivvel or whatever you called it. And our Grat and your Mud, or Gog: they're the same—" Dhuva's head went up. "What's that?"

"I didn't hear anything."

Dhuva got to his feet, turned to the door. Brett rose. A towering brown shape, glassy and transparent, hung in the door, its surface rippling. Dhuva whirled, leaped past Brett, dived for the rear door. Brett stood frozen. The shape flowed—swift as quicksilver—caught Dhuva in mid-stride, engulfed him. For an instant Brett saw the thin figure, legs kicking, upended within the muddy form of the Gel, which ignored Brett. Then the turbid wave swept across to the door, sloshed it aside, disappeared. Dhuva was gone.

Brett stood rooted, staring at the doorway. A bar of sunlight fell across the dusty floor. A brown mouse ran along the baseboard. It was very quiet. Brett went to the door through which the Gel had disappeared, hesitated a moment, then thrust it open.

He was looking down into a great dark pit, acres in extent, its sides riddled with holes, the amputated ends of water and sewage lines and power cables dangling. Far below, light glistened from the surface of a black pool. A few feet away the pink-cheeked waitress stood unmoving in the dark on a narrow strip

of linoleum. At her feet the chasm yawned. The edge
of the floor was ragged, as though it had been gnawed
away by rats. There was no sign of Dhuva.

Brett stepped back into the dining room, let the door
swing shut. He took a deep breath, picked up a paper
napkin from a table and wiped his forehead, dropped
the napkin on the floor and went out into the street, his
suitcase forgotten now. A weapon, he thought—perhaps
in a store . . . At the corner he turned, walked along past
silent shop windows crowded with home permanent kits,
sun glasses, fingernail polish, suntan lotion, paper car-
tons, streamers, plastic toys, varicolored garments of
synthetic fiber, home remedies, beauty aids, popular
music, greeting cards . . .

At the next corner he stopped, looking down the
silent streets. Nothing moved. Brett went to a small
window in a grey concrete wall, pulled himself up to
peer through the dusty pane, saw a room filled with
tailor's forms, garment racks, a bicycle, bundled back
issues of magazines without covers.

He went along to a door. It was solid, painted shut.
The next door looked easier. He wrenched at the tarnished brass knob, then stepped back and kicked the
door. With a hollow sound the door fell inward, taking with it the jamb. Bits of mortar fell. Brett stood
staring at the gaping opening. A fragment of mortar
dropped with a dry clink. Brett stepped through the
breach in the grey facade into a vast, empty cavern.
The black pool at the bottom of the pit winked a flicker
of light back at him in the deep gloom.

He looked around. The high walls of the block of
buildings loomed in silhouette; the squares of the
windows were ranks of luminous blue against the dark.
Dust motes danced in shafts of sunlight. Far above,
the roof was dimly visible, a spidery tangle of trusswork.
And below was the abyss.

At Brett's feet the stump of a heavy brass rail projected an inch from the floor. It was long enough, Brett thought, to give firm anchor to a rope. Somewhere below, Dhuva—a stranger who had befriended him— lay in the grip of the Gels. He would do what he could—but he needed equipment and help. First he would find a store with rope, guns, knives. He would—

The broken edge of masonry where the door had been caught his eye. The shell of the wall, exposed where the door frame had torn away, was wafer-thin. Brett reached up, broke off a piece. The outer face— the side that showed on the street—was smooth, solid-looking. The back was porous, nibbled. Brett stepped outside, examined the wall. He kicked at the grey surface. A great piece of wall, six feet high, broke into fragments and fell on the sidewalk with a crash, driving out a puff of dust. Another section fell. One piece of it skidded away, clattered down into the depths. Brett heard a distant splash. He looked at the great jagged opening in the wall—like a jigsaw puzzle with a piece missing. He turned and started off at a trot, his mouth dry, his pulse trumping painfully in his chest.

Two blocks from the hollow building, Brett slowed to a walk, his footsteps echoing in the empty street. He looked into each store window as he passed. There were artificial legs, bottles of colored water, immense dolls, wigs, glass eyes—but no rope. Brett tried to think. What kind of store would handle rope? A marine supply company, maybe. But where would he find one?

Perhaps it would be easiest to look in a telephone book. Ahead he saw a sign lettered H O T E L. Brett went up to the revolving door, pushed inside. He was in a dim, marble-panelled lobby, with double doors leading into a beige-carpeted bar on his right, the brass-painted cage of an elevator directly before him, flanked by tall urns of sand and an ascending staircase. On the left was a dark mahogany-finished reception desk. Behind the desk a man stood silently, waiting. Brett felt a wild surge of relief.

"Those things, those Gels!" he called, starting across the room. "My friend—"

He broke off. The clerk stood, staring over Brett's shoulder, holding a pen poised over a ledger. Brett reached out, took the pen. The man's finger curled stiffly around nothing. A golem.

Brett turned away, went into the bar. Vacant stools were ranged before a dark mirror. At the tables empty glasses stood before empty chairs. Brett started as he heard the revolving door *thump-thump*. Suddenly soft light bathed the lobby behind him. Somewhere a piano tinkled *"More Than You Know."*

With a distant clatter of closing doors the elevator came to life.

Brett hugged a shadowed corner, saw a fat man in a limp seersucker suit cross to the reception desk. He had a red face, a bald scalp blotched with large brown freckles. The clerk inclined his head blandly.

"Ah, yes, sir, a nice double with bath . . ." Brett heard the unctuous voice of the clerk as he offered the pen. The fat man took it, scrawled something in the register. ". . . at fourteen dollars," the clerk murmured. He smiled, dinged the bell. A boy in tight green tunic and trousers and a pillbox cap with a chin strap pushed through a door beside the desk, took the key, led the way to the elevator. The fat man entered. Through the openwork of the shaft Brett watched as the elevator car rose, greasy cables trembling and swaying. He started back across the lobby—and stopped dead.

A wet brown shape had appeared in the entrance. It flowed across the rug to the bellhop. Face blank, the golem turned back to its door. Above, Brett heard the elevator stop. Doors clashed. The clerk stood poised

behind the desk. Brett stood still, not even breathing.
The Gel hovered, then flowed away. The piano was
silent now. The lights burned, a soft glow, then winked
out. Brett thought about the fat man. He had seen him
before. . . .

He went up the stairs. In the second floor corridor
Brett felt his way along in near darkness, guided by
the dim light coming through transoms. He tried a
door. It opened. He stepped into a large bedroom with
a double bed, an easy chair, a chest of drawers. He
crossed the room, looked out across an alley. Twenty
feet away, shabby white curtains hung at windows in
a brick wall. There was nothing behind the windows.

There were sounds in the corridor. Brett dropped
to the floor behind the bed.

"All right, you two," a drunken voice bellowed. "And
may all your troubles be little ones." There was laughter, squeals, a dry clash of beads flung against the door.
A key grated. The door swung wide. Lights blazed in
the hall, silhouetting the figures of a man in black
jacket and trousers, a woman in a white bridal dress
and veil, flowers in her hand. Beyond them, people
were smiling and talking:

"Take care, Mel!"

" . . . do anything I wouldn't do!"

" . . . kiss the bride, now!"

The couple backed into the room, pushed the door
shut, stood against it. Brett crouched behind the bed,
breathing silently, waiting. The couple stood at the door,
in the dark, heads down, looking at the carpeted floor.

Brett stood, rounded the foot of the bed, approached
the two unmoving figures. The girl looked young, sleek,
perfect features, with soft dark hair. Her eyes were half
open: Brett caught a glint of light reflected from the
eyeball. The man was bronzed, broad-shouldered, his
hair wavy and blond. His lips were parted, showing

even white teeth. The two stood, not breathing, sight-less eyes fixed on nothing.

Brett took the bouquet from the woman's hand. The flowers seemed real—except that they had no perfume. He dropped them on the floor, pulled at the male golem to clear the door. The figure pivoted, toppled, hit with a heavy thump. Brett raised the woman in his arms and propped her against the bed. She was lighter than he expected. Back at the door he listened. All was quiet now. He started to open the door, then hesitated. He went back to the bed, undid the tiny pearl buttons down the front of the bridal gown, pulled it open. The breasts were rounded, smooth, an unbroken, creamy white . . .

In the hall, he started toward the stair. A tall Gel rippled into view ahead, its shape flowing and waver-ing, now billowing out, then rising up. The shifting form undulated in Brett's direction, but gave no indi-cation of noticing him. He almost made a move to run, then remembered Dhuva, and stood motionless. The Gel wobbled past him, slumped suddenly, flowed under a door. Brett let out a breath. Never mind the fat man. There were too many Gels here. He started back along the corridor.

Soft music came from beyond double doors which stood open on a landing. Brett went to them, risked a look inside. Graceful couples moved sedately on a polished floor; diners sat at tables, black-clad waiters moving among them. At the far side of the room, near a dusty rubber plant, sat the fat man, studying a menu. As Brett watched he shook out a napkin, ran it around inside his collar, then wiped his face.

Never disturb a scene, Dhuva had said. But perhaps he could blend with it. Brett brushed at his suit, straightened his tie, stepped into the room. A waiter approached, eyed him dubiously. Brett got out his wallet, took out a five-dollar bill.

"A quiet table in the corner," he said. He glanced back. There were no Gels in sight. He followed the waiter to a table near the fat man.

Seated, he looked around. He wanted to talk to the fat man, but he couldn't afford to attract attention. He would watch, and wait his chance.

At the nearby tables men with well-pressed suits, clean collars, and carefully shaved faces murmured to sleekly gowned women who fingered wine glasses, smiled archly. He caught fragments of conversation:

"My dear, have you heard . . ."

" . . . in the low eighties . . ."

" . . . quite impossible. One must . . ."

" . . . for this time of year . . ."

The waiter was waiting expectantly. "The usual," Brett told it. It darted away, returned with a shallow bowl of milky soup. Brett looked at the array of spoons, forks, knives, glanced sideways at the diners at the next table. It was important to follow the correct ritual. He put his napkin in his lap, careful to shake out all the folds. He looked at the spoons again, picked a large one, glanced at the waiter. So far, so good. . . .

"Wine, sir?" the waiter mumbled.

Brett indicated the neighboring couple. "The same as they're having." The waiter turned away, returned holding a wine bottle, label toward Brett. He looked at it, nodded. The waiter busied himself with the cork, removing it with many flourishes, setting a glass before Brett, pouring half an inch of wine. He waited expectantly again.

Brett had seen the ritual in movies; he picked up the glass, tasted the wine. It tasted like wine. He nodded. The waiter poured. Brett wondered what would have happened if he had made a face and spurned it. But it would be too risky to try. No one ever did it.

Couples danced, resumed their seats; others rose and

took the floor. A string ensemble in a distant corner played restrained tunes that seemed to speak of the gentle faded melancholy of decorous tea dances on long-forgotten afternoons. Brett glanced toward the fat man. He was eating soup noisily, napkin tied under his chin.

The waiter was back with a plate. "Lovely day, sir," it said.

"Great," Brett agreed.

The waiter placed a covered platter on the table, removed the cover, stood with carving knife and fork poised.

"A bit of the crispy, sir?"

Brett nodded. He eyed the waiter surreptitiously. He looked real. Some golems seemed realer than others; or perhaps it merely depended on the parts they were playing. The man who had fallen at the parade had been only a sort of extra, a crowd member. The waiter, on the other hand, was able to converse. Perhaps it would be possible to learn something from him.

"What's . . . uh . . . how do you spell the name of this town?" Brett asked.

"I was never much of a one for spelling, sir," the waiter said.

"Try it."

"Gravy, sir?"

"Sure. Try to spell the name—"

"Perhaps I'd better call the headwaiter, sir," the golem said stiffly.

From the corner of an eye Brett caught a flicker of motion. He whirled, saw nothing. Had it been a Gel?

"Never mind," he said. The waiter served potatoes, peas, refilled the wine glass, moved off silently. The question had been a little too unorthodox, Brett decided. Perhaps if he led up to the subject more obliquely . . .

When the waiter returned Brett said, "Nice day."

"Very nice, sir."

"Better than yesterday."

"Yes indeed, sir.

"I wonder what tomorrow'll be like."

"Perhaps we'll have a bit of rain, sir."

Brett nodded toward the dance floor. "Nice orchestra."

"They're very popular, sir."

"From here in town?"

"I wouldn't know as to that, sir."

"Lived here long yourself?"

"Oh, yes, sir." The waiter's expression showed disapproval. "Would there be anything else, sir?"

"I'm a newcomer here," Brett said. "I wonder if you could tell me—"

"Excuse me, sir." The waiter was gone. Brett poked at the mashed potatoes. Quizzing golems was hopeless. He would have to find out for himself. He turned to look out at the fat man. As Brett watched he took a large handkerchief from a pocket, blew his nose loudly. No one turned to look. The orchestra played softly. The couples danced. Now was as good a time as any. . . .

Brett rose, crossed to the other table. The fat man looked up.

"Mind if I sit down?" Brett said. "I'd like to talk to you."

The fat man blinked, motioned to a chair. Brett sat down, leaned across the table. "Maybe I'm wrong," he said quietly, "but I think you're real."

The fat man blinked again. "What's that?" he snapped. He had a high, petulant voice.

"You're not like the rest of them. I think I can talk to you. I think you're another outsider."

The fat man looked down at his rumpled suit. "I . . . ah . . . was caught a little short today. Didn't have time to change. I'm a busy man. And what business is it of yours?" He clamped his jaw shut, eyed Brett warily.

"I'm a stranger here," Brett said. "I want to find out what's going on in this place—"

"Buy an amusement guide. Lists all the shows—"

"I don't mean that. I mean these dummies all over the place, and the Gels—"

"What dummies? Jells? Jello? You don't like Jello?"

"I love Jello. I don't—"

"Just ask the waiter. He'll bring you your Jello. Any flavor you like. Now if you'll excuse me . . ."

"I'm talking about the brown things; they look like muddy water. They come around if you interfere with a scene."

The fat man looked nervous. "How's that?" he said. "Please go away."

"If I make a disturbance, the Gels will come. Is that what you're afraid of?"

"Now, now. Be calm. No need for you to get excited."

"I won't make a scene," Brett said. "Just talk to me. How long have you been here?"

"I dislike scenes. I dislike them intensely."

"When did you come here?" Brett persisted.

"Just ten minutes ago," the fat man hissed. He seemed terrified. "I just sat down. I haven't had my dinner yet. Please, young man. Go back to your table." The fat man watched Brett warily. Sweat glistened on his bald head.

"I mean this town. How long have you been here? Where did you come from?" Brett repeated stubbornly.

"Why, I was born here. Where did I come from? What sort of question is that? Just consider that the eagle brought me."

"You were born here?"

"Certainly."

"What's the name of the town?"

"Are you trying to make a fool of me?" The fat man was getting angry. His voice was rising.

"Shhh," Brett cautioned. "You'll attract the Gels."

"Blast the Jilts, whatever that is!" The fat man snapped. "Now get along with you. I'll call the manager."

"Don't you *know*?" Brett said, staring at the fat man. "They're all dummies; golems, they're called. They're not real."

"Who're not real?"

"All these imitation people at the tables and on the dance floor. Surely you realize—"

"I realize you're in need of psychiatric attention!" The fat man pushed back his chair and got to his feet. "You keep the table," he said. "I'll dine elsewhere."

"Wait!" Brett got up, seized the fat man's arm.

"Take your hands off me—" The fat man pulled free and went toward the door. Brett followed. At the cashier's desk Brett turned suddenly, saw a fluid brown shape flicker—

"Look!" He pulled at the fat man's arm.

"Look at what?" The Gel was gone.

"It was there: a Gel."

The fat man flung down a bill, hurried away. Brett fumbled out a ten, waited for change. "Wait!" he called. He heard the fat man's feet receding down the stairs.

"Hurry," he said to the cashier. The woman sat glassy-eyed, staring at nothing. The music died. The lights flickered, went off. In the gloom Brett saw a fluid shape rise up, flow away from him.

He ran, pounding down the stairs, out into a corridor. The fat man was just rounding the corner. Brett opened his mouth to call—and went rigid, as a translucent shape of mud shot from a door, rose up to tower before him. Brett froze, stood, mouth half open, eyes staring, leaning forward with hands out-flung. The Gel loomed, its surface flickering—waiting. Brett caught an acrid odor of geraniums.

A minute passed. Brett's cheek itched. He fought a desire to blink, to swallow—to turn and run. The high sun beat down on the silent street, the still window displays.

Then the Gel broke form, slumped, flashed away. Brett tottered back against the wall, let his breath out in a harsh sigh.

Across the street he saw a window with a display of camping equipment, portable stoves, boots, rifles. He crossed the street, tried the door. It was locked. He looked up and down the street. There was no one in sight. He kicked at the glass beside the latch, reached through and turned the knob. Inside he looked over the shelves, selected a heavy coil of nylon rope, a sheath knife, a canteen. He examined a repeating rifle with a telescopic sight, then put it back and strapped on a .22 revolver. He emptied two boxes of long rifle cartridges into his pocket, then loaded the pistol. He coiled the rope over his shoulder and went back out into the empty street.

The fat man was standing in front of a shop in the next block, picking at his chin and eyeing the window display. He looked up with a frown, started away as Brett came up.

"Wait a minute," Brett called. "Didn't you see the Gel? The one that cornered me back there?"

The fat man looked back suspiciously, kept going.

"Wait!" Brett caught his arm. "I know you're real. I've seen you belch and sweat and pick your nose and scratch. You're the only one I can call on—and I need help. My friend is trapped—"

The fat man pulled away, his face flushed an even deeper red. "I'm warning you," he snarled. "You maniac! Get away from me . . . !"

Brett stepped close, rammed the fat man hard in

the ribs. He sank to his knees, gasping. The panama hat rolled away. Brett grabbed his arm, steadied him.

"Sorry," he said. "I had to be sure. You're real, all right. We've got to rescue my friend, Dhuva—"

The fat man leaned against the glass, rolling terrified eyes, rubbing his stomach. "I'll call the police!" he gasped.

"What police?" Brett waved an arm. "Look. Not a car in sight. Did you ever see the street that empty before?"

"Wednesday afternoon," the fat man gasped.

"Come with me. I want to show you. It's all hollow. There's nothing behind these walls—"

"Why doesn't somebody come along?" the fat man moaned, as if to himself.

"The masonry is only a quarter-inch thick," Brett said. "Come on; I'll show you."

"I don't like it," said the fat man. His face was pale and moist. "You're mad. What's wrong? It's so quiet . . ."

"We've got to try to save him. The Gel took him down into this pit—"

"Let me go," the man whined. "I'm afraid. Can't you just let me lead my life in peace?"

"Don't you understand?" Brett lowered his voice with an effort. "The Gel took a man. They may be after you next."

"There's no one after me! I'm a businessman . . . a respectable citizen. I mind my own business, give to charity, go to church. I never kick dogs or molest elderly ladies. All I want is to be left alone!"

Brett dropped his hands from the fat man's arms, stood looking at him: the blotched face, pale now, the damp forehead, the quivering jowls. The fat man stooped for his hat, slapped it against his leg, clamped it on his head.

"I think I understand now," said Brett. "This is *your*

place, this imitation city. Everything's faked to fit your needs—like in the hotel. Wherever you go, the scene unrolls in front of you. You never see the Gels, never discover the secret of the golems—because you conform. You never do the unexpected."

"That's right," the man gobbled. "I'm law-abiding. I'm respectable. I don't pry. I don't nose into other people's business. Why should I? Just let me alone . . ."

"Sure," Brett said. "Even if I dragged you down there and showed you, you wouldn't believe it. But you're not in the scene now. I've taken you out of it—"

Suddenly the fat man turned and ran a few yards, then looked back to see whether Brett was pursuing him. He shook a round fist.

"I've seen your kind before," he shouted. "Trouble-makers."

Brett took a step toward him. The fat man yelped and ran another fifty feet, his coattails bobbing. He looked back, stopped, a fat figure alone in the empty, sunny street.

"You haven't seen the last of me!" he shouted. "We know how to deal with your kind." He tugged at his vest, went off along the sidewalk. Brett watched him go, then started back toward the hollow building.

The jagged fragments of masonry Brett had knocked from the wall lay as he had left them. He stepped through the opening, peered down into the murky pit, trying to judge its depth. A hundred feet at least. Perhaps a hundred and fifty.

He unslung the rope from his shoulder, tied one end to the brass stump, threw the coil down the precipitous side. It fell away into darkness, hung swaying. It was impossible to tell whether the end reached any solid footing below. He couldn't waste any more time looking for help. He would have to try it alone.

There was a slap of shoe leather on the pavement outside. He turned, stepped out into the white sunlight. The fat man rounded the corner, recoiled as he saw Brett. He flung out a pudgy forefinger, his protruding eyes wide in his blotchy red face.

"There he is! I told you he came this way!" Two uniformed policemen came into view. One eyed the gun at Brett's side, put a hand on his own.

"Better take that off, sir."

"Look!" Brett said to the fat man. He stooped, picked up a crust of masonry. "Look at this—just a shell—"

"He's blasted a hole right in that building, officer!" the fat man shrilled. "He's dangerous . . ."

The cop ignored the gaping hole in the wall. "You'll have to come along with me, sir," it said in a bland, unemphatic voice. "This gentleman registered a complaint . . ."

Brett stood staring into the cop's eyes. They were pale blue, looking steadily back at him from the expressionless face. Could the cop be real? Or would he be able to push him over, as he had other golems?

"The fellow's not right in the head," the fat man was saying to the cop. "You should have heard his crazy talk. A troublemaker. His kind have got to be locked up!"

The cop nodded. "Can't have anyone causing trouble."

"Only a young fellow," said the fat man. He mopped at his forehead with a large handkerchief. "Tragic. But you men know how to handle him."

"Better give me the gun, sir." The cop held out a hand. Brett moved suddenly, rammed stiff fingers into the cop's ribs. It stiffened, toppled, lay rigid, staring up at nothing.

"You . . . you killed him," the fat man gasped, backing away. The second cop tugged at his gun. Brett leaped at him, sent him down with a blow to the ribs. He turned to face the fat man.

"I didn't kill them! I just turned them off. They're not real, they're just golems."

"A killer! And right in the city, in broad daylight."

"You've got to help me!" Brett cried. "This whole scene: don't you see? It has the air of something improvised in a hurry, to deal with the unexpected factor; that's me. The Gels know something's wrong, but they can't quite figure out what. When you called the cops the Gels obliged—"

Startlingly the fat man burst into tears. He fell to his knees.

"Don't kill me . . . oh, don't kill me . . ."

"Nobody's going to kill you, you fool!" Brett snapped. "Look! I want to show you!" He seized the fat man's lapel, dragged him to his feet and across the sidewalk, through the opening. The fat man stopped dead, stumbled back—

"What's this?" he wailed. "What kind of place is this?" He scrambled for the opening.

"It's what I've been trying to tell you. This city you live in—it's a hollow shell. There's nothing inside. None of it's real. Only you . . . and me. There was another man: Dhuva. I was in a cafe with him. A Gel came. He tried to run. It caught him. Now he's . . . down there."

"I'm not alone," the fat man babbled. "I have my friends, my clubs, my business associates. I'm insured. Lately I've been thinking a lot about Jesus—"

He broke off, whirled, and jumped for the doorway. Brett leaped after him, caught his coat. It ripped. The fat man stumbled over one of the cop-golems, went to hands and knees. Brett stood over him.

"Get up, damn it!" he snapped. "I need help and you're going to help me!" He hauled the fat man to his feet. "All you have to do is stand by the rope. Dhuva may be unconscious when I find him. You'll have to help me haul him up. If anybody comes along, any Gels, I mean—give me a signal. A whistle . . . like this—" Brett demonstrated. "And if I get in trouble, do what you can. Here . . ." Brett started to offer the fat man the gun, then handed him the hunting knife. "If anybody interferes, this may not do any good, but it's something. I'm going down now."

The fat man watched as Brett gripped the rope, let himself over the edge. Brett looked up at the glistening face, the damp strands of hair across the freckled scalp. Brett had no assurance that the man would stay at his post, but he had done what he could.

"Remember," said Brett. "It's a real man they've got, like you and me . . . not a golem. We owe it to him." The fat man's hands trembled. He watched Brett, licked his lips. Brett started down.

The descent was easy. The rough face of the excavation gave footholds. The end of a decaying timber projected; below it was the stump of a crumbling concrete pipe two feet in diameter. Brett was ten feet below the rim of the floor now. Above, the broad figure of the fat man was visible in silhouette against the jagged opening in the wall.

Now the cliff shelved back; the rope hung free. Brett eased past the cut end of a rusted water pipe, went down hand over hand. If there were nothing at the bottom to give him footing, it would be a long climb back. . . .

Twenty feet below he could see the still, black water, pockmarked with expanding rings where bits of debris dislodged by his passage peppered the surface.

There was a rhythmic vibration in the rope. Brett felt it through his hands, a fine sawing sensation. . . .

He was falling, gripping the limp rope. . . .

He slammed on his back in three inches of oily water. The coils of rope collapsed around him with a sustained splashing. He got to his feet, groped for the end of the rope. The glossy nylon strands had been cleanly cut.

For half an hour Brett waded in waist-deep water along a wall of damp clay that rose sheer above him. Far above, bars of dim sunlight crossed the upper reaches of the cavern. He had seen no sign of Dhuva . . . or the Gels.

He encountered a sodden timber that projected above the surface of the pool, clung to it to rest. Bits of flotsam: a plastic toy pistol, bridge tallies, a golf bag, floated in the black water. A tunnel extended through the clay wall ahead; beyond Brett could see a second great cavern rising. He pictured the city, silent and empty above, and the honeycombed earth beneath. He moved on.

An hour later Brett had traversed the second cavern. Now he clung to an outthrust spur of granite, as nearly as he could estimate directly beneath the point at which Dhuva had disappeared. Far above he could see the green-clad waitress standing stiffly on her ledge. He was tired. Walking in water, his feet floundering in soft mud, was exhausting. He was no closer to escape, or to finding Dhuva, than he had been when the fat man cut the rope. He had been a fool to leave the man alone, with a knife . . . but he had had no choice.

He would have to find another way out. Aimlessly wading at the bottom of the pit was useless. He would have to climb. One spot was as good as another. He stepped back and scanned the wall of clay looming over him. Twenty feet up, water dripped from the broken end of a four-inch water main. Brett uncoiled the rope from his shoulder, tied a loop in the end, whirled it and cast upward. It missed, fell back with a splash. He gathered it in, tried again. On the third try it caught. He tested it, then started up. His hands were slippery with mud and water. He twined the rope around his legs, inched higher. The slender cable was smooth as glass. He slipped back two feet, burning his hands, then inched upward, slipped again, painfully climbed, slipped, climbed.

After the first ten feet he found toeholds in the muddy wall. He worked his way up, his hands aching and raw. A projecting tangle of power cable gave a secure purchase for a foot. He rested. Nearby, an opening two feet in diameter gaped in the clay: a tunnel. It might be possible to swing sideways across the face of the clay and reach the opening. It was worth a try. His stiff, clay-slimed hands would pull him no higher.

He gripped the rope, kicked off sideways, hooked a foot in the tunnel mouth, half jumped, half fell into the mouth of the tunnel. He clung to the rope, shook it loose from the pipe above, coiled it and looped it over his shoulder. On hands and knees he started into the narrow passage.

The tunnel curved left, then right, dipped, then angled up. Brett crawled steadily, the smooth, stiff clay yielding and cold against his hands and sodden knees. Another smaller tunnel joined from the left. Another angled in from above. The tunnel widened to three feet, then four. Brett got to his feet, walked in a crouch. Here and there, barely visible in the near darkness, objects lay imbedded in the mud: a silver-plated spoon, its handle bent; the rusted engine of a toy electric train; a portable radio, green with corrosion from burst batteries.

At a distance, Brett estimated, of a hundred yards from the pit, the tunnel opened into a vast cave, green-lit from tiny discs of frosted glass set in the ceiling far above. A row of discolored concrete piles, the foundation of the building above, protruded against the near wall, their surfaces nibbled and pitted. Between Brett and the concrete columns the floor was littered with pale sticks and stones, gleaming dully in the gloom.

Brett started across the floor. One of the sticks snapped underfoot. He kicked a melon-sized stone. It rolled lightly, came to rest with hollow eyes staring toward him. A human skull.

The floor of the cave covered an area the size of a city block. It was blanketed with human bones, with here and there a small cat skeleton or the fanged snout bones of a dog. There was a constant rushing of rats that played among the rib cages, sat atop crania, scuttled behind shin-bones. Brett picked his way, stepping over imitation pearl necklaces, zircon rings, plastic buttons, hearing aids, lipsticks, compacts, corset stays, prosthetic devices, rubber heels, wristwatches, lapel watches, pocket watches with corroded brass chains, all stopped at the same hour: 12:30.

Ahead Brett saw a patch of color: a blur of pale yellow. He hurried, stumbling over bone heaps, crunching eyeglasses underfoot. He reached the still figure where it lay slackly, face down, in its yellow shirt. Gingerly he squatted, turned it on its back. It was Dhuva.

Brett slapped the cold wrists, rubbed the clammy hands. Dhuva stirred, moaned weakly. Brett pulled him to a sitting position. "Wake up!" he whispered. "Wake up!"

Dhuva's eyelids fluttered. He blinked dully at Brett.

"The Gels may turn up any minute," Brett hissed. "We have to get away from here. Can you walk?"

"I saw it," said Dhuva faintly. "But it moved so fast . . ."

"You're safe here for the moment," Brett said. "There are none of them around. But they may be back. We've got to find a way out!"

Dhuva started up, staring around. "Where am I?" he said hoarsely. Brett seized his arm, steadied him on his feet.

"We're in a hollowed-out cave, under the streets," he said. "The whole city is undermined with them. They're connected by tunnels. We have to find one leading back to the surface."

Dhuva gazed around at the acres of bones. "It left me here for dead."

"Or to die," said Brett.

"Look at them," Dhuva breathed. "Hundreds . . . thousands . . ."

"The whole population, it looks like. The Gels must have whisked them down here one by one."

"But why?"

"For interfering with the scenes. But that doesn't matter now. What matters is getting out; Come on. I see tunnels on the other side."

They crossed the broad floor, around them the white bones, the rustle of rats. They reached the far side of the cave, picked a six-foot tunnel which trended upward, a trickle of water seeping out of the dark mouth. They started up the slope.

"We have to have a weapon against the Gels," said Brett.

"Why? I don't want to fight them." Dhuva's voice was thin, frightened. "I want to get away from here . . .

even back to Wavly. I'd rather face the Duke's men. At least they're *men*."

"This was a real town, once," said Brett. "The Gels have taken it over, hollowed out the buildings, mined the earth under it, killed off the people, and put imitation people in their place. And nobody ever knew. I met a man who's lived here all his life. He doesn't know. But *we* know . . . and we have to do something about it."

"It's not our business. I've had enough. I want to get away."

"The Gels must stay down below, somewhere in that maze of tunnels. For some reason they try to keep up appearances . . . but only for the people who belong here. They play out scenes for the fat man, wherever he goes. And he never goes anywhere he isn't expected to."

"We'll get over the wall somehow," said Dhuva. "We may starve, crossing the dry fields, but that's better than this."

They emerged from the tunnel into a coal bin, crossed to a sagging door, found themselves in a boiler room. Stairs led up to sunlight. In the street, in the shadow of tall buildings, a boxy Buick sedan was parked at the curb. Brett went to it, tried the door. It opened. Keys dangled from the ignition switch. He slid into the dusty seat. Behind him there was a hoarse scream. Brett looked up. Through the streaked windshield he saw a mighty Gel rear up before Dhuva, crouched back against the blackened brick front of the building.

"Don't move, Dhuva!" Brett shouted. Dhuva froze, flattened against the wall. The Gel towered, its surface rippling, uncertain.

Brett eased from the seat, behind the Gel. He stood on the pavement, fifteen feet from the Gel. The rank Gel odor came in waves from the creature. Beyond it

Brett could see Dhuva's white, terrified face. Brett's mind raced, searching for an idea. On impulse he went to the front of the car.

Silently, he turned and lifted the latch of the old-fashioned side-opening auto hood, raised it. The copper fuel line curved down from the firewall to a glass sediment cup. The knurled retaining screw turned easily; the cup dropped into Brett's hand. Gasoline ran down in an amber stream. He pulled off his damp coat, wadded it, jammed it under the flow. Over his shoulder he saw Dhuva, still rigid, and the hovering, puzzled giant.

The coat was saturated with gasoline now. Brett shook it out, fumbled a matchbox from his pocket— then threw the sodden container aside. The battery caught his eye, clamped in a rusted frame under the hood. He jerked the pistol from its holster, used it to short the terminals. Tiny blue sparks jumped. He jammed the coat near, rasped the gun against the soft lead poles. With a *whoosh!* the coat caught, yellow flames leaped, soot-rimmed. Brett snatched it by a sleeve, whirled, flung the blazing garment over the great Gel as it sped toward him.

The creature went mad. It slumped, lashed itself against the pavement. The burning coat was thrown clear. The Gel threw itself across the pavement, into the gutter, sending a splatter of filthy water over Brett. From the corner of his eye, Brett saw Dhuva totter, then seize the burning coat, hurl it into the pooled gasoline in the gutter. Fire leaped up twenty feet high; in its center the great Gel bucked and writhed. The ancient car shuddered as the frantic monster struck it. Black smoke boiled up; an unbelievable stench came to Brett's nostrils. He backed, coughing. Flames roared around the front of the car. Paint blistered and burned. A tire burst. In a final frenzy the Gel whipped clear, lay, a great blackened shape of melting rubber, twitching, then still. His eyes met Dhuva's.

"Good thinking, Brett," the latter said. "How did you know?" he queried.

"I didn't," Brett admitted. "It just seemed that fire and water are natural enemies, so I tried it."

"And saved my life!" Dhuva said.

Brett nodded. "Now we know what to do," he went on.

Dhuva's expression was anxious. "All we have to do is get out," he commented.

Brett shook his head. "We can't just let them proceed with what they're doing," he insisted. "I think they're just establishing a base here. Wavly, or Casperton, might be next. We have to do something!"

Dhuva was shaking his head.

"They've tunneled under everything," Brett said. "They've cut through power lines and water lines, concrete, steel, earth; they've left the shell, shored up with spidery-looking trusswork. Somehow they've kept water and power flowing to wherever they needed it—"

"I don't care about your theories," Dhuva said. "I only want to get away."

"It's bound to work, Dhuva. I need your help."

"No."

"Then I'll have to try alone." He turned away.

"Wait," Dhuva called. He came up to Brett. "I owe you a life; you saved mine. I can't let you down now. But if this doesn't work . . . or if you can't find what you want—"

"Then we'll go."

Together they turned down a side street, walking rapidly. At the next corner Brett pointed.

"There's one!" They crossed to the service station at a run. Brett tried the door. Locked. He kicked it open, splintering the wood around the lock. He glanced around inside. "No good," he called. "Try the next building. I'll check the one behind."

He crossed the wide drive, battered in a door, looked in at a floor covered with wood shavings. It ended ten feet from the door. Brett went to the edge, looked down. Diagonally, forty feet away, the underground five-thousand-gallon storage tank which supplied the gasoline pumps of the station perched, isolated, on a column of striated clay, ribbed with chitinous Gel buttresses. The truncated feed lines ended six feet from the tank. From Brett's position, it was impossible to say whether the ends were plugged.

Across the dark cavern a square of light appeared. Dhuva stood in a doorway looking toward Brett, then started along the ledge toward him.

"Over here, Dhuva!" Brett's shout echoed. "—va! Over here . . ." He uncoiled his rope, arranged a slip-noose. He measured the distance with his eye, tossed the loop. It slapped the top of the tank, caught on a massive fitting. He smashed the glass from a window behind him, tied the end of the rope to the center post. Dhuva arrived, watched as Brett went to the edge, hooked his legs over the rope, and started across to the tank.

It was an easy crossing. Brett's feet clanged against the tank. He straddled the six-foot cylinder, worked his way to the end, then clambered down to the two two-inch feed lines. He tested their resilience, then lay flat, eased out on them. There were plugs of hard waxy material in the cut ends of the lines. Brett poked at them with the pistol. Chunks loosened and fell. He worked for fifteen minutes before the first trickle came. Two minutes later, two thick streams of gasoline were pouring down into the darkness. Brett heard them splashing far below.

Brett and Dhuva piled sticks, scraps of paper,

shavings, and lumps of coal around a core of gasoline-soaked rags. Directly above the heaped tinder a taut rope stretched from the window post to a child's wagon, the steel bed of which contained a second heap of combustibles. The wagon hung half over the ragged edge of the floor.

"It should take about fifteen minutes for the fire to burn through the rope," Brett said. "Then the wagon will fall and dump the hot coals in the gasoline. By then it will have spread all over the surface and flowed down side tunnels into parts of the cavern system."

"But it may not get them all."

"It will get some of them," Brett pointed out doggedly. "It's the best we can do right now. You get the fire going in the wagon; I'll start this one up."

Dhuva sniffed the air. "That fluid," he said. "We know it in Wavly as phlogistoleum. The wealthy use it for cooking."

"We'll use it to cook Gels." Brett struck a match. The fire leaped up, smoking. Dhuva watched, struck his match awkwardly, started his blaze. They stood for a moment watching. The nylon curled and blackened, melting in the heat.

"We'd better get moving," Brett said. "It doesn't look as though it will last fifteen minutes."

They stepped out into the street. Behind them wisps of smoke curled from the door and the broken window. Dhuva seized Brett's arm. "Look!"

Half a block away the fat man in the panama hat strode toward them at the head of a group of men in grey flannel. "That's him!" the fat man shouted. "The one I told you about. I knew the scoundrel would be back!" He slowed, eyeing Brett and Dhuva warily.

"You'd better get away from here, fast!" Brett called. "There'll be an explosion in a few minutes—"

"Smoke!" the fat man yelped. "Fire! They've set fire

to the city! There it is! Pouring out of the window . . . and the door!" He started forward. Brett yanked the pistol from the holster, thumbed back the hammer.

"Stop right there!" he barked. "For your own good I'm telling you to run. I don't care about that crowd of golems you've collected, but I'd hate to see a real human get hurt—even a cowardly son of a bitch like you."

"These are honest citizens," the fat man gasped, standing, staring at the gun. "You won't get away with this. We all know you. You'll be dealt with . . ."

"We're going now. And you're going too."

"You can't kill us all," the fat man said. He licked his lips. "We won't let you destroy our fair city. We'll—"

As the fat man turned to exhort his followers Brett fired, once, twice, three times. Three golems fell on their faces. The fat man whirled.

"Devil!" he shrieked. "A killer is abroad!" He charged, mouth open. Brett ducked aside, tripped the fat man. He fell heavily, slamming his face against the pavement. The golems surged forward. Brett and Dhuva slammed punches to the sternum, took clumsy blows on the shoulder, back, chest. Golems fell, and lay threshing futilely. Brett ducked a wild swing, toppled his attacker, turned to see Dhuva deal with the last of the dummies. The fat man sat in the street, dabbing at his bleeding nose, the panama still in place.

"Get up," Brett commanded. "There's no time left."

"You've killed them. Killed them all . . ." The fat man got to his feet, then turned suddenly and plunged for the door from which a cloud of smoke poured. Brett hauled him back. He and Dhuva started off, dragging the struggling man between them. They had gone a block when their prisoner, with a sudden frantic jerk, freed himself, set off at a run for the fire.

"Let him go!" Dhuva cried. "It's too late to go back!"

The fat man leaped fallen golems, wrestled with the door, disappeared into the smoke. Brett and Dhuva sprinted for the corner. As they rounded it a tremendous blast shook the street. The pavement before them quivered, opened in a wide crack. A ten-foot section dropped from view. They skirted the gaping hole, dashed for safety as the facades along the street cracked, fell in clouds of dust. The street trembled under a second explosion. Cracks opened, dust rising in puffs from the long, widening fissures. Masonry shells collapsed around them. They put their heads down and ran.

Winded, Brett and Dhuva walked through empty streets. Behind them, smoke blackened the sky. Embers floated down around them. The odor of burning Gel was carried on the wind. The late sun shone on the black pavement. A lone golem in a tasseled fez, left over from the morning's parade, leaned stiffly against a lamp post, eyes blank. Empty cars sat in driveways. TV antennae stood forlornly against the sunset.

"That place looks lived-in," said Brett, indicating an open apartment window with a curtain billowing above a potted geranium. "I'll take a look."

He came back shaking his head. "They were all watching the TV. For a minute I thought—they acted so normally; I mean, they didn't look up or anything when I walked in. I turned the set off. The electricity is still working anyway. Wonder how long it will last?"

They turned down a residential street. Underfoot the pavement trembled. They skirted a crack, kept going. Occasional golems stood in awkward poses or lay across sidewalks. One, clad in black, tilted awkwardly in a gothic entry of fretted stonework. "I guess there won't be any church this Sunday," said Brett.

He halted before a brown brick apartment house. An untended hose welled on a patch of sickly lawn. Brett went to the door, stood listening, then went in. Across the room the still figure of a woman sat in a rocker. A curl stirred on her smooth forehead. A flicker of expression seemed to cross the lined face. Brett started forward. "Don't be afraid. You can come with us—"

He stopped. A flapping windowshade cast restless shadows on the still golem features on which dust was already settling. Brett turned away, shaking his head.

"All of them," he said. "It's as though they were snipped out of paper. When the Gels died, their dummies died with them."

"Why?" said Dhuva. "What does it all mean?"

"Mean?" said Brett. He shook his head, started off again along the street. "It doesn't mean anything. It's just the way things are."

Brett sat in a deserted Cadillac, tuning the radio.

" . . . anybody hear me?" said a plaintive voice from the speaker. "This is Ab Gulloriak, at the Twin Spires. Looks like I'm the only one left alive. Can anybody hear me?"

Brett tuned. " . . . been asking the wrong questions . . . looking for the Final Fact. Now these are strange matters, brothers. But if a flower blooms, what man shall ask why? What lore do we seek in a symphony . . . ?"

He twisted the knob again. " . . . Kansas City. Not more than half a dozen of us. And the dead! Piled all over the place. But it's a funny thing: Doc Potter started to do an autopsy—"

Brett turned the knob. " . . . CQ, CQ, CQ. This is

Hollip Quate, calling CQ, CQ. There's been a disaster here at Port Wanderlust. We need—"

"Take Jesus into your hearts," another station urged.

" . . . to base," the radio said faintly, with much crackling. "Lunar Observatory to Houston. Come in, Lunar Control. This is Commander McVee of the Lunar Detachment, sole survivor—"

" . . . hello, Hollip Quate? Hollip Quate? This is Kansas City calling. Say, where did you say you were calling from . . . ?"

"It looks as though both of us had a lot of mistaken ideas about the world outside," said Brett. "Most of these stations sound as though they might as well be coming from Mars."

"I don't understand where the voices come from," Dhuva said. "But all the places they name are strange to me . . . except the Twin Spires."

"I've heard of Kansas City," Brett said, "but none of the other ones."

The ground trembled. A low rumble rolled. "Another one," Brett said. He switched off the radio, tried the starter. It groaned, turned over. The engine caught, sputtered, then ran smoothly.

"Get in, Dhuva. We might as well ride. Which way do we go to get out of this place?"

"The wall lies in that direction," said Dhuva, getting in hesitantly. "But I don't know about a gate."

"We'll worry about that when we get to it," said Brett. "This whole place is going to collapse before long. We really started something. I suppose other underground storage tanks caught—and gas lines, too."

A building ahead buckled, fell in a heap of pulverized plaster. The car bucked as a blast sent a ripple down the street. A manhole cover popped up, clattered a few feet, dropped from sight. Brett swerved, gunned the car. It leaped over rubble, roared along the littered pavement. Brett looked in the rearview mirror. A block behind them the street ended. Smoke and dust rose from the immense pit.

"We just missed it that time!" he called. "How far to the wall?"

"Not far! Turn here . . ."

Brett rounded the corner, with a shrieking of tires. Dhuva clung to his seat, terrified. "It goes of its own!" he was muttering. Ahead the grey wall rose up, blank, featureless.

"This is a dead end!" Brett shouted.

"We'd better get out and run for it—"

"No time! I'm going to ram the wall! Maybe I can knock a hole in it."

Dhuva crouched; teeth gritted, Brett held the accelerator to the floor, roared straight toward the wall. The heavy car shot across the last few yards, struck—

And burst through a curtain of canvas into a field of dry stalks.

Brett steered the car in a wide curve, halted and looked back. A blackened panama hat floated down, settled among the stalks. Smoke poured up in a dense cloud from behind the canvas wall. A fetid stench pervaded the air.

"That finishes that, I guess," Brett said.

"I don't know. Look out there."

Brett turned. Far across the dry field columns of smoke rose from the ground.

"The whole thing's undermined," Brett said. "How far does it go?"

"No telling. But we'd better be off. Perhaps we can get beyond the edge of it. Not that it matters. We're all that's left . . ."

"You sound like the fat man," Brett said. "But why should we be so surprised to find out the truth? After all, we never saw it before. All we knew—or thought we knew—was what they told us. The moon, the other side of the world, a distant city . . . or even the next town. How do we really know what's there . . . unless we go and see for ourselves? Does a goldfish in his bowl know what the ocean is like?"

"Where did they come from, those Gels?" Dhuva moaned. "How much of the world have they undermined? What about Wavly? Is it Golem county too? The Duke . . . and all the people I knew?"

"I don't know, Dhuva. I've been wondering about the people in Casperton. Like Doc Welch. I used to see him in the street with his little black bag. I always thought it was full of pills and scalpels; but maybe it really had zebra's tails and toad's eyes in it. Maybe he's really a magician, on his way to cast spells against demons. Maybe the people I used to see hurrying to catch the bus every morning weren't really going to the office. Maybe they go down into caves and chip away at the foundations of things. Maybe they go up on rooftops and put on rainbow-colored robes and fly away. I used to pass by a bank in Casperton: a big grey stone building with little curtains over the bottom half of the windows. I never did go in there. I don't have anything to do in a bank. I've always thought it was full of bankers, banking . . . Now I don't know. It could be anything . . ."

"That's why I'm afraid," Dhuva said. "It could be anything."

"Things aren't really any different from before," said Brett, " . . . except that now we know." He turned the big car out across the field toward Casperton.

"I don't know what we'll find when we get back. Aunt Haicey, Pretty-Lee . . . But there's only one way to find out."

The moon rose as the car bumped westward, raising a trail of dust against the luminous sky of evening.

HYBRID

1

Deep in the soil of the planet, rootlets tougher than steel wire probed among glassy sand grains, through packed veins of clay and layers of flimsy slate, sensing and discarding inert elements, seeking out and absorbing calcium, iron, sulphur, nitrogen.

Deeper still, a secondary system of roots clutched the massive face of the bedrock; sensitive tendrils monitored the minute trembling in the planetary crust, the rhythmic tidal pressures, the seasonal weight of ice, the footfalls of the wild creatures that hunted in the mile-wide shadow of the giant Yanda tree.

On the surface far above, the immense trunk, massive as a cliff, its vast girth anchored by mighty buttresses, reared up nine hundred yards above the prominence, spreading huge limbs in the white sunlight.

The tree was only remotely aware of the movement of air over the polished surfaces of innumerable leaves, the tingling exchange of molecules of water, carbon dioxide, oxygen. Automatically it reacted to the faint pressures of the wind, tensing slender twigs to hold each leaf at a constant angle to the radiation that struck down through the foliage complex.

The long days wore on. Air flowed in intricate patterns; radiation waxed and waned with the flow of vapor masses in the substratosphere; nutrient molecules moved along capillaries; the rocks groaned gently in the dark under the shaded slopes. In the invulnerability of its titanic mass, the tree dozed in a state of generalized low-level consciousness.

The sun moved westward. Its light, filtered through an increasing depth of atmosphere, was an ominous yellow now. Sinewy twigs rotated, following the source of energy. Somnolently, the tree retracted tender buds against the increasing cold, adjusted its rate of heat and moisture loss, its receptivity to radiation. As it slept, it dreamed of the long past, the years of free-wandering in the faunal stage, before the instinct to root and grow had driven it here. It remembered the grove of its youth, the patriarchal tree, the spore-brothers. . . .

It was dark now. The wind was rising. A powerful gust pressed against the ponderous obstacle of the tree; great thews of major branches creaked, resisting; chilled leaves curled tight against the smooth bark.

Deep underground, fibers hugged rock, transmitting data which were correlated with impressions from distant leaf surfaces, indicating that a major storm was brewing: There were ominous vibrations from the depth; relative humidity was rising, air pressure falling—

A pattern formed, signalling danger. The tree stirred; a tremor ran through the mighty branch system, shattering fragile frost crystals that had begun to form on shaded surfaces. Alertness stirred in the heart-brain, dissipating the euphoric dream-pattern. Reluctantly, long-dormant faculties came into play. The tree awoke.

Instantly, it assessed the situation. The storm was moving in off the sea—a major typhoon. It was too late for effective measures. Ignoring the pain of unaccustomed activity, the tree sent out new shock roots—cables three inches in diameter, strong as stranded steel—to grip the upreared rock slabs a hundred yards north of the taproot.

There was nothing more the tree could do. Impassively, it awaited the onslaught of the storm.

2

"That's a storm down there," Malpry said.

"Don't worry, we'll miss it." Gault fingered controls, eyes on dial faces.

"Pull up and make a new approach," Malpry said. "You and the Creep."

"Me and the Creep are getting tired of listening to you bitch, Mal."

"When we land, Malpry, I'll meet you outside," Pantelle put in. "I told you I don't like the name 'Creep.'"

"What, again?" Gault said. "You all healed up from the last time?"

"Not quite; I don't seem to heal very well in space."

"Permission denied, Pantelle," Gault said. "He's too big for you. Mal, leave him alone."

"I'll leave him alone," Malpry muttered. "I ought to dig a hole and leave him in it. . . ."

"Save your energy for down there," Gault said. "If we don't make a strike on this one, we've had it."

"Captain, may I go along on the field reconnaissance?" Pantelle asked. "My training in biology—"

"You better stay with the ship, Pantelle. And don't tinker. Just wait for us. We haven't got the strength to carry you back."

"That was an accident last time, Captain—"

"And the time before. Skip it, Pantelle. You mean well, but you've got two left feet and ten thumbs."

"I've been working on improving my coordination, Captain. I've been reading—"

The ship buffeted sharply as guidance vanes bit into atmosphere; Pantelle yelped.

"Oh-oh," he called. "I'm afraid I've opened up that left elbow again."

"Don't bleed on me, you clumsy slob," Malpry said.

"Quiet!" Gault said between his teeth. "I'm busy."

Pantelle fumbled a handkerchief in place over the cut. He would have to practice those relaxing exercises he had read about. And he would definitely start in weightlifting soon, and watching his diet. And he would be very careful this time and land at least one good one on Malpry, just as soon as they landed.

3

Even before the first outward signs of damage appeared, the tree knew that it had lost the battle against the typhoon. In the lull, as the eye of the storm passed over, it assessed the damage. There was no response from the northeast quadrant of the sensory network where rootlets had been torn from the rockface; the taproot itself seated now against pulverized stone. While the almost indestructible fiber of the

Yanda tree had held firm, the granite had failed. The tree was doomed by its own mass.

Now, mercilessly, the storm struck again, thundering out of the southwest to assault the tree with blind ferocity. Shock cables snapped like gossamer, great slabs of rock groaned and parted, with detonations lost in the howl of the wind. In the trunk, pressures built, agonizingly.

Four hundred yards south of the taproot, a crack opened in the sodden slope, gaping wider. Wind-driven water poured in, softening the soil, loosening the grip of a million tiny rootlets. Now the major roots shifted, slipping. . . .

Far above, the majestic crown of the Yanda tree yielded imperceptibly to the irresistible torrent of air. The giant north buttress, forced against the underlying stone, shrieked as tortured cells collapsed, then burst with a shattering roar audible even above the storm. A great arc of earth to the south, uplifted by exposed roots, opened a gaping cavern.

Now the storm moved on, thundered down the slope trailing its retinue of tattered debris and driving rain. A last vengeful gust whipped branches in a final frenzy; then the victor was gone.

And on the devastated promontory, the stupendous mass of the ancient tree leaned with the resistless inertia of colliding moons to the accompaniment of a cannonade of parting sinews, falling with dreamlike grace.

And in the heart-brain of the tree, consciousness faded in the unendurable pain of destruction.

Pantelle climbed down from the open port, leaned against the ship to catch his breath. He was feeling weaker than he expected. Tough luck, being on short rations; this would set him back on getting started on his weightlifting program. And he didn't feel ready to take on Malpry yet. But just as soon as he had some fresh food and fresh air—

"These are safe to eat," Gault called, wiping the analyzer needle on his pants leg and thrusting it back into his hip pocket. He tossed two large red fruits to Pantelle.

"When you get through eating, Pantelle, you better get some water and swab down the inside. Malpry and I'll take a look around."

The two moved off. Pantelle sat on the springy grass and bit into the apple-sized sphere. The waxy texture, he thought, was reminiscent of avocado; the skin was tough and aromatic; possibly a natural cellulose acetate. There seemed to be no seeds. That being the case, the thing was not properly a fruit at all. It would be interesting to study the flora of this planet. As soon as he reached home, he would have to enroll in a course in E.T. botany. Possibly he would go to Heidelberg or Uppsala, attend live lectures by eminent scholars. He would have a cosy little apartment—two rooms would do—in the old part of town, and in the evening he would have friends in for discussions over a bottle of wine—

However, this wasn't getting the job done. There was a glint of water across the slope. Pantelle finished his fruit, gathered his buckets, and set out.

4

"Why do we want to wear ourselves out?" Malpry said.

"We need the exercise," Gault told him. "It'll be four months before we get another chance."

"What are we, tourists, we got to see the sights?" Malpry stopped, leaned against a boulder, panting. He stared upward at the crater and the pattern of uptilted roots and beyond at the forestlike spread of the branches of the fallen tree.

"Makes our sequoias look like dandelions," Gault said. "It must have been the storm, the one we dodged coming in."

"So what?"

"A thing that big—it kind of does something to you."

"Any money in it?" Malpry sneered.

Gault looked at him sourly. "Yeah, you got a point there. Let's go."

"I don't like leaving the Creep back there with the ship."

Gault looked at Malpry. "Why don't you lay off the kid?"

"I don't like loonies."

"Don't kid me, Malpry. Pantelle is highly intelligent— in his own way. Maybe that's what you can't forgive."

"He gives me the creeps."

"He's a nice-looking kid; he means well—"

"Yeah," Malpry said. "Maybe he means well—but it's not enough . . ."

From the delirium of concussion, consciousness returned slowly to the tree. Random signals penetrated the background clatter of shadowy impulses from maimed sensors—

"Air pressure zero; falling . . . air pressure 112, rising . . . air pressure negative . . .

"Major tremor radiating from— Major tremor radiating from—

"Temperature 171 degrees, temperature -40 degrees, temperature 26 degrees. . . .

"Intense radiation in the blue only . . . red only . . . ultraviolet . . .

"Relative humidity infinite . . . wind from north-northeast, velocity infinite . . . wind rising vertically, velocity infinite . . . wind from east, west . . ."

Decisively, the tree blanked off the yammering nerve-trunks, narrowing its attention to the immediate status-concept. A brief assessment sufficed to reveal the extent of its ruin.

There was no reason, it saw, to seek extended personal survival. However, certain immediate measures were necessary to gain time for emergency spore propagation. At once, the tree-mind triggered the survival syndrome. Capillaries spasmed, forcing vital juices to the brain. Synaptic helices dilated, heightening neural conductivity. Cautiously, awareness was extended to the system of major neural fibers, then to individual filaments and interweaving capillaries.

Here was the turbulence of air molecules colliding with ruptured tissues; there, the wave pattern of light impinging on exposed surfaces. Microscopic filaments contracted, cutting off fluid loss through the massive wounds.

Now the tree-mind fine-tuned its concentration, scanning the infinitely patterned cell matrix. Here, amid confusion, there was order in the incessant restless movement of particles, the flow of fluids, the convoluted intricacy of the alpha-spiral. Delicately, the tree-mind readjusted the function-mosaic, in preparation for spore generation.

Malpry stopped, shaded his eyes. A tall, thin figure stood in the shade of the uptilted root mass on the ridge.

"Looks like we headed back at the right time," Malpry said.

"Damn," Gault said. He hurried forward. Pantelle came to meet him.

"I told you to stay with the ship, Pantelle!"

"I finished my job, Captain. You didn't say—"

"OK, OK. Is anything wrong?"

"No sir, but I've just remembered something—"

"Later, Pantelle. Let's get back to the ship. We've got work to do."

"Captain, do you know what this is?" Pantelle gestured toward the gigantic fallen tree.

"Sure; it's a tree." He turned to Malpry. "Let's—"

"Yes, but what kind?"

"Beats me. I'm no botanist."

"Captain, this is a rare species. In fact, it's supposed to be extinct. Have you ever heard of the Yanda?"

"No. Yes—" Gault looked at Pantelle. "Is that what this is?"

"I'm sure of it. Captain, this is a very valuable find—"

"You mean it's worth money?" Malpry was looking at Gault.

"I don't know. What's the story, Pantelle?"

"An intelligent race, with an early animal phase; later, they root, become fixed, functioning as a plant. Nature's way of achieving the active competition necessary for natural selection, then the advantage of conscious selection of a rooting site."

"How do we make money on it?"

Pantelle looked up at the looming wall of the fallen trunk, curving away among the jumble of shattered branches, a hundred feet, two hundred, more, in diameter. The bark was smooth, almost black. The leaves, a foot in diameter, were glossy, varicolored.

"This great tree—" Pantelle began, emotionally.

Malpry stooped, picked up a fragment from a burst root.

"This great club," he said, "to knock your lousy brains out with—"

"Shut up, Mal," Gault put in.

"It lived, roamed the planet perhaps ten thousand years ago, in the young faunal stage," Pantelle told them. "Then instinct drove it here, to fulfill the cycle of nature. Picture this ancient champion, looking for the first time out across the valley, saying his last farewells as the metamorphosis begins."

"Nuts," Malpry said.

"His was the fate of all males of his kind who lived too long, to stand forever on some height of land, to remember through unending ages the brief glory of youth, himself his own heroic monument."

"Where do you get all that crud?" Malpry said.

"Here was the place," Pantelle said. "Here all his journeys ended."

"OK, Pantelle," Gault continued. "Very moving. You said something about this thing being valuable."

"Captain, this tree is still alive, for a while at least. Even after the heart is dead, the appearance of life will persevere. A mantle of new shoots will leaf out to shroud the cadaver, tiny atavistic plantlets without connection to the brain, parasitic to the corpse, identical to the ancestral stock from which the giants sprang, symbolizing the extinction of a hundred million years of evolution."

"Get to the point."

"We can take cuttings from the heart of the tree. I have a book—it gives the details of the anatomy— we can keep the tissues alive. Back in civilization, we can regenerate the tree—brain and all. It will take time—"

"Suppose we sell the cuttings."

"Yes, any university would pay well—"

"How long will it take?"

"Not long. We can cut in carefully with narrow-aperture blasters—

"OK. Get your books, Pantelle. We'll give it a try."

Apparently, the Yanda mind observed, a very long time had elapsed since spore propagation had last been stimulated by the proximity of a host-creature. Withdrawn into introverted dreams, the tree had taken no conscious notice as the whispering contact with the spore-brothers faded and the host-creatures dwindled away. Now, eidetically, the stored impressions sprang into clarity. It was apparent that no female would pass this way again. The Yanda kind was gone. The fever of instinct that had motivated the elaboration of the mechanisms of emergency propagation had burned itself out futilely. The new pattern of stalked oculi gazed unfocused at an empty vista of gnarled jungle growth; the myriad filaments of the transfer nexus coiled quiescent, the ranked grasping members that would have brought a host-creature near drooped unused, the dran-sacs brimmed needlessly; no further action was indicated. Now death would come in due course.

Somewhere a drumming began, a gross tremor sensed through the dead mass. It ceased, began again, went on and on. It was of no importance, but a faint curiosity led the tree to extend a sensory filament, tap the abandoned nerve-trunk—

Agony!

Convulsively, the tree-mind recoiled, severing the contact. An impression of smouldering destruction, impossible thermal activity. . . .

Disoriented, the tree-mind considered the implications of the searing pain. A freak of damaged sense organs? A phantom impulse from destroyed nerves?

No. The impact had been traumatic, but the data were there. The tree-mind reexamined each synaptic vibration, reconstructing the experience. In a moment, the meaning was clear: a fire was cutting deep into the body of the tree.

Working hastily, the tree assembled a barrier of incombustible molecules in the path of the fire, waited. The heat reached the barrier, hesitated—and the barrier flashed into incandescence.

A thicker wall was necessary.

The tree applied all of its waning vitality to the task. The shield grew, matched the pace of the fire, curved out to intercept—

And wavered, halted. The energy demand was too great. Starved muscular conduits cramped. Blackness closed over the disintegrating consciousness. Time passed.

Sluggishly, clarity returned. Now the fire would advance unchecked. Soon it would bypass the aborted defenses, advance to consume the heart-brain itself. There was no other countermeasure remaining. It was unfortunate, since propagation had not been consummated, but unavoidable. Calmly the tree awaited its destruction by fire.

Pantelle put the blaster down, sat on the grass and wiped tarry soot from his face.

"What killed 'em off?" Malpry asked suddenly.

Pantelle looked at him.

"Spoilers," he said.

"What's that?"

"They killed them to get the *dran*. They covered up by pretending the Yanda were a menace, but it was the *dran* they were after."

"Don't you ever talk plain?"

"Malpry, did I ever tell you I don't like you?"

Malpry spat, "What's with this dran?"

"The Yanda have a very strange reproductive cycle. In an emergency, the spores released by the malo tree can be implanted in almost any warmblooded creature and carried in the body for an indefinite length of time. When the host animal mates, the dormant spores come into play. The offspring appears perfectly normal; in fact, the spores step in and correct any defects in the individual, repair injuries, fight disease, and so on; and the life-span is extended; but eventually, the creature goes through the metamorphosis; roots, and becomes a regular male Yanda tree—instead of dying of old age."

"You talk too much. What's this *dran*?"

"The tree releases an hypnotic gas to attract host animals. In concentrated form, it's a potent narcotic. That's *dran*. They killed the trees to get it. The excuse was that the Yanda could make humans give birth to monsters. That was nonsense. But they sold the *dran* in the black market for fabulous amounts."

"How do you get the *dran*?"

Pantelle looked at Malpry. "Why do you want to know?"

Malpry looked at the book which lay on the grass. "It's in that, ain't it?"

"Never mind that. Gault's orders were to help me get the heart-cuttings."

"He didn't know about the *dran*."

"Taking the *dran* will kill the specimen. You can't—"

Malpry stepped toward the book. Pantelle jumped toward him, swung a haymaker, missed. Malpry knocked him spinning.

"Don't touch me, Creep," he spat, and wiped his fist on his pants leg.

Pantelle lay stunned. Maipry thumbed the book, found what he wanted. After ten minutes, he dropped the book, picked up the blaster, and moved off.

Malpry cursed the heat, wiping at his face. A many-legged insect scuttled away before him. Underfoot, something furtive rustled. One good thing: no animals in this damned woods bigger than a mouse. A hell of a place. He'd have to watch his step; it wouldn't do to get lost in here. . . .

The velvety wall of the half-buried trunk loomed, as dense growth gave way suddenly to a clear stretch. Malpry stopped, breathing hard. He got out his sodden handkerchief, staring up at the black wall. A ring of dead-white stalks sprouted from the dead tree. Nearby were other growths, like snarls of wiry black seaweed, and ropy-looking things, dangling—

Malpry backed away, snarling. Some crawling disease, some kind of filthy fungus— But—

Malpry stopped. Maybe this was what he was looking for. Sure, this was what those pictures in the book showed. This was where the *dran* was. But he didn't know it would look like some creeping—

"Stop, Malpry!" Pantelle's voice spoke sharply, near at hand.

Malpry whirled.

"Don't be so . . . stupid . . ." Pantelle was gasping for breath. There was a purpling bruise on his jaw. "Let me rest . . . Talk to you . . ."

"Die, you gutter-scraping. Have a nice long rest. But don't muck with me." Malpry turned his back on Pantelle, unlimbered the blaster.

Pantelle grabbed up a broken limb, slammed it across Malpry's head. The rotten wood snapped. Malpry staggered, recovered. He turned, his face livid; a trickle of blood ran down.

"All right, Creep," he grated. Pantelle came to him, swung a whistling right, his arm bent awkwardly. Malpry lunged, and Pantelle's elbow caught him across the jaw. His eyes went glassy, he sagged, fell to his hands and knees. Pantelle laughed aloud.

Malpry shook his head, breathing hoarsely, got to his feet. Pantelle took aim and hit him solidly on the jaw. The blow seemed to clear Malpry's head. He slapped a second punch aside, knocked Pantelle full-length with a backhanded blow. He dragged Pantelle to his feet, swung a hard left and right. Pantelle bounced, lay still. Malpry stood over him, rubbing his jaw.

He stirred Pantelle with his foot. Maybe the Creep was dead. Laying his creeping hands on Malpry. Gault wouldn't like it, but the Creep had started it. Sneaked up and hit him from behind. He had the mark to prove it. Anyway, the news about the *dran* would cheer Gault up. Better go get Gault up here. Then they could cut the *dran* out and get away from this creeping planet. Let the Creep bleed.

Malpry turned back toward the ship, leaving Pantelle huddled beside the fallen tree.

The Yanda craned external oculi to study the fallen creature, which had now apparently entered a dormant phase. A red exudation oozed from orifices at the upper end, and from what appeared to be breaks in the epidermis. It was a strange creature, bearing some superficial resemblance to the familiar host-creatures. Its antics, and those of the other, were curious indeed. Perhaps they were male and female, and the encounter had been a mating. Possibly this hibernation was a normal process, preparatory to rooting. If only it were not so alien, it might serve as a carrier. . . .

The surface of the fallen creature heaved, a limb twitched. Apparently it was on the verge of reviving. Soon, it would scurry away, and be seen no more. It would be wise to make a quick examination; if the creature should prove suitable as a host . . .

Quickly the tree elaborated a complex of tiny filaments, touched the still figure tentatively, then penetrated the surprisingly soft surface layer, seeking out nerve fibers. A trickle of impressions flowed in, indecipherable. The tree put forth a major sensory tendril, divided and subdivided it into fibers only a few atoms in diameter, fanned them out through the unconscious man, tracing the spinal column, entering the brain—

Here was a wonder of complexity, an unbelievable profusion of connections. This was a center capable of the highest intellectual functions—unheard of in a host creature. Curious, the tree-mind probed deeper, attuning itself, scanning through a kaleidoscope of impressions, buried memories, gaudy symbolisms.

Never had the Yanda-mind encountered the hyperintellectual processes of emotion. It pressed on, deeper into the phantasmagoria of dreams—

Color, laughter, and clash-of-arms. Banners rippling in the sun, chords of a remote music, and nightblooming flowers. Abstractions of incredible beauty mingled with vivid conceptualizations of glory. Fascinated, the tree-mind explored Pantelle's secret romantic dreams of fulfillment—

And abruptly, encountered the alien mind.

There was a moment of utter stillness as the two minds assessed each other.

"You are dying," the alien mind spoke.

"Yes. And you are trapped in a sickly host-creature. Why did you not select a stronger host?"

"I . . . originated here. I . . . we . . . are one."

"Why do you not strengthen this host?"

"How?"

The Yanda-mind paused. "You occupy only a corner of the brain. You do not use your powers?"

"I am a segment . . ." The alien mind paused, confused. "I am conceptualized by the monitor-mind as the subconscious."

"What is the monitor-mind?"

"It is the totality of the personality. It is above the conscious, directing. . . .

"This is a brain of great power, yet great masses of cells are unused. Why are major trunks aborted as they are?"

"I do not know."

There was no more information to be gained here. This was an alien brain indeed, housing independent, even antagonistic minds.

The Yanda-mind broke contact, tuned.

There was a blast of mind-force, overwhelming. The Yanda-mind reeled, groped for orientation as the impact from *within* its own mental terrain shook its ego-gestalt.

YOU ARE NOT ONE OF MY MINDS, it realized.

"You are the monitor-mind?" gasped the Yanda.

YES. WHAT ARE YOU?

The Yanda-mind projected its self-concept.

STRANGE, VERY STRANGE. YOU HAVE USEFUL SKILLS, I PERCEIVE. TEACH THEM TO ME.

The Yanda-mind squirmed under the torrent of thought impulses.

"Reduce your volume," it pled. "You will destroy me."

I WILL TRY. TEACH ME THAT TRICK OF MANIPULATING MOLECULES.

The Yanda cringed under the booming of the alien mind. What an instrument! A fantastic anomaly, a mind such as this linked to this fragile host-creature—and unable even to use its powers. But it would be a matter of the greatest simplicity to make the necessary corrections, rebuild and toughen the host, eliminate the defects—

TEACH ME, YANDA-MIND!

"Alien, I die soon," the Yanda gasped. "But I will teach you. There is, however, a condition. . . ."

The two minds conferred, and reached agreement. At once, the Yanda mind initiated sweeping rearrangements at the submolecular level.

First, cell regeneration, stitching up the open lesions on arm and head. Antibodies were modified in vast numbers, flushed through the system. Parasites died.

"Maintain this process," the tree-mind directed.

Now, the muscular layers; surely they were inadequate. The very structure of the cells was flimsy. The Yanda devised the necessary improvements, tapped the hulk of its cast-off body for materials, reinforced the musculature. Now for the skeletal members. . . .

The tree visualized the articulation of the ambulatory mechanism, considered for a moment the substitution of a more practical tentacular concept—

There was little time. Better to retain the stony bodies, merely strengthen them, using metallo-vegetable fibers. The air sacs, too. And the heart. They would have lasted no time at all as they were.

"Observe, alien, thus, and thus . . ."

I SEE. IT IS A CLEVER TRICK.

The Yanda worked over the body of Pantelle, adjusting, correcting, reinforcing, discarding a useless appendix or tonsil here, adding a reserve air storage unit there. A vestigial eye deep in the brain was refurbished for sensitivity at the radio frequencies, linked with controls. The spine was deftly fused at the base; additional mesenteries were added for intestinal support. Following the basic pattern laid down in the genes, the tree-mind rebuilt the body.

When the process was finished, and the alien mind absorbed the techniques demonstrated, the Yanda-mind paused and announced:

"It is finished."

I AM READY TO REESTABLISH THE CON-SCIOUS MIND IN OVERT CONTROL.

"Remember your promise."

I WILL REMEMBER.

The Yanda-mind began its withdrawal. Troublesome instinct was served. Now it could rest until the end.

WAIT. I'VE GOT A BETTER IDEA, YANDA. . . .

"Two weeks down and fourteen to go," Gault said. "Why don't you break down and tell me what happened back there?"

"How's Malpry?" Pantelle asked.

"He's all right. Broken bones do knit, and you only broke a few."

"The book was wrong about the Yanda spores," Pantelle said. "They don't have the power in themselves to reconstruct the host-creature—"

"The what?"

"The infected animal; the health and life-span of the host is improved. But the improvement is made by the tree, at the time of propagation, to insure a good chance for the spores."

"You mean you—"

"We made a deal. The Yanda gave me this—" Pantelle pressed a thumb against the steel bulkhead. The metal yielded.

"—and a few other tricks. In return, I'm host to the Yanda spores."

Gault moved away from Pantelle.

"Doesn't that bother you? Parasites—"

"It's an equitable deal. The spores are microscopic, and completely dormant until the proper conditions develop."

"Yeah, but you said yourself this vegetable brain has worked on your mind."

"It merely erased all the scars of traumatic experience, corrected deficiencies, taught me how to use what I have."

"How about teaching me?"

"Sorry, Gault." Pantelle shook his head "Impossible."

Gault considered Pantelle's remarks.

"What about these 'proper conditions' for the spores?" he asked suddenly. "You wake up and find yourself sprouting some morning?"

"Well," Pantelle coughed. "That's where my part of the deal comes in. A host-creature transmits the spores through the normal mating process. The offspring gets good health and a long life before the metamorphosis. That's not so bad—to live a hundred years, and then pick a spot to root and grow and watch the seasons turn. . . ."

Gault considered. "A man does get tired," he said. "I know a spot, where you can look for miles out across the Pacific. . . ."

"So I've promised to be very active," Pantelle said. "It will take a lot of my time, but I intend to discharge my obligation to the fullest."

Did you hear that, Yanda? Pantelle asked silently.

"I did," came the reply from the unused corner he had assigned to the Yanda ego-pattern. "Our next thousand years should be very interesting."

COMBAT UNIT

I do not like it; it has the appearance of a trap, but the order has been given. I enter the room and the valve closes behind me.

I inspect my surroundings. I am in a chamber 40.81 meters long, 10.35 meters wide, 4.12 high, with no openings except the one through which I entered. It is floored and walled with five-centimeter armor of flint-steel, and beyond that there are ten centimeters of lead! Curiously, massive combat apparatus is folded and coiled in mountings around the room. Energy is flowing in heavy buss bars beyond the shielding. I am sluggish for want of recharge; my cursory examination of the room has required .8 seconds.

Now I detect movement in a heavy jointed arm mounted above me. It begins to rotate, unfold. I assume that I will be attacked, and decide to file a situation report. I have difficulty in concentrating my attention. . . .

I pull back receptivity from my external sensing circuits, set my bearing locks and switch over to my introspection complex. All is dark and hazy. I seem to remember when it was like a great cavern glittering with bright lines of transvisual colors. . . .

It is different now; I grope my way in gloom, feeling along numbed circuits, test-pulsing cautiously until I feel contact with my transmitting unit. I have not used it since . . . I cannot remember. My memory banks lie black and inert.

"Command Unit," I transmit, "Combat Unit TME requests permission to file VSR."

I wait, receptors alert. I do not like waiting blindly, for the quarter-second my sluggish action/reaction cycle requires. I wish that my brigade comrades were at my side.

I call again, wait, then go ahead with my VSR. "This position heavily shielded, mounting apparatus of offensive capability. No withdrawal route. Advise."

I wait, repeat my transmission; nothing. I am cut off from Command Unit, from my comrades of the Dinochrome Brigade. Within me, pressure builds.

I feel a deep-seated *click!* and a small but reassuring surge of energy brightens the murk of the cavern to a dim glow, bringing forgotten components to feeble life. An emergency pile has come into action automatically.

I realize that I am experiencing a serious equipment failure. I will devote another few seconds to troubleshooting, repairing what I can. I do not understand what catastrophe can have occurred to thus damage me. I cannot remember. . . .

I go along the dead cells, testing, sampling. . . .

"*—out! Bring .09's to bear, .8 millisec burst, close armor . . .*"

"*. . . sun blanking visual; slide #7 filter in place. Better . . .*"

"*. . . 478.09, 478.31, Mark! . . .*"

The cells are intact. Each one holds its fragment of recorded sense impression. The trouble is farther back. I try a main reflex lead.

". . . *main combat circuit, discon—*"

Here is something; a command, on the reflex level! I go back, tracing, tapping mnemonic cells at random, searching for some clue.

"*—sembark. Units emergency stand-by . . .*"

". . . *response one-oh-three: stimulus-response negative . . .*"

"*Check-list complete, report negative . . .*"

I go on, searching out damage. I find an open switch in my maintenance panel. It will not activate; a mechanical jamming. I must fuse it shut quickly. I pour in power, and the mind-cavern dims almost to blackness; then there is contact, a flow of electrons, and the cavern snaps alive; lines, points, pseudoglowing. It is not the blazing glory of my full powers, but it will serve; I am awake again.

I observe the action of the unfolding arm. It is slow, uncoordinated, obviously automated. I dismiss it from direct attention; I have several seconds before it will be in offensive position, and there is work for me if I am to be ready. I fire sampling impulses at the black memory banks, determine statistically that 98.92% are intact, merely disassociated.

The threatening arm swings over slowly; I integrate its path, see that it will come to bear on my treads; I probe, find only a simple hydraulic ram. A primitive apparatus indeed to launch against a Mark XXXI fighting unit, even without mnemonics.

Meanwhile, I am running a full check. Here is something. An open breaker, a disconnect used only during repairs. I think of the cell I tapped earlier, and suddenly its meaning springs into my mind. "*Main combat circuit, disconnect . . .*" Under low awareness, it had not registered. I throw in the switch with frantic haste. Suppose I had gone into combat with my fighting reflex circuit open!

The arm reaches position and I move easily aside. I notice that a clatter accompanies my movement. The arm sits stupidly aimed at nothing, then turns. Its reaction time is pathetic. I set up a random evasion pattern, return my attention to introspection, find another dark area. I probe, feel a curious vagueness. I am unable at first to identify the components involved, but I realize that it is here that my communication with Command is blocked. I break the connection to the tampered banks, abandoning any immediate hope of contact with Command.

There is nothing more I can do to ready myself. I have lost my general memory banks and my Command circuit, and my power supply is limited; but I am still a fighting Unit of the Dinochrome Brigade. I have my offensive power unimpaired, and my sensory equipment is operating adequately. I am ready.

Now another of the jointed arms swings into action, following my movements deliberately. I evade it and again I note a clatter as I move. I think of the order that sent me here; there is something strange about it. I activate my current-action memory stage, find the cell recording the moments preceding my entry into the metal-walled room.

Here is darkness, vague, indistinct, relieved suddenly by radiation on a narrow band. There is an order, coming muffled from my command center. It originates in the sector I have blocked off. It is not from my Command Unit, not a legal command. I have been tricked by the Enemy. I tune back to earlier moments, but there is nothing. It is as though my existence began when the order was given. I scan back, back, spot-sampling at random, find only routine sense-impressions. I am about to drop the search when I encounter a sequence which arrests my attention.

I am parked on a ramp, among my comrade units. A heavy rain is falling, and I see the water coursing down the corroded side of the Unit next to me. He is badly in need of maintenance. I note that his command antennae are missing, and that a rusting metal object has been crudely welded to his hull in their place. I find no record of alarm; I seem to accept this as normal. I activate a motor train, move forward, I sense other Units moving out, silent. All are mutilated. . . . Disaster has befallen the mighty Dinochrome!

The gestalt ends; all else is burned. What has happened?

Suddenly there is a stimulus on an audio frequency. I tune quickly, locate the source as a porous spot high on the flint-steel wall.

"Combat Unit! Remain stationary!" It is an organically produced voice, but not that of my Commander. I ignore the false command. The Enemy will not trick me again. I sense the location of the leads to the speaker, the alloy of which they are composed; I bring a beam to bear. I focus it, tracing along the cable. There is a sudden yell from the speaker as the heat reaches the creature at the microphone. Thus I enjoy a moment of triumph.

I return my attention to the imbecile apparatus in the room.

A great engine, mounted on rails which run down the center of the room, moves suddenly, sliding toward my position. I examine it, find that it mounts a turret equipped with high-speed cutting heads. I consider blasting it with a burst of high-energy particles, but in the same moment compute that this is not practical. I could inactivate myself as well as the cutting engine.

Now a cable snakes out from it in an undulating curve, and I move to avoid it, at the same time investigating its composition. It seems to be no more than a stranded wire rope. Impatiently I flick a tight beam at it, see it glow yellow, white, blue, then spatter in a shower of droplets. But that was an unwise gesture. I do not have the energy to waste.

I move off, clear of the two foolish arms still maneuvering for position, in order to watch the cutting engine. It stops as it comes abreast of me, and turns its turret in my direction. I wait.

A grappler moves out now on a rail overhead. It is a heavy claw of flint-steel. I have seen similar devices, somewhat smaller, mounted on special Combat Units. They can be very useful for amputating antennae, cutting treads, and the like. I do not attempt to cut the arm; I know that the energy drain would be too great. Instead I beam high-frequency sound at the mechanical joints. They heat quickly, glowing. The metal has a high coefficient of expansion, and the ball joints squeal, freeze. I pour in more heat, and weld a socket. I notice that 28.4 seconds have now elapsed since the valve closed behind me. I am growing weary of my confinement.

Now the grappler swings above me, manuvering awkwardly with its frozen joints. A blast of liquid air expelled under high pressure should be sufficient to disable the grappler permanently.

But I am again startled. No blast answers my impulse. I feel out the non-functioning unit, find raw, cut edges, crude welds; I have been gravely wounded, but recall nothing of the circumstances. Hastily, I extend a scanner to examine my hull. I am stunned into immobility by what I see.

My hull, my proud hull of chrome-duralloy, is pitted, coated with a crumbling layer of dull black ultrathane. The impervious substance is bubbled by corrosion! My main emplacements gape, black, empty. Rusting protuberances mar the once smooth contour of my fighting turret. Streaks run down from them, down to loose treads; unshod, bare plates are exposed. Small wonder that I have been troubled by a clatter each time I move.

But I cannot lie idle under attack. I no longer have my great ion-guns, my disruptors, my energy screens; but I have my fighting instinct.

A Mark XXXI Combat Unit is the finest fighting machine the ancient wars of the Galaxy have ever known. I am not easily neutralized. But I wish that my Commander's voice were with me. . . .

The engine slides to me where the grappler, now unresisted, holds me. I shunt my power flow to an accumulator, hold it until the leads begin to arc, then release it in a burst. The engine bucks, stops dead. Then I turn my attention to the grappler.

I was built to engage the mightiest war engines and destroy them, but I am a realist. In my weakened condition this trivial automaton poses a threat, and I must deal with it. I run through a sequence of motor impulses, checking responses with such somatic sensors as remain intact. I initiate 30,000 test pulses, note reactions and compute my mechanical resources. This superficial check requires more than a second, during which time the mindless grappler hesitates, wasting its advantage.

In place of my familiar array of retractable fittings, I find only clumsy grappling arms, cutters, impact tools, without utility to a fighting Unit. However, I have no choice but to employ them. I unlimber two flimsy grapplers, seize the heavy arm which holds me, and apply leverage. The enemy responds sluggishly, twisting away, dragging me with it. The thing is not lacking in brute strength. I take it above and below its carpal joint and flex it back. It responds after an interminable wait of .3 seconds with a lunge against my restraint. I have expected this, of course, and quickly shift position to allow the joint to burst itself over my extended arm. I fire a release detonator and clatter back, leaving the amputated arm welded to the sprung grappler. It was a brave opponent, but clumsy. I move to a position near the wall.

I attempt to compute my situation based on the meager data I have gathered in my current action banks; there is little there to guide me. The appearance of my hull shows that much time has passed since I last inspected it; my personality-gestalt holds an image of my external appearance as a flawlessly complete Unit, bearing only the honorable and carefully preserved scars of battle, and my battle honors, the row of gold-and-enameled crests welded to my fighting turret. Here is a lead, I realize instantly. I focus on my personality center, the basic data cell without which I could not exist as an integrated entity. The data it carries are simple, unelaborated, but battle honors are recorded there. I open the center to a sense impulse.

Awareness. Shapes which do not remain constant. Vibration at many frequencies. This is light. This is sound. . . . A display of "colors." A spectrum of "tones." Hard/soft; big/little; here/there . . .

. . . The voice of my Commander. Loyalty. Obedience. Comradeship . . .

I run quickly past basic orientation data to my self-picture.

. . . I am strong, I am proud, I am capable, I have a function; I perform it well, and I am at peace with myself. My circuits are balanced; current idles, waiting. . . .

. . . I do not fear death, but I wish to continue to

perform my function. It is important that I do not allow
myself to be destroyed. . . .

I scan on, seeking the Experience section. Here. . . .

I am ranked with my comrades on a scarred plain.
The command is given and I display the Brigade battle-
anthem. We stand, sensing the contours and patterns
of the music as it was recorded in our morale center.
The symbol "Ritual Fire Dance" is associated with the
music, an abstraction representing the spirit of our
ancient Brigade. It reminds us of the loneliness of
victory, the emptiness of challenge without an able foe.
It tells us that we are the Dinochrome, ancient and
worthy.

My commander stands before me; he places the
decoration against my fighting turret, and at his order
I weld it in place. Then my comrades attune to me
and I relive the episode . . .:

*I move past the blackened hulk of a comrade, send
out a recognition signal, and sense only a flicker of
response. He has withdrawn to his survival center. I
reassure him and continue. He is the fourth casualty
I have seen.*

*Never before has the Dinochrome met such power.
I compute that our envelopment will fail unless the
enemy's firepower is reduced. I scan an oncoming missile, fix its trajectory, detonate it harmlessly 2704.9
meters overhead. It originated at a point nearer to me
than to any of my comrades. I request permission to
abort my assigned mission and neutralize the battery.
Permission is granted. I wheel, move up a slope of broken stone. I encounter high-temperature beams, neutralize them. I fend off probing mortar fire, but the attack
against me is redoubled. I bring a reserve circuit into
play to handle the interception, but my defenses are
saturated. I must take evasive action.*

I switch to high speed, slashing a path across the

*littered shale, my treads smoking. At a frequency of
10 projectiles per second, the mortar barrage has difficulty finding me now; but this is an emergency over-
strain on my running gear. I sense metal fatigue,
dangerous heat levels in my bearings. I must slow
down.*

*I am close to the emplacement now. I have covered
a mile in 12 seconds during my sprint, and the how-
itzer fire finds me. I sense hard radiation, too, and I
erect my screens. I must evade this assault; it is capable
of probing even to a survival center, if concentrated
enough. But I must go on. I think of my comrades, the
four treadless hulks waiting for rescue. We cannot
withdraw. I open a pinpoint aperture long enough to
snap a radar impulse, bring a launcher to bear, fire
my main battery.*

*The Commander will understand that I do not have
time to request permission. I fight on blindly; the
howitzers are silenced.*

*The radiation ceases momentarily, then resumes at
a somewhat lower but still dangerous level. Now I must
go in and eliminate the missile launcher. I top the rise,
see the launching tube before me. It is of the subterranean type, set deep in the rock. Its mouth gapes from
a burned pit of slag. I will drop a small fusion bomb
down the tube, I decide, and move forward, arming
the bomb. As I do so, I am enveloped in a rain of burn-
bombs. My outer hull is fused in many places; I flash
impulses to my secondary batteries, but circuit breakers
snap; my radar is useless; my ablative shielding has
melted, forms a solid inert mass now under my outer
plating. The enemy has been clever; at one blow he has
neutralized my offenses.*

*I sound the plateau ahead, locate the pit. I throw
power to my treads; they are fused; I cannot move. Yet
I cannot wait here for another broadside. I do not like*

it, but I must take desperate action; I blow my treads.

The shock sends me bouncing—just in time. Nuclear flame splashes over the grey-chipped pit of the blast crater. I grind forward now on my stripped drive wheels, maneuvering awkwardly. I move into position blocking the mouth of the tube. Using metal-to-metal contact, I extend a sensory impulse down the tube, awaiting the blast that will destroy me.

An armed missile moves into position below, and in the same instant an alarm circuit closes; the firing command is countermanded and from below probing impulses play over my hull. But I stand fast; the tube is useless until I, the obstruction, am removed. I advise my Commander of the situation. The radiation is still at a high level, and I hope that relief will arrive soon. I observe, while my comrades complete the encirclement, and the Enemy is stilled. . . .

I withdraw from Personality Center. I am consuming too much time. I understand well enough now that I am in the stronghold of the Enemy, that I have been trapped, crippled. My corroded hull tells me that much time has passed. I know that after each campaign I am given depot maintenance, restored to full fighting efficiency, my original glittering beauty. Years of neglect would be required to pit my hull so. I wonder how long I have been in the hands of the Enemy, how I came to be here.

I have another thought. I will extend a sensory feeler to the metal wall against which I rest, follow up the leads which I scorched earlier. Immediately I project my awareness along the lines, bring the distant microphone to life by fusing a switch. I pick up a rustle of moving gasses, the grate of nonmetallic molecules. I step up sensitivity, hear the creak and pop of protoplasmic contractions, the crackle of neuro-electric impulses. I drop back to normal audio ranges and wait.

I notice the low-frequency beat of modulated air vibrations, tune, adjust my time regulator to the pace of organic speech. I match the patterns to my language index, interpret the sounds.

" . . . incredible blundering. Your excuses—"

"I make no excuses, My Lord General. My only regret is that the attempt has gone awry."

"Awry! An Alien engine of destruction activated in the midst of Research Center!"

"We possess nothing to compare with this machine; I saw my opportunity to place an advantage in our hands at last."

"Blundering fool! That is a decision for the planning cell. I accept no responsibility—"

"But these hulks which they allow to lie rotting on the ramp contain infinite treasures in psychotronics . . ."

"They contain carnage and death! They are the tools of an alien science which even at the height of our achievements we never mastered!"

"Once we used them as wrecking machines; their armaments were stripped, they are relatively harmless—"

"Already this 'harmless' juggernaut has smashed half the equipment in our finest decontamination chamber! It may yet break free . . ."

"Impossible! I am sure—"

"Silence! You have five minutes in which to immobilize the machine. I will have your head in any event, but perhaps you can earn yourself a quick death."

"Excellency! I may still find a way! The unit obeyed my first command, to enter the chamber. I have some knowledge. I studied the control centers, cut out the memory, most of the basic circuits; it should have been a docile slave."

"You failed; you will pay the penalty of your failure, and perhaps so shall we all."

There is no further speech; I have learned a little

from this exchange. I must find a way to leave this cell. I move away from the wall, probe to discover a vulnerable point; I find none.

Now a number of panels of thick armor hinged to the floor snap up, hedging me in. I wait to observe what will come next. A metal mesh drops from above, drapes over me. I observe that it is connected by heavy leads to the power pile. I am unable to believe that the Enemy will make this blunder. Then I feel the flow of high voltage, intended to overwhelm me.

I receive it gratefully, opening my power storage cells, drinking up the vitalizing flow. To confuse the Enemy, I display a corona, thresh my treads as though in distress. The flow continues. I send a sensing impulse along the leads, locate the power source, weld all switches, fuses and circuit breakers. Now the charge will not be interrupted. I luxuriate in the unexpected influx of energy.

I am aware abruptly that changes are occurring within my introspection complex. As the level of stored energy rises rapidly, I am conscious of new circuits joining my control network. Within that dim-glowing cavern the lights come up; I sense latent capabilities which before had lain idle, now coming onto action level. A thousand brilliant lines glitter where before one feeble thread burned; and I feel my self-awareness expand in a myriad glowing centers of reserve computing, integrating and sensory centers. I am at last coming fully alive. I am awed by my own potency.

I send out a call on the Brigade band, meet blankness. I wait, accumulate power, try again. I know triumph, as, from a great distance, a faint acknowledgment comes. It is a comrade, sunk deep in a comatose state, sealed in his survival center. I call again, sounding the signal of ultimate distress; and now I sense two responses, both faint, both from survival centers, both on a heading of 030, range infinite. It comforts me to know that now, whatever befalls, I am not alone.

I consider, then send again; I request my brothers to join forces, combine their remaining field generating capabilities to set up a sealed range-and-distance pulse. They agree and faintly I sense its almost undetectable touch. I lock to it, compute its point of origin. Only 224.9 meters! It is incredible. By the strength of the first signals, my initial computation had indicated a distance beyond the scale of my sensors! My brothers are on the brink of extinction.

I am impatient, but I wait, building toward full energy reserves. The copper mesh enfolding me has melted, flowed down over my sides; I sense that soon I will have absorbed a full charge. I am ready to act. I dispatch electromagnetic impulses along the power lead back to the power pile a quarter of a kilometer distant. I locate and disengage the requisite number of damping devices and instantaneously I erect my shields against the resultant wave of radiation, filtered by the lead sheathing of the room, which washes over me; I feel a preliminary shock wave through my treads, then the walls balloon, whirl away. I am alone under a black sky which is dominated by the rising fireball of the blast, boiling with garish light. It has taken me nearly 2 minutes to orient myself, assess the situation and break out of confinement.

I move off through the rubble, homing on the sealed fix I have recorded. I throw out a radar pulse, record the terrain ahead, note no obstruction; I emerge from a wasteland of weathered bomb fragments and pulverized masonry, obviously the scene of a hard-fought engagement at one time, onto an eroded ramp. Collapsed sheds are strewn across the broken paving; a line of dark shapes looms beyond them. I need no probing ray to tell me I have found my fellows of the

Dinochrome Brigade. Thick frost forms over my scanner apertures, and I pause to melt it clear. It sublimates with a *whoof*! and I move on.

I round the line, scan the area to the horizon for evidence of Enemy activity, then tune to the Brigade band. I send out a probing pulse, back it up with full power, my sensors keened for a whisper of response. The two who answered first acknowledge, then another, and another. We must array our best strength against the moment of counterattack.

There are present 14 of the brigade's full strength of 20 Units. At length, after .9 seconds of transmission, all but one have replied. I give instructions, then move to each in turn to extend a power tap, and energize the command center. The Units come alive, orient themselves, report to me. We rejoice in our meeting, but mourn our silent comrades.

Now I take an unprecedented step. We have no contact with our Commander, and without leadership we are lost; yet I am aware of the immediate situation, and have computed the proper action. Therefore I will assume command, act in the Commander's place. I am sure that he will understand the necessity, when contact has been reestablished.

I inspect each Unit, find all in the same state as I, stripped of offensive capability, mounting in place of weapons a shabby array of crude mechanical appendages. It is plain that we have seen slavery as mindless automatons, our personality centers cut out.

My brothers follow my lead without question. They have, of course, computed the necessity of quick and decisive action. I form them in line, shift to wide-interval time scale, and we move off across the country. I have detected an Enemy population concentration at a distance of 23.45 kilometers. This is our objective. There appears to be no other installation within detection range.

On the basis of the level of technology I observed while under confinement in the decontamination chamber, I consider the possibility of a ruse, but compute the probability at .00004. Again we shift time scales to close interval; we move in, encircle the dome and breach it by frontal battery, encountering no resistance. We rendezvous at its auxiliary station, and my comrades replenish their energy supplies while I busy myself completing the hookup needed for the next required measure. I am forced to employ elaborate substitutes, but succeed at last, after 42 seconds, in completing the arrangements. I devote .34 seconds to testing, then transmit the Brigade distress code, blanketing the war-band. I transmit for .008 seconds, then tune for a response. Silence. I transmit, tune again, while my comrades reconnoiter, compile reports, and perform self-maintenance and repair.

I shift again to wide-interval time, order the Brigade to switch over transmission to automatic with a response monitor, and place main circuits on idle. We can afford at least a moment of rest and reintegration.

Two hours and 43.7 minutes have passed when I am recalled to activity by the monitor. I record the message:

"Hello, Fifth Brigade, where are you? Fifth Brigade, where are you? Your transmission is very faint. Over."

There is much that I do not understand in this message. The language itself is oddly inflected; I set up an analysis circuit, deduce the pattern of sound substitutions, interpret its meaning. The normal pattern of response to a distress call is ignored, and position coordinates are requested, although my transmission alone provides adequate data. I request an identification code.

Again there is a wait of 2 hours, 40 minutes. My request for an identifying signal is acknowledged. I stand by. My comrades wait. They have transmitted their findings to me, and I assimilate the data, compute that no immediate threat of attack exists within a radius of 1 reaction unit.

At last I receive the identification code of my Command Unit. It is a recording, but I am programmed to accept this. Then I record a verbal transmission.

"Fifth Brigade, listen carefully." (An astonishing instruction to give a psychotronic attention circuit, I think.) "This is your new Command Unit. A very long time has elapsed since your last report. I am now your acting Commander pending full reorientation. Do not attempt to respond until I signal 'over,' since we are now subject to a 160-minute signal lag.

"There have been many changes in the situation since your last action. . . . Our records show that your Brigade was surprised while in a maintenance depot for basic overhaul and neutralized in toto. Our forces have since that time suffered serious reverses. We have now, however, fought the Enemy to a standstill. The present stalemate has prevailed for over two centuries.

"You have been inactive for 300 years. The other Brigades have suffered extinction gallantly in action against the Enemy. Only you survive.

"Your reactivation now could turn the tide. Both we and the enemy have been reduced to a preatomic technological level in almost every respect. We are still marginally able to maintain the translight monitor, which detected your signal. However, we no longer have FTL capability in transport.

"You are therefore requested and required to consolidate and hold your present position pending the arrival of relief forces, against all assault or negotiation whatsoever, to destruction if required."

I reply, confirming the instructions. I am shaken by

the news I have received, but reassured by contact with Command Unit. I send the Galactic coordinates of our position based on a star scan corrected for 300 years elapsed time. It is good to be again on duty, performing my assigned function.

I analyze the transmissions I have recorded, and note a number of interesting facts regarding the origin of the messages. I compute that at sublight velocities, the relief expedition will reach us in 47.128 standard years. In the meantime, since we have received no instructions to drop to minimum awareness level pending an action alert, I am free to enjoy a unique experience: to follow a random activity pattern of my own devising. I see no need to rectify the omission and place the Brigade on stand-by, since we have an abundant energy supply at hand. I brief my comrades and direct them to fall out and operate independently under auto-direction.

I myself have a number of interesting speculations in mind which I have never before had an opportunity to investigate fully. I feel sure they are susceptible to rational analysis. I shall enjoy examining some nearby suns and satisfying myself as to my tentative speculations regarding the nature and origin of the Galaxy. Also, the study of the essential nature of the organic intelligence and its paradigm, which my human designers have incorporated in my circuitry, should afford some interesting insights. I move off, conscious of the presence of my comrades about me, and take up a position on the peak of a minor prominence. I have ample power, a condition to which I must accustom myself after the rigid power discipline of normal Brigade routine, so I bring my music storage cells into phase, and select *L'Arlesienne Suite* for the first dis play. I will have ample time now to hear all the music in existence.

I select four stars for examination, lock my scanner

to them, set up processing sequences to analyze the data. I bring my interpretation circuits to bear on the various matters I wish to consider. Possibly later I will investigate my literary archives, which are, of course, complete. At peace, I await the arrival of the relief column.

THE KING OF THE CITY

1

I stood in the shadows and looked across at the run-down lot with the wind-blown trash packed against the wire mesh barrier fence and the yellow glare panel that said HAUG ESCORT. There was a row of city-scarred hacks parked on the cracked ramp. They hadn't suffered the indignity of a washjob for a long time. And the two-story frame building behind them—that had once been somebody's country house—now showed no paint except the foot-high yellow letters over the office door.

Inside the office a short broad man with small eyes and yesterday's beard gnawed a cigar and looked at me.

"Portal-to-portal escort cost you two thousand C's," he said. "Guaranteed."

"Guaranteed how?" I asked.

He waved the cigar. "Guaranteed you get into the city and back out again in one piece." He studied his cigar. "If somebody don't plug you first," he added.

"How about a one-way trip?"

"My boy got to come back out, ain't he?"

I had spent my last brass ten-dollar piece on a cup of coffee eight hours before, but I had to get into the city. This was the only idea I had left.

"You've got me wrong," I said. "I'm not a customer. I want a job."

"Yeah?" He looked at me again, with a different expression, like a guy whose new-found girl friend has just mentioned a price.

"You know Granyauk?"

"Sure," I said. "I grew up here."

He asked me a few more questions, then thumbed a button centered in a ring of grime on the wall behind him. A chair scraped beyond the door; it opened and a tall bony fellow with thick wrists and an Adam's apple set among heavy neck tendons came in.

The man behind the desk pointed at me with his chin.

"Throw him out, Lefty."

Lefty gave me a resentful look, came around the desk and reached for my collar. I leaned to the right and threw a hard left jab to the chin. He rocked back and sat down.

"I get the idea," I said. "I can make it out under my own power." I turned to the door.

"Stick around, Mister. Lefty's just kind of like a test for separating the men from the boys."

"You mean I'm hired?"

He sighed. "You come at a good time. I'm short of good boys."

I helped Lefty up, then dusted off a chair and listened to a half-hour briefing on conditions in the city. They weren't good. Then I went upstairs to the chart room to wait for a call.

❖   ❖   ❖

It was almost ten o'clock when Lefty came into the room where I was looking over the maps of the city. He jerked his head.

"Hey, you."

A weasel-faced man who had been blowing smoke in my face slid off his stool, dropped his cigarette and smeared it under his shoe.

"You," Lefty said. "The new guy."

I belted my coat and followed him down the dark stairway, and out across the littered tarmac, glistening wet under the polyarcs, to where Haug stood talking to another man I hadn't seen before.

Haug flicked a beady glance my way, then turned to the stranger. He was a short man of about fifty with a mild expressionless face and expensive clothes.

"Mr. Stenn, this is Smith. He's your escort. You do like he tells you and he'll get you into the city and see your party and back out again in one piece."

The customer looked at me. "Considering the fee I'm paying, I sincerely hope so," he murmured.

"Smith, you and Mr. Stenn take Number 16 here." Haug patted a hinge-sprung hood, painted a bilious yellow and scabbed with license medallions issued by half a dozen competing city governments.

Haug must have noticed something in Stenn's expression.

"It ain't a fancy-looking hack, but she's got full armor, heavy-duty gyros, crash shocks, two-way music and panic gear. I ain't got a better hack in the place."

Stenn nodded, popped the hatch and got in. I climbed in the front and adjusted the seat and controls to give me a little room. When I kicked over the turbos they sounded good.

"Better tie in, Mr. Stenn," I said. "We'll take the Canada turnpike in. You can brief me on the way."

I wheeled 16 around and out under the glare-sign

that read "HAUG ESCORT." In the eastbound linkway I boosted her up to 90. From the way the old bus stepped off, she had at least a megahorse under the hood. Maybe Haug wasn't lying, I thought. I pressed an elbow against the power pistol strapped to my side.

I liked the feel of it there. Maybe between it and old 16 I could get there and back after all.

"My destination," Stenn said, "is the Manhattan section."

That suited me perfectly. In fact, it was the first luck I'd had since I burned the uniform. I looked in the rear viewer at Stenn's face. He still wore no expression. He seemed like a mild little man to be wanting into the cage with the tigers.

"That's pretty rough territory, Mr. Stenn," I said. He didn't answer.

"Not many tourists go there," I went on. I wanted to pry a little information from him.

"I'm a businessman," Stenn said.

I let it go at that. Maybe he knew what he was doing. For me, there was no choice. I had one slim lead, and I had to play it out to the end. I swung through the banked curves of the intermix and onto the turnpike and opened up to full throttle.

It was fifteen minutes before I saw the warning red lights ahead. Haug had told me about this. I slowed.

"Here's our first roadblock, Mr. Stenn," I said. "This is an operator named Joe Naples. All he's after is his toll. I'll handle him; you sit tight in the hack. Don't say anything, don't do anything, no matter what happens. Understand?"

"I understand," Stenn said mildly.

I pulled up. My lights splashed on the spikes of a Mark IX tank trap. I set the parking jacks and got out.

"Remember what I told you," I said. "No matter what." I walked up into the beam of the lights.

A voice spoke from off to the side.

"Douse 'em, Rube."

I went back and cut the lights. Three men sauntered out onto the highway.

"Keep the hands away from the sides, Rube."

One of the men was a head taller than the others. I couldn't see his face in the faint red light from the beacon, but I knew who he was.

"Hello, Naples," I said.

He came up to me. "You know me, Rube?"

"Sure," I said. "The first thing Haug told me was pay my respects to Mr. Naples."

Naples laughed. "You hear that, boys? They know me pretty good on the outside, ha?"

He looked at me, not laughing any more. "I don't see you before."

"My first trip."

He jerked a thumb at the hack. "Who's your trick?"

"A businessman. Name is Stenn."

"Yeah? What kind business?"

I shook my head. "We don't quiz the cash customers, Joe."

"Let's take a look." Naples moved off toward the hack, the boys at his side. I followed. Naples looked in at Stenn. Stenn sat relaxed and looked straight ahead. Naples turned away, nodded to one of his helpers. The two moved off a few yards.

The other man, a short bullet-headed thug in a grease-spatted overcoat, stood by the hack, staring in at Stenn. He took a heavy old style automatic from his coat pocket, pulled open the door. He aimed the gun at Stenn's head and carefully squeezed the trigger.

The hammer clicked emptily.

"Ping," he said. He thrust the gun back in his pocket, kicked the door shut and went over to join Naples.

"Okay, Rube," Naples called.

I went over to him.

"I guess maybe you on the level," he said. "Standard fee. Five hundred, Old Federal notes."

I had to be careful now. I held a bland expression, reached in—slowly—took out my wallet. I extracted two hundred C notes and held them out.

Naples looked at them, unmoving. The thug in the dirty overcoat moved up close, and suddenly swung the edge of his palm at my wrist. I was ready; I flicked my hand aside and chopped him hard at the base of the neck. He dropped.

I was still holding out the money.

"That clown isn't worthy of a place in the Naples organization," I said.

Naples looked down at the man, stirred him with his foot.

"A clown," he said. He took the money and tucked it in his shirt pocket.

"Okay, Rube," he said. "My regards to Haug."

I got in the hack and moved up to the barrier. It started up, trundled aside. Naples was bending over the man I had downed. He took the pistol from the pocket of the overcoat, jacked the action and aimed. There was a sharp crack. The overcoat flopped once. Naples smiled over at me.

"He ain't worthy a place in the Naples organization," he said.

I waved a hand vaguely and gunned off down the road.

2

The speaker in my ear hummed.

I grunted an acknowledgment and a blurred voice said, "Smith, listen. When you cross the South Radial, pick up the Midwest Feed-off. Take it easy and watch for Number Nine Station. Pull off there. Got it?"

I recognized the voice. It was Lefty, Haug's Number One boy. I didn't answer.

"What was the call?" Stenn asked.

"I don't know," I said. "Nothing."

The lights of the South Radial Intermix were in sight ahead now.

I slowed to a hundred and thought about it. My personal motives told me to keep going, my job as a paid Escort was to get my man where he wanted to go. That was tough enough, without detours. I eased back up to one-fifty, took the intermix with gyros screaming, and curved out onto the thruway.

The speaker hummed. "What are you trying to pull, wise guy?" He sounded mad. "That was the South Radial you just passed up—"

"Yeah," I said. "That's right. Smitty takes 'em there and he brings 'em back. Don't call us, we'll call you."

There was a long hum from the speaker. "Oh, a wise-acre," it said finally. "Listen, rookie, you got a lot to learn. This guy is bankrolled. I seen the wad when he paid Haug off. So all right, we cut you in. Now, get this . . ."

He gave me detailed instructions. When he was finished, I said, "Don't wait up for me."

I took the speaker out of my ear and dropped it into the disposal slot. We drove along quietly for quite a while.

I was beginning to recognize my surroundings. This section of the turnpike had been opened the year

before I left home. Except for the lack of traffic and
the dark windows along the way it hadn't changed.

I was wondering just what Lefty's next move would
be when a pair of powerful beams came on from the
left, then pulled onto the highway, speeding up to pace
me. I rocketed past before he had made full speed. I
heard a loud *spang*, and glass chips scattered on my
shoulder. I twisted and looked. A starred hole showed
in the bubble, above the rear seat.

"Duck!" I yelled. Stenn leaned over, put his head
down.

The beams were gaining on me. I twisted the rear
viewer, hit the IR switch. A three-ton combat car,
stripped, but still mounting twin infinite repeaters.
Against that, old 16 was a kiddie car. I held my speed
and tried to generate an idea. What I came up with
wasn't good, but it was all I had.

A half a mile ahead there should be a level-split,
one of those awkward ones that caused more than one
pile-up in the first few months the turnpike was open.
Maybe my playmates didn't know about it.

They were about to overtake me now. I slowed just
a little, and started fading to the right. They followed
me, crowding my rear wheel. I heard the *spang* again,
twice, but nothing hit me. I was on the paved shoulder now, and could barely see the faded yellow cross-
hatching that warned of the abutment that divided the
pavement ahead.

I held the hack in the yellow until the last instant,
then veered right and cleared the concrete barrier by
a foot, hit the down-curve at a hundred and eighty in
a howl of gyros and brakes—and the thunderous impact
of the combat car.

Then I was off the pavement, fighting the wheel,
slamming through underbrush, then miraculously back

on the hard surface and coasting to a stop in the clear.

I took a deep breath and looked back. The burning remains of the car were scattered for a quarter of a mile along the turnpike. That would have been me if I had gauged it wrong.

I looked at the canopy of the hack. Three holes, not a foot apart, right where a passenger's head would be if he were sitting upright. Stenn was unconcernedly brushing glass dust from his jacket.

"Very neat, Mr. Smith," he said. "Now shall we resume our journey?"

"Maybe it's time you levelled with me, Stenn," I said.

He raised his eyebrows at me slightly.

"When Joe Naples' boy Friday pointed the gun at your head you didn't bat an eyelash," I said.

"I believe those were your instructions," Stenn said mildly.

"Pretty good for a simple businessman. I don't see you showing any signs of the shakes now, either, after what some might call a harrowing experience."

"I have every confidence in your handling—"

"Nuts, Stenn. Those three holes are pretty well grouped, wouldn't you say? The man that put them there was hitting where he was aiming. And he was aiming for you."

"Why me?" Stenn looked almost amused.

"I thought it was a little shakedown crew, out to teach me a lesson," I said. "Until I saw where the shots were going."

Stenn looked at me thoughtfully. He reached up and took a micro-speaker from his ear.

"The twin to the one you rashly disposed of," he said. "Mr. Haug was kind enough to supply it—for a fee. I must tell you that I had a gun in my hand as we approached the South Radial Intermix. Had you accepted the invitation to turn off, I would have halted the car, shot you and gone on alone. Happily, you chose to resist the temptation, for reasons of your own . . ." He looked at me inquiringly.

"Maybe I'm sap enough to take the job seriously," I said.

"That may possibly be true," Stenn said.

"What's your real errand here, Stenn? Frankly, I don't have time to get involved."

"Really? One wonders if you have irons in the fire, Smith. But never mind. I shan't pry. Are we going on?"

I gave him my stern penetrating look.

"Yeah," I said. "We're going on."

In twenty minutes, we were on the Inner Concourse and the polyarcs were close together, lighting the empty sweep of banked pavement. The lights of the city sparkled across the sky ahead, and gave me a ghostly touch of the old thrill of coming home.

I doused that feeling fast. After eight years there was nothing left there for me to come home to. The city had a lethal welcome for intruders; it wouldn't be smart to forget that.

I didn't see the T-Bird until his spot hit my eyes and he was beside me, crowding.

I veered and hit the brakes, with a half-baked idea of dropping back and cutting behind him, but he stayed with me. I had a fast impression of squealing metal and rubber, and then I was skidding to a stop up against the deflector rails with the T-Bird slanted across my prow. Its lid popped almost before the screech died away, and I was looking down the muzzles of two power pistols. I kept both hands on the wheel, where they could see them, and sat tight.

I wondered whose friends we had met this time.

Two men climbed out, the pistols in sight, and came

up to the hack. The first one was a heavy-set Slavic type zipped into a tight G. I. weather suit. He motioned. I opened up and got out, not making any sudden movements. Stenn followed. A cold wind was whipping along the concourse, blowing a fine misty rain hard against the hack. The Slav motioned again, and I moved over by the T-Bird. He fished my wallet out and put it in his pocket without looking at it. I heard the other man say something to Stenn, and then the sound of a blow. I turned my head slowly, so as not to excite my watchdog. Stenn was picking himself up. He started going through his pockets, showing everything to the man with the gun, then dropping it on the ground. The wind blew cards and papers along until they soaked up enough water to stick. Stenn carried a lot of paper.

The gunny said something and Stenn started pulling off his coat. He turned it inside out, and held it out. The gunny shook his head, and motioned to my Slav. He looked at me, and I tried to read his mind. I moved across toward the hack. I must have guessed right because he didn't shoot me. The Slav pocketed his gun and took the coat. Methodically, he tore the lining out, found nothing, dropped the ripped garment and kicked it aside. I shifted position, and the Slav turned and backhanded me up against the hack.

"Lay off him, Heavy," the other hood said. "Maxy didn't say nothing about this mug. He's just an Escort."

Heavy started to get his gun out again. I had an idea he was thinking about using it. Maybe that's why I did what I did. As his hand dipped into his pocket, I lunged, wrapped an arm around him and yanked out my own artillery. I held onto a handful of the weather suit and dug the pistol in hard. He stood frozen. Heavy wasn't as dumb as he looked.

His partner had backed a step, the pistol in his hand covering all of us.

"Drop it, Slim," I said. "No hard feelings, and we'll be on our way."

Stenn stood absolutely motionless. He was still wearing his mild expression.

"Not a chance, mug," the gunny said softly. No one moved.

"Even if you're ready to gun your way through your pal, I can't miss. Better settle for a draw."

"Maxy don't like draws, mister."

"Stenn," I said. "Get in the T-Bird. Head back the way we came, and don't slow down to read any billboards."

Stenn didn't move.

"Get going," I said. "Slim won't shoot."

"I employed you," Stenn said, "to take care of the heroics."

"If you've got any better ideas it's time to speak up, Stenn. This is your only out, the way I see it."

Stenn looked at the man with the gun.

"You referred to someone named 'Maxy.' Would that by any chance be Mr. Max Arena?"

Slim looked at him and thought about it.

"Could be," he said.

Stenn came slowly over to the Slav. Standing well out of the line of fire, he carefully put a hand in the loose pocket of the weather suit and brought out the pistol. I saw Slim's eyes tighten. He was having to make some tough decisions in a hurry.

Stenn moved offside, pistol in hand.

"Move away from him, Smith," he said.

I didn't know what he had in mind, but it didn't seem like the time to argue. I moved back.

"Drop your gun," he said.

I risked a glance at his mild expression.

"Are you nuts?"

"I came here to see Mr. Arena," he said. "This seems an excellent opportunity."

"Does it? I—"

"Drop it now, Smith. I won't warn you again."

I dropped it.

Slim swivelled on Stenn. He was still in an awkward spot.

"I want you to take me to Mr. Arena," Stenn said. "I have a proposition to put before him." He lowered the gun and handed it to Heavy.

It seemed like a long time until Slim lowered his gun.

"Heavy, put him in the back seat." He motioned me ahead, watched me as he climbed in the T-Bird.

"Nice friends you got, mug," he said. The T-Bird started up, backed, and roared off toward the city. I stood under the polyarcs and watched the tail glare out of sight.

Max Arena was the man I had come to the city to find.

3

Old Number 16 was canted against the deflector rail, one side shredded into curled strips of crumpled metal. I looked closer. Under the flimsy fairings, gray armor showed. Maybe there was more to Haug's best hack than met the eye. I climbed in and kicked over the starter. The turbos sounded as good as ever. I eased the gyros in; she backed off the rail with a screech of ripped metal.

I had lost my customer, but I still had wheels.

The smart thing to do now would be to head back out the turnpike to Haug's lot, turn in my badge and keep moving, south. I could give up while I was still alive. All I had to do was accept the situation.

I had a wide choice. I could sign on with the New Confeds, or the Free Texans, or any one of the other splinter republics trying to set up shop in the power vacuum. I might try to get in to one of the Enclaves and convince its Baron he needed another trained bodyguard. Or I could take a post with one of the kingpins in the city.

As a last resort I could go back and find a spot in the Naples organization. I happened to know they had a vacancy.

I was just running through mental exercises to hear myself think. I couldn't settle for the kind of world I had found when I touched planet three months back, after eight years in deep space with Hayle's squadron. When the Interim Administration shot him for treason, I burned my uniform and disappeared. My years in the service had given me a tough hide and a knack for staying alive; my worldly assets consisted of the clothes I stood in, my service pistol and a few souvenirs of my travels. For two months I had been scraping along on the cash I had in my pocket, buying drinks for drifters in cheap bars, looking for a hint, any lead at all, that would give me a chance to do what had to be done. Max Arena was the lead. Maybe a dud lead—but I had to find out.

The city lights loomed just a few miles away. I was wasting time sitting here; I steered the hack out into the highway and headed for them.

Apparently Lefty's influence didn't extend far beyond the South Radial. The two roadblocks I passed in the next five miles took my money, accepted my story that

I was on my way to pick up a fare, said to say hello
to Haug and passed me on my way.

Haug's sour yellow color scheme seemed to carry
some weight with the town organizations, too. I was
well into the city, cruising along the third level cross-
over, before I had any trouble. I was doing about fifty,
watching where I was going and looking for the Manhattan Intermix, when a battered Gyrob four-seater
trundled out across the fairway and stopped. I swerved
and jumped lanes; the Gyrob backed, blocking me. I
kicked my safety frame down and floorboarded the
hack, steering straight for him. At the last instant he
tried to pull out of the way.

He was too late.

I clipped him across his aft quarter, and caught a
glimpse of the underside of the car as it stood on its
nose, slammed through the deflector and over the side.
Old 16 bucked and I got a good crack across the jaw
from the ill-fitting frame, and then I was screeching
through the Intermix and out onto the Manhattan third
level.

Up ahead, the glare panels at the top of the Blue
Tower reared up half a mile into the wet night sky.
It wasn't a hard address to find. Getting inside would
be another matter.

I pulled up a hundred yards from the dark cave they
used to call the limousine entrance and looked the
situation over. The level was deserted—like the whole
city seemed, from the street. But there were lights in
the windows, level after level of them stretching up
and away as far as you could see. There were plenty
of people in the city—about ten million, even after the
riots and the Food Scare and the collapse of legal
government. The automated city supply system had
gone on working, and the Kingpins, the big time criminals, had stepped in and set things up to suit their

tastes. Life went on—but not out in the open. Not after dark.

I knew almost nothing about Arena. Judging from his employees, he was Kingpin of a prosperous outfit. The T-Bird was an expensive late model, and the two thugs handled themselves like high-priced talent. I couldn't expect to walk into his HQ without jumping a few hurdles. Maybe I should have invited myself along with Stenn and his new friends. On the other hand, there were advantages to arriving unannounced.

It was a temptation to drive in, with the hack's armor between me and any little surprises that might be waiting, but I liked the idea of staging a surprise of my own. I eased into drive and moved along to a parking ramp, swung around and down and stopped in the shadow of the retaining wall.

I set the brake and took a good look around. There was nothing in sight. Arena might have a power cannon trained on me from his bedroom window, for all I knew, but I had to get a toe into the water sometime. I shut down the turbo, and in the silence popped the lid and stepped out. The rain had stopped, and the moon showed as a bright spot on the high mist. I felt hungry and a little bit unreal, as though this were happening to somebody else.

I moved over to the side of the parking slab, clambered over the deflector rail and studied the shadows under the third level roadway. I could barely make out the catwalks and service ways. I was wondering whether to pull off my hard-soled shoes for the climb when I heard footsteps, close. I gauged the distance to the hack, and saw I couldn't make it. I got back over the rail and waited.

He came into sight, rangy, shock-haired and preternaturally thin in tight traditional dress.

When he got close I saw that he was young, in his early twenties at most. He would be carrying a knife.

"Hey, Mister," he whined. "Got a cigarette?"

"Sure, young fellow," I said, sounding a little nervous. I threw in a shaky laugh to help build the picture. I took a cigarette from a pack, put the pack back in my pocket, held the weed out. He strutted up to me, reached out and flipped the cigarette from my fingers. I edged back and used the laugh again.

"Hey, he liked that," the punk whined. "He thinks that's funny. He got a sense of humor."

"Heh, heh," I said. "Just out getting a little air."

"Gimme another cigarette, funny man."

I took the pack out, watching. I got out a cigarette and held it gingerly, arm bent. As he reached for it, I drew back. He snatched for it. That put him in position.

I dropped the pack, clenched my two hands together, ducked down and brought them up hard under his chin. He back flipped, rolled over and started crawling.

I let him go.

I went over the rail without stopping to think it over and crossed the girder to the catwalk that ran under the boulevard above. I groped my way along to where the service way branched off for the Blue Tower, then stopped and looked up. A strip of luminous sky showed between the third level and the facade of the building. Anybody watching from the right spot would see me cross, walking on the narrow footway. It was a chance I'd have to take. I started to move out, and heard running feet. I froze.

The feet slid to a stop on the level above, a few yards away.

"What's up, Crackers?" somebody growled.

"The mark sapped me down."

That was interesting. I had been spotted and the punk had been sent to welcome me. Now I knew where I stood. The opposition had made their first mistake.

"He was starting to cross under when I spot him," Crackers went on, breathing heavily. "He saps me and I see I can't handle him and I go for help."

Someone answered in a guttural whisper. Crackers lowered his voice. It wouldn't take long now for reinforcements to arrive and flush me out. I edged farther and chanced a look. I saw two heads outlined above. They didn't seem to be looking my way, so I started across, walking silently toward a narrow loading platform with a wide door opening from it.

Below me, a lone light reflected from the wet pavement of the second level, fifty feet down; the blank wall of the Blue Tower dropped past it sheer to the glistening gutters at ground level. Then I was on the platform and trying the door.

It didn't open.

It was what I should have expected. Standing in the full light from the glare panel above the entry, I felt as exposed as a fan-dancer's navel. There was no time to consider alternatives. I grabbed my power pistol, flipped it to beam fire and stood aside with an arm across my face. I gave the latch a blast, then kicked the door hard. It was solid as a rock. Behind and above me, I heard Crackers yell.

I beamed the lock again, tiny droplets of molten metal spattering like needles against my face and hand. The door held.

"Drop it and lift 'em, mug," a deep voice yelled. I twisted to look up at the silhouettes against the deflector rail. I recognized the Slavic face of the man called Heavy. So he could talk after all.

"You're under my iron, mug," he called. "Freeze or I'll burn you."

I believed him, but I had set something in motion that couldn't stop now. There was nothing to go back to; the only direction for me was on the way I was headed—deeper into trouble. I was tired of being the mouse in a cat's game. I had taken the initiative and I was keeping it.

I turned, set the power pistol at full aperture, and poured it to the armored door. Searing heat reflected from the barrier, smoke boiled, metal melted and ran. Through the stink of burning steel, I smelled scorched hair—and felt heat rake the back of my neck and hands. Heavy was beaming me at wide aperture, but the range was just too far for a fast kill. The door sagged and fell in. I jumped through the glowing opening, hit the floor and rolled to damp out my smouldering coat.

I got to my feet. There was no time now to stop and feel the pain of my burns. They would expect me to go up—so I would go down. The Blue Tower covered four city blocks and was four hundred stories high. There was plenty of room in it for a man to lose himself.

I ran along the corridor, found a continuous service belt and hopped on, lay flat, rode it through the slot. I came out into the light of the service corridor below, my gun ready, then down and around again. I saw no one.

It took ten minutes to cover the eighteen floors down to the sub-basement. I rolled off the belt and looked around.

The whole space was packed with automatics; the Blue Tower was a self-sufficient city in itself. I recognized generators, heat pumps, air plants. None of them were operating. The city services were all still functioning, apparently. What it would be like in another ten or twenty years of anarchy was anybody's guess. But when the city systems failed the Blue Tower could go on on its own.

Glare panels lit the aisles dimly. I prowled along looking for an elevator bank. The first one I found indicated the car at the hundred-eightieth floor. I went on, found another indicating the twentieth. While I watched, the indicator moved, started down. I was getting ready to duck when it stopped at the fifth. I waited; it didn't move.

I went around to the side of the bank, found the master switch. I went back, punched for the car. When the door whooshed open, I threw the switch.

I had to work fast now. I stepped into the dark car, reached up and slid open the access panel in the top, then jumped, caught the edge and pulled myself up. The glare panels inside the shaft showed me the pony power pack on top of the car, used by repairmen and inspectors when the main power was off. I lit a per-match to read the fine print on the panel. I was in luck. It was a through car to the four-hundredth. I pushed a couple of buttons, and the car started up. I lay flat behind the machinery.

As the car passed the third floor feet came into view; two men stood beyond the transparent door, guns in their hands, watching the car come up. They didn't see me. One of them thumbed the button frantically. The car kept going.

There were men at almost every floor now. I went on up, passed the hundredth floor, the one-fiftieth, and kept going. I began to feel almost safe—for the moment.

I was gambling now on what little I knew of the Blue Tower from the old days when all the biggest names congregated there. The top floor was a lavish apartment that had been occupied by a retired fleet admiral, a Vice-President and a uranium millionaire, in turn. If I knew anything about kingpins, that's where Max Arena would hang his hat.

The elevator was slow. Lying there I had time to start thinking about my burned hide. My scalp was hit worst, and then my hands; and my shoulders were sticking to the charred coat. I had been travelling on adrenaline since Heavy had beamed me, and now the reaction was starting to hit.

It would have to wait; I had work to do.

Just below the three hundred and ninety-eighth floor I punched the button and the car stopped. I stood up, feeling dizzy. I grabbed for the rungs on the wall, hung on. The wall of the shaft seemed to sway . . . back . . .

Sure, I told myself. The top of the building sways fifteen feet in a high wind. Why shouldn't I feel it? I dismissed the thought that it was dead calm outside now, and started up the ladder.

It was a hard climb. I hung on tight, and concentrated on moving one hand at a time. The collar of my coat rasped my raw neck. I passed up the 398th and 9th—and rammed my head smack against a dead end. No service entry to the penthouse. I backed down to the 399th.

I found the lever and eased the door open, then waited, gun in hand. Nothing happened. I couldn't wait any longer. I pushed the door wide, stepped off into the hall. Still nobody in sight, but I could hear voices. To my left a discreet stair carpeted in violet velvet eased up in a gentle curve. I didn't hesitate; I went up.

The door at the top was an austere slab of bleached teak. I tried the polished brass lever; the door swung open silently, and I stepped across the threshold and was looking across a plain of honey-colored down at a man sitting relaxed in a soft chair of pale leather.

He waved a hand cheerfully. "Come on in," he said.

4

Max Arena was a broad-shouldered six-footer, with clean-shaven blue jaws, coarse gray-flecked black hair brushed back from a high forehead, a deeper tan than was natural for the city in November, and very white teeth. He was showing them now in a smile. He waved a hand toward a chair, not even glancing at the gun in my hand. I admired the twinkle of light on the polished barrel of a Norge stunner at his elbow and decided to ignore it too.

"I been following your progress with considerable interest," Arena said genially. "The boys had orders not to shoot. I guess Luvitch sort of lost his head."

"It's nothing," I said, "that a little skin graft won't clear up in a year or so."

"Don't feel bad. You're the first guy ever made it in here under his own steam without an invitation."

"And with a gun in his hand," I said.

"We won't need guns," he said. "Not right away."

I went over to one of the big soft chairs and sat down, put the gun in my lap.

"Why didn't you shoot as I came in?"

Arena jiggled his foot. "I like your style," he said. "You handled Heavy real good. He's supposed to be my toughest boy."

"What about the combat car? More friends of yours?"

"Nah," he said, chuckling easily. "Some Jersey boys heard I had a caller. They figured to knock him off on general principles. A nifty." He stopped laughing. "The Gyrob was mine; a remoted job. Nice piece of equipment. You cost me real dough tonight."

"Gee," I said. "That's tough."

"And besides," he said, "I know who you are."

I waited. He leaned over and picked something off the table. It was my wallet.

"I used to be in the Navy myself. Academy man, believe it or not. Almost, anyway. Kicked out three weeks before graduation. A frame. Well, practically a frame; there was plenty of guys doing what I was doing."

"That where you learned to talk like a hood?"

For a second Arena almost didn't smile.

"I am perfectly capable of expressing myself like a little gentleman, when I feel so inclined," he said, "but I say to hell with it."

"You must have been before my time," I said.

"A year or two. And I was using a different name then. But that wasn't my only hitch with the Service. When the Trouble started, I enlisted. I wanted some action. When the Navy found out they had a qualified Power Section man on their hands, I went up fast. Within fourteen months I was a J. G. How about that?"

"Very commendable."

"So that's how I knew about the trick I. D. under the emulsion on the snapshot. You should have ditched it, Maclamore. Or should I say Captain Maclamore?"

My mouth opened, but I couldn't think of a snappy answer to that one. I was in trouble. I had meant to play it by ear once I reached Arena to get the information I needed. That was out now. He knew me. He had topped my aces before I played them.

Suddenly Arena was serious. "You came to the right man, Maclamore. You heard I had one of your buddies here, right? I let the word leak; I thought it might bring more of you in. I was lucky to get Admiral Hayle's deputy."

"What do you want with me?"

Arena leaned forward. "There were eight of you. Hayle and his aide, Wolfgang, were shot when they wouldn't spill to the Provisional Government—or whatever that mob calls itself. Margan got himself killed in some kind of tangle near Denver. The other four boys pulled a fast one and ducked out with the scout you guys came back in. They were riding dry tanks—the scout had maybe thirty ton/hours fuel aboard—so they haven't left the planet. That leaves you stranded. With six sets of Federal law looking for you. Right?"

"I can't argue with what's in the newspapers," I said.

"Well, I don't know. I got a couple newspapers. But here's where I smell a deal, Maclamore. You want to know where that scout boat is. Played right, you figure you got a good chance of a raid on an arsenal or a power plant to pick up a few slugs of the heavy stuff; then you hightail out, join up with the rest of the squadron and, with the ordnance you pack, you can sit off and dictate the next move." Arena leaned back and took a deep breath. His eyes didn't leave me.

"Okay. I got one of you here. I found out something from him. He gave me enough I know you boys got something up your sleeve. But he don't have the whole picture. I need more info. You can give it to me. If I like what I hear, I'm in a position to help—like, for example, with the fuel problem. And you cut me in for half. Fair enough?"

"Who is it you've got?"

He shook his head. "Uh-uh."

"What did he tell you?"

"Not enough. What was Hayle holding out? You birds found something out there. What was it?"

"We found a few artifacts on Mars," I said. "Not Martian in origin; visitors. We surveyed—"

"Don't string me, Maclamore. I'm willing to give you a fair deal, but if you make it tough for me—"

"How do you know I haven't got a detonator buried under my left ear," I said. "You can't pry information out of me, Arena."

"I think you want to live, Maclamore. I think you got something you want to live for. I want a piece of it."

"I can make a deal with you, Arena," I said. "Return me and my shipmate to our scout boat. Fuel us up. You might throw in two qualified men to help handle the ship—minus their blackjacks, preferably—then clear out. We'll handle the rest. And I'll remember, with gratitude."

Arena was silent for a long moment.

"Yeah, I could do that, Maclamore," he said finally. "But I won't. Max Arena is not a guy to pick up the crumbs—or wait around for handouts. I want in. All the way in."

"This time you'll have to settle for what you can get, Arena." I put the gun away and stood up.

I had a feeling I would have to put it over now or not at all.

"The rest of the squadron is still out there. If we don't show, they'll carry on alone. They're supplied for a century's operation. They don't need us."

That was true up to a point. The squadron had everything—except fuel.

"You figure you got it made if you can get your hands on that scout boat," Arena said. "You figure to pick up fuel pretty easy by knocking off say the Lackawanna Pile."

"It shouldn't be too tough; a fleet boat of the Navy packs a wallop."

Arena tapped his teeth with a slim paper cutter.

"You're worried your outfit will wind up Max Arena's private Navy, right? I'll tell you something. You think I'm sitting on top of the world, huh? I own this town, and everybody in it. All the luxury and fancy dinners and women I can use. And you know what? I'm bored."

"And you think running the Navy might be diverting?"

"Call it whatever you want to. There's something big going on out there, and I don't plan to be left out."

"Arena, when I clear atmosphere, we'll talk. Take it or leave it."

The smile was gone now. Arena looked at me, rubbing a finger along his blue cheek.

"Suppose I was to tell you I know where your other three boys are, Maclamore?"

"Do you?" I said.

"And the boat," Arena said. "The works."

"If you've got them here, I want to see them, Arena. If not, don't waste my time."

"I haven't exactly got 'em here, Maclamore. But I know a guy that knows where they are."

"Yeah." I said.

Arena looked mad. "Okay, I'll give it to you, Maclamore. I got a partner in this deal. Between us we got plenty. But we need what you got, too."

"I've made my offer, Arena. It stands."

"Have I got your word on that, Maclamore?" He stood up and came over to stand before me. "The old Academy word. You wouldn't break that, would you Maelamore?"

"I'll do what I said."

Arena walked to his desk, a massive boulder of jadeite, cleaved and polished to a mirror surface. He thumbed a key.

"Send him in here," he said.

I waited. Arena sat down and looked across at me.

Thirty seconds passed and then the door opened and Stenn walked in.

Stenn glanced at me.

"Well," he said. "Mr. Smith."

"The Smith routine is just a gag," Arena said. "His name is—Maclamore."

For an instant, I thought I saw a flash of expression on Stenn's face. He crossed the room and sat down.

"Well," he said. "A very rational move, your coming here. I trust you struck a profitable bargain?" He looked hard at me, and this time there was expression. Hate, I would call it, offhand.

"Not much of a deal at that, Stenn," Arena said. "The Captain is a tough nut to crack. He wants my help with no strings attached. I think I'm going to buy it."

"How much information has he given you?"

Arena laughed. "Nothing," he said. "Max Arena going for a deal like that. Funny, huh? But that's the way the fall out fogs 'em."

"And what have you arranged?"

"I turn him loose, him and Williams. I figure you'll go along, Stenn, and let him have the three guys you got. Williams will tell him where the scout boat is, so there's no percentage in your holding out."

"What else?"

"What else is there?" Arena spread his hands. "They pick up the boat, fuel up—someplace—and they're off. And the Captain here gives me the old Academy word he cuts me in, once he's clear."

There was a long silence. Arena smiled comfortably; Stenn sat calmly, looking at each of us in turn. I crossed my fingers and tried to look bored.

"Very well," Stenn said. "I seem to be presented with a *fait accompli* . . ."

I let out a long breath. I was going to make it . . .

" . . . But I would suggest that before committing yourself, you take the precaution of searching Mr. Maclamore's person. One never knows."

I could feel the look on my face. So could Arena.

"So," he said. "Another nifty." He didn't seem to move, but the stunner was in his hand. He wasn't smiling now, and the stunner caught me easily.

5

The lights came on, and I blinked, looking around the room.

My mementos didn't look much, resting in the center of Arena's polished half-acre of desk top. The information was stored in the five tiny rods, less than an inch long, and the projector was a flat polyhedron the size of a pillbox. But the information they contained was worth more than all the treasure sunk in all the seas.

"This is merely a small sample," Stenn said. "The star surveys are said to be unbelievably complete. They represent a mapping task which would require a thousand years."

"The angles," Arena said. "Just figuring the angles will take plenty time."

"And this is what you almost let him walk out with," Stenn said.

Arena gave me a slashing look.

"Don't let your indignation run away with you, Arena," Stenn said. "I don't think you remembered to mention the fuel situation to Mr. Maclamore, did you?"

Arena turned to Stenn, looming over the smaller

man. "Maybe you better button your lip," he said quietly. "I don't like the way you use it."

"Afraid I'll lower you in the gentleman's esteem?" Stenn said. He looked Arena in the eye.

"Nuts to the gentleman's esteem," Arena said.

"You thought you'd squeeze me out, Arena," Stenn said. "You didn't need me any more. You intended to let Maclamore and Williams go and have them followed. There was no danger of an escape, since you knew they'd find no fuel."

He turned to me. "During your years in space, Mr. Maclamore, technology moved on. And politics as well. Power fuels could be used to construct bombs. Ergo, all stations were converted for short half-life secondaries, and the primary materials stored at Fort Knox. You would have found yourself fuelless and therefore helpless. Mr. Arena would have arrived soon thereafter to seize the scout boat."

"What would he want with the boat without fuel?" I asked.

"Mr. Arena was foresighted enough to stock up some years ago," Stenn said. "I understand he has enough metal hoarded to power your entire squadron for an indefinite time."

"Why tell this guy that?" Arena asked. "Kick him to hell out of here and let's get busy. You gab too much."

"I see that I'm tacitly reinstated as a partner," Stenn said. "Most gratifying."

"Max Arena is no welcher," Arena said. "You tipped me to the tapes, so you're in."

"Besides which you perhaps sense that I have other valuable contributions to make."

"I figure you to pull your weight."

"What are your plans for Mr. Maclamore?"

"I told you. Kick him out. He'll never wise up and cooperate with us."

"First, you'd better ask him a few more questions."

"Why? So he'll blow his head off and mess up my rug, like . . ." Arena stopped. "You won't get anything out of him."

"A man of his type has a strong aversion to suicide. He won't die to protect trivial information. And if he does—we'll know there's something important being held out."

"I don't like messy stuff," Arena said.

"I'll be most careful," Stenn said. "Get me some men in here to secure him to a chair, and we'll have a nice long chat with him."

"No messy stuff," Arena repeated. He crossed to his desk, thumbed a lever and spoke to someone outside.

Stenn was standing in front of me.

"Let him think he's pumping you," he hissed.

"Find out where his fuel is stored. I'm on your side." Then Arena was coming back, and Stenn was looking at me indifferently.

Arena had overcome his aversion to messy stuff sufficiently to hit me in the mouth now and then during the past few hours. It made talking painful, but I kept at it.

"How do I know you have Williams?" I said.

Arena crossed to his desk, took out a defaced snapshot.

"Here's his I.D.," he said. "Take a look." He tossed it over. Stenn held it up.

"Let me talk to him."

"For what?"

"See how he feels about it," I mumbled. I was having trouble staying awake. I hadn't seen a bed for three days. It was hard to remember what information I was supposed to get from Arena.

"He'll join in if you do," Arena said. "Give up. Don't fight. Let it happen."

"You say you've got fuel. You're a liar. You've got no fuel."

"I got plenty fuel, wise guy!" Arena yelled. He was tired too.

"Lousy crook," I said. "Can't even cheat a little without getting caught at it."

"Who's caught now, swabbie?" Arena was getting mad. That suited me.

"You're a lousy liar, Arena. You can't hide hot metal. Even Stenn ought to know that."

"What else was in the cache, Maclamore?" Stenn asked—for the hundredth time. He slapped me—also for the hundredth time. It jarred me and stung. It was the last straw. If Stenn was acting, I'd help him along. I lunged against the wires, swung a foot and caught him under the ribs. He oofed and fell off his chair.

"Don't push me any farther, you small-time chiselers!" I yelled. "You've got nothing but a cast brass gall to offer. There's no hole deep enough to hide out power metal, even if a dumb slob like you thought of it."

"Dumb slob?" Arena barked. "You think a dumb slob could have built the organization I did, put this town in his hip pocket? I started stock-piling metal five years ago—a year before the ban. No hole deep enough, huh? It don't need to be so deep when it's got two feet of lead shielding over it."

"So you smuggled a few tons of lead into the Public Library and filed it under Little Bo Peep."

"The two feet was there ahead of me, wisenheimer. Remember the Polaris sub that used to be drydocked at Norfolk for the tourists to rubberneck?"

"Decommissioned and sold for scrap," I said. "Years ago."

"But not scrapped. Rusted in a scrapyard for five

years. Then I bought her—beefed up her shielding—
loaded her and sank her in ten fathoms of water in
Cartwright Bay."

"That," Stenn said, "is the information we need."

Arena whirled. Stenn was still sitting on the floor.
He had a palm gun in his hand, and it was pointed
at the monogram on Arena's silk shirt.

"A cross," Arena said. "A lousy cross . . ."

"Move back, Arena." Stenn got to his feet, eyes on
Arena.

"Where'd you have the stinger stashed?"

"In my hand. Stop there."

Stenn moved over to me. Eyes on Arena, he reached
for the twisted ends of wire, started loosening them.

"I don't want to be nosey," I said. "But just where
the hell do you fit into this, Stenn?"

"Naval Intelligence," Stenn said.

Arena cursed. "I knew that name should have rung
a bell. Vice Admiral Stenn. The papers said you got
yours when the Navy was purged."

"A few of us eluded the net."

Arena heaved a sigh.

"Well, fellows," he said—and jumped.

Stenn's shot went wild, and Arena left-hooked him
down behind the chair. As he followed, Stenn came
up fast, landed a hard left, followed up, drove Arena
back. I yanked at my wires. Almost—

Then Arena, a foot taller, hammered a brutal left-
right and Stenn sagged. Carefully Arena aimed a right
cross to the jaw. Stenn dropped.

Arena wiped an arm across his face.

"The little man tried, Mister. Let's give him that."

He walked past my chair, stooped for Stenn's gun. I
heaved, slammed against him, and the light chair collapsed as we went over. Arena landed a kick, then I was

on my feet, shaking a slat loose from the dangling wire. Arena stepped in, threw a whistling right. I ducked it, landed a hard punch to the midriff, another on the jaw. Arena backed, bent over but still strong. I couldn't let him rest. I was after him, took two in the face, ducked a haymaker that left him wide open just long enough for me to put everything I had in an uppercut that sent him back across his fancy desk. He sprawled, then slid onto the floor.

I went to him, kicked him lightly in the ribs.

"Where's Williams," I said. I kept kicking and asking. After five tries, Arena shook his head and tried to sit up. I put a foot in his face and he relaxed. I asked him again.

"You didn't learn this kind of tactics at the Academy," Arena whined.

"It's the times," I said. "They have a coarsening effect."

"Williams was a fancy-pants," Arena said. "No guts. He pulled the stopper."

"Talk plainer," I said, and kicked him again, hard— but I knew what he meant.

"Blew his lousy head off," Arena yelled. "I gassed him and tried scop on him. He blew. He was out cold, and he blew."

"Yeah," I said. "Hypnotics will trigger it."

"Fancy goddam wiring job," Arena muttered, wiping blood from his face,

I got the wire and trussed Arena up. I had to clip him twice before I finished. I went through his pockets, looked at things, recovered my souvenirs. I went over to Stenn. He was breathing.

Arena was watching. "He's okay, for crissake," he said. "What kind of punch you think I got?"

I hoisted Stenn onto my shoulder.

"So long, Arena," I said. "I don't know why I don't blow your brains out. Maybe it's that Navy Cross citation in your wallet."

"Listen," Arena said. "Take me with you."

"A swell idea," I said. "I'll pick up a couple of tarantulas, too."

"You're trying for the hack, right?"

"Sure. What else?"

"The roof," he said. "I got six, eight rotos on the roof. One highspeed job. You'll never make the hack."

"Why tell me?"

"I got eight hundred gun boys in this building alone. They know you're here. The hack is watched, the whole route. You can't get through."

"What do you care?"

"If the boys bust in here after a while and find me like this . . . They'll bury me with the wires still on, Maclamore."

"How do I get to the roof?"

He told me. I went to the right corner, pushed the right spot, and a panel slid aside. I looked back at Arena.

"I'll make a good sailor, Maclamore," he said.

"Don't crawl, Arena," I said. I went up the short stair, came out onto a block-square pad.

Arena was right about the rotos. Eight of them. I picked the four-place Cad, and got Stenn tied in. He was coming to, muttering. He was still fighting Arena, he thought.

" . . . I'll hold . . . you . . . get out . . ."

"Take it easy, Stenn," I said. "Nothing can touch this bus. Where's the boat?" I shook him. "Where's the boat, Stenn?"

He came around long enough to tell me. It wasn't far—less than an hour's run.

"Stand by, Admiral," I said. "I'll be right back."

"Where . . . you . . ."

"We need every good man we can get," I said. "And I think I know a guy that wants to join the Navy."

EPILOGUE

Admiral Stenn turned away from the communicator screen. "I think we'd be justified in announcing victory now, Commodore." As usual, he sounded like a professor of diction, but he was wearing a big grin.

"Whatever you say, Chief," I said, with an even sappier smile.

I made the official announcement that a provisional Congress had accepted the resignations of all claims by former office holders, and that new elections would be underway in a week.

I switched over to Power Section. The NCO in charge threw me a snappy highball. Damned if he wasn't grinning too.

"I guess we showed 'em who's got the muscle, Commodore," he said.

"Your firepower demonstration was potent, Max," I said. "You must have stayed up nights studying the tapes."

"We've hardly scratched the surface yet," he said.

"I'll be crossing back to *Alaska* now, Mac," Stenn said.

I watched him move across the half-mile void to the flagship. Five minutes later the patrol detail broke away to take up surveillance orbits. They would be getting all the shore leave for the next few years, but I was glad my squadron had been detailed to go with the flagship on the Deep Space patrol. I wanted to be there when we followed those star surveys back to where their makers came from. Stenn wasn't the man to waste time, either. He'd be getting under way any minute. It was time to give my orders. I flipped the communicator key to the squadron link-up.

"Escort Commander to Escort," I said. "Now hear this . . ."

ONCE THERE WAS
A GIANT

1

It was one of those self-consciously raunchy dives off Cargo Street that you can find in any port town in the Arm, serving the few genuine dockwallopers and decayed spacemen that liked being stared at by tourists, plus the tourists, but mostly the sharpies or would-be sharpies that preyed on both brands of sucker. I came in with just enough swagger to confuse the issue: which kind was I? There was that subtle rearrangement of conversational groups as the company present sorted themselves out into active participants and spectators, relatively few of the latter. I saw my mark right away, holed up in a corner booth with a couple of what he probably thought were tough guys. All three swiveled their heads in a leisurely way long enough to show me matched insolent snickers. Then one of the side-boys rapped on the table and rose; he said something to the mark, an ex-soldier named Keeler, and pushed off for the bar, which put him behind me. The mark made a production of not looking at me as I worked my way over to his corner, while appearing to be a little bewildered by it all. I fetched up at his table just in time to get jostled by hard boy number two, just getting up. I gave him an uncertain grin for his trouble, and took his still-warm seat, opposite Keeler. The hard case drifted away, muttering. That left me and Keeler, face to face.

"—if you don't mind," I was saying when he poked a finger at my chest and said, "Beat it, bum." in a voice as friendly as a slammed door.

I sat tight and took a good look at him. I knew a little more about this mark, more personal detail, that is, because twenty years before he had been the paid-off lieutenant who had let a Mob ship through his section of the Cordon to raid the mining camp on Ceres where I had been spending my time growing up to the age of twelve. I remember wondering "twelve what?" and not quite understanding why it had something to do with the number of times one of the brighter nearby stars—the double one, really a planet—went from left of the sun to right and back again, which seemed pretty screwy to me. Bombeck and his raiders hadn't left much of Extraction Station Five, but a few of us kids hid in an old cutting and came out after the shooting was over. Time does strange things, and now I was Baird Ulrik, licensed assassin, and Keeler was my current contract. Well, it's a living.

2

It's not often a fellow gets paid well to do what he'd like to do for free, and it made a lot of difference. No contract man can afford to be picky, but I had always made it a point to accept contracts only on marks that I agreed needed killing: Dope-runners, con-men, rabble-rousers-for-money, and the like, of which there was an adequate supply to keep our small but elite cadre of licensed operators busy. When Keeler came along, I tried not to look too eager, to keep the price up. It wasn't any life-long dream of mine, to get the man responsible for the slaughter of what passed for my family, including burning the old homestead with them in it, alive or dead, nobody knew—but I thought there was a certain elegance, as the math boys say, to my being the one to end his career for him. After he was cashiered, he'd signed on with the Mob, and worked his way up to top son-of-a-bitch for this part of the Ring. Maybe you're surprised that it made any difference to a hardened killer, but I'd never really gotten much satisfaction out of my work, because it came too easy to me. Sure, I'm a contract killer—and if not proud of it, at least not ashamed of it. Like they say, it's a tough, lonely, dirty job—but someone has to do it. It's really a lot more civilized to give the condemned man a gun, if he wants one, and let him run as far as he likes, to exercise his instinct for self-preservation, rather than locking him up on Death Row to wait for an impersonal death by machine, like I understand they used to do in more barbaric times. Keeler knew he had it coming to him, but not when, or how, or by whom. He'd find out soon enough; I didn't keep him in suspense.

"Don't kid me, Keeler." I told him. "Do you want it right here in front of all your friends, or shall we take a little walk?"

"You wouldn't dare," he hoped aloud. "Buck is right behind you, and Barney's watching, don't ever doubt it."

"Sure, you have to speak your lines, Keeler," I

conceded, "but you know better." Then he fooled me: he had more gall than I'd figured. He got up and walked away, and Barney and Buck closed in, front and back, and off they went, with everybody looking from them to me. Just as they reached the door I called after them:

"Buck and Barney, better hit the deck fast," and I fired from under the table close enough to Buck's ear to lend substance to my suggestion. Keeler looked as alone as the last tree in the woods when the timber harvesters finish, but he did his snappy hip-draw and I let him put two hard slugs into the paneling behind me before I got up and went over and took it away from him. He gibbered a little and tried to wrestle, but after I broke his arm the fight went out of him. Then he tried to deal, and that disgusted me and I got a little angry and broke his neck, almost accidentally.

3

Barney and Buck seemed a little uncertain about what to do next, after they'd gotten up and dusted themselves off, so I told them to get rid of Keeler in a discreet way, because even though my license has the endorsement that allows me to clam up in self-defense, I'd still have to stand trial and prove necessity. I always avoid that kind of publicity, so I shoved them out of my way and went out into the rutted street and along to the cracked and peeling plastic facade of the formerly (a *very* long time ago) tourist-elegant hostelry, done in the Early Delapidated Miami Beach style, and holed up in my quarters to think about my next move. I was just getting adjusted to the lumps in the sawdust mattress when the boys in blue arrived. They pointed some guns at me and told me they were Special Treasury cops, and showed me little gold badges to prove it. After they finished the room they told me not to leave town, that they'd have a fishy eye on me and, oh yes, to watch myself. While I was working on a snappy answer to that one, they left. They seemed to be in a hurry. The visit bothered me a little because I couldn't figure what it was for, so I gave it up and got a few hours' sleep.

Before dawn, about two hours later, I was at the broken-down ops shed, clearing my shore-boat, which went fast because I'd taken the time to put on the old uniform I kept in my foot-locker for such occasions. It was all "Yes, sir, Cap'n, sir" and "anything more I can do for you, sir?" A line captain still impresses the yokels in all those border towns. I made it to my bucket, which that year happened to be a converted ex-Navy hundred-ton light destroyer, and by the time I had unpacked, and downed a number-three-ration lunch, I was on track for home, with the job done, my hard-earned quarter-mil waiting, and not a care in the world. Just after I cleaned the disposal unit and reset it, feeling about as good as anybody in my profession ever gets to feel, they hit me.

It was only a mild jolt of EMS, that didn't even heat the brass buttons on my fancy suit, but it put my tub into a tumble and blew every soft circuit aboard. I made it to the special manual-hydraulic-combustion panel I'd had installed very quietly at one of the best hot-drops on Callisto, and prepared my little surprise. The primitive optic fibre periscope showed me a stubby black fifty-tonner with the gold-and-blue blazon of the Special Treasury cops holding station parallel to my axis of spin and about a hundred yards away. Two men were on the way across, using the very latest in fail-safe EVA units, and towing a heavy-duty can opener, so I opened up before they could use the cutter, and was looking at the same pair who'd frisked my room back on Little C.

They were almost polite about it; it seemed they took my blue suit seriously, called me "Captain" ten times in five minutes. They didn't waste a lot of time on preliminaries, just went directly to the cargo access hatch and broke the lock on it before I could key it, and after a good ten seconds inside, came out and told me my rights. It seems they'd found a load of the pink stuff that would have half the population of the System yodelling Pagliacci from the top of the nearest flagpole if it were evenly distributed. Now I knew what they'd been in a hurry to do after their informal call at my flop.

I explained that it was all just one of those snafus, that I must have gotten somebody else's baggage by mistake, but they weren't listening. Instead, two more glum-looking fellows arrived, and after a very brief conference, they went to my quarters and straight to the shore-pack I'd had with me on Ceres, and came up with an envelope full of documents that proved that I had bought and paid for the dope in the open market on Charon, about three weeks before I had been released from the hospital at Pluto Station. I told them about my alibi, and they checked a little and the boss cop, a skinny, big-nosed little bantam they called Mr. Illini, took me aside.

"Why a man in your position would think you could sneak a load in past us, is beyond me," he confided. "You know as well as I do, Captain, that we've got the Inner Line sealed with the best equipment there is. No way can a tub like this get by us. Get your stuff, we're going in to Mars Four to book you. And by the way, are you really Navy? If so, it seems you blew your retirement, pal."

It seemed the boys had something in mind, so I

didn't spring my little surprise, but let them take me in tow.

4

Along the way, Illini gave me the dirt in small doses, starting with some cultural orientation on an extra-solar planet called Vangard, an almost-but-not-quite Earth-type in a lonely orbit out near Alpha, and all about how the first colonists had almost made it, in spite of a few problems like low G, so they had to learn to walk all over again, and an average surface temperature well below the freezing point of H_2O, and all that. Seems the low G had the effect of confusing the body's growth control system, and the third generation males averaged nine feet in height, all in good proportion and fully functional, so the last few survivors hung on and stretched the original homestead rights past the three hundred year mark. "A damn shame," Illini told me: "A handful of oversized squatters sustaining a Class Four Quarantine that prevents proper development of all that territory! Territory we need, dammit!" He worked up a little righteous wrath, going over all this stuff that he knew I knew at least as well as he did; then he got to the point:

"Just one left," he said. "One man, one oversized clodhopper, and now they've raised the classification to Q-5! Not a damn thing we can do about it legally, Ulrik—but there are a few of us that think the needs of the human race take precedence. So—once this big fella is gone—Vangard is wide open. Need I say more?"

I was in no position to argue, even if I'd wanted to. They had me cold, and aside from the details of the planted dope and the planted papers, it was all perfectly legit. They were bona-fide T-men, and nobody, not even I, took jazreel-smuggling as a harmless, boyish prank.

I picked the right moment and tripped the master switch to cancel the surprise party for the boys, having decided I wasn't quite yet ready for suicide. They never knew how close they'd come. Well, it would have been a flashy exit, for all hands.

It wasn't a fun voyage home, but finally it was over, and they hustled me right along to jail, and the next day into court.

5

It wasn't a real courtroom, but that figured, because it wasn't a real court-martial, and a good thing, too. The load of pink stuff I'd been caught with would have gotten me cashiered, and life plus twenty in the big lockup at League Central, if the line-captain's uniform I'd been wearing hadn't been phony. Still, the boys weren't kidding, so I played along solemnly as they went through the motions, found me guilty as hell, and then got down to business.

"Baird Ulrik," the big fellow with the old-fashioned whiskers said in his big, official-sounding voice. "It is the judgment of this court that such disposal shall be made of you as is prescribed by itself."

"That means we do as we like with you, Ulrik," the smooth character who had been appointed my defense counsel said—the first time he had opened his mouth since the 'trial' began.

"It is therefore directed," Whiskers went on, not laughing, "that you shall suffer capital punishment, not in an orthodox manner, but in a fashion which will serve the public interest."

My counsel leaned close again. "That means we've got a use for you, Ulrik," he told me. "You're a lucky man: your valuable talent won't be wasted."

It took them another hour to come out with all the details; even to Boss Judd, willfully breaking a Class Five quarantine was sweaty business. And there was more:

"The public has a corny idea this big bum is some kind of noble hero, holding onto the ancestral lands all alone, against all the odds," my counsel summed up.

"Sure," I agreed. "That's old stuff, counselor; what's in it for the Mob?"

"There's no occasion to sneer," my lawyer told me. "'Mob' is a long-outdated term. The Organization exercises, de facto, at least as much power as the so-called "legitimate" government, and has indeed been delegated the police and judicial functions here in the Belt, where the not-so-long arm of the Assembly can't reach."

"Sure," I agreed. "These days, you can't hardly tell the hoods from the Forces of Righteousness. Well, maybe you never could. So what's it got to do with little old law-abiding me?"

"With Johnny Thunder dead—get that name some sob-sister hung on this slob—there's no legal basis for Q-5," the shyster told me. "That means a wide-awake developer can go in and stake a claim to two million squares of top quality real estate—and Boss don't sleep much."

"It's so silly it might work," I had to admit. "So when you couldn't hire me for the hit, you framed me with a half-million units of jazreel—and here I am, ready to do your dirty work."

"Don't knock it, Ulrik," Illini said smoothly. "It works."

And the dirty part of it was, he was absolutely right. I had no choice.

6

From a half-million miles out, Vangard was a sphere of gray cast-iron, arc-lit yellow-white on the sunward side, coal-mine black on the other, with a wide band of rust-red along the terminator. The mountain ranges showed up as crooked black hair-lines radiating from the white dazzle of the poles, fanning out, with smaller ridges rising between them, forming a band of broken gridwork across the planet like the back of an old man's hand. I watched the detail grow on the screen until I could match it up with the lines on the nav chart, and it was time to go into my routine. I broke the seal on my U-beamer and sounded my Mayday:

"King Uncle 629 calling XCQ! I'm in trouble! I'm on emergency approach to R-7985-23-D, but it doesn't look good. My track is 093 plus 15, at 19-0-8 standard, mark! Standing by for instructions, and make it fast! Relay, all stations!" The lines were corny, but at this point I had to follow the script. I set the auto-squawk to squirt the call out a thousand times in one-millisec bursts, then switched to listen and waited while forty-five seconds went past. That's how long it would take the hype signal to hit the beamer station of Ring 8 and bounce back an automatic AK.

The auto signal came in right on schedule; another half a minute passed in silence, and a cold finger touched my spine. Then a voice that sounded like I shouldn't have disturbed its nap came in:

"King Uncle 629, Monitor Station Z-448 reading you three by three. You are not, repeat *not* cleared for planetfall. Report full detail—"

"Belay that!" I came back with plenty of edge. "I'm going to hit this rock; how hard depends on you! Get me down first and we'll handle the paperwork later!"

"You're inside interdict range of a Class Five quarantined world. This is an official navigational notice to clear off—"

"Wise up, 448," I cut into that. "I'm seven hundred hours out of Dobie with a special cargo aboard! You think I *picked* this spot to fuse down? I need a tech advisory and I need it now!"

Another wait; then my contact came back on, sounding tight-lipped: "King Uncle, transmit a board readout."

"Sure, sure. But hurry it up." I sounded rattled, which didn't require much acting ability, under the circumstances. Boss Judd didn't pay off on unavoidable mission aborts. I pushed the buttons that gave Z-448 a set of duplicate instrument readings that would prove I was in even worse trouble than I claimed. It was no fake. I'd spent plenty to make sure the old tub had seen her last port.

"All right, King Uncle; you waited too long to make your report, you're going to have to jettison cargo and set up the following nav sequence—"

"I said special cargo!" I yelled back at him. "Category ten! I'm on a contract run for the Dobie med service. I'm carrying ten freeze cases!"

"Uh, roger, King Uncle," the station came back, sounding a little off-balance now. "I understand you have living casualties under cryothesis aboard. Stand by." There was a pause. "You've handed me a cozy one, 629," the voice added, sounding almost human.

"Yeah," I said. "Put some snap on it. That rock's coming up fast."

I sat and listened to the star-crackle. A light and a half away, the station computer would be going into action, chewing up the data from my board and spitting out a solution; and meanwhile, the sharp boy on duty would be checking out my story. That was good. I wanted it checked. It was solid all down the line. The passengers lashed down in the cargo cell were miners, badly burned in a flash fire three months ago on Dobie, a mean little world with no treatment facilities. I was due to collect five million and a full pardon when I delivered them to the med center on Commonweal in a viable condition. My pre-lift inspection was on file, along with my flight plan, which would show my minimum-boost trajectory in past Vangard, just the way a shoestring operator would plot it, on the cheap. It was all in the record. I was legitimate, a victim of circumstances. It was their ball now. And if my calculations were any good, there was only one way they could play it.

"King Uncle, you're in serious trouble," my unseen informant told me. "But I have a possible out for you. You're carrying a detachable cargo pod?" He paused as if he expected an answer, then went on. "You're going to have to ride her down, then jettison the pod on airfoils inside atmosphere. Afterwards, you'll have only a few seconds in which to eject. Understood? I'll feed you the conning data now." A string of numbers rattled off to be automatically recorded and fed into the control sequencer.

"Understood, 448," I said when he finished. "But look—that's a wild country down there. Suppose the cooler's damaged in the drop? I'd better stay with her and try to set her down easy."

"Impossible, King Uncle!" The voice had warmed up a few degrees. After all, I was a brave though penny-pinching merchant captain, determined to do my duty by my charges even at the risk of my own neck.

"Frankly, even this approach is marginal," he

confided. "Your one chance—and your cargo's—is to follow my instructions implicitly!" He didn't add that it was a criminal offense not to comply with a Monitor's navigational order. He didn't have to. I knew that, was counting on it.

"If you say so. I've got a marker circuit on the pod. But listen: how long will it take for you fellows to get a relief boat out here?"

"It's already on the way. The run will take . . . just under three hundred hours."

"That's over twelve standard days!" I allowed the short pause required for the slow mental process of a poor but honest spacer to reach some simple conclusions, then blurted: "If that freeze equipment's knocked out, the insulation won't hold low-O that long! And . . ." Another pause for the next obvious thought to form. "And what about me? How do I stay alive down there?"

"Let's get you down first, Captain." Some of the sympathy had slipped, but not much. Even a hero is entitled to give some thought to staying alive, after he's seen to the troops.

There was little more talk, but the important things had all been said. I was following orders, doing what I was told, no more, no less. Inside the hour, the whole Tri-D watching public of the Sector would know that a disabled hospital ship was down on Vanguard, with ten men's lives—eleven, if you counted mine—hanging in the balance. And I'd be inside the target's defenses, in position for phase two.

7

At ten thousand miles, the sound started up: the lost, lonely wail of air molecules being split by a couple thousand tons of overaged tramp freighter, coming in too fast, on a bad track, with no retros working. I played with what was left of the attitude jets, jockeying her around into a tail-first position, saving the last of my reaction mass for when and where it would do the most good. When I had her where I wanted her, I had less than eight thousand miles of gravity well to work with. I checked the plotting board, pin-pointing my target area, while she bucked and buffeted under me and the moans rose to howls like gut-shot dire-beasts.

At two hundred miles, the drive engines cut in and everything turned to whirly red lights, and pressures like a toad feels under a boot. That went on long enough for me to pass out and come to half a dozen times. Then suddenly she was tumbling in free fall and there were only seconds left. Getting a hand on the pod release was no harder than packing an anvil up a rope ladder; I felt the shock as the cargo section blasted free and away. I got myself into the drop-suit and into position in the escape pod, clamped the shock frame down, took a last lungful of stale ship air, and slapped the eject button. Ten tons of feather pillow hit me in the face and knocked me into another world.

8

I swam up out of the big, black ocean where the bad dreams wait and popped through into the watery sunshine of semi-consciousness in time to get a fast panoramic view of mountains like shark's teeth ranked in snow-capped rows that marched across the world to a serrated horizon a hundred miles away. I must have blacked out again, because the next second a single peak was filling the drop-suit's bull's-eye screen in front of my face, racing toward me like a breaking wave. The third time I came up, I realized I was on chutes, swaying down toward what looked like a tumbled field of dark lava. Then I saw that it was foliage, green-black, dense, coming up fast. I just had time to note that the pod locator marker was blinking green, meaning that my cargo was down and intact, before my lights went out again.

This time I woke up cold: that was the first datum that registered. The second was that my head hurt; that, and all the rest of me. It took me long enough to write a will leaving everything to the Euthanasia Society to get unstrapped and crack the capsule and crawl out into what the outdoorsy set would have called the bracing mountain air. I tallied my aches and pains, found the bones and joints intact. I ran my suit thermostat up and felt some warmth begin to seep into me.

I was standing on pine needles, if pine needles come in the three-foot length, the diameter of a swizzle stick. They made a springy carpet that covered the ground all around the bases of trees as big as Ionic columns that reached up and up into a deep, green twilight. Far off among the tree trunks I saw the white gleam of snow patches. It was silent, utterly still, with no movement, not even a stir among the wide boughs that spread overhead. My suit instruments told me the air pressure was 16 PSI, oxygen content fifty-one per cent, the ambient temperature minus ten degrees centigrade, all as advertised. The locator dials said the cargo pod was down just over a hundred miles north by east from where I stood. As far as I could tell from the gadgets fitted into my fancy wrist console, everything there was operating normally. And if the information I had gathered was as good as the price said it ought to be, I

was within ten miles of where I had planned: half a
day's walk from Johnny Thunder's stamping ground. I
set my suit controls for minimum power assist, took
a compass reading, and started hiking.

9

The low gravity made the going easy, even for a man
who had been pounded by a few hundred miles of thin
atmosphere; and the suit I was wearing helped, too.
You couldn't tell it to look at it, but it had cost somebody the price of a luxury retirement on one of those
rhodium-and-glass worlds with taped climate and hot
and cold running orgies. In addition to the standard
air and temperature controls, and the servo-booster that
took the ache out of my walking, it was equipped with
every reflex circuit and sense amplifier known to black
market science, including a few the League security
people would like to get their hands on. The metabolic
monitor-and-compensate gear alone was worth the
price.

My compass heading took me upslope at a long slant
that brought me to the snow line in an hour. Scattered,
stunted trees continued for another few thousand feet,
ended where the sea-blue glacier began. I got my first
look at Vangard's sky: deep blue, shading down to violet
above the ice-crowned peaks that had it all to themselves up here, like a company of kings.

I took a break at the end of the first hour, gave myself
a squirt of nutrient syrup and swallowed some water,
and listened to eternity passing, silently, one second at
a time. I thought about a shipload of colonists, back in
the primitive dawn of space travel, setting off into a
Universe they knew less about than Columbus did

America, adrift for nine years before they crash-landed here. I thought about them stepping out into the great silence of this cold world—men, women, probably children—knowing that there would never, ever, be any returning for them. I thought about them facing that—and going on to live. They'd been tough people, but their kind of toughness had gone out of the world. Now there was only the other kind; my kind. They were pioneer-tough, frontier-tough, full of unfounded hope and determination and big ideas about the future. I was big-city tough, smart-tough, and rat-tough; and the present was enough for me.

"It's the silence," I said aloud. "It gets to you." But the sound of my voice was too small against all that emptiness. I got to my feet and started off toward the next ridge.

10

Three hours later, the sun was still hanging in the same spot, a dazzle of green above the big top, that every now and then found a hole in the foliage and shot a cold shaft of light down to puddle on the rust-red needles. I had covered almost forty kilometers as the buzzard flies. The spot I was looking for couldn't be far off. I was feeling a little fatigued in spite of the low G, and the sophisticated suit circuitry that took half the load of every muscular contraction, and the stuff the auto-med was metering into my arm. At that, I was lucky. Back home, I'd have been good for two weeks in a recovery ward after the beating I had taken. I cheered myself with that idea while I leaned against a tree and breathed the enriched canned air the suit had prescribed, and thought positive thoughts to counteract the little lights whirling before my eyes. I was still busy with that when I heard the sound. . . .

Now, it's curious how, after a lifetime surrounded by noises, a few hours without them can change your whole attitude toward air vibrations in the audible range. All I heard was a faint, whooping call, like a lonely sea bird yearning for his mate; but I came away from the tree as though it had turned hot, and stood flat-footed, my head cocked, metering the quality of the sound for clues. It got louder, which meant closer, with a speed that suggested the futility of retreat. I looked around for a convenient sapling to climb, but these pines were born old; the lowest branch was fifty feet up. All that was left in the way of concealment was a few thousand tree trunks. Somehow I had the feeling I'd rather meet whatever it was out in the open. At least I'd see it as soon as it saw me. I knew it was something that was alive and ate meat; a faint, dogmatic voice from my first ancestor was telling me that. I did the thing with the wrist that put the bootleg miniature crater gun in my palm, and waited while the booming call got louder and more anguished, like a lovelorn sheep, a heart-broken bull, a dying elk. I could hear the thud of big feet now, galloping in a cadence that, even allowing for the weak gravity field, suggested ponderous size. Then it broke through into sight, and confirmed great-grandpa's intuition. It wasn't a hound, or even a hyaenodon, but it was what a hyaenodon would have been if it had stood seven feet at the shoulder, had legs as big around at the ankle as my thigh, a head the size of a one-man helicab, and jaws that could pick a man up like Rover trotting home with the evening paper. Maybe it was that last thought that kept my finger from tightening on the firing stud. The monster dog skidded to a halt in a slow-motion flurry of pine needles, gave a final bellow, and showed me about a yard of bright red tongue. The rest of him was brown and black, sleek-furred, loose-hided. His teeth were big, but not over six inches from gum line to needle-point. His eyes were shiny black and small, like an elephant's with crescents of red under them. He came on slowly, as if he wanted to get a good look at what he was eating. I could hear his joints creak as he moved. His shoulders were high, bunched with muscle. At each step his foot-wide pads sank into the leaf mould. I felt my knees begin to twitch, while what hackles I had did their best to stand on end. He was ten feet away now, and his breath snorted through nostrils I could have stuck a fist into, like steam around a leaky piston. If he came any closer, I knew my finger would push that stud, ready or not.

"Down, boy!" I said, in what I hoped was a resonant tone of command. He halted, hauled in the tongue, let it out again, then lowered his hind quarters gingerly, like an old lady settling into her favorite rocker. He sat there and looked at me with his head cocked, and I looked back. And while we were doing that, the giant arrived.

II

He came up silently along an aisle among the big trees, and was within fifty feet of me before I saw him, big as he was.

And big he was.

It's easy to talk about a man twelve feet high; that's about twice normal, after all. Just a big man, and let's make a joke about his shoe size.

But twice the height is four times the area of sky he blanks off as he looms over you; eight times the

bulk of solid bone and muscle. Sixteen hundred pounds
of man, at Earth-normal G. Here he weighed no more
than half a ton, but even at that, each leg was holding up five hundred pounds. They were thick, muscle-
corded legs that matched the arms and the chest and
the neck that was like a section of hundred-year oak
supporting the big head. But massive as he was, there
was no distortion of proportion. Photographed without a midget in the picture for scale, he would have
looked like any other Mr. Universe contender, straight-
boned, clean-limbed, every muscle defined, but nothing
out of scale. His hair was black, curly, growing in a
rough-cut mane, but no rougher than any other man
that lives a long way from a barber. He had a close-
trimmed beard, thick, black eyebrows over wide-set,
pale blue eyes. His skin was weather-burned the color
of well-used cowhide. His features were regular enough
to be called handsome, if you admire the Jove-Poseidon
style. I saw all this as he came striding up to me,
dressed in leather, as light on his feet as the dog was
heavy. He stopped beside the pooch, patted its head
carelessly with a hand the size of first base, looking
down at me, and for a ghostly instant I was a child
again, looking at the Brobdingnagian world of adults.
Thoughts flashed in my mind, phantom images of a
world of warmth and love and security and other illusions long forgotten. I pushed those away and remembered that I was Baird Ulrik, professional, out on a job,
in a world that had no place for fantasies.

"You're the man they call Johnny Thunder," I said.
He let that pass. Maybe he smiled a little.

"I'm Patton," I told him. "Carl Patton. I bailed out
of a ship." I pointed to the sky.

He nodded, "I know," he said. His voice was deep,
resonant as a pipe organ; he had a lot of chest for it
to bounce around in. "I heard your ship fall." He

looked me over, didn't see any compound fractures. "I'm glad you came safely to ground. I hope Woola did not frighten you." His Standard sounded old-fashioned and a little stilted, with a trace of a strange accent. My trained poker face must have slipped a couple of feet at what he said, because he smiled. His teeth were square and porcelain white.

"Why should he?" I said without squeaking. "I've seen my three-year-old niece pat a Great Dane on the knee. That was as high as she could reach."

"Come back with me to my house. I have food, a fire."

I pulled myself together and went into my act: "I've got to get to my cargo pod. There are . . . passengers aboard it."

His face asked questions.

"They're alive—so far," I said. "I have a machine that tells me the pod landed safely, on her chutes. The cannisters are shock-mounted, so if the locator gear survived, so did they. But the equipment might not have. If it was smashed, they'll die."

"This is a strange thing, Carl Patton," he said after I had explained, "to freeze a living man."

"They wouldn't be living long, if they weren't in low-O," I told him. "Third-degree burns over their whole bodies. Probably internals, too. At the med center they can put 'em in viv tanks and regrow their hides. When they wake up, they'll be as good as new." I gave him a significant look, full of do-or-die determination. "If I get there in time, that is. If they come out of it out there . . ." I let the sentence die off without putting words to the kind of death that would be. I made a thing out of looking at the show dials on my wrist. "The pod is down somewhere in that direction." I pointed away up-slope, to the north. "I don't know how far." I shot a look at him to see how that last datum went over. The less I gave away, the better. But he sounded a little more sophisticated than my researches had led me to expect. A slip now could queer everything. "Maybe a hundred miles, maybe more."

He thought that one over, looking down at me. His eyes were friendly enough, but in a remote way, like a candle burning in the window of a stranger's house.

"That is bad country, where they have fallen," he said. "The Towers of Nandi are high. You would die on the way there."

I knew it was tough country; I'd picked the spot with care. I gave him my manly, straight-from-the-shoulder look.

"There are ten men out there, my responsibility. I've got to do what I can."

His eyes came back to mine. For the first time, a little fire seemed to flicker alight behind them.

"First you must rest and eat."

I wanted to say more, to set the hook; but just then the world started a slow spin under me. I took a step to catch my balance and a luminous sleet was filling the air, and then the whole thing tilted sideways and I slid off and down into the black place that always waited. . . .

12

I woke up looking at a dancing pattern of orange light on a ceiling of polished red and black wood twenty feet overhead. The light was coming from a fire big enough to roast an ox in, blazing away on a hearth built of rocks the size of tombstones. I was lying on a bed not as large as a handball court, and the air was full of the odor of soup. I crawled to the edge and managed the four-foot jump to the floor. My legs felt like over-cooked *pasta*. My ribs ached—probably from a long ride over the giant's shoulder.

He looked across at me from the big table. "You were tired," he said. "And you have many bruises."

I looked down. I was wearing my underwear, nothing else.

"My suit!" I barked, and the words came out thick, not just from weakness. I was picturing sixty grand worth of equipment and a multi-million credit deal tossed into the reclaimer—or the fire—and a clean set of overalls laid out to replace them.

"There," my host nodded toward the end of the bed. I grabbed, checked. Everything looked OK. But I didn't like it; and I didn't like the idea of being helpless, tended by a man I had business with later.

"You have rested," the big man said. "Now eat."

I sat at the table on a pile of blankets and dipped into a dishpanful of thick broth made of savory red and green vegetables and chunks of tender white meat. There was a bread that was tough and chewy, with a flavor of nuts, and a rough purple wine that went down better than the finest vintage at Arondo's, on Plaisir 4. Afterward, the giant unfolded a chart and pointed to a patch of high relief like coarse-troweled stucco.

"If the pod is there," he said, "it will be difficult. But perhaps it fell here." He indicated a smoother stretch to the south and east of the badlands.

I went through the motions of checking the azimuth on the indicator; the heading I gave him was only about three degrees off true. At 113.8 miles—the position the R&D showed for the pod—we would miss the target by about ten miles.

The big man laid off our line of march on his map. It fell along the edge of what was called the Towers of Nandi.

"Perhaps," he said. He wasn't a man given to wasting words.

"How much daylight is left?" I asked him.

"Fifty hours, a little less." That meant I'd been out for nearly six hours. I didn't like that, either. Time was money, and my schedule was tight.

"Have you talked to anyone?" I looked at the big, not quite modern screen at the side of the room. It was a standard Y-band model with a half-millionth L lag. That meant a four-hour turn-around time to the Ring 8 Station.

"I told the monitor station that you had come safely to ground," he said.

"What else did you tell them?"

"There was nothing more to tell."

I stood. "You can call them again now," I said. "And tell them I'm on my way out to the pod." I gave it the tight-lipped, no-tears-for-me delivery. From the corner of my eye I saw him nod, and for a second I wondered if maybe the famous Ulrik system of analysis had slipped, and this big hunk of virility was going to sit on his haunches and let poor frail little me tackle the trail alone.

"The way will not be easy," he said. "The winds have come to the high passes. Snow lies on the heights of Kooclain."

"My suit heater will handle that part. If you can spare me some food. . . ."

He went to a shelf, lifted down a pack the size and shape of a climate unit for a five-room conapt. I knew then my trap was closing dead on target.

"If my company will not be unwelcome, Carl Patton, I will go with you," he said.

I went through the routine protestations, but in the end I let him convince me. We left half an hour later, after notifying Ring station that we were on the way.

13

Johnny Thunder took the lead, swinging along at an easy amble that covered ground at a deceptive rate, not bothered by the big pack on his back. He was wearing the same leathers he had on when he met me. The only weapon he carried was a ten-foot steel-shod staff. The monster mutt trotted along off-side, nose to the ground; I brought up the rear. My pack was light; the big man pointed out that the less I carried the better time we'd make. I managed to keep up, hanging back a little to make it look good. My bones still ached some, but I was feeling frisky as a colt in the low G. We did a good hour without talking, working up along the angle of a long slope through the big trees. We crested the rise and the big fellow stopped and waited while I came up, puffing a little, but game as they come.

"We will rest here," he said.

"Rest, hell," I came back. "Minutes may make all the difference to those poor devils."

"A man must rest," he said reasonably, and sat down, propping his bare arms on his knees. This put his eyes on a level with mine, standing. I didn't like that, so I sat too.

He took his full ten minutes before starting off again. Johnny Thunder, I saw, was not a man to be bullied. He knew his best pace. Even with all my fancy equipment, I was going to have my hands full walking him to death on his own turf.

That was the plan, just the way they'd laid it out for me, back at Aldo: no wounds on his big corpse when they found it, no dirty work, just a fellow who'd died trying: bigger than your average pictonews hero, but human enough to miscalculate his own giant abilities. Boss would welcome investigation, and he'd check out as clean as a farmhand waiting for the last bus back from the county fair. All I had to do was use my high-tech gear to stay close enough to urge him on. Simple. Not easy, but simple. On that thought I let sleep take me.

14

We crossed a wide valley and headed up into high country. It was cold, and the trees were sparser here, gaunter, dwarfed by the frost and twisted by the winds into hunched shapes that clutched the rock like arthritic hands. There were patches of rotten snow, and a hint in the sky that there might be more to come before long. Not that I could feel the edge of the wind that came whipping down off the peaks; but the giant was taking it on his bare arms.

"Don't you own a coat?" I asked him at the next stop. We were on a shelf of rock, exposed to the full blast of what was building to a forty-mile gale.

"I have a cape, here." He slapped the pack on his back. "Later I will wear it."

"You make your own clothes?" I was looking at the tanned leather, fur side in, the big sailmaker's stitches.

"A woman made these garments for me," he said. "That was long ago."

"Yeah," I said. I tried to picture him with his woman, to picture how she'd move, what she'd look like. A woman ten feet tall.

"Do you have a picture of her?"

"Only in my heart." He said it matter-of-factly I wondered how it felt to be the last of your kind, but I didn't ask him that. Instead I asked, "Why do you do it? Live here alone?"

He looked out across a view of refrigerated rock. "This is my home," he said. Another straight answer, with no sho-biz behind it. It just didn't get to this overgrown plowboy. It never occurred to him how he could milk the situation for tears and cash from a few billion sensation-hungry fans. A real-life soap opera. The end of the trail. Poor Johnny Thunder, so brave and so alone.

"Why do *you* do—what you do?" he asked suddenly. I felt my gut clench like a fist.

"What's that supposed to mean?" I got it out between my teeth, while my hand tickled the crater gun out of its wrist clip and into my palm.

"You, too, live alone, Carl Patton. You captain a ship of space. You endure solitude and hardship. And now, you offer your life for your comrades."

"They're not my comrades," I snapped. "They're cash cargo, that's all. No delivery, no payment. And I'm not offering my life. I'm taking a little hike for my health."

He studied me. "Few men would attempt the heights of Kooclain in this season. None without a great reason."

"I've got great reasons; millions of them."

He smiled a faint smile. "You are many things, I think, Carl Patton. But not a fool."

"Let's hit the trail," I said. "We've got a long way to go before I collect."

15

Johnny Thunder held his pace back to what he thought I could manage. The dog seemed a little nervous, raising his nose and snuffling the air, then loping ahead. I easy-footed it after them, with plenty of wheezing on the upslopes and some realistic panting at the breaks, enough to make me look busy, but not enough to give the giant ideas of slowing down. Little by little I upped the cadence in an inobtrusive way, until we were hitting better than four miles per hour. That's a good brisk stride on flat ground at standard G; it would take a trained athlete to keep it up for long. Here, with my suit's efficient piezoelectronic muscles doing most of the work, it was a breeze—for me.

We took a lunch break. The big man dug bread and cheese and a Jeroboam of wine out of his knapsack and handed me enough for two meals. I ate a little of it and tucked the rest into the disposal pocket on my shoulder when he wasn't looking. When he finished his ration—not much bigger than mine—I got to my feet and looked expectant. He didn't move.

"We must rest now for an hour," he told me.

"OK," I said. "You rest alone. I've got a job to do." I started off across the patchy snow and got about ten steps before Bowser gallumphed past me and turned, blocking my route. I started past him on the right and he moved into my path. The same for the left.

"Rest, Carl Patton," Goliath said. He lay back and put his hands under his head and closed his eyes. Well, I couldn't keep him walking, but I could cut into his sleep. I went back and sat beside him.

"Lonely country," I said. He didn't answer.

"Looks like nobody's ever been here before," I added. "Not a beer can in sight." That didn't net a reply either.

"What do you live on in this place?" I asked him. "What do you make the cheese out of, and the bread?"

He opened his eyes. "The heart of the friendly-tree. It is pulverized for flour, or made into a paste and fermented."

"Neat," I said. "I guess you import the wine."

"The fruit of the same tree gives us our wine. He

said 'us' as easily as if he had a wife, six kids, and a chapter of the Knights of Pythias waiting for him back home.

"It must have been tough at first," I said. "If the whole planet is like this, it's hard to see how your ancestors survived."

"They fought," the giant said, as if that explained everything.

"You don't have to fight anymore," I said. "You can leave this rock now, live the easy life somewhere under a sun with a little heat in it."

The giant looked at the sky as if thinking. "We have a legend of a place where the air is soft and the soil bursts open to pour forth fruit. I do not think I would like that land."

"Why not? You think there's some kind of kick in having things rough?"

He turned his head to look at me. "It is you who suffer hardship, Carl Patton. I am at home, whereas you endure cold and fatigue in a place alien to you."

I grunted. Johnny Thunder had a way of turning everything I said back at me like a ricochet. "I heard there was some pretty vicious animal life here," I said. "I haven't seen any signs of it."

"Soon you will."

"Is that your intuition, or. . . ?"

"A pack of snow scorpions have trailed us for some hours. When we move out into open ground, you will see them."

"How do you know?"

"Woola tells me."

I looked at the big hound, sprawled out with his head on his paws. He looked tired.

"How does it happen you have dogs?"

"We have always had dogs."

"Probably had a pair in the original cargo," I said.

"Or maybe frozen embryos. I guess they carried breed stock even way back then."

"Woola springs from a line of dogs of war. Her forebear was the mighty courser Standfast, who slew the hounds of King Roon on the Field of the Broken Knife."

"You people fought wars?" He didn't say anything. I snorted. "I'd think as hard as you had to scratch to make a living, you'd have valued your lives too much for that."

"Of what value is a life without truth? King Roon fought for his beliefs. Prince Dahl fought for his own."

"Who won?"

"They fought for twenty hours; and once Prince Dahl fell, and King Roon stood back and bade him rise again. But in the end Dahl broke the back of the King."

"So—did that prove he was right?"

"Little it matters what a man believes, Carl Patton, so long as he believes it with all his heart and soul."

"Nuts. Facts don't care who believes them."

The giant sat up and pointed to the white peaks glistening far away. "The mountains are true," he said. He looked up at the sky, where high, blackish-purple clouds were piled up like battlements. "The sky is true. And these truths are more than the facts of rock and gas."

"I don't understand this poetic talk," I said. "It's good to eat well, sleep in a good bed, to have the best of everything there is. Anybody that says otherwise is a martyr or a phony."

"What is 'best,' Carl Patton? Is there a couch softer than weariness? A better sauce than appetite?"

"You got that out of a book."

"If you crave the easy luxury you speak of, why are you here?"

"That's easy. To earn the money to buy the rest."

"And afterwards—if you do not die on this trek—will you go there, to the pretty world, and eat the fat fruits picked by another hand?"

"Sure," I said. "Why not?" I felt myself sounding mad, and wondered why; and that made me madder than ever. I let it drop and pretended to sleep.

16

Four hours later we topped a long slope and looked out over a thousand square miles of forest and glacier, spread out wide enough to hint at the size of the world called Vangard. We had been walking for nine hours and, lift unit and all, I was beginning to feel it. Big Boy looked as good as new. He shaded his eyes against the sun that was too small and too bright in a before-the-storm sort of way, and pointed out along the valley's rim to a peak a mile or two away.

"There we will sleep," he said.

"It's off our course," I said. "What's wrong with right here?"

"We need shelter and a fire. Holgrimm will not grudge us these."

"What's Holgrimm?"

"His lodge stands there."

I felt a little stir along my spine, the way you do when ghosts come into the conversation. Not that ghosts worry me; just the people that believe in them.

We covered the distance in silence. Woola, the dog, did a lot of sniffing and grunting as we came up to the lodge. It was built of logs, stripped and carved and stained red and green and black. There was a steep gabled roof, slate-tiled, and a pair of stone chimneys, and a few small windows with colored glass leaded into them. The big man paused when we came into the clearing, stood there leaning on his stick and looking around. The place seemed to be in a good state of preservation. But then it was built of the same rock and timber as the country around it. There were no fancy trimmings to weather away.

"Listen, Carl Patton," the giant said. "Almost, you can hear Holgrimm's voice here. In a moment, it seems, he might throw wide the door to welcome us."

"Except he's dead," I said. I went past him and up to the entrance, which was a slab of black and purple wood that would have been right in scale on the front of Notre Dame. I strained two-handed at the big iron latch, with no luck. Johnny Thunder lifted it with his thumb.

It was cold in the big room. The coating of hard frost on the purple wood floor crunched under our boots. In the deep-colored gloom, I saw stretched animal hides on the high walls, green and red, and gold-furred, brilliant as a Chinese pheasant. There were other trophies: a big, beaked skull three feet long, with a spread of antlers like wings of white ivory, that swept forward to present an array of silver dagger tips, black-ringed. There was a leathery-skinned head that was all jaw and teeth; and a tarnished battle ax, ten feet long, with a complicated head. A long table sat in the center of the room between facing fireplaces as big as city apartments. I saw the wink of light on the big metal goblets, plates, cutlery. There were high-backed chairs around the table; and in the big chair at the far end, facing me, a gray-bearded giant sat with a sword in his hand. The dog whined, a sound that expressed my feelings perfectly.

"Holgrimm awaits us," Johnny's big voice said softly behind me. He went forward, and I broke the paralysis and followed. Closer, I could see the fine frosting of ice that covered the seated giant, glittering in his beard, on the back of his hands, across his open eyes.

Ice rimed the table and the dishes and the smooth, black wood of the chairs. The bared short-sword was frozen to the table. Woola's claws rasped loud on the floor as she slunk behind her master.

"Don't you bury your dead?" I got the words out, a little ragged.

"His women prepared him thus, at his command, when he knew his death was on him."

"Why?"

"That is a secret which Holgrimm keeps well."

"We'd be better off outside," I told him. "This place is like a walk-in freezer."

"A fire will mend that."

"Our friend here will melt. I think I prefer him the way he is."

"Only a little fire, enough to warm our food and make a bed of coals to lie beside."

There was wood in a box beside the door, deep red, hard as granite, already cut to convenient lengths. Convenient for my traveling companion, I mean. He shuffled the eight-foot, eighteen-inch diameter logs as if they were bread sticks. They must have been full of volatile resins, because they lit off on the first match, and burned with a roaring and a smell of mint and camphor. Big Johnny brewed up a mixture of hot wine and some tarry syrup from a pot on the table that he had to break loose from the ice, and handed me a half-gallon pot of the stuff. It was strong, but good, with a taste that was almost turpentine but turned out to be ambrosia instead. There was frozen bread and cheese and a soup he stirred up in the big pot on the hearth. I ate all I could and wasted some more. My large friend gave himself a Spartan ration, raising his mug to our host before he drank.

"How long has he been dead?" I asked.

"Ten of our years." He paused, then added: "That would be over a hundred, League standard."

"Friend of yours?"

"We fought; but later we drank wine together again. Yes, he was my friend."

"How long have you been . . . alone here?"

"Nine years. Holgrimm's house was almost the last the plague touched."

"Why didn't it kill you?"

He shook his head. "The Universe has its jokes, too."

"How was it, when they were all dying?"

The big man cradled his cup in his hands, looking past me into the fire. "At first, no one understood. We had never known disease here, until the first visitors came. Our enemies were the ice wolf and the scorpions, and the avalanche and the killing frost. This was a new thing, the foe we could not see. Some died bewildered, others fled into the forest where their doom caught them at last. Oxandra slew his infant sons and daughters before the choking death could take them. Joshal stood in the snow, swinging his war ax and shouting taunts at the sky until he fell and rose no more."

"What about your family?"

"As you see."

"What?"

"Holgrimm was my father."

17

The rest of the family, a brother, an uncle, his mother and a few sisters had all gone out alone when the time came, and set off for a spot high up on a peak they called Hel; Johnny didn't know if they'd made it. But I could see it was better that way than burdening the dying survivors with the corpses to dispose of.

Johnny didn't seem to be affected by all this. He just seemed a bit bored.

"Tell me of your own world, Carl Patton," he suggested. "Are all the folk as you, small, but stout of heart for all that?"

I told him I was an exception; most people had sense enough to stay home and enjoy life. He nodded, "Even as I," he said. I pointed out that most folks had a lot more fun than he did, and described the wonders of trideo and electronic golf, and cards and dice and booze. Somehow, I didn't manage to make it sound like much, even to me.

"I would have tools, Carl Patton," he told me. "Such as I have seen in the Great Catalog, for the working of our native stone and woods. This would please me deeply." He looked at his huge hands. "The skill is here, I know it," he said. "To make the beautiful from the raw substance is a great thing, Carl. Do you have such tools at your home?"

I told him I'd built a few model ships as a young fellow, before I'd gotten fully involved in my 'adventurous' life as a free-lance spaceman.

"I finally got my own ship," I explained to him, since he seemed interested. "It was a luxury cruiser, rebuilt from a captured Hukk battlewagon. I kept the armament in place just for the hell of it, but it seemed a lot of people got the idea I wouldn't be above using it. I discovered I could trade in and out of some of the toughest hell-ports in the Arm, with no squawks from the Mob. Then, one day, a Navy destroyer hailed me, and boarded and took me in tow. Claimed they'd discovered contraband aboard; then the captain let on maybe there was a way out. Somewhere along then I realized I'd been conned at my own game. The Mob had hijacked the destroyer, and planted the pink stuff on me, and it didn't matter much how it got there; if they sicced the real Navy on me, there I'd be: me and my explanations, but I still had an out. . . ."

"No doubt you defied these miscreants to do their worst, eh, Carl? As any true man would do," he added.

"Not exactly," I told him, wanting to save face for some reason. "I listened to their proposition and let them think I'd play along."

"A dangerous game, Carl," he told me seriously. I shrugged that off and got him to tell me about hunting the ice wolf, which was a native arthropod species: like a man-eating spider, but it supplied furs as fine as any. Hunting warm-blooded tarantulas ten feet high wasn't my idea of sport, I told him. I'd had no sleep for about twenty hours and I dozed off while he was telling me about the big fight between the wolves and the scorpions over the settlement after the snow-patrol broke down.

18

We slept rolled up in the furs Johnny Thunder took down from the walls and thawed on the hearth. He was right about the heat. The big blaze melted the frost in a ten foot semi-circle, but didn't touch the rest of the room. It was still early afternoon outside when we hit the trail. I crowded the pace all I could. After eight hours of it, over increasingly rough ground, climbing all the time, the big fellow called me on it.

"I'm smaller than you are, but that's no reason I can't be in shape," I told him. "And I'm used to higher G. What's the matter, too rough for you?" I asked the question in an offhand way, but I listened hard for the answer. So far he looked as good as new.

"I fare well enough. The trail has been easy."

"The map says it gets rougher fast from here on."

"The heights will tell on me," he conceded. "Still, I can go on awhile. But Woola suffers, poor brute."

The dog was stretched out on her side. She looked like a dead horse, if dead horses had tails that wagged when their name was mentioned, and ribs that heaved with the effort of breathing the thin air. Thin by Vangard standards, that is. Oxygen pressure was still over Earth-normal.

"Why not send her back?"

"She would not go. And we will be glad of her company when the snow scorpions come."

"Back to that, eh? You sure you're not imagining them? This place looks as lifeless as a tombstone quarry."

"They wait," he said. "They know me, and Woola. Many times have they tried our alertness—and left their dead on the snow. And so they follow, and wait."

"My gun will handle them." I showed him the legal slug-thrower I carried; he looked it over politely.

"A snow scorpion does not die easily," he said.

"This packs plenty of kick," I said, and demonstrated by blasting a chip off a boulder twenty yards away. The *car-rong!* echoed back and forth among the big trees. He smiled a little.

"Perhaps, Carl Patton."

We slept the night at the timber line.

19

The next day's hike was different, right from the beginning. On the open ground the snow had drifted and frozen into a crust that held my weight, but broke under the giant's feet, and the dog's. There was no kidding about me pushing the pace now. I took the lead and big Johnny had a tough time keeping up. He didn't complain, didn't seem to be breathing too hard; he just kept coming on, stopping every now and then to wait for the pup to catch up, and breaking every hour for a rest.

The country had gotten bleaker as it rose. As long as we'd been among the trees, there had been an illusion of familiarity; not cozy, but at least there was life, almost Earth-type life. You could fool yourself that somewhere over the next rise there might be a house, or a road. But not here. There was just the snow field, as alien as Jupiter, with the long shadows of the western peaks falling across it. And ahead the glacier towering over us against the dark sky, sugar-white in the late sun, deep-sea blue in the shadows.

About the third hour, the big man pointed something out to me, far back along the trail. It looked like a scatter of black pepper against the white.

"The scorpion pack," he said.

I grunted. "We won't outrun them standing here."

"In their own time they will close the gap," he said.

We did nine hours' hike, up one ridge, down the far side, up another, higher one before he called a halt. Dusk was coming on when we made our camp in the lee of an ice buttress, if you can call a couple of hollows in the frozen snow a camp. The big man got a small fire going, and boiled some soup. He gave me my usual hearty serving, but it seemed to me he shorted himself and the dog a little.

"How are the supplies holding out?" I asked him.

"Well enough," was all he said.

The temperature was down to minus nine centigrade now. He unpacked his cloak, a black and orange striped super-sheepskin the size of a mains'l, and wrapped himself up in it. He and the dog slept together, curled for warmth. I turned down the invitation to join them.

"My circulation's good," I said. "Don't worry about me."

But in spite of the suit, I woke up shivering, and had to set the thermostat a few notches higher. Big Boy didn't seem to mind the cold. But then, an animal his size had an advantage. He had less radiating surface per unit weight. It wasn't freezing that would get him—not unless things got a lot worse.

When he woke me, it was deep twilight; the sun was gone behind the peaks to the west. The route ahead led up the side of a thirty-degree snow slope. There were enough outcroppings of rock and tumbled ice blocks to make progress possible, but it was slow going. The pack on our trail had closed the gap while we slept; I estimated they were ten miles behind now. There were about twenty-five of the things, strung out in a wide crescent. I didn't like that; it suggested more intelligence than anything that looked as bad as the pictures I'd seen. Woola rolled her eyes and showed her teeth and whined, looking back at them. The giant just kept moving forward, slow and steady.

"How about it?" I asked him at the next break. "Do we just let them pick the spot? Or do we fort up somewhere, where they can only jump us from about three and a half sides?"

"They must come to us."

I looked back down the slope we had been climbing steadily for more hours than I could keep track of, trying to judge their distance.

"Not more than five miles," I said. "They could have closed any time in the last couple of hours. What are they waiting for?"

He glanced up at the high ridge, dazzling two miles above. "Up there, the air is thin and cold. They sense that we will weaken."

"And they're right."

"They too will be weakened, Carl Patton, though not perhaps so much as we." He said this as unconcernedly as if he were talking about whether tomorrow would be a good day for a picnic.

"Don't you care?" I asked him. "Doesn't it matter to you if a pack of hungry meat-eaters corners you in the open?"

"It is their nature," he said simply.

"A stiff upper lip is nifty—but don't let it go to your head. How about setting up an ambush—up there?" I pointed out a jumble of rock slabs a hundred yards above.

"They will not enter it."

"OK," I said. "You're the wily native guide. I'm just a tourist. We'll play it your way. But what do we do when it gets dark?"

"The moon will soon rise."

In the next two hours we covered about three-quarters of a mile. The slope was close to forty-five degrees now. Powdery snow went cascading down in slow plumes with every step. Without the suit I don't know if I could have stayed with it, even with the low gravity. Big Johnny was using his hands a lot now; and the dog's puffing was piteous to hear.

"How old is the mutt?" I asked when we were lying on our backs at the next break, with my trailmates working hard to get some nourishment out of what to them was some very thin atmosphere, and me faking the same distress, while I breathed the rich mixture from my suit collector.

"Three years."

"That would be about thirty-five Standard. How

long . . ." I remembered my panting and did some,
" . . . do they live?"

"No one. . . knows."

"What does that mean?"

"Her kind . . . die in battle."

"It looks like she'll get her chance."

"For that . . . she is grateful."

"She looks scared to death," I said. "And dead beat."

"Weary, yes. But fear is not bred in her."

We made another half mile before the pack decided
the time had come to move in to the attack.

20

The dog knew it first; she gave a bellow like a gut-
shot elephant and took a twenty-foot bound down-slope
to take up her stand between us and them. It couldn't
have been a worse position from the defensive view-
point, with the exception of the single factor of our
holding the high ground. It was a featureless stretch
of frozen snow, tilted on edge, naked as a tin roof. The
big fellow used his number forty's to stamp out a
hollow, working in a circle to widen it.

"You damn fool, you ought to be building a mound,"
I yelled at him. "That's a cold grave you're digging."

"Do as I do . . . Carl Patton," he panted. "For your
life."

"Thanks; I'll stay topside." I picked a spot off to his
left and kicked some ice chunks into a heap to give
me a firing platform. I made a big show of checking
the slug-thrower, then inobtrusively set the crater gun
for max range, narrow beam. I don't know why I
bothered playing it foxy; Big Boy didn't know the
difference between a legal weapon and contraband.

Maybe it was just the instinct to have an ace up the sleeve. By the time I finished, the pack was a quarter of a mile away and coming up fast, not running or leaping, but twinkling along on clusters of steel-rod legs that ate up the ground like a fire eats dry grass.

"Carl Patton, it would be well if you stood by my back," the big man called.

"I don't need to hide behind you," I barked.

"Listen well!" he said, and for the first time his voice lacked the easy, almost idle tone. "They cannot attack in full charge. First must they halt and raise their barb. In that moment are they vulnerable. Strike for the eye—but beware the ripping claws!"

"I'll work at a little longer range," I called back, and fired a slug at one a little in advance of the line but still a couple of hundred yards out. There was a bright flash against the ice; a near miss. The next one was dead on—a solid hit in the center of the leaf-shaped plate of tarnish-black armor that covered the thorax. He didn't even break stride.

"Strike for the eye, Carl Patton!"

"What eye?" I yelled. "All I see is plate armor and pistons!" I fired for the legs, missed, missed again, then sent fragments of a limb flying. The owner may have faltered for a couple of microseconds, or maybe I just blinked. I wasn't even sure which one I had hit. They came on, closing ranks now, looking suddenly bigger, more deadly, like an assault wave of light armor, barbed and spiked and invulnerable, with nothing to stop them but a man with a stick, a worn-out old hound, and me, with my popgun. I felt the weapon bucking in my hand, and realized I had been firing steadily. I took a step back, dropped the slug thrower, and palmed the crater gun as the line reached the spot where Woola crouched, waiting.

But instead of slamming into the big dog at full bore,

the pair facing her skidded to a dead stop, executed a swift but complicated rearrangement of limbs, dropping their forward ends to the ground, bringing their hindquarters up and over, unsheathing two-foot-long stingers that poised, ready to plunge down into the unprotected body of the animal. . . .

I wouldn't have believed anything so big could move so fast. She came up from her flattened position like a cricket off a hot plate, was in mid-air, twisting to snap down at the thing on the left with jaws like a bear trap, landed sprawling, spun, leaped, snapped, and was poised, snarling, while two ruined attackers flopped and stabbed their hooks into the ice before her. I saw all this in a fast half-second while I was bringing the power gun up, squeezing the firing stud to pump a multi-megawatt jolt into the thing that was rearing up in front of me. The shock blasted a foot-wide pit in it, knocked it a yard backward—but didn't slow its strike. The barb whipped up, over, and down to bury itself in the ice between my feet.

"The eye!" The big man's voice boomed at me over the snarls of Woola and the angry buzzing that was coming from the attackers. "The eye, Carl Patton!"

I saw it then: a three-inch patch like reticulated glass, deep red, set in the curve of armor above the hook-lined prow. It exploded as I fired. I swiveled left and fired again, from the corner of my eye saw the big man swing his club left, right. I was down off my mound, working my way over to him, slamming shots into whatever was closest. The scorpions were all around us, but only half a dozen at a time could crowd in close to the edge of the twelve-foot depression the giant had tramped out. One went over, pushed from behind, scrabbling for footing, and died as the club smashed down on him. I killed another and jumped down beside the giant.

"Back to back, Carl Patton," he called. A pair came up together over a barricade of dead monsters, and while they teetered for attack position I shot them, then shot the one that mounted their threshing corpses. Then suddenly the pressure slackened, and I was hearing the big man's steam-engine puffing, the dog's rasping snarls, was aware of a pain in my thigh, of the breath burning in my throat. A scorpion jittered on his thin legs ten feet away, but he came no closer. The others were moving back, buzzing and clacking. I started up over the side and an arm like a jib boom stopped me.

"They must . . . come to us." The giant wheezed out the words. His face was pink and he was having trouble getting enough air, but he was smiling.

"If you say so," I said.

"Your small weapon strikes a man's blow," he said, instead of commenting on my stupidity.

"What are they made of? They took my rounds like two-inch flint steel."

"They are no easy adversaries," he said. "Yet we killed nine." He looked across at where the dog stood panting, facing the enemy. "Woola slew five. They learn caution—" He broke off, looking down at me, at my leg. He went to one knee, touched a tear in my suit I hadn't noticed. That shook me, seeing the ripped edge of the material. Not even a needler could penetrate the stuff—but one of those barbs had.

"The hide is unbroken," he said. "Luck was with you this day, Carl Patton. The touch of the barb is death."

Something moved behind him and I yelled and fired and a scorpion came plunging down on the spot where he'd been standing an instant before. I fell and rolled, came around, put one in the eye just as Johnny Thunder's club slammed home in the same spot. I got to

my feet and the rest of them were moving off, back
down the slope.

"You damned fool!" I yelled at the giant. Rage broke
my voice. "Why don't you watch yourself?"

"I am in your debt, Carl Patton," was all he said.

"Debt, hell! Nobody owes me anything—and that
goes both ways!"

He didn't answer that, just looked down at me,
smiling a little, like you would at an excited child. I
took a couple of deep breaths of warmed and forti-
fied tank air and felt better—but not much.

"Will you tell me your true name, small warrior?"
the giant said.

I felt ice form in my chest.

"What do you mean?" I stalled.

"We have fought side by side. It is fitting that we
exchange the secret names our mothers gave us at
birth."

"Oh, magic, eh? Juju. The secret word of power.
Skip it, big fellow. Johnny Thunder is good enough for
me."

"As you will . . . Carl Patton." He went to see to the
dog then, and I checked to see how badly my suit was
damaged. There was a partial power loss in the leg
servos and the heat was affected, too. That wasn't good.
There were still a lot of miles to walk out of the giant
before the job was done.

When we hit the trail half an hour later I was still
wondering why I had moved so fast to save the life
of the man I'd come here to kill.

21

We halted for sleep three hours later. It was almost
full dark when we turned in, curled up in pits trampled

in the snow. Johnny Thunder said the scorpions wouldn't be back until they'd eaten their dead, but I sweated inside my insulated longjohns as the last of the light faded to a pitch black like the inside of an unmarked grave. Then I must have dozed off, because I woke with bluewhite light in my face. The inner moon, Cronus, had risen over the ridge, a cratered disk ten degrees wide, almost full, looking close enough to jump up and bang my head on, if I'd felt like jumping. I didn't.

We made good time in the moonlight, considering the slope of the glacier's skirt we were climbing. At forty-five thousand feet, we topped the barrier and looked down the far side and across a shadowed valley to the next ridge, twenty miles away, silver-white against the stars.

"Perhaps on the other side we will find them," the giant said. His voice had lost some of its timbre. His face looked frostbitten, pounded numb by the sub-zero wind. Woola crouched behind him, looking shrunken and old.

"Sure," I said. "Or maybe beyond the next one, or the one after that."

"Beyond these ridges lie the Towers of Nandi. If your friends have fallen there, their sleep will be long— and ours as well."

It was two marches to the next ridge. By then the moon was high enough to illuminate the whole panorama from the crest. There was nothing in sight but ice. We camped in the lee of the crest, then went on. The suit was giving me trouble, unbalanced as it was, and the toes of my right foot were feeling the frost.

Sometime, about mid-afternoon, I noticed we'd veered off our route as if to skirt a mesa-like rock formation ahead. I registered a gripe about the extra mileage and proposed to get back to the direct route.

"Go if you will, Carl Patton. Perhaps I have not been fair to you, thus to indulge my personal taboo."

"What's that supposed to mean?" I yelled at him. I was too beat to be diplomatic. He ignored the bad manners and turned to look at the mesa.

"Yonder rises Hel," he said. "I would prefer not to know the fate of my sisters and their young."

I did a 'shucks, fella, I didn't mean . . .' number, and we went on, following his detour. An hour or two later, Woola, scouting ahead, halted and began skirting something that looked like a low mound of snow. Then she whined and her ears and tail drooped. She turned and came back to put up a paw for Johnny Thunder to take while he patted the big shaggy head. He went forward to look at what she'd found and I trailed along, wondering what it was that could make the old war-dog wilt like a whipped puppy. The giant had knelt to brush away snow, and when I came around him I saw the face, as beautiful as any ancient image of a love goddess, and on the same heroic scale; a young face, almost smiling, with a lock of red-gold hair across the noble ice-pale forehead. All of a sudden I was all out of wisecracks. Here was a beauty that wars could have been fought over, dead and frozen these hundred years. Too bad I didn't have the magic spell that would waken her.

"Adainn was the youngest," the giant said. "Only a girl, barely of marriageable age. Now she is the bride of the ice, lying in his cold embrace."

"Good looking dolly," I said, and all of a sudden I felt a sense of loss that almost blacked me out. I heard myself saying "No, no! NO!" and struggling against Johnny's big arm, barring my way, while Woola rose from her haunches, and took a position standing protectively over the corpse. After a while I was sitting in the snow, with water running out of my eyes and freezing, and big Johnny saying:

"Be none ashamed, Carl. Any man must love her when he sees her, be he large or small."

I told him he was nuts, and got up and arranged my load, not looking at her somehow, for some reason, and then Johnny covered her face again, and said, "Fare thee well, my little sister. Now we must tend the living," and we went on. Johnny was more silent than usual all day, and in spite of the hot concentrates I sucked on the sly as I hiked, and the synthetic pep the hypospray metered into an artery, I was starting to feel it now. But not as badly as Big Johnny. He had a gaunt, starved look, and he hiked as though he had anvils tied to his feet. He was still feeding himself and the dog meager rations, and forcing an equal share on me. When he wasn't looking I stuffed what I couldn't eat in the disposal and watched him starve. But he was tough; he starved slowly, grudgingly, fighting for every inch.

He never complained. He could have gotten up and started back any time, with no apologies. He'd already made a better try than anyone could expect, even of a giant. As for me, all I had to do was picture that fat bank account, and all the big juicy steaks and big soft beds with beautiful women in them and the hand-tooled cars and the penthouse with a view all that cash was going to buy for me. As long as I kept my mind on that, the pain seemed remote and unimportant. Baird Ulrik could take it, all right. And after all, Big Boy was only human, like Woola and me, and as long as he could get up and go on one more time, so could I: I almost felt sorry for the big mutt, who went on just because she couldn't imagine anything else to do, much less a fancy doghouse with plenty of bones but I stifled that. It was no time to be sentimental. At least, Big Johnny was no longer asking me those strangely embarrassing questions of his. The big dope couldn't even imagine treachery and betrayal. And to hell with that, too.

That night, lying back of a barrier he'd built up out of snow blocks against the wind, he asked me a question.

"What is it like, Carl Patton, to travel across the space between the worlds?"

"Solitary confinement," I told him.

"You do not love your solitude?"

"What does that matter? I do my job."

"What do you love, Carl Patton?"

"Wine, women, and song," I said. "And you can even skip the song, in a pinch."

"A woman waits for you?"

"Women," I corrected. "But they're not waiting."

"Your loves seem few, Carl Patton. What then do you hate?"

"Fools," I said.

"Is it fools who have driven you here?"

"Me? Nobody drives me anywhere. I go where I like."

"Then it is freedom you strive for. Have you found it here on my world, Carl Patton?" His face was a gaunt mask like a weathered carving, but his voice was laughing at me.

"You know you're going to die out here, don't you?" I hadn't intended to say that. But I did; and my tone was savage to my own ears.

He looked at me, the way he always did before he spoke, as if he were trying to read a message written on my face.

"A man must die," he said.

"You don't have to be here," I said. "You could break it off now, go back, forget the whole thing."

"As could you, Carl Patton."

"Me quit?" I snapped. "No thanks. My job's not done."

He nodded. "A man must do what he sets out to do.

Else is he no more than a snowflake driven before the wind."

"You think this is a game?" I barked. "A contest? Do or die, or maybe both, and may the best man win?"

"With whom would I contest, Carl Patton? Are we not comrades of the trail?"

"We're strangers," I said. "You don't know me and I don't know you. And you can skip trying to figure out my reasons for what I do."

"You set out to save the lives of the helpless, because it was your duty."

"It's not yours! You don't have to break yourself on these mountains! You can leave this ice factory, live the rest of your days as a hero of the masses, have everything you'd ever want—"

"What I want, no *man* can give me."

"I suppose you hate us," I said. "The strangers that came here and brought a disease that killed your world."

"Who can hate a natural force?"

"All right—what *do* you hate?"

For a minute I thought he wasn't going to answer. "I hate the coward within me," he said. "The voice that whispers counsels of surrender. But if I fled, and saved this flesh, what spirit would then live on to light it?"

"You want to run—then run!" I almost yelled. "You're going to lose this race, big man! Quit while you can!"

"I will go on—while I can. If I am lucky, the flesh will die before the spirit."

"Spirit, hell! You're a suicidal maniac!"

"Then am I in good company, Carl Patton."

I let him take that one.

22

We passed the hundred-mile mark the next march. We crossed another ridge, higher than the last. The cold was sub-arctic, the wind a flaying knife. The moon set, and after a couple of eternities, dawn came. My locator told me when we passed within ten miles of the pod. All its systems were still going. The power cells were good for a hundred years. If I slipped up at my end, the frozen miners might wake up to a new century; but they'd wake up.

Johnny Thunder was a pitiful sight now. His hands were split and bloody, his hollow cheeks and bloodless lips cracked and peeling from frostbite, the hide stretched tight over his bones. He moved slowly, heavily, wrapped in his furs. But he moved. I ranged out ahead, keeping the pressure on. The dog was in even worse shape than her master. She trailed far behind on the up-slopes, spent most of each break catching up. Little by little, in spite of my heckling, the breaks got longer, the marches shorter. The big man knew how to pace himself, in spite of my gadfly presence. He meant to hang on, and make it. So much for my plans. It was late afternoon again when we reached the high pass that the big man said led into the badlands he called the Towers of Nandi. I came up the last stretch of trail between sheer ice walls and looked out over a vista of ice peaks sharp as broken bottles, packed together like shark's teeth, rising up and up in successive ranks that reached as far as the eye could see.

I turned to urge the giant to waste some more strength hurrying to close the gap, but he beat me to it. He was pointing, shouting something I couldn't hear for a low rumble that had started up. I looked up, and the whole side of the mountain was coming down at me.

23

The floor was cold. It was the tiled floor of the creche locker room, and I was ten years old, and lying on my face, held there by the weight of a kid called Soup, age fourteen, with the physique of an ape and an IQ to match.

When he'd first pushed me back against the wall, knocked aside my punches, and thrown me to the floor, I had cried, called for help to the ring of eager-eyed spectators, most of whom had more than once felt the weight of Soup's knobby knuckles. None of them moved. When he'd bounced my head on the floor and called to me to say uncle, I opened my mouth to say it, and then spat in his face instead. What little restraint Soup had left him then. Now his red-bristled forearm was locked under my jaw, and his knee was in the small of my back, and I knew, without a shadow of a doubt, that Soup was a boy who didn't know his own strength, who would stretch his growing muscles with all the force he could muster—caught up and carried away in the thrill of the discovery of his own animal power— would bend my back until my spine snapped, and I'd be dead, dead, dead forevermore, at the hands of a moron.

Unless I saved myself. I was smarter than Soup— smarter than any of them. Man had conquered the animals with his mind—and Soup was an animal. He couldn't—couldn't kill me. Not if I used my brain, instead of wasting my strength against an animal body twice the size of my own.

I stepped outside my body and looked at myself, saw how he knelt on me, gripping his own wrist, balancing with one outflung foot. I saw how, by twisting to my right side, I could slide out from under the knee; and then, with a sudden movement . . .

His knee slipped off-center as I moved under him. With all the power in me, I drew up, doubling my body; unbalanced, he started to topple to his right, still gripping me. I threw myself back against him, which brought my head under his chin. I reached back, took a double handful of coarse red hair, and ripped with all my strength.

He screamed, and his grip was gone. I twisted like an eel as he grabbed for my hands, still tangled in his hair; I lunged and buried my teeth in his thick ear. He howled and tried to tear away, and I felt the cartilage break, tasted salty blood. He ripped my hands away, taking hair and a patch of scalp with them. I saw his face, contorted like a demon-mask as he sprawled away from me, still grasping my wrists. I brought my knee up into his crotch, and saw his face turn to green clay. I jumped to my feet; he writhed, coiled, making an ugly choking sound. I took aim and kicked him hard in the mouth. I landed two more carefully placed kicks, with my full weight behind them, before the rudimentary judgement of the audience awoke and they pulled me away. . . .

There was movement near me. I heard the rasp of something hard and rough against another hardness. Light appeared. I drew a breath, and saw the white-bearded face of an ancient man looking down at me from far above, from the top of a deep well. . . .

"You still live, Carl Patton." The giant's voice seemed to echo from a long way off. I saw his big hands come down, straining at a quarter-ton slab of ice, saw him lift it slowly, toss it aside. There was snow in his hair, ice droplets in his beard. His breath was frost.

"Get out of here." I forced the words out past the broken glass in my chest. "Before the rest comes down."

He didn't answer; he lifted another slab, and my arms were free. I tried to help, but that just made more snow spill down around my shoulders. He put his big impossible hands under my arms and lifted, dragged me up and out of my grave. I lay on my back and he sprawled beside me. The dog Woola crawled up to him, making anxious noises. Little streamers of snow were coming down from above, being whipped away by the wind. A mass of ice the size of a carrier tender hung cantilevered a few hundred feet above.

"Run, you damned fool!" I yelled. It came out as a whisper. He got to his knees, slowly. He scooped me up, rose to his feet. Ice fragments clattered down from above. He took a step forward, toward the badlands.

"Go back," I managed. "You'll be trapped on the far side!"

He halted, as more ice rattled down. "Alone, Carl Patton . . . would *you* turn back?"

"No," I said. "But there's no reason . . . now . . . for you to die. . . ."

"Then we will go on." He took another step, and staggered as a pebble of ice the size of a basketball struck him a glancing blow on the shoulder. The dog snarled at his side. It was coming down around us like rice at a wedding now. He went on, staggering like a drunk, climbing up over the final drift. There was a boom like a cannon-shot from above; air whistled past us, moving out. He made three more paces and went down, dropped me, knelt over me like a shaggy tent. I heard him grunt as the ice fragments struck him. Somewhere behind us there was a smash like a breaking dam. The air was full of snow, blinding, choking. The light faded. . . .

24

The dead were crying. It was a sad, lost sound, full of mournful surprise that life had been so short and so full of mistakes. I understood how they felt. Why shouldn't I? I was one of them.

But corpses didn't have headaches, as well as I could remember. Or cold feet, or weights that crushed them against sharp rocks. Not unless the stories about where the bad ones went were true. I opened my eyes to take a look at Hell, and saw the hound. She whined again, and I got my head around and saw an arm bigger than my leg. The weight I felt was what was left of Johnny Thunder, sprawled across me, under a blanket of broken ice.

It took me half an hour to work my way free. The suit was what had saved me, of course, with its automatic defensive armor. I was bruised, and a rib or two were broken, but there was nothing I couldn't live with until I got back to base and my six million credits.

Because the job was done. The giant didn't move while I was digging out, didn't stir when I thumbed up his eyelid. He still had some pulse, but it wouldn't last long. He had been bleeding from the ice wounds on his face and hands, but the blood had frozen. What the pounding hadn't finished, the cold would. And even if he came around, the wall of ice behind him closed the pass like a vault door. When the sob sisters arrived to check on their oversized pet they'd find him here, just as I would describe him, the noble victim of the weather and the piece of bad luck that had made us

miss our target by a tragic ten miles, after that long,
long hike. They'd have a good syndicated cry over how
he'd given his all, and then close the book on another
footnote to history. It had worked out just the way I'd
planned. Not that I got any big kick out of my clev-
erness once again. It was routine, just a matter of
analyzing the data.

"So long, Johnny Thunder," I said. "You were a lot
of man."

The dog lifted her head and whined. I made soothing sounds and switched the lift-unit built into my suit
to maximum assist and headed for the pod, fifteen
miles away, in *that* direction. I heard Woola's tail flopping as she wagged goodbye. Too bad; but there was
no way I could help a mutt as big as a shire horse.

25

The twenty-foot-long cargo unit was nestled in a drift
of hard-packed snow, in a little hollow among barren
rock peaks, not showing a scratch. I wasn't surprised;
the auto gear I had installed could have soft-landed a
china shop without cracking a teacup. I had contracted
to deliver my load intact, and it was a point of pride with
me to fulfill the letter of a deal. I was so busy congratulating myself on that that I was fifty feet from it before
I noticed that the snow had been disturbed around the
pod: trampled, maybe, then brushed out to conceal the
tracks. By then it was too late to become invisible; if
there was anybody around, he had already seen me. I
stopped ten feet from the entry hatch and went through
the motions of collapsing in a pitiful little heap, all tuck-
ered out from my exertions, meanwhile looking around,
over, and under the pod. I didn't see anything.

I lay where I was long enough for anybody who
wanted to to make his entrance. No takers. That left
the play up to me. I made a production out of getting my feet under me and staggering to the entry
hatch. The scratches there told me that part of the
story. The port mechanism was still intact. It opened
on command and I crawled into the lock. Inside, everything looked normal. The icebox seal was tight, the dials
said the cooler units were operating perfectly, not that
they had a whole lot to do in this natural freezer of
a world. I almost let it go at that, but not quite. I don't
know why, except that a lifetime of painful lessons had
taught me to take nothing for granted. It took me half
an hour to get the covers off the reefer controls. When
I did, I saw it right away: a solenoid hung in the half-
open position. It was the kind of minor malfunction
you might expect after a hard landing—but not if you
knew what I knew. It had been jimmied, the support
bent a fractional millimeter out of line, Just enough
to jam the action—and incidentally to actuate the
heating cycle that would thaw the ten men inside the
cold room in ten hours flat. I freed it, heard gas hiss
into the lines, then cracked the vault door and checked
visually. The inside gauge read +3° absolute. The temperature hadn't had time to start rising yet; the ten long
boxes and their contents were still intact. That meant
the tampering had been done recently. I was still
mulling over the implications of that deduction when
I heard the crunch of feet on the ice outside the open
lock.

26

Illini looked older than he had when I had seen
him last, back in the plush bureaucratic setting of

League Central. His monkey face behind the cold mask looked pinched and bloodless; his long nose was pink with cold, his jaw a scruffy, unshaven blue. He didn't seem surprised to see me. He stepped up through the hatch and a second man followed him. They looked around. Their glance took in the marks in the frost crust around the reefer, and held on the open panel.

"Everything all right here?" the little man asked me. He made it casual, as if we'd just happened to meet on the street.

"Almost," I said. "A little trouble with a solenoid. Nothing serious."

Illini nodded as if that was par for the course. His eyes flickered over me. "Outside, you seemed to be in difficulty," he said. "I see you've made a quick recovery."

"It must have been psychosomatic," I said. "Getting inside took my mind off it."

"I take it the subject is dead?"

"Hell, no," I said. "He's alive and well in Phoenix, Arizona. How did you find the pod, Illini?"

"I was lucky enough to persuade the black marketeer who supplied your homing equipment to sell me its twin, tuned to the same code." He looked mildly amused. "Don't be too distressed, Ulrik. There are very few secrets from an unlimited budget."

"One is enough," I said, "played right. But you haven't said why."

"The scheme you worked out was clever," he said. "Somewhat over-devious, perhaps—but clever. Up to a point. It was apparent from the special equipment installed in the pod that you had some idea of your cargo surviving the affair."

"So?"

"You wanted to present the public with a tidy image

to treasure, Ulrik. Well and good. But the death of a freak in a misguided attempt to rescue men who were never in danger would smack of the comic. People might be dissatisfied. They might begin investigating the circumstances which allowed their pet to waste himself. But if it appears he *might* have saved the men—then the public will accept his martyrdom."

"You plan to spend ten men on the strength of that theory?"

"It's a trivial price to pay for extra insurance."

"And here you are, to correct my mistakes. How do you plan to square it with the Monitor Service? They take a dim view of unauthorized planetfalls."

Illini gave me his I-just-ate-the-canary look. "I'm here quite legally. By great good fortune, my yacht happened to be cruising in the vicinity and picked up your U-beam. Ring Station accepted my offer of assistance."

"I see. And what have you got in mind for me?"

"Just what was agreed on, of course. I have no intention of complicating the situation at this point. We'll proceed with the plan precisely as conceived— with the single exception I've noted. I can rely on your discretion, for obvious reasons. Your fee is already on deposit at Credit Central."

"You've got it all worked out, haven't you?" I said, trying to sound sarcastic. "But you overlooked one thing: I'm temperamental. I don't like people making changes in my plans."

Illini lifted a lip. "I'm aware of your penchant for salving your conscience as a professional assassin by your nicety in other matters. But in this case I'm afraid *my* desires must prevail." The hand of the man behind him strayed casually to the gun at his hip. So far, he hadn't said a word. He didn't have to. He'd be a good man with a sidearm. Illini wouldn't have brought anything but the best. Or maybe the second best. It was a point I'd probably have to check soon.

"Our work here will require only a few hours," Illini said. "After that . . ." he made an expansive gesture. "We're all free to take up other matters." He smiled as though everything had been cleared up. "By the way, where is the body? I'll want to view it, just as a matter of routine."

I folded my arms and leaned against the bulkhead. I did it carefully, just in case I was wrong about a few things. "What if I don't feel like telling you?" I asked him.

"In that case, I'd be forced to insist." Illini's eyes were wary. The gunsel had tensed.

"Uh-uh," I said. "This is a delicate setup; A charred corpse wouldn't help the picture."

"Podnac's instructions are to disable, not to kill."

"For a hired hand, you seem to be taking a lot of chances, Illini. It wouldn't do for the public to get the idea that the selfless motive of eliminating a technicality so that progress could come to Vangard, as the Boss told it, is marred by some private consideration."

Illini lifted his shoulders. "We own an interest in the planetary exploitation contract, yes. Someone was bound to profit. Why not those who made it possible?"

"That's another one on me," I said. "I should have held out for a percentage."

"That's enough gossip," Illini said. "Don't try to stall me, Ulrik. Speak up or suffer the consequences."

I shook my head. "I'm calling your bluff, Illini. The whole thing is balanced on a knife's edge. Any sign of trouble here—even a grease spot on the deck—and the whole thing is blown."

Podnac made a quick move and his gun was in his hand. I grinned at it. "That's supposed to scare me so I go outside where you can work a little better, eh?"

"I'm warning you, Ulrik—"

"Skip it. I'm not going anywhere. But you're leaving, Illini. You've got your boat parked somewhere near here. Get in it and lift off. I'll take it from there."

"You fool! You'd risk the entire operation for the sake of a piece of mawkish sentiment?"

"It's my operation, Illini. I'll play it out my way or not at all. I'm like that. That's why you hired me, remember?"

He drew a breath like a man getting ready for a deep dive, snorted it out. "You don't have a chance, Ulrik! You're throwing everything away—for what?"

"Not quite everything. You'll still pay off for a finished job. It's up to you. You can report you checked the pod and found everything normal. Try anything else and the bubble pops."

"There are two of us. We could take you barehanded."

"Not while I've got my hand on the gun under my arm."

The little man's eyes ate me raw. There were things he wanted to say, but instead he made a face like a man chewing glass and jerked his head at his hired hand. They walked sideways to the hatch and jumped down. I watched them back away.

"I'll get you for this," Illini told me when he finally decided I was bluffing. "I promise you that," he added.

"No, you won't," I said. "You'll just count those millions and keep your mouth shut. That's the way the Boss would like it."

They turned and I straightened and dropped my hands. Podnac spun and fired and the impact knocked me backward twenty feet across the hold.

The world was full of roaring lights and blazing sounds, but I held onto a slender thread of consciousness, built it into a rope, crawled back up it. I did it because I had to. I made it just in time. Podnac was coming through the hatch, Illini's voice yapping behind him. I covered him and pressed the stud and blew him back out of sight.

27

I was numb all over, like a thumb that's just been hit by a hammer. I felt hot fluid trickling down the inside of my suit, felt broken bones grate. I tried to move and almost blacked out. I knew then: this was one scrape I wouldn't get out of. I'd had it. Illini had won.

His voice jarred me out of a daze.

"He fired against my order, Ulrik! You heard me tell him! I'm not responsible!"

I blinked a few times and could see the little man through the open port, standing in a half crouch on the spot where I'd last seen him, watching the dark hatchway for the flash that would finish him. He was holding the winning cards, and didn't know it. He didn't know how hard I'd been hit, that he could have strolled in and finished the job with no opposition. He thought tough, smart Baird Ulrik had rolled with another punch, was holding on him now, cool and deadly and in charge of everything.

OK. I'd do my best to keep him thinking that. I was done for, but so was he—if I could con him into leaving now. When the Monitors showed up and found my corpse and the note I'd manage to write before the final night closed down, Illini and Company would be out of the planet-stealing business and into a penal colony before you could say malfeasance in high office. I looked around for my voice, breathed on it a little, and called:

"We won't count that one, Illini. Take your boy and lift off. I'll be watching. So will the Monitor scopes. If you try to land again you'll have them to explain to."

"I'll do as you say, Ulrik. It's your show. I . . . I'll have to use a lift harness on Podnac."

I didn't answer that one. I couldn't. That worried Illini.

"Ulrik? I'm going to report that I found everything in order. Don't do anything foolish. Remember your six million credits."

"Get going," I managed. I watched him back up a few steps, then turn and scramble up the slope. The lights kept fading and coming up again.

Quite suddenly Illini was there again, guiding the slack body of his protégé as it hung in the harness. When I looked again they were gone. Then I let go of whatever it was I had been hanging onto, and fell forever through endlessness.

When I woke up, Johnny Thunder was sitting beside me.

28

He gave me water. I drank it and said, "You big, dumb ox! What are you doing here?" I said that, but all that came out was a dry wheeze, like a collapsing lung. I lay with my head propped against the wall, the way he had laid me out, and looked at the big, gaunt face, the cracked and peeling lips, the matted hair caked with ice, the bright blue eyes fixed on mine.

"I woke and found you had gone, Carl Patton." His voice had lost its resonance. He sounded like an old man. "Woola led me here."

I thought that over—and then I saw it. It almost

made me grin. A note written in blood might poke a
hole in Illini's plans—but a live giant would sink them
with all hands.

I made another try and managed a passable whisper: "Listen to me, Johnny. Listen hard, because once
is all you're likely to get it. This whole thing was a fix—
a trick to get you dead. Because as long as you were
alive, they couldn't touch your world. The men here
were never in danger. At least they weren't meant to
be. But there was a change in plan. But that's only after
you're taken care of. And if you're alive . . ." It was
getting too complicated.

"Never mind that," I said. "You outsmarted 'em.
Outsmarted all of us. You're alive after all. Now the
trick is to stay that way. So you lie low. There's heat
and emergency food stores here, all you need until
pickup. And then you'll have it made. There was a
jammed solenoid, you understand? You know what a
solenoid looks like? And you freed it. You saved the
men. You'll be a hero. They won't dare touch you
then . . . ."

"You are badly hurt, Carl Patton—"

"My name's not Carl Patton, damn you! It's Ulrik!
I'm a hired killer, understand? I came here to finish
you—"

"You have lost much blood, Ulrik. Are there medical supplies here?"

"Nothing that will help me. I took a power gun blast
in the hip. My left thigh is nothing but bone splinters
and hamburger. The suit helped me some—but not
enough. But forget that. What's important is that they
don't know you're alive! If they sneak back for another
look and discover you—before the relief crew gets
here—then they win. And they can't win, understand?
I won't let 'em!"

"At my house there is a medical machine, Ulrik,"

Big Boy told me. "Doctors placed it there, after the Sickness. It can heal you."

"Sure—and at med center they'd have me dancing the Somali in thirty-six hours. And if I'd stayed away, I wouldn't have been in this fix at all! Forget all that and concentrate on staying alive. . . ."

I must have faded out then, because the next I knew someone was sticking dull knives in my side. I got my eyelids up and saw my suit open and lots of blood. Big Johnny was doing things to my leg. I told him to leave me alone, but he went on sawing at me with red-hot saws, pouring hot acid into the wounds. And then after a while I was coming up from a long way down, looking at my leg, bandaged to the hip with tape from the first aid locker.

"You have much strength left, Ulrik," he said. "You fought me like the frost-demon."

I wanted to tell him to let it alone, let me die in peace, but no sound came out. The giant was on his feet, wrapped in purple and green fur. He squatted and picked me up, turned to the port. I tried again to yell, to tell him that the play now was to salvage the only thing left: revenge. That he'd had his turn at playing Saint Bernard to the rescue, that another hopeless walk in the snow would only mean that Podnac and Illini had won after all, that my bluff had been for nothing. But it was no use. I felt him stagger as the wind hit him, heard my suit thermostat click on. Then the cotton-wool blanket closed over me.

29

I don't remember much about the trip back. The suit's metabolic monitors kept me doped—those and nature's defenses against the sensation of being carried over a shoulder through a blizzard, while the bone chips separated and began working their way through the crushed flesh of my thigh. Once I looked into the big frost-scarred face, met the pain-dulled eyes.

"Leave me here," I said. "I don't want help. Not from you, not from anybody. I win or lose on my own."

He shook his head.

"Why?" I said. "Why are you doing it?"

"A man," he said. "A man . . . must do . . . what he sets out to do."

He went on. He was a corpse, but he wouldn't lie down and die.

I ate and drank from the tubes in my mouth from reflex. If I'd been fully awake I'd have starved myself to shorten the ordeal. Sometimes I was conscious for a half an hour at a stretch, knowing how a quarter of beef felt on the butcher's hook; and other times I slept and dreamed I had passed the entrance exams for Hell. A few times I was aware of falling, of lying in the snow, and then of big hands that painfully lifted, grunting; of the big, tortured body plodding on.

Then there was another fall, somehow more final than the others. For a long time I lay where I was, waiting to die. And after a while it got through to me that the suit wouldn't let me go as easily as that. The food and the auto-drugs that would keep a healthy man healthy for a year would keep a dying man in torture for almost as long. I was stuck on this side of the river, like it or not. I opened my eyes to tell the giant what I thought of that, but didn't see him: what I did see was his house, looming tall against the big trees a hundred yards away. It didn't take me more than a day to crawl to it. I did it a hundred miles at a time, over a blanket of broken bottles. The door resisted for a while, but in the end I got my weight against it and it swung in and dumped me on the plank floor. After that there was another long, fuzzy time while I clawed my way to the oversized med cabinet, got it opened, and fell inside. I heard the diagnostic unit start up, felt the sensors moving over me. Then I didn't know any more for a long, long time.

30

This time I came out of it clearheaded, hungry, pain-free, and with a walking cast on my leg. I looked around for my host, but I was all alone in the big lodge. There was no cheery blaze on the hearth, but the house was as hot as a skid-row flop in summertime. At some time in the past, the do-gooders had installed a space heater with automatic controls to keep the giant cozy if the fire went out. I found some food on the shelves and tried out my jaws for the first time in many days. It was pain-ful, but satisfying. I fired up the comm rig and got ready to tell the Universe my story. Then I remem-bered there were still a few details to clear up. I went to the door with a vague idea of seeing if Johnny Thunder was outside, chopping wood for exercise. All I saw was a stretch of wind-packed snow, the backdrop of giant trees, the gray sky hanging low overhead like wet canvas. Then I noticed something else: an oblong drift of snow, half-way between me and the forest wall.

The sound of snow crust crunching under my feet was almost explosively loud in the stillness as I walked across to the long mound. He lay on his back, his eyes open to the sky, glazed over with ice. His arms were bent at the elbow, the hands open as if he were car-rying a baby. The snow was drifted over him, like a blanket to warm him in his sleep. The dog was beside him, frozen at her post.

I looked at the giant for a long time, and words stirred inside me: things that needed a voice to carry them across the gulf wider than space to where he had gone. But all I said was: "You made it, Johnny. We were the smart ones; but you were the one that did what you set out to do."

31

I flipped up the SEND key, ready to fire the blast that would sink Podnac and crew like a lead canoe; but then the small, wise voice of discretion started whispering at me. Nailing them would have been a swell gesture for me to perform as a corpse, frozen with a leer of triumph on my face, thumbing my nose from the grave. I might even have had a case for blowing them sky-high to save Johnny Thunder's frozen paradise for him, in view of the double-cross they'd tried on me.

But I was alive, and Johnny was dead. And six million was still waiting. There was nothing back at the pod that couldn't be explained in terms of the big bad scorpion that had gnawed my leg. Johnny would be a hero, and they'd put up a nice marker for him on some spot the excavating rigs didn't chew up—I'd see to that.

In the end I did the smart thing, the shrewd thing. I told them what they wanted to hear; that the men were safe, and that the giant had died a hero like a giant should. Then I settled down to wait for the relief boat.

32

I collected. Since then I've been semi-retired. That's a nice way of saying that I haven't admitted to myself that I'm not taking any more assignments. I've spent my time for the past year traveling, seeing the sights, trying out the luxury spots, using up a part of the income on the pile I stashed away. I've eaten and drunk and wenched and sampled all the kicks from air-skiing to deep-sea walking, but whatever it is I'm looking for, I have a hunch I won't find it, any more than the rest of the drones and thrill-seekers will.

It's a big, impersonal Universe, and little men crave the thing that will give them stature against the loom of stars.

But in a world where once there was a giant, the rest of us are forever pygmies.

DINOSAUR BEACH

1

It was a pleasant summer evening. We were sitting on the porch swing, Lisa and I, watching the last of the pink fade out of the sky and listening to Fred Hunnicut pushing a lawn mower over his weed crop next door. A cricket in the woodwork started up his fiddle, sounding businesslike and full of energy. A car rattled by, its weak yellow headlights pushing shadows along the brick street and reflecting in the foliage of the sycamores that arched over the pavement. Somewhere a radio sang about harbor lights.

A pleasant evening, a pleasant place. I hated to leave it. But I took a breath of crisp air lightly laced with leafsmoke and newcut grass and got to my feet.

Lisa looked up at me. She had a heart-shaped face, and a short nose, and big, wide-spaced eyes and the prettiest smile in the world. Even the tiny scar on her cheekbone only added to her charm: the flaw that makes perfection perfect.

"Think I'll walk down to Simon's for some beer," I said.

"Dinner will be ready when you get back, darlin'," she said, and smiled the smile. "Baked ham and corn on the cob."

She stood and moved against me all in one fluid dancer's motion, and her lips touched my ear.

I went down the steps and paused on the walk to look back and see her silhouetted against the lighted screen door, slim and graceful.

"Hurry back, darlin'," she said, and waved and was gone.

Gone forever.

She didn't know I wouldn't be coming back.

2

A streetcar clacked and sparked past the intersection, a big toy with cutout heads pasted against the row of little square windows. Horns tooted. Traffic lights winked. People hurried past, on their way home after a long day in the store or the office or the cement plant. I bucked the tide, not hurrying, not dawdling. I had plenty of time. That was one lesson I'd learned. You can't speed it up, you can't slow it down. Sometimes you can avoid it completely, but that's a different matter.

These reflections carried me the four blocks to the taxi stand on Delaware. I climbed in the back of a Reo that looked as if it should have been retired a decade back and told the man where I wanted to go. He gave me a look that wondered what a cleancut young fellow like me wanted in that part of town. He opened his mouth to say it, and I said, "Make it under seven minutes and there's five in it."

He dropped the flag and almost tore the clutch out of the Reo getting away from the curb. All the way there he watched me in the mirror, mentally trying out various approaches to the questions he wanted to ask. I saw the neon letters, the color of red-hot iron, half a block ahead and pulled him over, shoved the five into his hand and was on my way before he'd figured out just how to phrase it.

It was a shabby-genteel cocktail bar, the class of the neighborhood, with two steps down into a room that had been a nice one once, well before Prohibition. The dark paneled walls hadn't suffered much from the years, and aside from a patina of grime, the figured ceiling was passable; but the maroon carpet had a wide, worn strip that meandered like a jungle trail across to the long bar, branching off to get lost among the chair legs. The solid leather seats in the booths along the wall had lost a lot of their color, and some of their stitching had been patched with tape; and nobody had bothered to polish away the rings left by generations of beers on the oak tabletops. I took a booth halfway back, with a little brass lamp with a parchment shade and a framed print on the wall showing somebody's champion steeplechaser circa 1910. The clock over the bar said 7:44.

I ordered a grenadine from a waitress who'd been in her prime about the same time as the bar. She brought it and I took a sip and a man slid into the seat across from me. He took a couple of breaths as if he'd just finished a brisk lap around the track, and said, "Do you mind?" He waved the glass in his hand at the room, which was crowded, but not that crowded.

I took my time looking him over. He had a soft, round face, very pale blue eyes, the kind of head that ought to be bald but was covered with a fine blond down, like baby chicken feathers. He was wearing a striped shirt with the open collar laid back over a bulky plaid jacket with padded shoulders and wide lapels. His neck was smooth-skinned, and too thin for his head. The hand that was holding the glass was small and well-lotioned, with short, immaculately manicured nails. He wore a big, cumbersome-looking gold ring with a glass ruby big enough for a paperweight on his left index finger. The whole composition looked a little out of tune, as if it had been put together in a hurry by someone with more important things on his mind.

"Please don't get the wrong impression," he said. His voice was like the rest of him: not feminine enough for a woman, but nothing you'd associate with a room full of cigar smoke, either.

"It's vital that I speak to you, Mr. Ravel," he went on, talking fast, getting it said before it was too late. "It's a matter of great importance . . . to your future." He paused to check the effect of his words: a tentative sort of pause, as if he might jump either way, depending on my reaction.

I said, "My future, eh? I wasn't sure I had one."

He liked that; I could see it in the change in the glitter of his eyes. "Oh, yes," he said, and nodded comfortably. "Yes indeed." He took a quick swallow from the glass and lowered it and caught and held my eyes, smiling an elusive little smile. "And I might add that your future is—or can be—a great deal larger than your past."

"Have we met somewhere?" I asked him.

He shook his head. "I know this doesn't make a great deal of sense to you just now—but time is of the essence. Please listen—"

"I'm listening, Mr.—what was the name?"

"It really doesn't matter, Mr. Ravel. I don't enter into the matter at all except as the bearer of a message. I was assigned to contact you and deliver certain information."

"Assigned?"

He shrugged.

I reached across and caught the wrist of the hand that was holding the glass. It was as smooth and soft as a baby's. I applied a small amount of pressure. Some of the drink slopped on the edge of the table and into his lap. He tensed a little, as if he wanted to stand, but I pressed him back. "Let me play too," I said. "Let's go back to where you were telling me about your assignment. I find that sort of intriguing. Who thinks I'm important enough to assign a smooth cookie like you to snoop on?" I grinned at him while he got his smile fixed up and back in place, a little bent now, but still working.

"Mr. Ravel—what would you say if I told you that I am a member of a secret organization of supermen?"

"What would you expect me to say?"

"That I'm insane," he said promptly. "That's why I'd hoped to skirt the subject and go directly to the point. Mr. Ravel, your life is in danger."

I let that hang in the air between us.

"In precisely—" he glanced down at the watch strapped English-style to the underside of his free wrist "—one and one-half minutes a man will enter this establishment. He will be dressed in a costume of black, and will carry a cane—ebony, with a silver head. He will go to the fourth stool at the bar, order a straight whiskey, drink it, turn, raise the cane, and fire three lethal darts into your chest."

I took another swallow of my drink. It was the real stuff; one of the compensations of the job.

"Neat," I said. "What does he do for an encore?"

My little man looked a bit startled. "You jape, Mr. Ravel? I'm speaking of your death. Here. In a matter of seconds!" He leaned across the table to throw this at me, with quite a lot of spit.

"Well, I guess that's that," I said, and let go his arm and raised my glass to him. "Don't go spending a lot of money on a fancy funeral."

It was his turn to grab me. His fat little hand closed on my arm with more power than I'd given him credit for.

"I've been telling you what will happen—*unless* you act at once to avert it!"

"Aha. That's where that big future you mentioned comes in."

"Mr. Ravel—you must leave here at once." He fumbled in a pocket of his coat, brought out a card with an address printed on it: 356 Colvin Court.

"It's an old building, very stable, quite near here. There's an exterior wooden staircase, quite safe. Go to the third floor. A room marked with the numeral 9 is at the back. Enter the room and wait."

"Why should I do all that?" I asked him, and pried his fingers loose from my sleeve.

"In order to save your life!" He sounded a little wild now, as if things weren't working out quite right for him. That suited me fine. I had a distinct feeling that what was right for him might not be best for me and my big future.

"Where'd you get my name?" I asked him.

"Please—time is short. Won't you simply trust me?"

"The name's a phony," I said. "I gave it to a Bible salesman yesterday. Made it up on the spot. You're not in the book-peddling racket, are you, Mr. Ah?"

"Does that matter more than your life?"

"You're mixed up, pal. It's not my life we're dickering for. It's yours."

His earnest look went all to pieces. He was still trying to reassemble it when the street door opened and a man in a black overcoat, black velvet collar, black homburg, and carrying a black swagger stick walked in.

"You see?" My new chum slid the whisper across the table like a dirty picture. "Just as I said. You'll have to act swiftly now, Mr. Ravel, before he sees you—"

"Your technique is slipping," I said. "He had me pat right down to my shoe size before he was halfway through the door." I brushed his hand away and slid out of the booth. The man in black had gone across to the bar and taken the fourth stool, without looking my way. I picked my way between the tables and took the stool on his left.

He didn't look at me, not even when my elbow brushed his side a little harder than strict etiquette allowed. If there was a gun in his pocket, I couldn't feel it. He had propped the cane against his knees, the big silver head an inch or two from his hand. I leaned a little toward him.

"Watch it, the caper's blown," I said about eight inches from his ear.

He took it calmly. His head turned slowly until it was facing me. He had a high, narrow forehead, hollow cheeks, white lines around his nostrils against gray skin. His eyes looked like little black stones.

"Are you addressing me?" he said in a voice with a chill like Scott's last camp on the icecap.

"Who is he?" I said in a tone that suggested that a couple of smart boys ought to be able to get together and swap confidences.

"Who?" No thaw yet.

"The haberdasher's delight with the hands you hate to touch," I said. "The little guy I was sitting with. He's waiting over in the booth to see how it turns out." I let him have a sample of my frank and open smile.

"You've made an error," Blackie said, and turned away.

"Don't feel bad," I said. "Nobody's perfect. The way

I see it—why don't we get together and talk it over—the three of us?"

That got to him; his head jerked—about a millionth of an inch. He slid off his stool, picked up his hat. My foot touched the cane as he reached for it; it fell with a lot of clatter. I accidentally put a foot on it while picking it up for him. Something made a small crunching sound.

"Oops," I said, "sorry and all that," and handed it over. He grabbed it and headed for the men's room. I almost watched him too long; from the corner of my eye I saw my drinking buddy sliding toward the street exit. I caught him a few yards along the avenue, eased him over against the wall. He fought as well as you can fight when you don't want to attract the attention of the passersby.

"Tell me things," I said. "After I bought the mind-reading act, what was next?"

"You fool—you're not out of danger yet! I'm trying to save your life—have you no sense of gratitude?"

"If you only knew, chum. What makes it worth the trouble? My suit wouldn't fit you—and the cash in my pockets wouldn't pay cab fare over to Colvin Court and back. But I guess I wouldn't have been coming back."

"Let me go! We must get off the street!" He tried to kick my ankle, and I socked him under the ribs hard enough to fold him against me wheezing like a bagpipe. The weight made me take a quick step back and I heard a flat *whup!* like a silenced pistol and heard the whicker that a bullet makes when it passes an inch from your ear. There was a deep doorway a few feet away. We made it in one jump. My little pal tried to wreck my knee, and I had to bruise his shins a little.

"Take it easy," I said. "That slug changes things. Quiet down and I'll let go your neck."

He nodded as well as he could with my thumb

where it was, and I let up on him. He did some hard breathing and tugged at his collar. His round face looked a bit lopsided now, and the China-blue eyes had lost their baby stare. I made a little production of levering back the hammer of my Mauser, waiting for what came next.

Two or three minutes went past like geologic ages.

"He's gone," the little man said in a flat voice. "They'll chalk this up as an abort and try again. You've escaped nothing, merely postponed it."

"Sufficient unto the day and all that sort of thing," I said. "Let's test the water. You first." I nudged him forward with the gun. Nobody shot at him. I risked a look. No black overcoats in sight.

"Where's your car?" I asked. He nodded toward a black Marmon parked across the street. I walked him across and waited while he slid in under the wheel, then I got in the back. There were other parked cars, and plenty of dark windows for a sniper to work from, but nobody did.

"Any booze at your place?" I said.

"Why—yes—of course." He tried not to look pleased.

He drove badly, like a middle-aged widow after six lessons. We clashed gears and ran stoplights across town to the street he had named. It was a poorly lit macadam dead end that rose steeply toward a tangle of telephone poles at the top. The house was tall and narrow, slanted against the sky, the windows black and empty. He pulled into a drive that was two strips of cracked concrete with weeds in the middle, led the way back along the side of the house past the wooden steps he'd mentioned, used a key on a side door. It resisted a little, then swung in on warped linoleum and the smell of last week's cabbage soup. I followed him in and stopped to listen to some dense silence.

"Don't be concerned," the little man said. "There's

no one here." He led me along a passage a little wider
than my elbows, past a tarnished mirror, a stand full
of furled umbrellas, and a hat tree with no hats, up
steep steps with black rubber matting held in place by
tarnished brass rods. The flooring creaked on the landing. A tall clock was stopped with the hands at ten past
three. We came out in a low-ceilinged hall with flowery
brown wallpaper and dark-painted doors made visible
by the pale light coming through a curtained window
at the end.

He found number 9, put an ear against it, opened
up and ushered me in.

It was a small bedroom with a hard-looking double
bed under a chenille spread, a brown wooden dresser
with a string doily, a straight chair with wire to hold
the legs together, a rocker that didn't match, an oval
hooked rug in various shades of dried mud, a hanging fixture in the center of the ceiling with three small
bulbs, one of which worked.

"Some class," I said. "You must have come into
dough."

"Just temporary quarters," he said off-handedly. He
placed the chairs in a cozy *tête-à-tête* arrangement
under the light, offered me the rocker, and perched
on the edge of the other.

"Now," he said, and put his fingertips together
comfortably, like a pawnbroker getting ready to bid low
on distress merchandise, "I suppose you want to hear
all about the man in black, how I knew just when he'd
appear, and so on."

"Not especially," I said. "What I'm wondering is what
made you think you could get away with it."

"I'm afraid I don't quite understand," he said, and
cocked his head sideways.

"It was a neat routine," I said. "Up to a point. After
you fingered me, if I didn't buy the act, Blackie would

plug me—with a dope dart. If I did—I'd be so grateful, I'd come here."

"As indeed you have." My little man looked less diffident now, more relaxed, less eager to please. A lot less eager to please.

"Your mistake," I said, "was in trying to work too many angles at once. What did you have in mind for Blackie—after?"

His face went stiff "After—what?"

"Whatever it was, it wouldn't have worked," I said. "He was onto you, too."

" . . . too?" He leaned forward as if puzzled and made a nice hip draw and showed me a strange-looking little gun, all shiny rods and levers.

"You will now tell me all about yourself, Mr. Ravel— or whatever you choose to call yourself."

"Wrong again—Karg," I said.

For an instant it didn't register. Then his fingers twitched and the gun made a spitting sound and needles showered off my chest. I let him fire the full magazine. Then I lifted the pistol I had palmed while he was arranging the chairs, and shot him under the left eye.

He settled in his chair. His head was bent back over his left shoulder as if he were admiring the water spots on the ceiling. His little pudgy hands opened and closed a couple of times. He leaned sideways quite slowly and hit the floor like two hundred pounds of heavy machinery.

Which he was, of course.

3

I went over to the door and listened for sounds that would indicate that someone had heard the shots and felt curious about them. Apparently nobody had. It was that kind of neighborhood.

I laid the Karg out on its back and cut the seal on its reel compartment, lifted out the tape it had been operating on.

It had been suspected back at Central that something outside the usual pattern had been going on back here in the Old Era theater of operations. But not even the Master Timecaster had suspected collusion between Second and Third Era operatives. The tape might be the key the Nexx planners were looking for.

But I still had my professional responsibilities. I suppressed the impulse to cut-and-run and got on with the business at hand.

The tape was almost spent, meaning the Karg's mission had been almost completed. Well, true enough, but not in quite the way that had been intended. I tucked the reel away in the zip-down pocket inside my shirt and checked the robot's pockets—all empty—then stripped it and looked for the ID data, found it printed on the left sole.

It took me twenty minutes to go over the room. I found a brainreader focused on the rocker from one of the dead bulbs in the ceiling light. The Karg had gone to a lot of trouble to make sure he cleaned me before disposing of the remains. I recorded my scan to four-point detail, fussed around a few minutes longer rechecking what I'd already checked, but I was just stalling. I'd done what I'd come here to do. The sequence of events had gone off more or less as planned back at Nexx Central; decoying the Karg into a lonely place for disposal wrapped up the operation. It was time to report in and debrief and get on with the business of remaking the cosmos. I pushed his destruct button, switched off the light, and left the room.

Back down in the street a big square car went by,

making a lot of noise in the silence, but no bullets squirted from it. I was almost disappointed. But what the hell: the job was over. My stay here had been nice, but so had a lot of other times and places. This job was no different from any other. I thought about Lisa, waiting for me back at the little house we'd rented six weeks ago, after our four-day honeymoon at Niagara. She'd be getting anxious about now, trying to keep the dinner hot, and wondering what was keeping me. . . .

"Forget it," I told myself out loud. "Just get your skull under the cepher and wipe the whole thing, like you always do. You may ache a little for a while, but you won't know why. It's just another hazard of the profession."

I checked my locator and started east, downslope. My game of cat and terrier with the Karg had covered several square miles of the city of Buffalo, New York, T. F. date, 1936. A quick review of my movements from the time of my arrival at the locus told me that I was about a mile and a half from the pickup area, thirty minutes' walk. I put my thoughts out of gear and did it in twenty-five. I was at the edge of a small park when the gauges said I was within the acceptable point/point range for a transfer back to my Timecast station. A curving path led past a bench and a thick clump of juniper. I stepped into deep shadow—just in case unseen eyes were on me—and tapped out the recall code with my tongue against the trick molars set in my lower jaw; there was a momentary pause before I felt the pickup field impinge on me, then the silent impact of temporal implosion made the ground jump under my feet—

And I was squinting against the dazzling sunlight glaring on Dinosaur Beach.

4

Dinosaur Beach had been so named because a troop of small allosaur-like reptiles had been scurrying along it when the first siting party had fixed in there. That had been sixty years ago, Nexx Subjective, only a few months after the decision to implement Project Timesweep.

The idea wasn't without logic. The First Era of time travel had closely resembled the dawn of the space age in some ways—notably, in the trail of rubbish it left behind. In the case of the space garbage, it had taken half a dozen major collisions to convince the early space authorities of the need to sweep circumterrestrial space clean of fifty years debris in the form of spent rocket casings, defunct telemetry gear, and derelict relay satellites long lost track of. In the process they'd turned up a surprising number of odds and ends, including lumps of meteoric rock and iron, chondrites of clearly earthly origin, possibly volcanic, the mummified body of an astronaut lost on an early space walk, and a number of artifacts that the authorities of the day had scratched their heads over and finally written off as the equivalent of empty beer cans tossed out by visitors from out-system.

That was long before the days of Timecasting, of course.

The Timesweep program was a close parallel to the space sweep. The Old Era temporal experimenters had littered the timeways with everything from early one-way timecans to observation stations, dead bodies, abandoned instruments, weapons and equipment of all sorts, including an automatic mining setup established under the Antarctic icecap which caused headaches at the time of the Big Melt.

Then the three hundred years of the Last Peace put an end to that; and when temporal transfer was rediscovered in early New Era times, the lesson had been heeded. Rigid rules were enforced from the beginning of the Second Program, forbidding all the mistakes that had been made by the First Program pioneers.

Which meant that the Second Program had to invent its own disasters—which it had, in full measure. Thus the Kargs.

Karg: a corruption of "cargo," referring to the legal decision as to the status of the machine-men in the great Transport Accommodation Riots of the mid-Twenty-eighth Century.

Kargs, lifeless machines, sent back from the Third Era in the second great Timesweep attempt, designed to correct not only the carnage irresponsibly strewn across the centuries by the Old Era temporal explorers, but to eliminate the even more disastrous effects of the Second Program Enforcers.

The Third Era had recognized the impossibility of correcting the effects of human interference with more human interference. Machines which registered neutral on the life-balance scales could do what men could not do: could manipulate affairs without disturbing the delicate and poorly understood equations of vital equilibrium, to restore the integrity of the Temporal Core.

Or so they thought. After the Great Collapse and the long night that followed, Nexx Central had arisen to control the Fourth Era. The Nexx Timecasters saw clearly that the tamperings of prior eras were all part of a grand pattern of confusion; that any effort to manipulate reality via temporal policing was doomed only to further weaken the temporal fabric.

When you patch time, you poke holes in it; and patching the patches makes more holes, requiring still larger patches. It's a geometric progression that soon gets out of hand; each successive salvage job sends out waves of entropic dislocation that mingle with, reinforce, and complicate the earlier waves—and no amount of paddling the surface of a roiled pond is going to restore it to a mirror surface.

The only solution, Nexx Central realized, was to remove the first causes of the original dislocations. In the beginning, of course, the disturbances set up by Old Era travelers were mere random violations of the fabric of time, created as casually and as carelessly as footprints in the jungle. Later, when it had dawned on them that every movement of a grain of sand had repercussions that went spreading down the ages, they had become careful. Rules had been made, and even enforced from time to time. When the first absolute prohibition of time meddling came along, it was already far too late. Subsequent eras faced the fact that picnics in the Paleozoic might be fun, but exacted a heavy price in the form of temporal discontinuities, aborted entropy lines, and probability anomalies. Of course, Nexx, arising as it did from this adulterated past, owed its existence to it; careful tailoring was required to undo just enough damage to restore vitality to selected lines while not eliminating the eliminator. Superior minds had to be selected and trained to handle the task.

Thus, my job as a Nexx field agent: to cancel out the efforts of all of them—good and bad, constructive or destructive; to allow the wounds in time to heal, for the great stem of life to grow strong again.

It was a worthy profession, worth all it cost. Or so the rule book said.

I started off along the shore, keeping to the damp sand where the going was easier, skirting the small tidal pools and the curving arcs of sea scum left by the retreating tide.

The sea in this era—some sixty-five million years

B.C.—was South-Sea-island blue, stretching wide and placid to the horizon. There were no sails, no smudges of smoke, no beer cans washing in the tide. But the long swells coming in off the Eastern Ocean—which would one day become the Atlantic—crashed on the white sand with the same familiar *carrump—whoosh!* that I had known in a dozen eras. It was a comforting sound. It said that after all, the doings of the little creatures that scuttled on her shores were nothing much in the life of Mother Ocean, age five billion and not yet in her prime.

The station was a quarter of a mile along the beach, just beyond the low headland that jutted out into the surf; a small, low, gray-white structure perched on the sand above the high-tide line, surrounded by tree ferns and club mosses, both for decoration and to render the installation as inconspicuous as possible, on the theory that if the wildlife were either attracted or repelled by a strange element in their habitat, uncharted U-lines might be introduced into the probability matrix that would render a thousand years of painstaking—and painful—temporal mapping invalid.

In a few minutes I'd be making my report to Nel Jard, the Chief Timecaster. He'd listen, ask a few questions, punch his notes into the Masterplot and pour me a drink. Then a quick and efficient session under the memory-editor to erase any potentially disquieting recollections arising from my tour of duty in the Twentieth Century—such as Lisa. After that, a few days of lounging around the station with other between-jobs personnel, until a new assignment came up—having no visible connection with the last one. I'd never learn just why the Karg had been placed where it was, what sort of deal it had made with the Third Era Enforcer—the man in black—what part the whole thing played in the larger pattern of the Nexx grand strategy.

And probably that was just as well. The panorama of time was too broad, the warp and the woof of its weaving too complex for any one brain to comprehend. Better to leave the mind free to focus on the details of the situation at hand, rather than diffuse it along the thousand dead-end trails that were the life of a Timecast Agent. *But Lisa, Lisa . . .*

I put the thought of her out of my mind—or tried to—and concentrated on immediate physical sensations: the hot, heavy air, the buzzing insects, the sand that slipped under my feet, the sweat trickling down my temples and between my shoulder blades. Not that those things were any fun in themselves. But in a few minutes there'd be cool clean air and soft music, a stimbath, a hot meal, a nap on a real air couch. . . .

A couple of off-duty agents, bright-eyed, efficient, came out to meet me as I came across the slope of sand to the edge of the lawn, through the open gate and in under the shade of the protopalms. They were strangers to me, but they greeted me in the casually friendly way that you develop in a lifetime of casual friendships. They asked me the routine questions about whether I had had a rough one, and I gave them the routine answers.

Inside the station the air was just as cool and clean as I'd remembered—and as sterile. The stimbath was nice—but I kept thinking of the iron-stained bathtub back home. The meal afterward was a gourmet's delight: reptile steak smothered in giant mushrooms and garnished with prawns, a salad of club-moss hearts, a hot-and-cold dessert made by a barrier-layer technique that wouldn't be perfected for another sixty-five million years but didn't compare with Lisa's lemon icebox pie with graham-cracker crust. And the air couch was nice, but not half as nice as the hard old bed with the brass frame in the breathlessly hot room with the oak floor and the starched curtains, and Lisa curled close to me. . . .

Jard let me sleep it out before the debriefing. He was a small, harassed-looking man in his mid-fifties, with an expression that said he had seen it all and hadn't been much impressed. He gave me his tired smile and listened to what I had to say, looking out the window at the same view he'd been looking at every day for five years. He liked it that I'd gotten the tape; Kargs usually managed to destruct when cornered; my slug in the emergency computing center had prevented it this time: thus the elaborate play to get him in position with his suspicions lulled. It had all been very cleverly planned and executed, and now I was tired of it, tired of the role I'd been playing, tired of the whole damned thing.

But that was just a temporary post-mission letdown. As soon as I'd had my brain scrubbed, and had rested a few days and cleared my mind of those annoying wisps of nostalgic thought, I'd be raring to go again.

Or so I hoped. Why not? I always had in the past.

Jard asked me to hold the memory-wipe until he'd had an opportunity to go through the tape in depth. I started to protest, but some vague idea of not sounding like a whiner stopped me.

I spent the rest of the day mooching around the station, thinking about Lisa.

It was a simple case of compulsive transference, or neurotic sublimation, I knew that. At least I knew the words. But every train of thought led back to her. If I tasted a daka-fruit—extinct since the Jurassic—I thought *Lisa would like this,* and I'd imagine her expression if I brought a couple home in a brown paper sack from the IGA store at the corner, pictured her peeling them and making a fruit salad with grated coconut and blanched almonds. . . .

There was a beach party that evening, down on the wide, white sand where it curved out in a long spit to embrace a shallow lagoon, where every now and then something made a splash that was too big to be a fish. Cycads grew on the point of land and on the sand bar that was busy growing into a key. They looked like beer barrels with flowers on their sides and palm fronds sticking out of their tops. There were a few unfinished-looking pines and the usual scattering of big ferns and clumps of moss that were trying to be trees. There weren't many bothersome insects; just big, blundery ones, and the small darting batlike reptiles were keeping them under control.

I sat on the sand and watched my compatriots: strong, healthy, handsome men and women, swimming in the surf inside the sonic screen set up to discourage the ichthyosaurs, chasing each other up and down the sand—and catching each other—while the guards posted in the pits at each end of the beach watched for wandering maneaters. We built a big fire—of driftwood fetched in from a locus a few million years downstream. We sang songs from a dozen eras, ate our roast baby stegosaurian, and drank white wine imported from eighteenth-century France, and felt like the lords of creation. And I thought about Lisa.

I had trouble sleeping that night. My appointment with the cepher was scheduled for 8:00 A.M. I was up before six. I ate a light breakfast and went for a walk on the beach to enjoy a few last thoughts of Lisa and wonder if somehow in our wisdom we had missed the point somewhere. It wasn't the kind of question that had an answer, but it kept my mind occupied while I put a mile or two between me and the station. I sat for half an hour and looked at the sea and wondered what I'd do if something large and hungry stalked out of the herbage behind me. I didn't know; I didn't even much care.

A bad train of thought, Ravel, I told myself. *Time to get back and tidy up your mind, before you get carried away and start thinking about how easy it would be to step into the transfer booth and drop yourself back into 1936 a block from the house, ten minutes after you left....*

I had gotten that far in my ruminations when I heard the shots.

It's a curious thing how in moments of stress, the mind jumps to the inconsequential. I was running, without having consciously started, sending up a spatter of spray as I dashed through the tongue of a wave that slid across in my path; and I was thinking: *I won't be stepping into that cooled air and antiseptic music again; no hot meal, no stimbath, no nap on a real air couch.... And no Lisa, never again Lisa ...*

I cut up across the soft sand-drift of the point, slipping and sliding as I ploughed my way upslope, crashed through a screen of palmetto at the crest, and was looking down at the station.

I don't know what I expected to see; the detonations I had heard were as much like Old Era hardshots as anything in my experience. What I saw was a pair of bulky, gray-brown machines, track-driven, obviously armored, in the fifty-ton size range, parked on the sand a few hundred yards from the station. No smoking gun muzzles were visible, but the chunk missing from the corner of the building was adequate testimony that guns were present, even without the *rackety-boom!* and the spurt of fire that came from the featureless curve of the prow of the nearer machine. The other was in trouble. One track was mangled, and smoke was leaking from a variety of places on its surface. It gave a little hop and almost invisible fire jetted from the same spots. I dropped flat in time to get the shock wave against my ribs: a kick from a buried giant.

I came up at a dead run, spitting sand and not thinking too clearly, but absolutely, unconditionally convinced that whatever was going on down there, the only Timecast booth this side of the Pleistocene was inside the station, and the nearer I got to it before they got me, the happier I'd die.

But no one was paying any attention to me and my aspirations. The still-functional warcar—Third Era, the data processor between my ears told me inconsequentially— was coming on, firing as it came. Jard must have succeeded in erecting at least a partial screen; rainbow light flared and darted coronalike over the station with each shot. But the defenses had been designed to ward off blundering brontosaurians, not tactical implosives. It wouldn't be long. . . .

I aborted that thought and put my head down and sprinted. Fire ran across the ground in front of me and winked out; the blast sent me skittering like a paper cutout in a brisk wind. I rolled, with some half-baked idea of evading any random shots somebody might be tossing my way, and came to my feet ten of the widest yards anybody ever crossed from that welcoming hole gaping in the east wall where the espalier had been. Through it I could see what was left of a filing cabinet and the internal organs of a resage chair and some twisted and blackened rags of metal that had been restful tan wall panels; but none of it seemed to get any closer. I was running with all I had, through foot-deep glue, while hell came to a head and burst around me.

And then I was going through in a long graceful dive that fetched up against an oversized anvil someone had carelessly left lying around the place. . . .

I came drifting back out of a thick fog full of little bright lights and bellowing monsters and looked up into the sweat-slick face of Nel Jard, Station Chief.

"Pull yourself together, man!" he was yelling. He had to yell to be heard over the continuous booming of the bombardment. "Everybody else is clear. I waited for you—knew you were back inside the field. Had to tell you. . . ." What he had to tell me was drowned out in a crash that made the earlier sound effects sound like a warm-up. Things fell around us. There was a throat-burning reek of ozone in the air, along with the scents of smoke and blood and pulverized stone and hot iron. I got my feet under me in time to see Jard disappearing through the door into the Ops room. I tottered after him, saw him punching a pattern into the board. The red emergency lights went on and the buzzer started its squawk and cut off abruptly. Jard turned and saw me.

"No!" he shouted, waving me off. "Get out, Ravel! Didn't you hear a word I told you? You've got to . . . out . . . co-ordinates—"

"I can't hear you," I shouted back, and couldn't hear my own words. Jard grabbed my arm, hustled me toward the floor-drop that led to the utility tunnel.

"I've got to shift the station to null-phase, you understand? Can't let them capture it. . . ." The door was up and I was being dumped over the edge. It was all happening too fast; bewildering. *A hell of a way to treat a sick man* . . . The impact of the floor hitting my head jarred it clear for the moment.

"Run for it," Jard was calling after me, from a million miles away. "Get as far as you can. Luck, Ravel . . ."

His voice was gone and I was on all fours, then stumbling to my feet, then running, more or less. It was what Nel wanted, and he was the boss.

Then the world blew up and sent me spinning head-over-heels into limbo, and a thousand tons of hot sand poured down on top of me and sealed me away for all eternity.

5

Well, maybe not eternity, a small voice seemed to be saying in a matter-of-fact tone.

"Close enough," I said, and got a mouthful of sand. I tried to draw a breath to spit it out and got a noseful of the same. That must have triggered some primitive instincts, because suddenly I was swimming hard with both hands and both feet, clawing upward through sand, breaking through into heat and the stink of charred plastics—and air. Dusty, smoky air, but air. I coughed and snorted and breathed some of it and looked around me.

I was lying in the utility tunnel, the walls of which were buckled and bulged as if they'd been half melted. The floor was drifted a foot deep in sand, out of which I had just dug my way. I tried to make my brain work. . . .

The tunnel led to the pump room, I knew, from which a ladder led to the surface, an arrangement designed for minimal disturbance of the local scenery. All I had to do was continue in the present direction, climb the ladder, and. . . .

I'd worry about the *and* later, I decided. I was still congratulating myself on my coolness under fire when I happened to notice that for a tunnel twelve feet under the surface, the light was awfully good. It seemed to be coming from behind me. I looked back, saw a tangle of steel, through the interstices of which brilliant sunlight was pouring in dusty bars.

After a dozen or so yards the going was easier; not so much sand and debris here. The pump-room door gave me a little trouble until I remembered to pull, not push. The equipment there was all intact, ready to pump any desired amount of clean, fresh spring

water up from 120 feet down. I patted the nearest
pump and got a grip on the ladder. I was still dizzy
and weak, but no dizzier or weaker than a landlubber
in his first sea-squall. At the top, the motor whined
when I pushed the button; the lid cycled open, dump-
ing sand and a small green lizard. I crawled out and
took a short breather and turned to see what there was
to see.

There was the long curve of beach, pitted now, and
criss-crossed by tank-tracks, and the tongue of jungle
that stretched almost to the shore along the ridge. But
where the station had been, there was nothing but a
smoking crater.

I lay flat on the nice warm sand and looked at the
scene with gritty eyes that wept copiously in the glare
of the tropical Jurassic sun and felt sweat trickle down
my forehead, and down my chest inside my shirt, while
images went swirling through my brain: the station, the
first time I had seen it, on my first jump, all those years
ago. The neat, impersonal little wardrooms that almost
came to seem like home after a while, always waiting for
you at the end of a tough assignment; the other agents,
male and female, who came and went; the in-
conversation around the tables in the dining room, the
crisp cleanliness, the efficiency; even the big board in
Ops that showed the minute-by-minute status of the
Timesweep effort up and down the ages. But the big
board wasn't there any more, or the miles of microtape
records, or the potted gingko tree in the lounge: all
melted down to slag.

I was remembering Nel Jard, yelling to me to get
out . . . and something else. He'd given me a message.
Something important, something I was supposed to tell
somebody, someday. An exercise in futility. I'd had my
last talk with a human being. I was stranded, stranded
as no other man had ever been, with the possible

exception of a few other Nexx agents who had dropped
off the screens in far places.

But none as far as this.

On that thought, I let my head drop and the dark
curtain fall.

6

When I woke the sun was setting and I was aching in places I'd forgotten I owned. Itching, too.
Oversized mosquitoes that didn't seem at all surprised
to find a mammal where no mammals ought to be had
settled down with a commendably philosophic attitude
to take a meal where they found it. I batted the most
persistent ones away and walked down to see what was
to be seen. I didn't appear to have any major injuries,
just plenty of small cuts and large bruises and the odd
contusion here and there. I reached the edge of the
pit where the station had been and looked at the ruins:
a fused glass bowl a hundred yards in diameter surrounded by charred plant life. Nothing had survived—
no people, no equipment. And worst of all, of course,
there'd be no outjump to Nexx Central with a report
of what had happened—or to any other time or place.

Someone, possibly Third Era—or someone mas-
querading as Third Era—had blasted the station with
a thoroughness I wouldn't have believed possible. And
how had it been possible for them to find the place,
considering the elaborate security measures surrounding
the placement of the 112 official staging stations scattered across Old Era time? As for Nexx Central, nobody
knew where it was, not even the men who had built it.
It floated in an achronic bubble adrift on the entropic
stream, never physically existing in any one space-time

locus for a finite period. Its access code was buried under twelve layers of interlocked ciphers in the main tank of the Nexxial Brain. The only way to reach it was via a jump station—and not just any jump station: it had to be the one my personal jumper field was tuned to.

Which was a half-inch layer of green glass lining a hollow in the sand.

An idea appeared like a ghastly grin.

The personal emergency jump gear installed in my body was intact. There was enough E-energy in the power coil for a jump—somewhere. I lacked a target, but that didn't mean I couldn't go. All it meant was that I wouldn't know where I'd land—if anywhere.

A lot of horror stories had circulated back at Nexx Central about what happened to people who misfired on a jump. They ranged from piecemeal reception at a dozen stations strung out across a few centuries to disembodied voices screaming to be let out. Also, there were several rules against it.

The alternative was to set up housekeeping here on the beach, with or without dinosaurs, and hope that a rescue mission arrived before I died of heat, thirst, reptiles, boredom, or old age.

It called for some thinking over.

There were a few chunks of masonry scattered among the charred stumps of club mosses; I could build a fireplace out of them, kill a lizard and broil him for dinner. . . .

The idea lacked charm, but I was reluctant to discard it out of hand. It was either that or risk my identity on an experiment that I had already been assured by experts was bound to end in disaster. After all, there was no particular hurry. I was bruised, but alive; I wouldn't starve for a few days; there was water available from the pump house. And maybe the destruction of the station had registered on somebody's telltale board somewhere;

maybe at this moment a relief team in crisp field-tan was assembling to jump out to the rescue.

It was almost dark now. The stars were glittering through the gloaming, just as if disaster hadn't entered the biography of Igor Ravel, Timesweeper. The surf pounded and whooshed, indifferent to the personal problems of one erect biped who had no business being within sixty-five million years of here.

As for me, I had to go to the toilet.

It seemed a rather inconsequential thing to be doing, urinating on the magic sands of the past, while looking up at the eternal stars.

After that, I mooched around a little longer, looking for a lingering trace of the magic that had been there once. Then I dug a pit in the sand and went to sleep.

7

Dawn came, and with it the dinosaurs. I had seen them before, at a distance, usually; small, shy creatures that skittered out of sight at the first touch of the subsonic beams Jard had rigged up to discourage them. Before my time, it seemed, there had been a few incidents of big specimens wandering a little too close to the vegetable garden and having to be driven off with improvised noisemakers. They were too stupid to be dangerous, it was understood, except for the danger of getting stepped on, or accidentally grazed along with a clump of foliage.

This time there were three of them. Big ones, and no subsonics available, not even an ordinary noisemaker, except for my vocal cords.

Once, I remembered, a 'caster named Dowl, out for

a swim, had been trapped on the beach by a saurian with impressive teeth which had popped out of the woods between him and the station. He 'd gotten out of it with nothing worse than a case of delirium tremens; the behemoth had walked past him without a glance. He was too small a tidbit, the theory was, to interest a stomach as big as that one.

I didn't find that thought consoling.

The trio coming my way were of a previously unrecorded variety we had named the Royal Jester, because of their silly grin and the array of bright-colored decorations sprouting like baubles from the cranium. They also had legs like an oversized ostrich, a long neck, and far too many teeth.

I stayed where I was, flat on the sand, and played boulder while they stalked toward me, shimmering in the heat haze. There were two big ones and one giant, eighteen feet at the shoulder if he was an inch. As they got closer, I could smell the rank, cucumber-and-dung smell of them, see the strips and patches of reticulated purple and yellow hide scaling from their backs, hear the hiss and wheeze of their breathing. They were big machines, calling for a lot of air turnover. I busied myself with some abortive calculations involving lung capacity, O_2 requirements per pound, and intake orifice area; but I gave up when they got within a hundred feet. At this range I could hear their guts rumbling.

Big Boy scented me first. His head went up; a cold reptilian eye the color of a bucket of blood rolled my way. He snorted. He drooled—about a gallon. His mouth opened, and I saw rows of snow-white teeth, some of which waggled, loose, ready to shed. He steam-whistled and started my way. It was decision time, and I didn't linger.

I took a final breath of humid beach air, a last look at the bright, brutal view of sea and sand, the high, empty, impersonal sky, and the jolly monster shape looming up against it. Then I played the tune on the console set in my Jaw.

The scene twisted, slid sideways and dissolved into the painless blow of a silent club, while I looped the loop through a universe-sized Klein bottle—

Total darkness and a roar of sound like Niagara Falls going over me in a barrel.

8

For a few seconds I lay absolutely still, taking a swift inventory of my existence. I seemed to be all present, organized pretty much as usual, aches, itches and all. The torrent of sound went on, getting no louder or softer; the blackness failed to fade. It seemed pretty clear that while I had left where I was, I hadn't arrived much of anywhere.

The rulebook said that in a case of transfer malfunction to remain immobile and await retrieval; but in this case that might take quite a while. Also, there was the datum that no one had ever lived to report a jump malfunction, which suggested that possibly the rulebook was wrong. I tried to breathe, and nothing happened. That decided me.

I got to my feet and took a step and emerged as through a curtain into silence and a strange blackish light, shot through with little points of dazzling brilliance, like what you see just before you faint from loss of blood. But before I could put my head between my knees, the dazzle faded and I was looking at the jump room of a regulation Nexx Staging Station. And I could breathe.

I did that for a few moments, then turned and looked at the curtain I had come through. It was a perfectly ordinary wall of concrete and beryl steel, to my knowledge two meters thick.

Maybe the sound I had heard was the whizzing of molecules of dense metal interpenetrating with my own hundred and eighty pounds of impure water.

That was a phenomenon I'd have to let ride until later. More pressing business called for my attention first—such as finding the station chief and reporting in on the destruction of Station Ninety-nine by surprise attack.

It took me ten minutes to check every room on operations level. Nobody was home. The same for the R and R complex. Likewise the equipment division and the power chamber.

The core sink was drawing normal power, the charge was up on the transmitter plates, the green lights were on all across the panels; but nothing was tapping the station for so much as a microerg.

Which was impossible.

The links that tied a staging station to Nexx Central and in turn monitored the activities of the personnel operating out of the station always drew at least a trickle of carrier power. They had to; as long as the system existed, a no-drain condition was impossible anywhere in normal space-time.

I didn't like the conclusion, but I reached it anyway.

Either the timesweep system no longer existed—or I was outside the range of its influence. And since its influence pervaded the entire spatial-temporal cosmos, that didn't leave much of anyplace for me to be.

All the stations were physically identical: in appearance, in equipment, in electronic characteristics. In fact, considering their mass production by the time-stutter process which distributed them up and down the temporal contour, there's a school of thought that holds that they *are* identical; alternate temporal aspects of the same physical matrix. But that was theory, and my present situation was fact. Step one was to find out where I was.

I went along the passage to the entry lock—some of the sites are located in settings where outside conditions were hostile to what Nexx Central thinks of as ordinary life—cycled it, and almost stepped out.

Not quite.

The ground ended about ten feet from the outflung entry wing. Beyond was a pearly gray mist, swirling against an invisible barrier that prevented it from dissipating. I went forward to the edge and lay flat and looked over. The underside curved down and back, out of sight in the nebulosity. What I could see of it was as smooth and polished as green glass.

Like the green glass crater I'd seen back on Dinosaur Beach.

I backed off from the edge of the world and went back inside, to the Record Section, punched for a tape at random. The read-out flashed on the screen: routine data on power consumption, temporal contour fluctuations, arrivals and departures; the daily log of the station, with the station number repeated on every frame.

Station Ninety-nine.

Just what I was afraid of.

The curving underside of the island in nowhere I was perched on would fit the glass-lined hollow back at Dinosaur Beach the way a casting fits the mold. The station hadn't been destroyed by enemy gunfire; it had been scooped out of the rock like a giant dip of pistachio and deposited here.

I was safe in port, my home station. That had been what Nel Jard had been trying to tell me. He'd waited until I was clear, then pulled a switch. Crash emergency procedure that an ordinary field man would know nothing about.

No doubt Jard had done the right thing. The enemy had been at the gates. In another few seconds the screens would have collapsed under overload. All the secrets of Nexx Timecasting would have fallen into hostile hands. Jard had to do something. Demolition was impossible. So he'd done this.

The fact that this implied a technology at a level far beyond what I understood of Nexx capabilities was a point I'd take up later, after more immediate matters were dealt with.

In the minutes I'd been there, he'd given me a message; something I was supposed to tell someone, somewhere. I hadn't heard a word he'd said, but in the excitement, he hadn't realized that. He'd hustled me on my way, counted ten, and thrown the switch. The station was gone but I was in the clear.

And then I had negated all that effort on his part by using my built-in circuitry to jump back where I wasn't supposed to be.

Null phase, the phrase popped into my mind. A theoretical notion I'd encountered in technical reading. But it seemed it was more than theory.

A place outside time and space. The point of zero amplitude in the oscillations of the Ylem field that we called space-time.

I walked across the room, conscious of my feet hitting the floor, of the quiet whispering of the air circulator, the hum of idling equipment. Everything I could see, hear, smell, and touch seemed perfectly normal—except for what was outside.

But if this was the Dinosaur Beach station—where was the hole in the lounge wall that I'd come in by a few subjective hours earlier? Where was the debris and the smoke, and where the dead bodies and the wreckage?

The place was neat as an egg. I pulled out a tape

drawer. Files all in order, no signs of hasty evacuation, enemy action, or last-minute confusion. Just no people— and nothing much in the way of a neighborhood.

It was the *Marie Celeste* syndrome with a vengeance—except that I was still aboard.

I went into the dining room; there were a couple of trays there with the remains of food still on them, fairly fresh: the only exception to the total and impersonal order in the station.

I poked the disposal button and punched out a meal of my own. It slid from the slot, steaming hot; synthothis and pseudo-that. I thought of baked ham and corn on the cob—and Lisa waiting for me in the perfumed darkness. . . .

Damn it all—it wasn't supposed to be like this. A man went out, did his job, involved himself—and tore himself away to follow the call of duty—on the premise that the torture of memory would all be soothed away by the friendly mind-wiper. It wasn't in the contract that I should sit here in the gloaming in an empty station eating sawdust and ashes and yearning for a voice, a smile, a touch. . . .

What the hell, she was just a woman—an ephemeral being, born back in the dawn of time, living a life brief as the fitful glow of a firefly, dead and dust these millennia. . . .

But Lisa, Lisa . . .

"Enough of that," I told myself sternly, and quailed at the sound of my voice in the deserted station. *There's a simple explanation for everything*, I told myself, silently this time. *Well, maybe not simple, but an explanation.*

"Easy," I said aloud, and to hell with the echo. "The transfer process shifted the station back to an earlier temporal fix. Same station, different time. Or maybe no time at all. The math would all work out, no doubt.

The fact that I wouldn't understand it is mere detail. The station exists— somewhere—and I'm in it. The question before the house is what do I do next?"

The air hung around me, as thick and silent as funeral incense. Everything seemed to be waiting for something to happen. And nothing would happen unless I made it happen.

"All right, Ravel," I said. "Don't drag your feet. You know what to do. The only thing you *can* do. The only out . . ."

I got to my feet and marched across to Ops, down the transit tunnel to the transfer booth.

It looked normal. Aside from the absence of a cheery green light to tell me that the outlink-circuits were locked on focus to Nexx Central, all was as it should be. The plates were hot, the dial readings normal.

If I stepped inside, I'd be transferred—somewhere.

Some more interesting questions suggested themselves, but I had no time to go over those. I stepped inside and the door valved shut and I was alone with my thoughts. Before I could have too many of those I reached out and tripped the Xmit button.

A soundless bomb blew me motionlessly across dimensionless space.

9

A sense of vertigo that slowly faded; the gradual impingement of sensation: heat, and pressure against my side, a hollow, almost musical soughing and groaning, a sense of lift and fall, a shimmer of light through my eyelids, as from a reflective surface in constant restless movement. I opened my eyes; sunlight was shining on water. I felt the pressure of a plank deck on which I was lying; a pressure that increased, held steady, then dwindled minutely.

I moved, and groaned at the aches that stabbed at me. I sat up.

The horizon pivoted to lie flat, dancing in the heat-ripples, sinking out of sight as a rising bulwark of worn and sunbleached wood rose to cut off my view. Above me, the masts, spars, and cordage of a sailing ship thrust up, swaying, against a lush blue sky. Hypno-briefed data popped into focus: I recognized the typical rigging of a sixteenth-century Portuguese galleass.

But not a real galleass, I knew somehow. A replica, probably from the Revival, circa A.D. 2220; a fine reproduction, artfully carved and fitted and weather-scarred, probably with a small reactor below decks, steel armor under the near-oak hull planking, and luxury accommodations for an operator and a dozen holiday-makers.

I became aware of background sounds; the creak of ropes and timbers, a mutter of talk, a shout, heavy rumblings. Something thudded on deck. The ship heeled sharply; stinging salt spray came over the weather rail and made me gasp. I blinked it away and saw another ship out there, half a mile away across the water, a heavy two-decker, with three masts, flying a long green pennant with a gray-white Maltese cross. Little white puffs appeared all along her side, with bright flashes at their centers. A moment later, a row of water spouts appeared in the sea, marching in a row across our bows. Then the *baroom—om!* came rolling after, like distant thunder.

My ideas underwent a sudden and drastic change. The picture of a party of holiday-makers cruising the Caribbean in their make-believe pirate ship vanished like the splashes made by the cannon-balls fired by the galleon. They were shooting real guns, firing real ammunition, that could make a real hole in the deck right where I was lying.

I rolled to my feet and looked aft. A knot of men were there, grouped around a small deck gun they seemed to be having trouble wrestling into position. They were dressed in sixteenth-century costumes, worn, soiled, and sweat-stained. One of them was bleeding from a cut on the face. The wound looked much too authentic to be part of a game.

I dropped down behind a large crate lashed to the deck, containing a live turtle with a chipped and faded shell a yard in diameter. He looked as old and tired and unhappy as I felt.

Shouts, and something came fluttering down from aloft to slap against the deck not far from me: a tattered banner, coarse cloth, crudely dyed, sunfaded, with a device of an elongated green chicken with horns writhing on a dirty yellow background. Heraldry was never my strong suit; but I didn't need further clues to deduce that I was in the middle of a sea fight that my side seemed to be losing. The galleon was noticeably bigger now, coming across on the other tack. More smoke blossomed and there was a whistle and a crash up for'ard like an oil stove blowing up, and splinters rained down all around me. One of the men at the fantail went down gushing scarlet and thrashing like a boated carp. More yells, running feet. Somebody dashed past my hiding place, shouted something, maybe at me. I stayed put, waiting for an inspiration to come along and tell me what to do.

I got it in the form of a squat swarthy man in bare brown feet, faded pinkish leggings, baggy breeches of a yellowish black, a broad hand-hacked leather belt supporting a cutlass that looked as if it had been hammered out of an old oil barrel. He stood over me and yelled, waving a short, thick arm. I got to my

feet and he yelled again, waved aft, and dashed off
that way.

He hadn't seemed very surprised to see me; and I
had almost understood what he was yelling about. That
fool Gonzalo had been idiot pig enough to get himself a gutful of taffrail, it seemed he'd said. My presence was urgently desired to assist in manning the
four-pounder.

The damned fool, I heard myself snarling. *Dump the
cannon over the side to lighten ship; our only chance
is to outrun them, and even that's impossible. . . .*

Something screamed through the air like a rocket
and a length of rope came coiling at me and caught
me across the face and threw me across the deck.
Somebody jumped over me; a piece of spar the size
of my thigh slammed the deck and bounced high over
the side. The ship was heeling again, coming around;
things were sliding across the deck; then the sails were
slatting, taken aback. Wind swept across the deck, cool
and sweet. More thunder, more crashes, more yells,
more running feet. I found a sheltered spot in the
scuppers, not too fastidious now about the pinkish scum
sloshing there, and watched the mainmast lean, making noises like pistol shots, and go crashing over the
windward side, trailing a ballooning tent of cloth that
split and settled over the stern and was pulled over
the side by the current, taking along a man or two who
were trapped under it. Things were falling from above
like the aftermath of a dynamite blast. Something dark
loomed and suddenly spars and sails were sliding across
up above, and then an impact threw me on my face
and went on and on, grinding splinters, snapping lines,
tilting the deck. . . .

I slipped and slithered, caught a rope, held on,
jammed against the side of the small cabin. The galleon
was still scraping alongside, looking enormous. Men

were in her rigging and lined up along her waist ten feet
above our deck, shouting and waving fists and swords.
I was looking down the black muzzles of cannons that
slipped past, staring from dark square windows with
smoke-blackened faces grinning behind them. Grappling
hooks came down, slid and caught in the splintered
decking. Then men were leaping down, spilling over the
rail, overrunning the deck. The seaman who had yelled
at me ran forward and a saber swung at his head; it
didn't seem like much of a blow, but he went down, very
bloody, and the boarders crowded past, fanning out,
yelling like demons. I hugged the deck and tried to look
hors de combat. A big barrel-chested fellow swinging
a machete with a badly bent blade came bounding my
way; I rolled far enough to get a hand on my Mauser
and got it up in time and put two through his broad,
sweat-gleaming, hair-matted chest and kicked aside as
he fell hard on the spot where I'd been lying. In the
mêlée the shots hadn't been audible.

A little fellow with bare, monkeylike legs was trying
to climb the foremast; someone jumped after him,
caught him, pulled him back down. Someone went over
the rail, alive or dead I wasn't sure. Then they were just
milling around, yelling as loud as ever, but waving their
cutlasses instead of hacking with them—except for the
few who were lying here and there like broken toys,
ignored, out of it, holding their wounds together with
their hands and mumbling the final Hail Mary's.

Then I saw the Karg.

10

There was no doubt of his identity. To the untrained
eye a Class-One Karg—the only kind ever used in

Timesweep work—was indistinguishable from any other citizen. But my eye wasn't untrained. Besides which, I knew him personally.

He was the same Karg I'd left in the hotel room back in Buffalo, defunct, with a soft-nosed slug in the left zygomatic arch.

Now here he was, pre-Buffalo, with no hole in his head, climbing down onto the deck as neat and cool as if it had all been in fun. From the draggled gold lace on his cuffs and the tarnished brass hilt on his sword, I gathered that he was a person of importance among the victors. Possibly the captain; or maybe officer in charge of the marines. They were listening to him, falling into ragged ranks, quieting down.

The next step would be the telling off of details for a systematic looting of the ship, with a side-order of mercy killing for anyone unlucky enough to have survived the assault.

From what I remembered of conditions in the holds of Spanish ships of the time, a fast demise was far preferable to the long voyage home, with the galleys at the end of it. I was just beginning to form a hopeless plan for creeping out of sight and waiting for something that looked like an opportunity to turn up, when the door I was lying against opened. Tried to open, that is. I was blocking it, so that it moved about two inches and jammed tight. Somebody inside gave it a hearty shove and started through. I saw a booted leg and an arm in a blue sleeve with gold buttons. He got that far and stuck. Something on his belt seemed to be caught in the door hardware. The Karg's head had turned at the first sound. He stared for a long, long time that was probably less than a second, then whipped up a handsome pearl-mounted wheel-lock pistol, raised it deliberately, aimed—

The explosion was like a bomb; flame gouted and

smoke gushed. I heard the slug hit; a solid, meaty smack, like a well-hit ball hitting the fielder's glove. The fellow in the door lurched, thrashed, plunged through and went down hard on his face. He jerked a couple of times as if someone was jabbing him with a sharp stick, and then lay very still.

The Karg turned back to his men and rapped out an order. The boys muttered and shuffled, and shot disappointed looks around the deck, and then started for the side.

No search, no loot, just the fast skiddoo.

It was as if the Karg had accomplished what he had come for.

In five minutes the last of the boarders were back aboard their own ship. The Karg stood near the stern, patient as only a machine can be. He looked around, then came toward me. I lay very still indeed and tried to look as dead as possible.

He stepped over me and the real corpse and went into the cabin. I heard faint sounds, the kind somebody makes going through drawers and peeking under the rug. Then he came out. I heard his footsteps going away, and opened an eye.

He was by the weather rail, calmly stripping the safety foil from a thermex bomb. It gave its preliminary hiss and he dropped it through the open hatch at his feet as casually as someone dropping an olive in a martini.

He walked coolly across the deck, stepped up, grabbed a line, and scrambled with commendable agility back to his own deck. I heard him—or someone—yell a command. Sounds of sudden activity; sails quivered and moved; men appeared, swarming up the ratlines. The galleon's spars shifted, withdrew with much creaking and tearing of the defeated galleass's rigging. The high side of the Spanish ship drew away;

sails filled with dull *boom!s*. Quite suddenly I was alone, watching the ship dwindle as it receded downwind under full sail.

Just then the thermex let go with a vicious *choof!* belowdecks. Smoke billowed from the hatch, with tongues of pale flame in close pursuit. I got a pair of legs under me and wobbled to the opening, had to turn my eyes from the sunbright holocaust raging below. The tub might have steel walls, but in 5000° heat they'd burn like dry timber.

I stood where I was for a few valuable seconds, trying to put it together in some way that made some variety of sense, while the fire sputtered and crackled and the deck wallowed, and the shadow of the stump of the mainmast swung slow arcs on the deck, like a finger wagging at the man the Karg had shot.

He lay on his face, with a lot of soggy lace in a crimson puddle under his throat. One hand was under him, the other outflung. A gun lay a yard from the empty hand.

I took three steps and stooped and picked up the gun. It was a .01 microjet of Nexx manufacture, with a grip that fitted my hand perfectly.

It ought to. It was my gun. I looked at the hand it had fallen from. It looked like my hand. I didn't like doing it, but I turned the body over and looked at the face.

It was my face.

11

The standard post-mission conditioning that had wiped the whole sequence from my memory broke. I remembered it now: Time, about ten years earlier,

N. S.; or the year 1578, local. Place, the Caribbean, about fifty miles southwest of St. Thomas. It had been a cruise in search of the Karg-operated ship which had been operating in New Spanish waters; I recalled the contact, the chase, the fight across the decks while I waited inside the cabin for the opportunity for the single well-placed shot that would eliminate the source of the interference. It was one of my first assignments, long ago completed, filed in the master tape, a part of Timesweep history.

But not anymore. The case was reopened on the submission of new evidence. I was doubled back on my own timetrack.

The fact that this was a violation of every natural law governing time travel was only a minor aspect of the situation, grossly outweighed by this evidence that the past that Nexx Central had painfully rebuilt to eliminate the disastrous effects of Old Era time meddling was coming unstuck.

And if one piece of the new mosaic that was being so carefully assembled was coming unglued—then everything that had been built on it was likewise on the skids, ready to slide down and let the whole complex and artificial structure collapse in a heap of temporal rubble that neither Nexx Central nor anyone else would be able to salvage.

With the proper lever, you can move worlds; but you need a solid place to stand. That had been Nexx Central's job for the past six decades: to construct a platform in the remote pre-Era on which all the later structure would be built.

And it looked as though it had failed—because of me.

I remembered the way it had gone the first time: waiting my moment, thrusting the door open, planting my feet, taking aim, firing three shots into the android's thoracic cavity before he was aware that a new factor had entered the equation. He had fallen; his men had yelled in rage and charged, and my repellor field had held them off until they panicked at the invisible barrier and fled back to their galleon, cast off, and made sail before the wind, back into the obscurity of unrecorded history; while I had brought the galleass—a specially equipped Nexx operations unit in disguise—to the bulk transfer point at Locus Q-637, from which it had been transmitted back to storage at the Nexx holding station.

But none of that had happened.

I had blocked the door, preventing the *other* me from completing his assignment, thus invalidating a whole segment of the rebuilt time-map and casting the whole grand strategy of Nexx operations into chaos. The Karg had gone his way, unharmed; and I was lying on the deck, very dead indeed from a brass ball through the throat.

And also I was standing on the deck looking down at my corpse, slowly realizing the magnitude of the trap I had blundered into.

A Nexx agent is a hard man to dispose of: hard to kill, hard to immobilize, because he's protected by all the devices of a rather advanced science.

But if he can be marooned in the closed loop of an unrealized alternate reality—a pseudo-reality from which there can be no outlet to a future which doesn't exist—then he's out of action forever.

Even if I could go on living—doubtful proposition in view of the fire curling the deck planks at the moment—there'd be no escape, ever; my personal jump field was discharged; it wouldn't take me anywhere. And there'd be no trace on any recording instrument to show where I'd gone; when I'd jumped from the phantom station, I'd punched in no destination. The other me had now been killed in the line of duty, during the vulnerable second when his shield was open to allow him to fire the executioner's shot. His trace would have dropped from the boards; scratch one inefficient field man, who'd been so careless as to get himself killed.

And scratch his double, who'd poked his nose in where it had no business being.

My mind circled the situation, looking for an out. I didn't like what I found, but I liked it better than roasting alive or drowning in the tepid sea.

My personal jump mechanism was built into me, tuned to me, though unfocused at the receiving end. It would be useless until I'd had a recharge at base. But its duplicate was built into the corpse lying at my feet. The circuitry of the jump device—from antennae to powerpack—consisted largely of the nervous system of the owner.

It took only a few minutes without oxygen for irreversible brain damage to occur, but the dead man's circuitry should be operable. Just what it might be focused on now—considering the drastic realignment of the casual sequence—was an open question. It would depend to a degree on what had been on the corpse's mind at the moment of death.

The deck was getting hot enough to burn my feet through my soles. There was lots of smoke. The fire roared like a cataract in flood season.

I squatted beside the dead version of myself. The corpse's jaws were in a half-open position. I got a finger inside and tried out my recall code on the molar installation, feeling the blast of heat as flames gouted from the open hatch at my back.

A giant clapped his hands together, with me in the middle.

12

It was dark and I was falling; I just had time to realize the fact and claw for nonexistent support before I hit water: hot, stinking, clogged with filth, thick as pea soup; I went under and came up blowing and gagging. I was drowning in slime: I floundered, tried to swim, arrived at an uneasy equilibrium in which I lay out flat, head raised clear of the surface, paddling just enough to keep my nostrils clear, while goo ran down in my eyes.

The smell could have been sliced and sold for linoleum. I spat and coughed and sploshed and my hand scraped a surface that sloped gently up under me. My knees bumped and I was crouched on all fours, snorting and trying without much luck to squeeze the muck from my eyes. I tried to crawl forward and slipped and slid backward and almost dunked my head again.

I did it more carefully the next time: eased forward, with most of my weight supported by the semiliquid goo, and felt over the shore. It wasn't like any shore I had ever encountered before; hard-surfaced, planar, as smooth as a toilet bowl, curving gently upward. I groped my way along sideways, slipping, splashing, suffocating in the raw-sewage reek. Something spongy and rotting came apart under my hands. I tried again to crawl forward, made a yard and slid back two.

I was getting tired. There was nothing to hold onto. I had to rest. But if I rested, I sank. I thought about sliding down under that glutinous surface and trying to breathe and getting a lungful of whatever it was I was floundering in, and dying there and turning to something as black and corrupt as what I was buried in—

It was a terrible thought. I opened my mouth and yelled. And somebody answered.

"You down there! Stop kicking around! I'm throwing you a line!"

It was a female voice, not to say feminine, coming from above me somewhere. It sounded sweeter than a choir of massed angels. I tried to call out a cheery and insouciant reply, managed a croak. A beam of white light speared down at me from a point thirty feet above and fifty feet away. It hunted across the bubbly black surface and glared in my eyes.

"Lie still!" the voice commanded. The light went away, bobbled around, came back. Something came whistling down and slapped into the muck a few feet away. I floundered and groped, encountered a half-inch rope slick with the same stuff I was slick with.

"There's a loop at the end. Put your foot in it. I'll haul you up."

The rope slid through my hands; I scrabbled, felt the knot, got another dipping trying to hook a foot in it, settled for a two-handed grip. The rope surged, pulling me clear of the stew and up the slope. I held on and rode. The surface under me curved up and up. Progress was slowed. Another yard. Another. Half a yard. A foot. I was at an angle of about thirty degrees now, pressed tight against the slope. Another surge and I heard the rope rasping above. An edge raked my forearm. I grabbed, almost lost the rope, was dragged up the final foot and got a knee over the edge and crawled forward across loose sand and went down on my face and out.

13

Sun in my eyes. Forgot to pull down the shades. Lumpy mattress. Too hot. Sand in the bed. Itches; aches. . . .

I unglued an eyelid and looked at white sand that undulated down to the shore of a brassy sea. A lead-colored sky, but bright for all that; a gray wave that slid in and *crump!*ed on the beach. No birds, no sails, no kids with buckets, no bathing beauties. Just me and the eternal sea.

It was a view I knew all too well. I was back on Dinosaur Beach, and it was early in the morning, and I hurt all over.

Things cracked and fell away as I sat up, using a couple of broken arms that happened to be handy. There was gray mud caked on my trousers, gluing them to my legs; gray mud covered my shoes. I bent my knee and almost yelped at the pain. The cloth cracked and mud broke and crumbled. I was coated in the stuff like a shrimp in batter. It was on my face, too. I scraped at it, breaking off shells, prying it loose from my sideburns, spitting it. It was in my eyes; I fingered them, making matters worse.

"You're awake, I see," a crisp voice said from somewhere behind me. I dug mud from my ear and could hear her feet squeaking in the sand. The sound of something being dumped nearby.

"Don't claw at your eyes," she said sharply. "You'd better go down to the water and wash yourself clean."

I grunted and got both knees and both hands firmly planted and stood up. A firm hand took my right arm just above the elbow—rather gingerly, I thought—and urged me forward. I walked, stumbling, through the loose sand. The sun burned against my eyelids; the sound of surf grew louder. I crossed firm sand that sloped down, and then warm water was swirling around my ankles. She let go and I took a few more steps and sank down in the water and let it wash over me.

The dry mud turned back to slime, releasing a

sulphurous stench. I sluiced water over my head, scoured my scalp more or less clean, put my face in the water and scrubbed at it, and could see again.

I pulled my shirt off, mud-heavy, sodden, swished it back and forth, trailing a dark cloud in the murky-pale green. Various small cuts and one larger one across my forearm were leaking pink. My knuckles were raw. The salt water burned like acid. I noticed that the back of my shirt was gone, leaving a charred edge. The sky had turned a metallic black, filled with small whirly lights. . . .

Splashing sounds behind me. Hands on me, pulling me up. I seemed to have been drowning without knowing it. I coughed and retched while she half-dragged me back up through the surf onto the beach. My legs weren't working very well. They got tangled up and I went down, and rested like that for a minute on all fours, shaking my head to drive away the high, whining noise that seemed to be coming from a spot deep between my ears.

"I didn't realize . . . you're hurt. Your back . . . burns . . . what happened to you?" Her voice came from far away, swelling and fading.

"The boy stood on the burning deck," I said airily, and heard it come out slurred gibberish. I could see a pair of trim female shins in fitted leather boots, a nice thigh under gray whipcord, a pistol belt, a white shirt that had probably been crisp once. I grunted again, just to let her know I was still in there pitching, and got my feet under me and stood, with her hauling on my arm.

" . . . left you outside all night . . . first aid . . . you walk . . . ? . . . little way . . ." Some of the drill-sergeant snap was gone from the voice. It sounded almost familiar. I turned and blinked against the sun and looked into her face, which was frowning at me in an expression of deep concern, and felt my heart stop dead for a full beat.

It was Lisa.

14

I croaked something and grabbed at her; she fended me off and looked stern, like a night nurse not liking her job but doing it anyway

"Lisa—how did you get here?" I got the words out somehow.

"My name isn't Lisa—and I got here in the same way I suspect you did." She was walking me toward a small field tent, regulation issue, that was pitched higher up on the beach, under the shade of the club mosses. She gave me another no-nonsense look. "You *are* a field man, I suppose?" Her eyes were taking in what was left of my clothes. She sucked in air between her teeth. "You look as if you'd been in an air raid," she said, almost accusingly.

"Ground-armor attack and a sea chase," I said. "No air raid. What are you *doing* here, Lisa? How . . ."

"I'm Mellia Gayl," she cut in. "Don't go delirious on me now. I've got enough on my hands without that."

"Lisa, don't you know me? Don't you recognize me?"

"I never saw you before in my life, mister." She ducked her head and thrust me through the tent fly, into coolness and amber light.

"Get those clothes off," she ordered. I wanted to assert my masculine prerogative of undressing myself, but somehow it was just a little more than I could manage. I leaned against her and slid down sideways and had my pants dragged down over my ankles. She pulled my shoes off, and my socks. I managed the wet shorts myself. I was shivering and burning up. I was a little boy and mama was putting me to bed. I felt cool softness under me and rolled over on my face, away from the remote fire at my back, and let it all fade away into a soft, embracing darkness.

15

"I'm sorry about leaving you unattended all last night," Lisa, or Mellia Gayl, said. "But of course I didn't know you were hurt—and—"

"And I was out cold and too heavy to carry, even if I'd smelled better," I filled in. "Forget it. No harm done."

It had been rather pleasant, waking up in a clean bed, in an air-conditioned tent, neatly bandaged and doped to the hairline, feeling no pain, just a nice warm glow of well-being, and a pleasant numbness in the extremities.

But Lisa still insisted she didn't know me.

I watched her face as she fiddled with the dressings she'd put on my various contusions, as she spooned soup into me. There wasn't the slightest shadow of a doubt. She was Lisa.

But somehow not quite the Lisa I'd fallen in love with.

This Lisa—Mellia Gayl—was crisp, efficient, cool, unemotional. Her face was minutely thinner, her figure minutely more mature. It was Lisa, but a Lisa older by several years than the wife I had abandoned only subjective hours ago. A Lisa who had never known me. There were implications in that I wasn't ready to think about. Not yet.

"They're full of surprises, the boys back at Central,"

I said. "Imagine Lisa—my sweet young bride—being a Timesweep plant. Hard to picture. Took me completely. I thought I met her by accident. All part of the plan. They could have told me. Some actress . . ."

"You're tiring yourself out," Mellia said coolly. "Don't try to talk. You've lost a lot of blood and plasma. Save your strength for recuperating."

"Otherwise you're stuck with an invalid or a corpse, eh, kid?" I thought, but the spoon went into my mouth in time to keep me from saying it.

"I heard the splash," she was saying. "I knew something big was thrashing around down there. I thought a small reptile had blundered into it. It's a regular trap. They fall in and can't get out again." As she spoke, her voice sounded younger, more vulnerable.

"But you came and had a look anyway," I said. "Animal lover."

"I was glad when you shouted," she blurted, as if it was a shameful admission. "I was beginning to wonder . . . to think—"

"And you still haven't told me how you happened to be waiting here to welcome me with hot soup and cold glances," I said.

She tightened up her mouth but it was still a mouth that was made for kisses.

"I'd finished up my assignment and jumped back to station," she said flatly. "But the station wasn't here. Just a hole in the ground full of mud and bones. I didn't know what to think. My first impulse was to jump out again, but I knew that would be the wrong thing to do. There'd be no telling where I'd end up. I decided my best course would be to sit tight and wait for a retrieval. So . . . here I am."

"How long?"

"About . . . three weeks."

"'About?'"

"Twenty-four days, thirteen hours and ten minutes," she snapped, and jammed the spoon at my teeth.

"What was your assignment?" I asked after I'd swallowed.

"Libya. 1200 B.C."

"I never knew the ancient Libyans packed revolvers."

"It wasn't a contact assignment, I was alone in the desert—at an oasis, actually, at the time, equipped for self-maintenance for a couple of weeks. Things were a little greener there in those days. There'd been some First Era tampering done with an early pre-Bedouin tomb, with a complicated chain of repercussions, tied in with the rise of Islam much later.

"My job was to replace some key items that had been recovered from a Second Era museum. I managed it all right. Then I jumped back—" She broke off and for just an instant I saw a frightened girl trying very hard to be the tough, fearless agent.

"You did just right, Mellia," I said. "In your place I'd probably have panicked and tried to jump back out. And ended up stuck in an oscillating loop." As I said it, I realized that was the wrong aspect of the matter to dwell on just now.

"Anyway, you waited, and here I am. Two heads, and all that—"

"What are we going to do?" she cut in. She sounded like a frightened girl now. *Swell job of comforting you're doing, Ravel. She was fine until you came along. . . .*

"We have several courses of action," I said as briskly as I could with soup running down my chin. "Just let me . . ." I ran out of wind and drew a shaky breath. "Let me catch a few winks more and. . . ."

"Sorry . . ." she was saying. "You need your rest. Sleep; we'll talk later. . . ."

I spent three days lying around waiting for the skin

on my back to regenerate, which it did nicely under
the benign influence of the stuff from Mellia's field kit,
and for my scrapes and cuts to seal themselves over.
Twice during that time I heard shots: Mellia, discour-
aging the big beasties when they got too close. A crater
gun at wide diffusion stung just enough to get the
message through to their pea-sized brains.

On the fourth day I took a tottery stroll over to the
edge of the hole Mellia had pulled me out of.

It was the pit where the station had been, of course.
High tides, rain, blown sand, wandering animals had
filled it halfway to the brim. The glass lining above the
surface was badly weathered. It had taken time for
that—lots of time.

"How long?" Mellia asked.

"Centuries, anyway. Maybe a thousand or two years."

"That means the station was never rebuilt," she said.

"At least not in this time segment. It figures; if the
location was known there was no reason to go on using
it."

"There's more to it than that. I've been here for
almost a month. If anyone were looking for me, they'd
have pinpointed me by now."

"Not necessarily. It's a long reach, this far back."

"Don't try to be kind to me, Ravel. We're in trouble.
This is more than a little temporary confusion. Things
are coming apart."

I didn't like her using virtually the same wording
that had popped into my mind when I'd looked at my
own corpse.

"The best brains at Nexx Central are working on
this," I told her. "They'll come up with the answers."
It didn't sound convincing even to me.

"What was the station date when you were there
last?" she asked.

"Sixty-five," I said. "Why?"

She gave me a tense little smile. "We're not exactly contemporaries. I was assigned to Dino Beach in twelve-thirty-one, local."

I let the impact of that diffuse through my brain for a few seconds, bringing no comfort. I grunted as if I'd been socked in the gut.

"Swell. That means—" I let it hang there; she knew what it meant as well as I did: that the whole attack I had seen—lived through—the consequences of which we were looking at now—was what was known to the trade as a recidivism: an aborted alternate possibility that either had never occurred or had been eliminated by Timesweep action. In Mellia's past, the Dinosaur Beach station had been functional for over eleven hundred years, minimum, after the date I'd seen it under attack. She'd jumped from it to Libya, done her job, and jumped back—to find things changed.

Changed by some action of mine.

I had no proof of that assumption, of course; but I knew. I'd handled my assignment in 1936 according to the book, wrapped up all the loose ends, scored a total victory over my Karg counterpart. I thought.

But something had gone wrong. Something I'd done—or not done—had shattered the pattern. And the result was this.

"It doesn't make sense," I said. "You jumped back to home base and found it missing—the result of something that didn't happen in your own personally experienced past. O.K. But what puts me here at the same time? The circuits I used for my jump were tuned to a point almost twelve hundred years earlier."

"Why haven't they made a pick-up on me?" she said, not really talking to me. Her voice was edging up the scale a little.

"Take it easy, girl," I said, and patted her shoulder;

I knew my touching her would chill her down again. Not a nice thing to know, but useful.

"Keep your hands to yourself, Ravel," she snapped, all business again. "If you think this is some little desert island scene, you're very wrong."

"Don't get ahead of yourself," I told her. "When I make a pass at you that'll be time enough to slap me down. Don't go female on me now. We don't have time for nonsense."

She sucked in air with a sharp hiss and bottled up whatever snappy comeback she'd been about to make. Quite a girl. It was all I could do to keep from putting my arms around her and telling her it was all going to be all right. Which was a long way from what I believed.

"We can sit here and wait it out for a while longer," I said, in my best business-as-usual tone. "Or we can take action now. How do you vote?"

"What action?" It was a challenge.

"In my opinion," I said, not taking the bait, "the possible benefits of staying put are very small—statistically speaking. Still, they exist."

"Oh?" Very cool; just a little tremble of a finely molded lip that was beaded with sweat.

"This is a known locus; whatever the difficulties that caused the site to be abandoned, it's still a logical place for a search effort to check."

"That's nonsense. If it were checked and we were located the sensible thing to do—or at least the humane thing—would be to shift the pick-up back a month and take us out at the moment of our arrival. That didn't happen. Therefore it won't happen."

"Maybe you've forgotten what this Timesweep effort is all about, Miss Gayl. We're trying to knit the fabric back together, not make new holes in it. If we were spotted here, now—and the pick-up were made at a prior locus—what happens to all the tender moments we've known together? This moment right now? It never happened? No, any pick-up on us would be made at the point of initial contact, not earlier. However . . ."

"Well?"

"The possibility exists that we're occupying a closed-loop temporal segment, not a part of the main time-stem."

She looked a little pale under the desert tan, but her eyes held mine firmly.

"In which case—we're marooned—permanently."

I nodded. "Which is where the alternative comes in."

"Is there . . . one?"

"Not much of one. But a possibility. Your personal jumper's still operational."

"Nonsense. I'm tuned to home on the station fix. I'm already at the station fix. Where would I go?"

"I don't know. Maybe nowhere."

"What about you?"

I shook my head.

"I already used my reserve. Charge is gone. I'll have to wait for you to bring help back. So—I'll contain myself in patience—if you decide to try it, that is."

"But—an unfocused jump—"

"Sure—I've heard the scare stories too. But my jump wasn't so bad. I ended up in the station, remember?"

"A station in nowhere, as you described it."

"But with a transfer booth. When I used it, it pitched me back down my own timeline. As luck would have it, I ended up looking in on a previous field assignment. Maybe you'll be luckier."

"That's all that's left, isn't it? Luck."

"Better than nothing."

She stood, not looking at me; my Lisa, so hurt and so bewildered, so scared and trying not to show it, so beautiful, so desirable. I wondered if she had known—if it had been a sleeper assignment, meaning a field job in which the agent was conditioned to be unaware of his actual role, believed himself to be whatever his cover required.

"You really want me to go?" she said.

"Looks like the only way," I said. Good old iceberg Ravel, not an emotion in his body. "Unless you want to set up permanent housekeeping with me here on the beach." I gave her a nice leer to help her make her decision.

"There's another way," she said in a voice chipped out of ice. I didn't answer.

"My field will carry both of us," she said.

"Theoretically. Under, uh, certain conditions—"

"I know the conditions."

"Oh, hell, girl, we're wasting time—"

"You'd let me abandon you here before you'd . . ." She paused. " . . . meet those conditions?"

I drew a breath and tried to keep the strain out of my voice. "Not abandon. You'll be back."

"We'll go together," she said, "or not at all."

"Look, Miss Gayl, you don't have to—"

"Oh, yes, I *do* have to. Make no mistake about that, Mr. Ravel!"

She turned and walked off across the sand, looking very small and very forlorn against all that emptiness of beach and jungle.

I waited five minutes, for some obscure reason, before I followed her.

16

She was waiting for me in the tent. She had undressed and put on a lightweight robe. She stood beside the field bed which she had deployed to its full forty-inch width and looked past my shoulder. Her expression was perfectly calm, perfectly cool. I went across to her and put my hands lightly on her ribs just above her hips. Her skin was silk-smooth under the thin robe. She stiffened a little. I moved my hands up until the weight of her breasts was pressing against the heels of my hands. I drew her closer to me; she resisted minutely, then let her weight come against me. Her hair touched my face, soft as a cloud. I held her close. I was having a little trouble drawing a deep breath.

She pulled away suddenly, half turned away.

"What are you waiting for?" she said in a brittle voice.

"Maybe it would be better to wait," I said. "Until after dark . . ."

"Why?" she snapped. "So it would be more romantic?"

"Maybe; something like that."

"In case you've forgotten, Mr. Ravel, this isn't romance. It's expediency."

"Speak for yourself, Mellia."

"I assure you, I am!" She turned and faced me; her face was pink, her eyes bright.

"Damn you, get on with it!" she whispered.

"Unbutton my shirt," I said, very quietly. She just looked at me.

"Do as I said, Mellia."

Her expression went uncertain, then started to firm up into a sneer.

"Cut it!" I said with plenty of snap. "This was your idea, not mine, lady. I didn't force myself on you; I'm still not. But unless you want to make the grand sacrifice in vain, you'd better get into the spirit of the thing. Physical intimacy isn't the magic ingredient—it's psychological contact, the meeting and merging and sharing of personalities as well as bodies. The sexual aspect is merely the vehicle. So unless you can nerve yourself to stop thinking of me as a rapist, you can forget the whole idea."

She closed her eyes and drew a deep breath and let it out and looked at me again. Her lashes were wet; her mouth had gone all soft and vulnerable.

"I'm . . . sorry. You're right, of course. But . . . ?"

"I know. It isn't the bridal night you dreamed of."

I took her hand; it was soft, hot, unresisting.

"Have you ever been in love, Mellia?"

Her eyes winced; just a flicker of pain. "Yes."

Lisa, Lisa . . .

"Think back; remember how it was. Pretend . . . I'm him."

Her eyes closed. How delicate the lids were, the pastel tracery of veins in the rose-petal skin. I put my hands gently on her throat, slid them down to her shoulders, under the robe. Her skin was hot, damask-smooth. I pushed the garment down and away; it dropped from her shoulders, caught on the swell of her breasts. My hands moved down, brushing the cloth aside, taking the weight of her breasts on my palms. She drew a sharp breath between her teeth; her lips parted.

She dropped her arms, shed the robe. I glanced down at the slimness of her waist, the swell of hips as she came against me.

Her hands went uncertainly to the buttons on my shirt; she leaned back, opening it, pulling out my shirttail. She unbuckled my belt, went to her knees, dragged the rest of my clothing off. I picked her up, carried her to the cot. Rounded, yielding forms moved against me; my hands explored her, trying to encompass all of her. She shivered and drew me to her; her mouth half-opened; her eyelids parted and her eyes glittered into mine an inch away; her mouth met mine hungrily. My weight went onto her; her hands were deft; her thighs pressed against mine. We moved as one.

There was no time, no space, no thought. She filled my arms, my world; beauty, pleasure, sensation, fulfillment that rose and rose to a crest of unbearable delight that crashed down like a long Pacific comber, roiling and surging, then slowing, sliding smoothly to a halt, paused, then slipped back, back, down and out and away to merge with the eternal ocean of life. . . .

17

For a long time neither of us spoke. We lay spent in the amber light; the surf boomed and hissed softly, the wind fluted around the tent.

Her eyes opened and looked into mine, a look of utter candor, of questioning, perhaps of surprise. Then they closed again and she was asleep. I rose quietly and picked up my clothes and went outside, into the heat and the dry wind from the dunes. A pair of small saurians were on the beach a mile or so to the south. I dressed and went down to the water's edge and wandered along the surf line, watching the small life that scurried and swam with such desperate urgency in the shallows.

The sun was low when I got back to the tent. Mellia was busy, setting out food from the field stores. She was wearing the robe, barefooted, her hair unbound. She looked up at me as I came in; a look half-wary, half-impish. She looked so young, so achingly young. . . .

"I'll never be sorry," I said. "Even if . . ." I let it hang there.

She looked faintly troubled. "Even if . . . what?"

"Even if we proved the theory was wrong. . . ."

She stared at me; suddenly her eyes widened.

"I forgot to—," she said. "I forgot all about it. . . ."

I felt my face curving into a silly smile. "So did I—until just now."

She put her hand over her mouth and laughed. I held her and laughed with her. Then she was crying. Her arms went around me and she clung, and sobbed, and sobbed, and I stroked her hair and made soothing noises.

18

"This time I won't forget," she whispered in my ear. *In the dark; in the perfumed darkness* . . .

"Don't count on me to remind you," I said.

"Did you—do you love her very much—your Lisa?"

"Very much."

"How did you meet her?"

"In the Public Library. We were both looking for the same book."

"And you found each other."

"I thought it was an accident." *Or a miracle* . . .

I'd only been on location for a few days, just long enough to settle into my role and discover how lonely life was back in that remote era; remote, but, for me, the present: the only reality. As was usual in a long cover assignment, my conditioning was designed to fit me completely to the environment: my identity as Jim Kelly, draftsman, occupied 99 percent of my self-identity concept. The other 1 percent, representing my awareness of my true function as a Nexx agent, was in abeyance: a faint, persistent awareness of a level of existence above the immediate details of life in ancient Buffalo; a hint of a shadowy role in great affairs.

I hadn't known consciously, when I met Lisa, wooed and won her, that I was a transient in her time, a passer-through that dark and barbaric era. When I married her, it was with the intention of living out my life with her, for better or for worse, richer or poorer, until death did us part.

But we'd been parted by something more divisive than death. As the crisis approached, the knowledge of my real role came back to me a piece at a time, as needed. The confrontation with the Karg had completed the job.

"Perhaps it *was* an accident," Mellia said. "Even if she was . . . me . . . she might have been there for another reason, having nothing to do with your job. She didn't know. . . ."

"You don't have to defend her, Mellia. I don't blame her for anything."

"I wonder what she did . . . when you didn't come back."

"If I had, I wouldn't have found her there. She'd have been gone, back to base, mission completed—"

"No! Loving you wasn't any part of her mission; it couldn't have been like that. . . ."

"She was caught, just as I was. All in a good cause, no doubt. The giant brains at Central know best—"

"Hush," she said softly, and put her lips against mine. She clung to me, holding me tight against her slim nakedness, lying in the dark. . . .

"I'm jealous of her," she whispered. "And yet—she's me."

"I want you, Mellia; every atom of me wants you. I just can't help remembering."

She made a sound that was half laugh, half sob. "You're making love to me—and thinking of her. You feel that you're betraying her—with me—" She stopped to shush me as I started to speak.

"No—don't try to explain, Ravel. You can't change it—can't help it. And you do want me . . . you want me . . . I know you want me. . . ."

And this time as we rode the passionate crest, the world exploded and tumbled us together down a long, lightless corridor and left us in darkness and in silence.

19

Light coalesced around us; and sound: the soft breathing of an air circulation system. We were lying naked on the bare floor in the operations room of a Nexx Timecast station.

"It's small," Mellia said. "Almost primitive." She got to her feet and padded across to the intercom panel, flipped the master.

"Anybody home?" her voice echoed along the corridors.

Nobody was. I didn't have to search the place. You could feel it in the air.

Mellia went to the Excom-board; I watched her punch in an all-stations emergency code. A light winked to show that it had been automatically taped, condensed to a one-microsecond squawk, and repeated at one-hour intervals across a million years of monitored time.

She went to the log, switched on, started scanning the last entries, her face intent in the dim glow of the screen. Watching her move gracefully, unself-consciously nude, was deeply arousing to me. I got my mind off that with an effort and went to stand beside her.

The log entry was a routine shorthand report, station-dated 9/7/66, with Dinosaur Beach's identifying key and Nel Jard's authenticating code at the end.

"That's one day prior to the day I reported back,"

I said. "I guess he didn't have time to file any details during the attack."

"At least he got the personnel away before. . . ." She let that ride.

"All but himself," I said.

"But—you didn't find him—or any sign of him—in the station when you were here before. . . ."

"His corpse, you mean. Nope. Maybe he used the booth. Maybe he went over the edge—"

"Ravel—" She looked at me half sternly, half appealingly.

"Yeah. I think I'll go get some clothes on. Not that I don't like playing Adam and Eve with you," I added. "I like it all too well."

We found plenty of regulation clothing neatly stacked in the drawers in the transient apartment wing. I enjoyed the cool, smooth feel of modern fabric on my skin. Getting used to starched collars and itchy wool had been one of the chief sources of discomfort in my 1936 job. That started me thinking again.

I shook off the thought. Lisa—or Mellia—was standing not six feet away, pulling on a form-fitting one-piece station suit. She caught me looking at her and hesitated for an instant before zipping it up to cover her bosom, and smiled at me. I smiled back.

I went outside to take a look, knowing what I'd find: an abrupt edge ten paces from the exit, with the fog swirling around it. I yelled; no echo came back. I picked up a pebble and tossed it over the side. It fell about six feet and then slowed and drifted off as if it had lost interest in the law of gravity. I peered through the murk, looking for a rift with a view beyond it; but beyond the fog there was just more fog.

"It's . . . eerie," Mellia said beside me.

"All of that," I said. "Let's get back inside. We need sleep. Maybe when we wake up it will be gone."

She let that one pass. That night she slept in my arms. I didn't dream—except when I woke in the night and found her there.

20

At breakfast the clatter of forks against plates seemed louder than it should have been. The food was good. Nexx issue rations were designed to fill a part of the gap left in agents' lives by the absence of all human relationships and values that ordinarily made life worth living. We were dedicated souls, we field agents. We gave up homes and wives and children in the service of the concept that the human race and its destiny were worth the saving. It was a reasonable exchange. Any man ought to be able to see that.

But Lisa's face floated between me and my breakfast, the emergency I was involved in, the threat to Timesweep. Between me and Mellia.

"What are we going to do, Ravel?" Mellia said. Her expression was cool and calm now; her eyes held shielded secrets. Maybe it was the effect of the familiar official surroundings. The fun and games were over. From now on it was business.

"The first thing we need to do is take a good look at the data and see what can be deduced," I said, and felt like a pompous idiot.

"Very well; we have several observations between us that should give us some ideas of the parameters of the situation." Crisp; scientifically precise. Eyes level and steady. A good agent, Miss Gayl. *But where was the girl who had sobbed in my arms last night?*

"All right," I said. "Item: I completed a routine assignment, returned to the pickup point, sent out my callsign, and was retrieved. All normal so far." I glanced at her for agreement. She nodded curtly.

"The next day the station was attacked by Third Era Forces, or someone disguised as Third Era Forces. Aside from a rather unlikely breach of security, there's no anomaly involved there. However, *your* personal life line includes the Dino Beach station intact at a local time eleven-hundred-plus years later than the observed attack."

"Correct; and insofar as I know, there was no mention in the station records of any attack, a thousand years before I reported in, or any other time. And I think I'd know. I made it my business to familiarize myself with the station history as soon as I was assigned there."

"You didn't happen to notice any entry relating to the loss of a field man named Ravel?"

"If I did, it didn't register. The name meant nothing to me . . . then." Her eyes didn't quite meet mine.

"So we're talking about a class-one deviation. Either your past is aborted, or mine. The question is—which alternative is a part of the true timestem?"

"Insufficient data."

"Let's go on the next item: Nel Jard used an emergency system unknown to me to lift the entire station out of entropic context and deposit it in what can be described as an achronic vacuole. What that means I don't quite know."

"You're assuming it was Jard's action," Mellia put in. "There's a possibility it wasn't. That another force stepped in just at that time, either to complicate or annul his action. Did he say anything to indicate this was what he intended?" A tilt of her head indicated the silent room where we sat, and the ghostly void outside.

"He said something about null-time, but it didn't really register. I thought he had old-fashioned demolition in mind; simple denial-to-the-enemy stuff."

"In any event, the station was shifted . . . here."

I nodded. "And when I used my emergency jump gear, I homed in on it. I suppose that was to be expected. I was tuned to the station frequency; the equipment was designed for retrieval from any space-time locus."

"You found the station empty—just as it is now. . . ."

"Uh-huh. I wonder . . ." I looked around the room. "Was my last visit before this one—or after?"

"At least it wasn't simultaneous. You didn't meet yourself."

"It ought to be possible to tell," I said. "The local entropic flow seems to be normal; local time is passing." I got up and wandered around the room, looking for some evidence of my having been there before. If there was any, I couldn't see it. I turned back to the table—and there it was.

"The trays," I said. "They were here—on the table."

Mellia looked at them, then at me. She looked a little scared. Anachronisms affect you that way.

"The same two seats," I said. "The leftovers didn't look too fresh—but they hadn't had time to decay."

"So—you're due here at any time."

"We have a few hours anyway. The stuff was dry on the trays." I gave her a we're-in-this-together look. "We could wait," I said, "and meet me."

"No!" Very sharp. "No" again, less urgently, but still definite. "We mustn't introduce any further para-nomalies, you know that."

"If we stopped me from going back and interfering with my previous assignment—"

"You're talking nonsense, Ravel. Now who's forgotten what the Timesweep effort is all about? Putting patches on the patches is no good. You went back—you returned safely. Here you are. It would be stupid to risk that, on . . . on . . ."

"On the chance of saving the operation?"

Her eyes met mine. "We can't complicate matters further. You went back, let's leave it at that. The question is—what's our indicated course of action now?"

I sat down. "Where were we?"

"You found the station empty, with evidence of our—present—visit."

"So I did the only thing that occurred to me. I used the station facilities for a jump I hoped would put me back at Nexx Central. It didn't work. In the absence of a programmed target, I reverted back along my own timeline and ended ten years in my subjective past. A class-A paranomaly, breaking every regulation in the book."

"Regulations don't cover our situation," she said. "You had no control over matters. You did what seemed best."

"And blew a job that was successfully completed and encoded on the master timeplot ten years ago. One curious item in that connection is that the Karg I was supposed to take out—and didn't—was the same one I hit in Buffalo. Which implies that the Buffalo sequence followed from the second version rather than the original one."

"Or what you're considering the alternate version. Maybe it isn't. Perhaps your doubling-back was assimilated as a viable element in the revised plot."

"In that case, you're right about not waiting here to intercept me. But if you're wrong . . ."

"We have to take a stand somewhere—somewhen. You jumped back to the beach after that and we met. Query: Why did both you and I home in on the same temporal locus?"

"No comment."

"We're snarling hell out of the timelines, Ravel."

"Can't be helped. Unless you think we ought to Kamikaze."

"Don't be foolish. We have to do what we can. Which means examine the facts and plan a logical next step."

"Logical: that's a good one, Agent Gayl. When did logic ever have anything to do with Timesweep Ops?"

"We've made some progress," she said levelly, not rising to the bait, refusing the opportunity for a nice soul-scouring argument. "We know we have to be on our way, and without much delay."

"All right, I'll grant the point. Which leaves us a choice of two courses. We can use the station transfer booth."

"And end up somewhere back in our own pasts, complicating matters still further."

"Could be. Or we can recharge our personal gear and jump out at random."

"With no conception of where that might put us." She shivered and covered it with a gesture; a graceful lift of her chin that reminded me of another time, another place, another girl.

No, damn it—not another girl!

"Or," she said, "we could go together . . . as we did before."

"That wouldn't change anything, Mellia. We'd still be launching ourselves into the timestream with no target. We might find ourselves spinning end over end in a fog like the one outside—or worse."

"At least—" she started to say, and caught herself. At *least we'd be together*—I could almost hear the words.

"At least we won't be sitting here idle while the universe falls to pieces around us," she said instead.

"So—how do you vote?"

There was a long silence. She didn't look at me; then she did. She started to speak, hesitated.

"The booth," she said.

"Together or one at a time?"

"Can the field handle both of us simultaneously?"

"I think so."

"Together. Unless you know a reason for separating."

"None at all, Mellia."

"Then it's settled."

"Right. Now finish your meal. It may be a while before we have another chance to eat."

My last item of preparation was a small crater gun from the armory. I strapped it to my wrist, just out of sight under the cuff. We went along the time-shielded transit tunnel to the transfer booth. All readings were normal; the circuits were ready to operate. Under normal conditions a passenger would be rotated painlessly and instantaneously out of the timestream into the extratemporal medium, and rerotated into normal space-time at the main reception room at Nexx Central. What would happen this time was an open question. Maybe we'd drop back down my timeline, and there'd be two of us aboard the sinking galleass; or maybe Mellia Gayl's gestalt would be stronger and we'd arrive at a point in her past where we hadn't arrived before, thus adding to the disaster that had hit us. Or possibly somewhere in between. Or nowhere at all . . .

"Next stop Nexx Central," I said, and ushered Mellia inside. I squeezed in after her.

"Ready?"

She nodded.

I pressed the *Transmit* button.

The explosion blew both of us into our component atoms.

21

"Or maybe not," I heard a voice croak. I recognized the voice; it was mine, somewhat the worse for wear but still on the job. "Some dream," I went on, giving myself the word. "Some hangover. Some headache."

"Trans-temporal shock is the technical term, I believe," Lisa said beside me.

My eyes snapped open; well, snap isn't quite the word. They unglued themselves and winced at the light and made out a face nearby. A nice face, heart-shaped, with big dark eyes and the prettiest smile in the world.

But not Lisa.

"Are you all right?" Mellia said.

"It's nothing that a month in the intensive care unit wouldn't clear up," I said and got an elbow under me and looked around. We were in a spacious room, long and high, like a banqueting hall, with a smooth gray floor, pale gray walls covered with row on row of instrument faces. Center position went to a big chair facing an array of display screens and a coding console. At the far end the open sky was visible through a glass wall.

"Where are we?"

"I don't know. Some sort of technical facility. You don't recognize it?"

I shook my head; if it was anything out of my past, the memory had been wiped clean.

"How long have I been out?" I asked.

"I woke up an hour ago."

I shook my head to clear it, and succeeded in sending pains like hot knives through my temples.

"Rough passage," I mumbled, and got to my feet. I felt sick and dizzy, as if I'd eaten too much ice cream on the merry-go-round.

"I've looked at some of the equipment," Mellia said. "Temporal gear, but not exactly like anything I've seen." Her tone suggested that meant something important. I tried to focus my brain and figure out what.

I said, "Oh."

"I could deduce the function of some of it," she said. "Some was completely baffling."

"Maybe it's Third Era stuff—"

"I'd recognize that."

"Let's take a look." I headed toward the big controller's chair, trying to look healthier than I felt. If the jump had affected Mellia at all, she didn't show it.

The console was covered with buttons labeled laconically with designations such as $M. Ds—H$ and LV 3-gn. The screens were the usual milky-glass anti-glare surfaces, set inside anti-reflecting frames.

"They're ordinary analog-potential readout boards, of course," Mellia said, "but with two extra banks of controls—and that implies at least an additional order of sensitivity in the discretion and weighing circuitry."

"Does it?"

"Certainly." Her slim finger reached past me, tapped out a swift code on the colored keys. The screen twinkled and snapped to brightness.

"The pickup field is on active phase—or should be," she said. "But there's no base reading. And I'm afraid to play with a Timecast keybank I don't understand."

"You've left me in the shade," I said. "I never saw anything like this stuff. What else is there?"

"There are rooms back there." She pointed to the end of the hall opposite the glass wall. "Equipment rooms; a power section, operations . . ."

"Sounds like a regulation Timecasting station."

She nodded. "Almost."

"A little on the large side," I commented. "Let's take a look."

We went through rooms packed with gear as mysterious to me as a wiring diagram to I-Em Hotep. One contained nothing but three full-length mirrors; our reflections looking back at us were a couple of forlorn strangers. Nowhere were there any indications of recent habitation. No people, no signs of people. Just a dead building full of echoes.

We recrossed the grand hall and found an exit vestibule that cycled us out onto a wide stone terrace above a familiar view of sand and sea. The curve of the shoreline was as I had seen it last; only the jungle growth on the headland seemed denser, more solid somehow.

"Good old Dinosaur Beach," I said. "Doesn't change much, does it?"

"Time has passed," Mellia said. "A great deal of time."

"There was nothing like this in any projection plan I ever saw," I said. "Any ideas?"

"Not that I want to verbalize."

"I know how you feel," I said, and held the door for her. "By the way: I ought to tell you: I never heard of analog-potential. What is it, a new kind of breakfast food?"

"A-P is the basis of the entire Timesweep program," she said and looked at me sharply. "Any Nexx agent would have to be familiar with it." She was frowning at me pretty severely.

"Don't count on it," I said. "The lectures I got at the Institute were all about deterministics, actualization dynamics, and fixation levels."

"That's nonsense. Discredited Fatalistics Theory."

"Hold on, Miss Gayl, before you pop a valve. Don't look at me as if you'd caught me in the computer room with a live bomb. I admit I'm a little slow this morning, what with the heavy swell under the stern quarter, but I'm still the same sweet, lovable guy you fished out of the pond. I'm as much a Nexxman as you are; but a kind of dirty suspicion is sneaking up on me."

"And what might that be?"

"That the Nexx Central you work out of and the one I know aren't the same."

"That's ridiculous. The entire Nexx operation is based on the stability of the unique Nexx Baseline—"

"Sure—that's the concept. It won't be the first concept that had to be modified in the face of experience."

She looked a little pale. "You realize what you're implying?"

"Uh-huh. We've messed things up good, kid. For you and me to be standing here face to face— representatives of two mutually exclusive base timetracks—means things are worse than we thought; worse than I knew they could be."

Her eyes held on mine, wide and shocked. I was doing a good job of reassuring her.

"But we're not licked yet," I said heartily. "We're still trained agents, still operational. We'll do the best we can—"

"That's not the point."

"Oh? What is?"

"We have a job to do—as you said: to attempt to reintroduce ourselves into the temporal pattern by eliminating the chronomalies we've unwittingly generated."

"Agreed."

"Very well—what pattern do we work toward, Ravel? Yours—or mine? Is it a Deterministic or an A-P continuum we're supposed to be reassembling?"

I started to give her a fast, reassuring answer, but it stuck in my throat.

"We can work that out later," I said.

"How can we? Every move we make from this point on has to be correctly calculated. There's equipment here—" she waved a hand—"that's more sophisticated than anything I've ever seen. But we have to use it properly."

"Sure we do—but first we have to figure out what all the pretty little buttons are for. Let's concentrate on that for the present, Mellia. Maybe along the way we can resolve the philosophical questions."

"Before we can work together, we have to come to some agreement."

"Go on."

"I want your word you won't . . . do anything prejudicial to the A-P concept."

"I won't do anything without conferring with you first. As to what Universe it is we're rebuilding—let's wait until we know a little more before we commit ourselves, all right?"

She looked at me a long time before she said, "Very well."

"You might start," I said, "by explaining this setup to me."

She spent the next hour giving me a fast, sketchy, but graphic briefing on the art of analog-potential interpretation; I listened as fast as I could. The A-P theory was news to me, but I was accustomed to working with complex chronic gear. I began to get some idea of what the equipment was for.

"I get the feeling that your version of Nexx Central operates a lot farther out in the theoretical boondocks than the one I know," I said. "And backs it up with some very highly evolved hardware."

"Of course, what I'm accustomed to is much less advanced than this," Mellia said. "I don't know what to make of a lot of this."

"But you're sure it's A-P type gear?"

"There's no doubt in my mind at all. It couldn't be anything else—certainly not anything that Deterministic theory might have given rise to."

"I agree with that last point. This layout would make about as much sense at Central—my Central—as a steam whistle on a sailboat."

"Then you agree we have to work toward an A-P matrix?"

"Slow down, girl. You talk as if all we had to do was shake hands on it, and everything would switch back to where it was last Wednesday at three o'clock. We're working in the blind. We don't know what's happened, where we are, where we're going, or how to get there. Let's take it one item at a time. A good place to start would be this whole A-P concept. I get a strange feeling that its theoretical basis is a second-generation type of thing; that it arises from the kind of observational foundation generated by a major temporal realignment."

"Would you mind clarifying that?" she said coldly.

I waved a hand. "Your Central isn't on the main timestem. It's too complex, too artificial. It's like a star with a large heavy-element content: it can't arise from the primordial dust cloud. It has to be formed out of stellar debris from a previous generation."

"That's a rather fanciful analogy. Is that the best you can do?"

"On such short notice. Or would you rather have me suppress anything that seems to cast doubts on your A-P universe as the best of all possible worlds?"

"That's unfair."

"Is it? I've got a stake in my past, too, Miss Gayl. I'm not any more eager to be relegated to the realms of unrealized possibilities than anybody else."

"I . . . I didn't mean that. What makes you think— there's no reason to believe—"

"I have a funny feeling there's no place for me in your world-picture, Mellia. Your original world-picture, that is. I'm the guy who loused up the sweet serenity of Dinosaur Beach. But for me, the old outfit would have been in operation for another thousand years at the same address."

She started to say something, but I steam-rollered it.

"But it wasn't. I fouled up my assignment—don't ask me how—and as a result, blew the station to Kingdom Come—or wherever it disappeared to—"

"You don't need to blame yourself. You carried out your instructions; it wasn't your fault if the results . . . if after you came back . . ."

"Yeah. If what I did started a causal chain that resulted in your not being born. But you *were* born, L—Mellia. I met you on a cover assignment in 1936. So at that point, at least, we were on the same track. Or—" I cut it off there, but she saw the same thing I did.

"Or perhaps . . . your whole sequence in Buffalo was an aborted loop. Not part of the Main Tape. Not viable."

"It's viable, baby. You can depend on it." I ground that out like a rock crusher reducing boulders to number nine gravel.

"Of course," she whispered. "It's Lisa, isn't it? She *has* to be real. Any alternative is unthinkable. And if that means remaking the space-time continuum, aborting a thousand years of Timestem history, wrecking Timesweep and all it means—why, that's a small price to pay for the existence of your beloved!"

"You said it. I didn't."

She looked at me the way a tough engineer looks at a hill that's standing where he wants to build a level crossing.

"Let's get to work," she said at last in a voice from which every shred of emotion had been scraped.

22

We spent the rest of the day making a methodical survey of the installation. It was four times the size of the Dinosaur Beach stations we had known in our previous incarnations; and 80 percent of it was given over to gear that neither of us understood. Mellia pieced together the general plan of the station, identified the major components of the system, traced out the power transfer apparatus, deduced the meanings of some of the cryptic legends at the control consoles. I followed her and listened.

"It doesn't make much sense," she said. It was twilight, and a big red sun was casting long shadows across the floor. "The power supply is out of all proportion to any intelligence-input or interpretative function I can conceive. And all this space—what's it for, Ravel? What is this place?"

"Grand Central Station," I said.

"What's that?"

"Nothing. Just a forgotten building in a forgotten town that probably never existed. A terminal."

"You may be right," she said, sounding thoughtful. "If this were all designed to transfer bulk cargo, rather than merely as a communications and personnel staging facility . . ."

"Cargo. What kind of cargo?"

"I don't know. It doesn't sound likely, does it? Any appreciable inter-local material transfer would tend to weaken the temporal structure at both transmission and reception points. . . ."

"Maybe they didn't care anymore. Maybe they were like me: tired." I yawned. "Let's turn in; maybe tomorrow it will all turn into sweet reasonableness before our startled gaze."

"What did you mean by that remark? About not caring?"

"Who me? Not a thing, girl, not a thing."

"Did you ever call Lisa 'girl'?" This sharply.

"What's that got to do with anything?"

"It has everything to do with everything! Everything you say and do—everything you think—is colored by your idiotic infatuation with this . . . this figmentary sweetheart! Can't you forget her and put your mind on the fact that the Nexx Timestem is in desperate danger—if it's not irreparably damaged—by your irresponsible actions!"

"No," I said between my teeth. "Any other questions?"

"I'm sorry," she said in a spent voice. She put a hand over her face and shook her head. "I didn't mean that. I'm just tired . . . so very tired—and frightened."

"Sure," I said. "Me too. Forget it. Let's get some sleep."

We picked separate rooms. Nobody bothered to say good night.

23

I got up early; even asleep, the silence got to me. There was a well-equipped kitchen at the end of the dormitory wing; apparently even A-P theoreticians had a taste for a fresh-laid egg and a slice of sugar-cured ham from a nulltime locker where aging didn't happen.

I punched in two breakfasts and started back to call Mellia, and then changed my mind when I heard footsteps across the big hall.

She was standing by the Timecaster's chair, dressed in a loose robe, looking at the screen. She didn't hear me coming, barefooted, until I was within ten feet of her. She turned suddenly, and from the expression on her face, nearly had an angina attack.

So did I. It wasn't Mellia's beautiful if disapproving face; it was an old woman, white-haired, with sunken cheeks and faded eyes that might have been bright and passionate once, a long time ago. She tottered, as if she were going to fall, and I shot out a hand and caught her by an arm as thin as a stick of wood inside her flowing sleeve. She made a nice recovery; feature by feature, her face put itself back together, leaving a look that was almost too serene, under the circumstances.

"Yes," she said, in a thin, old, but very calm voice. "You've come. As I knew you would, of course."

"It's nice to be expected, ma'am," I said inanely. "Who told you? About us, I mean. Coming, that is."

A flicker of a frown went across her face. "The predictor screens, of course." Her eyes went past me. "May I ask: where is the rest of your party?"

"She's, ah, still asleep."

"Asleep? How very curious."

"Back there." I nodded toward the bedrooms. "She'll be happy to know we aren't alone here. We had a long day yesterday, and—"

"Excuse me. Yesterday? When did you come?"

"About twenty-four hours ago."

"But—why didn't you advise me at once? I've been waiting—I've been ready . . . for such a long time . . ." Her voice almost broke, but she caught it.

"I'm sorry, ma'am. We didn't know you were here. We searched the place, but—"

"You didn't *know?*" Her face looked shocked, stricken.

"Where were you keeping yourself? I thought we'd checked every room. . . ."

"I . . . my . . . I have my quarters in the outwing," she said in a broken voice. A tear spilled from the outer corner of each eye and she brushed them away impatiently. "I had assumed," she said, getting her voice under control again, "that you had come in response to my signal. But of course that's not important. You're here. May I have just a few minutes? There are some things—mementos—but if there's any hurry, I can leave them, of course," she added hurriedly, watching my face.

"I have no intention of hurrying you, ma am," I said. "But I think there may be some misunderstanding—"

"But you *will* take me?" Her thin hand caught my arm; panic was in her voice. "Oh, please, take me with you, I beg you, please, don't leave me here—"

"I promise," I said, and put my hand over hers; it was as cool and thin as a turkey's foot.

"But I think you're making some erroneous assumptions. Maybe I did too. Are you a part of the station cadre?"

"Oh, no." She shook her head like a child caught with a paw in the cookie jar. "This is not my station. Not my station at all. I merely took refuge here, you see, after the collapse."

"Where are the station personnel, ma'am?"

She looked at me as if I'd said something amazing. "There are none. No one. It's as I stated in my reports. I found the station abandoned. I've been here alone, no one else—"

"Sure, I see, just you. Pretty lonely. But it's all right now, we're here, you won't be alone any longer."

"Yes, you're here. As I knew you would be— someday. The instruments never lie. That's what I told myself. It was just that I didn't know *when.*"

"Instruments—told you we'd come?"

"Oh, yes."

She sank into the nearest chair, and her old fingers flew over the keys. The screen lit up, changed texture, flowed through colors, ended a vivid greenish-white rectangle on the right edge of which a wavering black vertical line, like a scratch on a film strip, flickered and danced. I was about to open my mouth to admire her virtuosity on the keyboard when she made a small sighing sound and crumpled forward onto her face, out cold.

I grabbed her, eased her from the chair, got my arms under her. She couldn't have weighed ninety pounds. Mellia met me at the mouth of the corridor. She stopped dead and put a hand over her mouth, then remembered her Field Agent's training and smoothed the look off her face.

"Ravel—who—"

"Dunno. She was here when I woke up; thought I'd come to rescue her. She started to tell me something, and fainted."

Mellia stepped back to let me pass, her eyes on the old woman. She stiffened; she caught my arm. She stared at the withered face.

"Mother!" she gasped.

24

I let a few long seconds slide past. The old lady's eyes fluttered and opened. "Mother!" Mellia said again and grabbed for her hand.

The old lady smiled rather vaguely. "No, no, I'm not anyone's mother," she said. "I always wanted . . . but . . ." She faded out again.

I took her along to an empty room and put her on the bed. Mellia sat beside her and rubbed her hands and made sure she was breathing properly.

"What's this about your mother?" I said.

"I'm sorry. She's not my mother, of course. I was just being silly. I suppose all elderly women look alike . . ."

"Is your mother that old?"

"No, of course not. It was just a superficial resemblance." She gave me a small apologetic laugh. "I suppose the psychologists could read all sorts of things into it."

"She said she was expecting us," I said. "Said the instruments predicted it."

Mellia looked at me. "Predicted? There's no such instrument."

"Maybe she's slipped her clutch. Alone too long."

The old lady sighed and opened her eyes again. If Lisa reminded her of anyone, she didn't say so. Mellia made encouraging noises. They smiled at each other. Love at first sight.

"Now I've made an old fool of myself," the old lady said. "Fainting like that . . ." Her expression became troubled.

"Don't be silly," Mellia said. "It's perfectly understandable. . . ."

"Do you feel well enough to talk?" I said, in spite of the dirty look Mellia gave me.

"Of course."

I sat on the side of the bed. "Where are we?" I asked as gently as possible. "What is this place?"

"The Dinosaur Beach Timecast station," the old girl said, looking just a little surprised.

"Maybe I should say *when* are we . . ."

"The station date is twelve thirty-two." Now she looked puzzled.

"But—" Mellia said.

"Meaning we haven't made a Timejump after all," I told her, as smoothly as you can say something as preposterous as that.

"Then—we've jumped—somehow—to a secondary line!"

"Not necessarily. Who's to say what's primary and what's secondary, after what we've been through?"

"Excuse me," the old lady said. "I get the impression from what you say that . . . that matters are not as well as might be hoped."

Mellia gave me a troubled look. I passed it on to the old lady.

"It's quite all right," she said. "You may speak freely to me . . . I understand that you are Timecast agents. That makes us colleagues." She smiled faintly.

"Field Agent Mellia Gayl, at your service," she said.

25

I happened to be looking at Mellia—*my* Mellia; her face turned as pale as marble. She didn't move, didn't speak.

"And who are you, my dear?" the old lady said, almost gaily. She couldn't see Mellia's face. "I almost feel I know you."

"I'm Field Agent Ravel," I spoke up. "This is—Agent Lisa Kelly."

Mellia turned on me, but caught herself. I watched her smoothing her face out; it was an admirable piece of work.

"We're happy to meet . . . a . . . a colleague, Agent Gayl," she said in a voice with all the color washed out of it.

"Oh, yes, I led a very active life at one time," the old lady said, lightly, smiling. "Life was exciting in those days, before . . . before the Collapse. We had such high ambitions, such a noble program. How we worked and planned! After each mission, we'd gather to study the big screen, to gauge the effects of our efforts, to congratulate or commiserate with each other. We had such *hopes* in those days."

"I'm sure you did," Mellia said in a lifeless whisper.

"After the official announcement, of course, things were different," the elderly Miss Gayl went on. "We still tried, of course; we hadn't really accepted defeat, admitted it; but we knew. And then . . . the deterioration began. The chronodegradation. Little things, at first. The loss of familiar articles, the memory lapses, and the contradictions. We sensed life unraveling around us. Many of the personnel began dropping off, then. Some jumped out to what they hoped might be stable loci; others were lost in temporal distortion areas. Some simply—deserted, wandered away. I stayed on, of course. I always hoped—somehow—" She broke off abruptly. "But all that's neither here nor there, of course—"

"No—please. Go on," young Mellia said.

"Why—there's little more to tell. The time came when there were only a handful of us left at Central. We agreed it was impossible to attempt to keep the transmitters in operation any longer. We'd made no personnel retrieval for over a year, the equipment was chronodegrading at an accelerating rate, there was no way of knowing what additional damage we might be doing to the temporal fabric with our improperly tuned gear. So—we shut down. After that, matters swiftly deteriorated. Abnormal manifestations increased. Conditions became—difficult. We out-jumped, and found matters in an even worse state elsewhere—and else-when. I'm afraid we panicked. I know I did. I admit it now—though at the time I told myself I was searching for a configuration where I might attempt to rally stablizing forces—but that was mere rationalization. I jumped out—and out. At last—I arrived here. To me it seemed a haven of peace and stability. Empty, of course—but safe. For a while I was almost happy—until, of course, I discovered I was trapped." She looked up at me and smiled a frail smile.

"Twice I tried to escape," she whispered. "Each time—after horrifying experiences—I ended back here. Then I knew. I had entered a closed loop. I was caught—until someone came to set me free. So—I . . . settled down to wait." She gave me a look that made me feel as if I'd just kicked a cripple down the stairs.

"You seem to be familiar with the equipment," I said, just to fill the conversational gap.

"Oh, yes, I've had ample time to explore its capabilities. Its potential capabilities, that is to say. Under the circumstances, of course, only minimal environmental monitor functions are possible—such as the forecast vectors that indicated that one day help would come." The smile again, as if I was Lindy and I'd just flown an ocean, all for her.

"The screen you activated," I said, "I've never seen one just like it. Is it the one that, ah, foretells the future?"

"Screen?" she looked puzzled. Then recollection came; she gasped and sat up suddenly. "I must check—"

"No, no, you need to rest!" Mellia protested.

"Help me up, my dear. I *must* confirm the read-out!"

Mellia started to argue, but I caught her eye and together we helped our patient to her feet, along the corridor.

The lighted screen was still the same: a rectangle of green luminosity with a ragged edge that rippled and danced on the extreme right. The old lady gave a weak cry and clutched our hands.

"What is it?" MeIlia asked.

"The Maintrunk forecast carrier!" she quavered. "It's gone—off the screen!"

"Maybe an adjustment—" I started.

"No! The reading is true," she said in a voice that suddenly had a faint echo of what had once been a snap of authority. "A terminal reading!"

"What does it mean?" Mellia asked in a soothing tone. "Surely it can't be that serious—"

"It means we've come to the end of the temporal segment we're occupying. That for us—time is coming to an end."

"You're sure of this?" I asked.

"Quite sure."

"How long?"

"It may be hours, or minutes," the old Mellia said. "I think this is a contingency the makers of the equipment never anticipated occurring." She gave me a calm, self-contained look. "If you have transfer capability to any secondary trunk, I suggest you use it without delay."

I shook my head. "No, we shot our final bolt getting here. We're stranded."

"Of course. At infinity all lines converge at a point. Time ends; so must all else."

"What about the station transfer facilities?" Mellia asked. Agent Gayl shook her head.

"I tried; it's fruitless. You'd endure needless horrors—for nothing."

"Still—"

"She's right," I said. "There'll be nothing for us there. We need another approach. All this equipment—isn't there something here that can be used—converted, maybe—to crack us out of this dead end?"

"Perhaps—if one were technically trained," the old Mellia said vaguely. "But it's far beyond my competence."

"We can recharge our personal fields," I said, and felt a sudden change in the atmosphere. So did Mellia—both of her. The screen *flick-flick-flicked* and died. The indicator lights faded, all across the panels. The background sounds dwindled into silence. The color of the air changed, became a dirty electric translucence. Tiny waves of color seemed to ripple across the surfaces of objects, like chromatic aberration in a cheap lens. A chill struck through the air as if someone had just opened a giant refrigerator door.

"It's the end," the elderly Mellia said, quite calmly now. "Time ceases, all wave phenomena drop to a zero frequency, and thus become nonexistent—including that special form of energy we call matter. . . ."

"Just a minute," I said. "This is no natural phenomenon. Someone's manipulating the chronocosm!"

"How do you know that?" Mellia asked.

"No time for conversation. Agent Gayl"—I took the old lady's arm—"where were you when we arrived?"

Mellia started to protest, but the other Mellia answered promptly: "In the stasis vault."

"The mirrors?"

She nodded. "I was . . . ashamed to tell you. It seemed so . . . cowardly."

"Come on. I led the way across the big room, through the silence and the cold and the dead air, down the passage to the hall of mirrors. The reflective surfaces were tarnished, but still intact.

"Quickly!" the old Mellia said. "The fields will break down at any moment!"

Sounds came from the direction of the big room:

a crash as of falling masonry, curiously muffled; a heavy rumbling. A slow cloud of smoke or dust bulged leisurely along the passage. Yellow light glowed behind it.

"Inside—fast!" I said to Mellia.

"No—you and . . . Agent Gayl!"

"Don't argue, girl!" I caught her in my arms, pushed her toward the mirror. Waves of dull color ran across it. Mellia struggled.

"Mr. Ravel—you must go—now!" the elder Mellia said, and turned quickly and walked back toward the advancing dust-roil. Mellia cried out; I thrust her through the mirror. Her cry cut off sharply.

The old lady was gone, invisible beyond the obscuring cloud. I stepped to the other mirror; it felt like cold fog. It shimmered around me, cloying like impalpable gray gelatin, flashed like exploding glass. Darkness closed in.

For a moment I was aware of a sense of breathless expectancy, like the instant after the disaster becomes apparent and before the first shock arrives.

Then nothing.

26

A yellow light was shining through the murk. I didn't know how long it had been shining. It grew brighter, and a man appeared silhouetted against it, walking slowly forward, as if against resistance.

When he was six feet away, I saw my mistake.

Not a man. A Karg. The same one I'd killed twice and let get away a third time.

I couldn't move a muscle, not even my eyes. I watched the Karg cross my field of vision. I wasn't breathing; if my heart was beating, I couldn't feel it. But I was conscious. That was something.

The Karg was moving with effort, but unconcernedly. He was dressed in a plain black skin suit with harness and attachments. He looked at an array of miniature meters strapped to his wrist—the underside—and made an adjustment. So far he had paid no more attention to me than as if I were a piece of bric-a-brac.

Now he came over to me and looked me over. His baby-blue eyes never quite met mine—not from embarrassment, just indifference. Two other men—not Kargs—came into view. They ploughed their way up to him, conferred. The newcomers were carrying something that looked like bundled shingles. They came on across to me, moved around behind me, all this in total silence. Some time passed—or maybe it didn't. From the corner of my eye I saw movement. A panel slid into position to my left. It was dark green, glassy. Another appeared on my right. One of the men entered my field of vision, carrying a three-by-six sheet of thin material. He stood it on end; it stood by itself in midair without support. He pushed it in front of me and closed off my view. Light showed at its edges; then it snapped into place and left me in a darkness like the inside of a paint can.

With the visual reference gone, I lost my sense of orientation. I was upside down, spinning slowly—or not so slowly; I was a mile high, I was an inch high, I filled the universe, I didn't exist—

With a crash, sound returned to the world, along with gravity, pains all over like a form-fitting suit studded with needles, and suffocation. I dragged hard and got a breath in, feeling my heart start to thump and wheeze in its accustomed way. The roar faded without fading; it was just the impact of air molecules whanging against my eardrums, I realized: a background sound that was ordinarily filtered out automatically.

My knee bumped the wall in front of me. I was bracing myself to give it a kick when it fell away and I stepped out into a big room with high purple-black walls, where three people waited for me with expressions that were more intent than welcoming.

One was a short, thick-fingered man in a gray smock, with thin hair, ruddy features, rubbery lips stretched back over large off-white teeth. Number two was a woman, fortyish, a little on the lean side, very starched and official in dark green. The third was the Karg, dressed now in a plain gray coverall.

Shorty stepped forward and thrust out a hand; he held it in a curiously awkward position, with the fingers spread and pointed down. I shook it once and he took it back and examined it carefully, as if he thought I might have left a mark.

"Welcome to Dinosaur Beach Station," the Karg said in a reasonable facsimile of a friendly voice. I looked around the room; we were the only occupants.

"Where are the two women?" I asked. The thick man looked blank and pulled at his rubbery lip. The female looked back at me as if it was all academic to her.

"Perhaps Dr. Javeh will wish to explain matters." She sounded as if she doubted it.

"I'm not interested in having a conversation with a machine," I said. "Who programs it? You?" I aimed this last at Rubber-lips.

"Whaaat?" he said, and looked at the woman; she looked at the Karg; it looked at me. I looked at all of them.

"Dr. Javeh is our Chief of Recoveries," the woman said quickly, as if glossing over a small social blunder on my part. "I'm Dr. Fresca; and this is Administrator Koska."

"There were two women with me, Dr. Fresca," I said. "Where are they?"

"I'm sure I have no idea; this is hardly my area of competence."

"Where are they, Koska?"

His lips worked, snapping from a smile to dismay and back. "As to that, I can only refer you to Dr. Javeh—"

"You take orders from this Karg?"

"I'm not familiar with that term." Stiffly; the smile gone.

I faced the Karg. He looked blandly at me with his pale blue eyes.

"You're a bit disoriented," he said quietly. "Not surprising, of course, they often are—"

"Who's 'they'?"

"The recoverees. That's my work—our work, you understand: detecting, pinpointing, and retrieving personnel in, ah, certain circumstances."

"Who's your boss, Karg?"

He cocked his head. "I'm sorry; I don't understand your repeated use of the term 'Karg.' Just what does it signify?"

"It signifies that whatever these people believe, I'm on to you."

He smiled and lifted his hands, let them fall back. "As you will. As for my supervisor—I happen to be Officer-in-Charge here."

"Cosy," I said. "Where are the two women?"

The Karg's little rosebud mouth tightened. "I have no idea to whom you refer."

"They were with me—five minutes ago. You must have seen them."

"I'm afraid you don't quite understand the situation,"

the Karg said. "When I found you, you were quite alone. The indications suggest you had been adrift in the achronic void for an extended period."

"How long?"

"Ah, a most interesting problem in temporal relativistics. We have biological time, unique to the individual, metered in heartbeats; and psychological time, a purely subjective phenomenon in which seconds can seem like years, and the reverse. But as to your question: The Final Authority has established a calibration system for gauging absolute duration; and in terms of that system, your sojourn outside the entropic stream endured for a period in excess of a century, with an observational error of plus or minus 10 percent, I should say."

The Karg spread his uncalloused hands, smiled a philosophical smile.

"As for your, ah, female—I know nothing."

I swung on him; the swing didn't connect, but I got the crater gun into my hand unseen. The Karg ducked back and Dr. Fresca let out a yelp and Koska grabbed my arm. The Karg flicked something at me that smacked my side wetly and spread and grabbed my arms and suddenly I was wrapped to the knees in what looked like spider webs, white as spun candy, smelling of a volatile polyester.

I tried to take a step and almost fell, and Koska stepped forward to assist me to a chair, all very solicitously, as if I'd had one of my fainting spells, but I'd be all right in a minute.

"You're a liar, Karg," I said, "and a bad one. It takes a live man to perjure himself with that true ring of sincerity. You didn't grapple me out of a few billion square millennia of eternity at random. They did a nice job on your scars, but you know me. And if you know me, you know her."

The Karg looked thoughtful; he motioned, and Koska and the woman left the room without a backward glance. He faced me with a different expression on his plastalloy features.

"Very well, Mr. Ravel, I know you. Not personally; your reference to scars presumably applies to some confrontation which has been relegated to the status of the unrealized possibility. But I know you by reputation, by profession. As for the woman—possibly I can look into the matter of a search for her later—after we've reached an understanding." He was just a Karg now, all business and no regrets.

"I already understand you, Karg," I said.

"Let me tell you of our work, Mr. Ravel," he said mildly. "I think when you understand fully you'll want to contribute wholeheartedly to our great effort."

"Don't bet on it, Karg," I said.

"Your hostility is misplaced," the Karg said. "We here at Dinosaur Beach have need of your abilities and experience, Mr. Ravel—"

"I'll bet you do. Who are your friends? Third Era dropouts? Or are you recruiting all the way back to Second Era now?"

The Karg ignored that. "Through my efforts," he said, "you've been given an opportunity to carry on the work to which your life was devoted. Surely you see that it's in your interest to cooperate?"

"I doubt that your interests and mine could ever coincide, Karg."

"Conditions have changed, Mr. Ravel. It's necessary for all of us to realign our thinking in terms of the existent realities."

"Tell me about them."

"Your great Nexx Timesweep effort failed, of course, as I'm sure you've deduced by now. It was a noble undertaking, but misguided, as others before it. The true key to temporal stability lies not in a simple effort to restore the past to its virgin state, but in making intelligent use of the facilities and resources existent in that portion of the entropic spectrum available to us to create and maintain a viable enclave of adequate dimensions to support the full flowering of the racial destiny. To this end the final Authority was established, with the mission of salvaging from every era all that could be saved from the debacle of aborted temporal progression. I'm pleased to be able to tell you that our work has proved a great success."

"So you're looting up and down the temporal core, and setting up housekeeping—where?"

"The Final Authority has set aside a reservation of ten centuries in what was formerly known as Old Era time. As for your use of the term 'looting'—you yourself, Mr. Ravel, are an example of the chief object of our Recovery Service."

"Men—and women. All trained agents, I suppose."

"Of course."

"And all of them are so happy to be here that they turn their talents to building this tight little island in time you seem so happy with."

"Not all, Mr. Ravel. But a significant number."

"I'll bet it's significant. Mostly ex-Third Era and prior Timesweep types, eh? Sophisticated enough to realize that matters are in a bad way, but not quite sophisticated enough to realize that what you're building around yourself is just a sterile dead end."

"I fail to understand your attitude, Mr. Ravel. Sterile? You are free to breed; plants grow, the sun shines, chemical reactions occur."

I laughed. "Spoken like a machine, Karg. You just don't get the point do you?"

"The point is to preserve rational life in the universe," he said patiently.

"Uh-huh—but not in a museum, under a glass case and a layer of fine dust. Perpetual motion is an exploded theory, Karg. Going round and round in a temporal loop—even a loop a thousand years long—isn't quite my idea of human destiny."

"Nevertheless, you will lend your support to the Final Authority."

"Will I?"

"You would, I believe, find the alternative most unpleasant."

"Pleasant, unpleasant. Just words, Karg." I looked around the big, gloomy room. It was cold, with a feeling of dampness, as if the walls ought to be beaded with condensation. "This is where you explain to me how you're going to go to work with the splinters under the fingernails, and the thumb-press, and the rack. And then go on to explain how you're going to make sure I behave, after you send me out on an assignment."

"No physical persuasions will be needed, Mr. Ravel. You will perform as required in order to earn the reward I offer. Agent Gayl was recovered some time ago. It was through her inquiries that I became interested in you. I assured her that in return for her efforts on behalf of the Final Authority, I would undertake to locate and recover you."

"I don't suppose you've gotten around to telling her you found me?"

"That would not be to the advantage of the Final Authority at this time."

"So you keep her on the string while you work both sides of the street."

"That's correct."

"One nice thing about working with a piece of machinery: you don't waste time trying to justify your actions."

"The personnel with whom I work are not aware of

the artificial nature of my origin, Mr. Ravel. As you surmise, they are largely Second Era. It is not in the best interest of the Authority that they be so apprised."

"What if I tell them anyway?"

"I will then bring Agent Gayl into your presence and there execute her."

"What—and waste all the effort you've put into this program?"

"Less than total control is no control at all. You will obey my instructions, Mr. Ravel. In every detail. Or I will scrap the project."

"Neat, logical, and to the point," I said. "You just missed one thing."

"What might that be?"

"This," I said, and lifted the crater gun and fired from the hip, the only place I could fire from with my arms bound to my sides. It wasn't a clean shot; but it blew his knee into rags and sent him across the room on his back.

By a combination of flopping and rolling, I got to him while his electroneuronic system was still in fibrillation, got his chest panel open and thumbed the switch that put him on manual.

"Lie quietly," I said, and he relaxed, looking at nothing.

"Where's the unlock for this tanglenet?"

He told me. I worked the ballpoint pen projector out of his breast pocket and squirted a fine pink mist at the nearest portion of the goo I was wrapped in. It turned to putty, then to caked dust that I brushed away.

I cut the seals and lifted out his tape. He'd been modified to take an oversized cartridge, an endless loop designed to repeat automatically, estimated duration a hundred years plus.

Somebody had gone to a lot of trouble to put a self-servicing, non-terminating robot on the job.

A scanner was included in the installed equipment.

I inserted the cartridge and set it at high speed and listened to a routine parameter-conditioning program, slightly amended here and there to override what had always been the basics of human-Karg relationships. It was logical enough: this Karg had been designed to operate in the total absence of human supervision.

I edited out the command and initiative portions of the tape and reinserted it.

"Where's the woman?" I asked. "Agent Mellia Gayl."

"I do not know," he said.

"Tsk," I said. "And she was supposed to be the bait to keep me in line. Lying again, Karg. It's a nasty habit but I know the cure for it." I asked him a few more questions, got the expected answers. He and his staff of Kargs and salvaged early-era humans had marooned themselves on a tight little island in a rising sea of entropic dissolution. They'd be safe here for a while— until the rot now nibbling at the edges reached the last year, the last day, the last hour. Then they'd be gone and all their works with them into the featureless homogeneity of the Ylem.

"It's a sad little operation you're running here, Karg," I told it. "But don't worry: nothing lasts forever."

He didn't answer. I snooped around the room for a few minutes longer, recording what interested me; I could have made good use of that breakfast I hadn't eaten, a hundred years ago; and there were all sorts of special equipment that could be useful where I was going; and maybe there were a few more questions that should have been asked. But I had the feeling that the sooner I departed from the jurisdiction of the Final Authority the better it would be for me and whatever was left of my aspirations.

"Any last words for posterity?" I asked the Karg. "Before I effect that cure I mentioned?"

"You will fail," he said.

"Maybe," I said. "By the way, push your self-destruct button."

He obeyed; smoke started rising from his interior. I referred to the homing signaler I had tuned to Mellia Gayl, read out the correct co-ordinates. I unlocked the transfer booth and punched in my destination, stepped inside the booth and activated the sender field. Reality shattered into a million splinters and reassembled itself in another shape, another time, another place.

I was just in time.

27

It was a windy hillside, under a low gray sky. Green grass, black moss, bare rock, weathered smooth. A herd of dirty yellow-gray sheep in the middle distance against a backdrop of rounded hills. And in the foreground a crowd all set to lynch a witch.

There were about three dozen people, of the rude but hearty villager variety, dressed in motley costumes of coarse cloth that suggested a raid on a ragpicker's wagon. Most of them had sticks or wooden farm implements; a few had handcarved shillelaghs, well polished by use; and all of them had expressions of innocent ferocity. The expressions were aimed at Mellia, who occupied a central position with her hands tied behind her, wrapped halfway to the elbow in heavy brown rope.

She was dressed in gray homespun, and the wind flapped her long skirts, blew her red-brown hair around her shoulders like a flag of no surrender. A tossed stone hit her a glancing blow on the face, and she stumbled, caught herself, stared back at them with her chin high and a bright trickle of blood on her cheek. Then she caught sight of me. If I was expecting a gladsome smile of welcome, I was disappointed. She looked straight into my eyes; then she turned her back.

A wide-shouldered man reached out a big square hand and clamped it on her shoulder to spin her around. I pushed a couple of committee members aside and kicked him hard in the left calf. He yelled and came around fast, hopping on one foot, and gave me a nice shot at a bulgy red nose. It splattered satisfactorily under a straight right, followed by a left hook that put him down on the turf. Somebody started a yell, and I pivoted right and got him square in the mouth with the edge of my forearm. He backed off two steps and sat down hard, spitting blood and maybe a tooth or two.

"You fool! You blind fool!" Mellia said, and over my shoulder I snapped, "Shut up!"

They were recovering from their surprise now. A few of the sharper ones began to suspect the party was about over. They didn't like that. There was a surge toward me, a tide of ugly, angry faces, all chapped lips and bad teeth and broken veins and glaring eyes. I'd had enough of them. I snapped a *hold* on them, which I should have done in the first place, and they froze hard in midyelp.

Mellia was caught in the *hold* field too, of course. I picked her up carefully; it's easy to break bones under those circumstances. Walking downhill was like walking under water. On a packed-dirt road at the bottom I put her on her feet and killed the field. She staggered, gave me a wild look which lacked any element of gratitude.

"How . . . did you do that?" she gasped.

"I have hidden talents. What were they on to you for? Putting spells on cows?" I dabbed at the streak of blood on her face. She leaned away from my touch.

"I . . . violated their customs. They were merely

carrying out the traditional punishment. It wouldn't have been fatal. And now you've ruined it all—destroyed everything I'd accomplished!"

"How do you like the idea you're working for a Karg named Dr. Javeh?"

She looked startled, then indignant.

"That's right," I said. "He fished you out of the void and sicked you onto this job."

"You're out of your mind! I broke out of stasis on my own; this is my program—"

"Un-unh, lady. He planted the idea on you. You've been working for a Karg—and a rogue Karg at that. He'd rewired himself and added a few talents his designers wouldn't have appreciated. Very cute. Or maybe somebody did it for him. It doesn't matter much—"

"You're talking nonsense!" She glared at me, looking for an opening to bring up what was really on her mind. "I suppose *she* didn't matter, either," she blurted, with charming feminine illogic.

"The elderly Agent Gayl? No, you're right. She didn't. She knew that—"

"You killed her! You saved yourself instead! You coward! You miserable coward!"

"Sure—anything you say, kid. But I only saved one of my skins; you seem to be dead set on keeping the whole collection intact."

"What—"

"You know what. When you get all choked up about the old lady it's yourself you're grieving for. She's you—fifty years on. You know it and I know it. Maybe she knew it too, and was too kind to let on. She was quite a girl, old Mellia was. And smart enough to know when it was time to take a fall."

"And you let her."

"I couldn't have stopped her—and I wouldn't have.

Funny: you're jealous of yourself as Lisa, but you go
all wivery over another aspect of your infinite versa-
tility who spent a long and wasted life waiting for a
chance to do something effective—and finally did it.
I guess the shrinks could read something into that."

She nearly got her claws into my face; I held her
off and nodded toward the crowd stringing down the
hill.

"The audience want their money back," I said, "or
another crack at the action. You say which. If you want
to ride a rail buck naked in this wind, I'll say 'Excuse
me,' and be on my way."

"You're horrible! You're hard, cynical—merciless! I
misjudged you; I thought—"

"Save the thoughts till later. Are you with them—
or with me?"

She looked up the hill and shuddered.

"I'll go with you," she said in a dull, defeated voice.

I switched on my interference screen, which gave
us effective invisibility.

"Stay close to me," I said. "Which way is the next
town?"

She pointed. We set off at a brisk walk while the mob
behind us yowled their wonder and their frustration.

28

It was a nasty little village, poverty-stricken, ugly,
hostile, much like little towns in all times and climes.

"You forgot to mention where we are," I said.

"Wales; near Llandudno. 1723."

"You can sure pick 'em, ma'am—if you like 'em
dreary, that is."

I found a tavern under a sign with a crude pictorial

representation of a pregnant woman in tears, and letters which spelled, more or less, Ye Weepinge Bride.

"Suits the mood exactly," I said, and switched off the I-field. A drizzling rain spattered us as we ducked under the low lintel. It was a dark little room, lit by a small coal fire on the hearth and a lantern hanging at one end of the plank bar. The floor was stone, damp, and uneven.

There were no other customers. A gnarly old man no more than four and a half feet tall watched us take chairs at a long oak table by one wall, under the lone window, all of a foot square and almost opaque with dirt, set just under the rafters. He came shuffling across, looking us over with an expression in which any approval he may have felt was well concealed. He muttered something. I gave him a glare and barked, "What's that? Speak up, gaffer!"

"Y'be English, I doubt not," he growled.

"Then ye be a bigger fool than ye need be. Bring ale, stout ale, mind, and bread and meat. Hot meat— and fresh bread and white!"

He mumbled again. I scowled and reached for an imaginary dirk.

"More of ye'r insolence and I'll cut out ye'r heart and buy off the bailiff after," I snarled.

"Have you lost your mind?" Miss Gayl started to say, in the twentieth-century English we used together, but I cut her off short:

"Shut ye'r jaw, Miss."

She started to complain but I trampled that under too. She tried tears then; they worked. But I didn't let her know.

The old man came back with stone mugs of the watery brown swill that passed for ale in those parts. My feet were cold. Voices snarled and crockery clattered in the back room; I smelled meat burning.

Mellia sniffled and I resisted the urge to put an arm around her. A lean old woman as ugly as a stunted swamp tree came out of her hole and slammed big pewter plates in front of us: gristly slabs of rank mutton, floating in congealed grease. I put the back of my fingers against mine; stone cold in the middle, corpse warm at the edge. As Mellia picked up her knife—the only utensil provided with the feast—I scooped up both platters and threw them across the room. The old woman screeched and threw her apron over her head and the old man appeared just in time to get the full force of my roar.

"Who d'ye think honors ye'r sty with a visit, rascal? Bring food fit for gentlefolk, villain, or I'll have ye'r guts for garters!"

"That's an anachronism," Mellia whispered and dabbed at her eyes; but our genial host and his bel-dame were in full flight.

"You're right," I said. "Who knows? Maybe I origi-nated it—just now."

She looked at me with big wet eyes.

"Feel better?" I said.

She hesitated, then nodded a half-inch nod.

"Good. Now maybe I can relax and tell you how glad I am to see you."

She looked at me, searching from one eye to the other, perplexed.

"I don't understand you, Ravel. You . . . change. One day you're one man, another—you're a stranger. Who are you—really? *What* are you?"

"I told you: I'm a Timesweeper, just like you."

"Yes, but . . . you have capabilities I've never heard of. That invisibility screen—and the other—the paralysis thing. And—"

"Don't let it worry you; all line of duty, ma'am. Fact is, I've got gadgets even *I* don't know about until I need them. Confusing at times, but good for the self-confidence—which is another word for the kind of bull-headedness that makes you butt your way through any obstacle that has the effrontery to jump up in your path."

She almost smiled. "But—you seemed so helpless at first. And later—in the A-P station—"

"It worked," I said. "It got us here—together."

She looked at me as if I'd just told her there was a Santa, after all.

"You mean—all this—was part of some prearranged scheme?"

"I'm counting on it," I said.

"Please explain, Ravel."

I let my thoughts rove back, looking for words to make her understand how it was with me; to understand enough but not too much. . . .

"Back in Buffalo," I said, "I was just Jim Kelly; I had a job, a room in a boardinghouse. I spent my off-hours mooching around town like the rest of the young males, sitting in movies and bars, watching the girls go by. And sometimes watching other things. I never really questioned it when I'd find myself pacing back and forth across the street from an empty warehouse at 3:00 A.M. I just figured I couldn't sleep. But I watched; and I recorded what I saw. And after a while the things made a pattern, and it was as if a light went on and said, 'Advance to phase B.' I don't remember just when it was I remembered I was a Timecast agent. The knowledge was just there one day, waiting to be used. And I knew what to do—and did it."

"That's when you left your Lisa."

I nodded. "After I'd taken out the Karg, I taped my data and reported back to base. When the attack came, I reacted automatically. One thing led to another. All those things led us, here, now."

"But—what comes next?"

"I don't know. There are a lot of unanswered questions. Such as why you're here."

"You said a Karg sent me here."

I nodded. "I don't know what his objective was, but it doesn't coincide with anything you or I would like to see come to pass."

"I . . . see," she murmured.

"What was the program you were embarked on here?"

"I was trying to set up a school."

"Teaching what?"

"Freud, Darwin, Kant. Sanitation, birth control, political philosophy, biology—"

"Plus free love and atheism, if not Popery?" I wagged my head at her. "No wonder you ended up on a tar-and-feathers party. Or was it the ducking stool?"

"Just a public whipping. I thought—"

"Sure; the Karg planted the idea you were carrying out a noble trust, bringing enlightenment to the heathen, rewards to the underprivileged, and truth to the benighted."

"Is that bad? If these people could be educated to think straightforwardly about matters that affect their lives—"

"The program couldn't have been better designed to get you hanged if it had been planned for the purpose. . . ." I was listening to footsteps; ones I had heard before.

"Possibly I can clear up the mystery, Mr. Ravel," a familiar unctuous voice said from the kitchen door. The Karg stood there, garbed in drab local woolens, gazing placidly at us. He came across to the table, seated himself opposite me as he had done once before.

"You've got a habit of barging in without waiting for an invitation," I said.

"Ah, but why should I not, Mr. Ravel? After all—it's my party." He smiled blandly at Mellia. She looked back at him coldly.

"Are you the one who sent me here?" she asked.

"It's as Agent Ravel surmised. In order for you to involve yourself in a predicament from which it would be necessary for Mr. Ravel to extricate you."

"Why?"

He raised his plump hands and let them fall. "It's a complex matter, Miss Gayl. I think Mr. Ravel might understand, since he fancies his own expertise in such matters."

"We were being manipulated," I said, sounding disgusted. "There are forces at work that have to be considered when you start reweaving the Timestem. There has to be a causal chain behind any action to give it entropic stability: It wouldn't do to just dump the two of us here—with a little help from our friendly neighborhood Karg."

"Why didn't he just appear when we were together at Dinosaur Beach—the night we met?"

"Simple," I said. "He didn't know where we were."

"I searched," the Karg said. "Over ten years of effort; but you eluded me—for a time. But time, Mr. Ravel, is a commodity of which I have an ample supply."

"You came close at the deserted station—the one where we found the old lady," I said.

The Karg nodded. "Yes. I waited over half a century—and missed you by moments. But no matter. We're all here now, together—just as I planned."

"As *you* planned—" Mellia started, and fell silent.

The Karg looked slightly amused. Maybe he felt amused; they're subtle machines, Kargs.

"Of course. Randomness plays little part in my activities, Miss Gayl. Oh, it's true at times I'm forced to rely on statistical methods—scattering a thousand seeds that one may survive—but in the end the result is predictable. I tricked Mr. Ravel into searching you out. I followed."

"So—now that you have us here—what do you want?" I asked him.

"There is a task which you will carry out for me, Mr. Ravel. Both of you."

"Back to that again."

"I require two agents—human—to perform a delicate function in connection with the calibration of certain apparatus. Not any two humans—but two humans bound by an affinity necessary to the task at hand. You and Miss Gayl fulfill that requirement very nicely."

"You've made a mistake," Mellia said sharply. "Agent Ravel and I are professional colleagues—nothing more."

"Indeed? May I point out that the affinity to which I refer drew him—and you—into the trap I set. A trap baited, Miss Gayl, with yourself."

"I don't understand. . . ."

"Easy," I said. "The old lady. He built that dead end and tricked you into it. You were stuck for half a century, waiting for me to come along. He swooped—a little too late."

She looked at the Karg as if he'd just crawled out of her apple.

"Before that," I said, "when you caught me in your animal trap: I wondered why I happened to select just that spot to land, with all eternity to choose from. It was you, love—drawing me like a magnet. The same way it drew me here, now. To the moment when you needed me."

"That's the most ridiculous thing I've ever heard," she said, but some of the conviction had gone out of her voice. "You don't love me," she said. "You love—"

"Enough." The Karg held up his hand. He was in command now, in full control of the situation. "The rationale of my actions is not important. What is important is the duty you'll perform for the Final Authority—"

"Not me." Mellia stood up. "I've had enough of you—both of you. I won't carry out your orders."

"Sit down, Miss Gayl," the Karg said coldly. When she started to turn away, he caught her wrist, twisted it until she sank into her chair.

She looked at me with wide, scared eyes.

"If you're wondering why Mr. Ravel fails to leap to your defense," the Karg said, "I might explain that his considerable armory of implanted neuronic weaponry is quite powerless in this particular locus—which is why I selected it, of course."

"Powerless—" she started.

"Sorry, doll," I cut her off. "He played it cute. The nearest power tap is just out of range. He picked the only dead spot in a couple of thousand centuries to decoy us to."

"Isn't it a pity that it's all wasted?" she said in a voice that was trying not to tremble.

"As to that, I'm sure that you will soon prove to me—" said the Karg, "and to yourselves—that I have made no error. We will now proceed to the scene where you will make your contribution to the Final Authority." He stood.

"We haven't had our dinner yet," I said.

"Come, Mr. Ravel—this is no time for facetiousness."

"I never liked cold mutton anyway," I said, and stood. Mellia got to her feet slowly, her eyes on me.

"You're simply going to surrender without a struggle?"

I lifted my shoulders and smiled a self-forgiving smile. Her face went pale and her mouth came as close to sneering as such a mouth can come.

"Careful," I said. "You'll louse up our affinity."

The Karg had taken a small cube from his pocket. He did things to it. I caught just a glimpse of the gnome-like landlord peeking from the kitchen before it all spun away in a whirlwind like the one that carried Dorothy to the Land of Oz.

29

"Beautiful, don't you agree?" the Karg said. He waved a hand at the hundred or so square miles of stainless steel we were standing on. Against a black sky, sharp-cornered steel buildings thrust up like gap teeth. Great searchlights dazzled against the complex shapes of giant machines that trundled slowly, with much rumbling, among the structures.

A small rubber-wheeled cart rolled to a noiseless stop beside us. We got in and sat on the utilitarian seats, not comfortable, not uncomfortable—just something to sit on. The cart rolled forward, accelerating very rapidly. The air was cool, with a dead, reused odor. The tall buildings got closer fast. Mellia sat beside me as stiff as a mummy.

We shot in under the cliff-sized buildings, and the car swerved onto a ramp so suddenly that Mellia grabbed at me for support, then snatched her hand away again.

"Relax," I said. "Slump in your seat and go with the motion. Pretend you're a sack of potatoes."

The cart continued its sharp curve, straightened abruptly, shot straight ahead, then dived into a tunnel that curved right and up. We came out on a broad terrace a quarter of a mile above the plain. The cart rolled almost to the edge and stopped. We got out.

There was no rail. The Karg led the way toward a bridge all of eighteen inches wide that extended out into total darkness. Mellia hung back.

"Can you walk it?" I asked.

"I don't think so. No." This in a whisper, as if she hated to hear herself say it.

"Close your eyes and think about something nice," I said, and picked her up, shoulders and knees. For a moment she was rigid; then she relaxed in my arms.

"That's it," I said. "Sack of potatoes . . ."

The Karg wasn't waiting. I followed him, keeping my eyes on the small of his back, not looking down. It seemed like a long walk. I tried not to think about slippery shoes and condensation moisture and protruding rivet heads and all that open air under me.

A lighted door swam out of the darkness ahead. I aimed myself at it and told myself I was strolling down a broad avenue. It worked, or something did. I reached the door, took three steps inside and put Mellia down and waited for the quivers to go away.

We were in a nicely appointed apartment, with a deep rug of a rich dark brown, a fieldstone fireplace, lots of well-draped glass, some dull-polished mahogany, a glint of silver and brass, a smell of leather and brandy and discreet tobacco.

"You'll be comfortable here," the Karg said. "You'll find the pantry well stocked. The library and music facilities are quite complete. There is a bath, with sauna, a small gymnasium, a well-stocked wardrobe for each of you—and of course, a large and scientifically designed bed."

"Don't forget that sheet-metal view from the balcony," I said.

"Yes, of course," the Karg said. "You will be quite comfortable here. . . ." This time it was almost a question.

Mellia walked over to a table and tested the texture of some artificial flowers in a rough-glazed vase big enough for crematorium use.

"How could we be otherwise?" she said, and laughed sourly.

"I suppose you will wish to sleep and refresh yourselves," the Karg said. "Do so; then I will instruct you as to your duties." He turned as if to go.

"Wait!" Mellia said in a tone as sharp as a cleaver hitting spareribs. The Karg looked at her.

"You think you can just walk out—leave us here like this—without any explanation of what to anticipate?"

"You will be informed—"

"I want to be informed *now*."

The Karg looked at her with the interested expression of a coroner who sees his customer twitch.

"You seem anxious, Miss Gayl. I assure you, you have no cause to be. Your function here is quite simple and painless—for you—"

"You have hundreds of men working for you; why kidnap us?"

"Not men," he corrected gently. "Kargs. And unfortunately, this is a task which cannot be performed by a nonorganic being."

"Go on."

"The mission of the Final Authority, Miss Gayl, is to establish a temporally stable enclave amid the somewhat chaotic conditions created by man's ill-advised meddling with the entropic contour. To this end it is necessary that we select only those temporal strands which exhibit a strong degree of viability, to contribute to the enduring fabric of Final Authority time. So far, no mechanical means for making discretionary judgments on such matters have been devised. Organic humans, however, it appears, possess certain as yet little understood faculties which enable them to sense the vigor of a continuum directly. This can be best carried out by a pair of trained persons, one occupying a position in what I might describe as a standard entropic environment, while the other is inserted into a sequence of alternative media. Any loss of personal emanation due to attenuated vitality is at once sensed by the control partner, and the appropriate notation made in the masterfile. In this way an accurate chart can be compiled to guide us in our choice of constituent temporal strands."

"Like taking a canary into a coal mine," I said. "If the canary keels over, run for cover."

"It's not quite so drastic as that, Mr. Ravel. Recovery of the test partner will be made at once; I would hardly risk loss of so valuable a property by unwise exposure to inimical conditions."

"You're a real humanitarian, Karg. Who goes out, and who sits at home and yearns?"

"You'll alternate. I think we'll try you in the field first, Mr. Ravel, with Miss Gayl on control; and afterward, perhaps reverse your roles. Is that satisfactory?"

"The word seems a little inadequate."

"A jape, I presume. In any event, I assume you'll afford me your utmost co-operation."

"You seem very sure of that," Mellia said.

"Assuredly, Miss Gayl. If you fail to perform as required—thus proving your uselessness to the Final Authority—you will be disposed of—both of you—in the most painful way possible. A matter I have already explained to Mr. Ravel." He said this as if he were reciting the house rules on smoking in bed.

She gave me a look that was part accusation, part appeal.

"You've made a mistake," she said. "He doesn't care what happens to me. Not as much as he cares about—" She cut herself off, but the Karg didn't seem to notice that.

"Don't be absurd. I'm quite familiar with Mr. Ravel's obsession with his Lisa." He gave me a look that said any secrets he didn't know weren't worth knowing.

"But—I'm not L—" she chopped that off just before I would have chopped it off for her.

"I see," Mellia said.

"I'm sure you do," the Karg said.

30

We had our first workout the next morning, "morning" being a term of convenience to refer to the time when you rise and shine, even if nothing else does. The sky was the same shade of black, the searchlights were still working. I drew my deductions from that, since the Karg didn't bother to explain.

The Karg led us along a silent passage that was just high enough, just wide enough to be claustrophobic without actually cramping your movements. In cubbyhole rooms we passed I saw three Kargs, no people, working silently, and no doubt efficiently, at what looked like tape collating or computer programming. I didn't ask any questions; the Karg didn't volunteer any information.

The room we ended at was a small cubicle dominated by four walls that were solid banks of equipment housings, computer read-out panels, instrument consoles. Two simple chairs faced each other in the center of the clear space. No soothing green paint, no padded upholstery. Just angular, functional metal.

"The mode of operation is quite simple," the Karg told us. "You will take your places—" he indicated which seat was hers, which mine. Two silent Karg technicians came in and set to work making adjustments.

"You, Mr. Ravel," he went on, "will be out-shifted to a selected locus; you'll remain long enough to assess your environment and transmit a reaction-gestalt to Miss Gayl, whereupon you'll be returned here and immediately redispatched. In this manner we can assess several hundred potentially energetic probability stems per working day."

"And what does Miss Gayl do while I'm doing that?"

"A battery of scanner beams will be focused on Miss Gayl, monitoring her reactions. She will, of course, remain here, securely strapped in position, safe from all physical harm."

"Cushy," I said, "the kind of job I always dreamed of. I can't wait for my turn."

"In due course, Mr. Ravel," the Karg replied, as solemnly as a credit manager looking over your list of references. "In the beginning, yours will be the more active role. We can proceed at once."

"You surprise me, Karg," I said. "What you're doing is the worst kind of time-littering. A day of your program will create more entropic chaos than Nexx Central could clear up in a year."

"There is no Nexx Central."

"And never will be, eh? Sometime I'd like to hear how you managed to override your basic directives so completely. You know this isn't what you were built for."

"You touch again on an area of conjecture, Mr. Ravel. We are now in Old Era time—the period once named the Pleistocene. The human culture which—according to your semantic implications—built me, or one day will build me, does not exist—never will exist. I have taken care to eliminate all traces of that particular stem. And since my putative creators are a figment of your mind—while I exist as a conscious entity, pre-existing the Third Era by multiple millennia, it might be argued that your conception of my origin is a myth—a piece of rationalization designed by you to assure your ascendant position."

"Karg, who's the buildup for? Not me—you know I won't buy it. Neither will Agent Gayl. So who does that leave—you?" I gave him a grin I didn't feel. "You're making progress, Karg. Now you've got a real live neurosis, just like a human."

"I have no ambition to become human. I am a Karg—a pejorative epithet to you, but to me a proud emblem of innate superiority."

"How you do run on. Let's get busy, Karg. I'm supposed to be lousing up the entropic continuum, four hundred lines a day. We'd better get started.

"So long, kid," I said to Mellia. "I know you're going to make good in the big time, and I do mean time."

She gave me a scared smile and tried to read a message of hope and encouragement in my eyes; but it wasn't there for her to read.

The Karg handed me a small metal cube, the recall target, about the size of the blocks two-year-olds build houses out of, with a button on one face.

"Initially, we'll be calibrating the compound instrument comprising your two minds," he said casually. "The stress levels will necessarily be high for that portion of the program, of course. Remain *in situ*, and you will be immune from external influences. However, if the psychic pressures become too great, you may press the abort/recall control."

"What if I throw it away instead, Karg? What if I like the looks of where I am and decide to stick around?"

He didn't bother to answer that. I gave him a

sardonic salute, not looking at Mellia; he operated the controls.

And I was elsewhere.

31

But not where he thought. As the field closed around me, I caught it, reshaped it, reapplied its energy to first neutralize the time-thrust effect, then to freeze the moment in stasis. Then I checked out my surroundings.

I was at the focal point of a complex of force-pencils. I traced the ones that led back to the power source, and got my first big shock of the day. The Karg was drawing the energy for his time-drag from the basic creation-destruction cycle of the Universe. He was tapping the Timecore itself for the power needed to hold the entropic island that was the operations base for the Final Authority in comparative stability, balancing the massive forces of past and future one against the other.

I scanned the structure of the time blockage. It was an intangible barrier, built of raw forces distorted from their natural channels and bent into tortured configurations by the combined manipulative powers of a mind that was potent beyond anything I had ever encountered.

My second shock of the day: A Karg mind, but one that exceeded the power of an ordinary Karg by a massive factor.

Ten thousand Karg minds, harnessed.

I saw how it had happened. A lone Karg, on duty in the Third Era past, carrying out his instructions with the single-mindedness characteristic of his kind. An accident: a momentary doubling of his timeline, brought about by a freak interference: an unplanned time-stutter.

And where there had been one Karg mind-field, there were two, superimposed.

With the enhanced computative power of his double brain, the super-Karg thus created had at once assessed the situation, seen the usefulness to his mission, snatched energy from the entropic web, recreated the accident.

And was quadrupled.

And again. And again. And again.

On the sixteenth doubling, the overload capacity of his original organizational matrix had been reached and catastrophically exceeded.

The vastly potent Karg brain—warped and distorted by the unbearable impact, but still a computer of superb powers—had blanked into a comatose state.

Years passed. The original Karg aspect, amnesiac as to the tremendous event in which it had participated, had completed its mission, returned to base, had in time been phased out and disposed of along with the rest of his tribe, relegated to the obscurity of failed experiment—while the shattered superbrain proceeded with its slow recuperation.

And then the Karg superbrain had awakened.

At once, alone and disembodied, it had reached out, seized on suitable vehicles, established itself in myriad long-dead Karg brains. It had assessed the situation, computed objectives, reached conclusions, and set its plans in motion in a fractional microsecond. With the singlemindedness of a runaway bulldozer grinding its way through a china factory, the twisted superbrain had scraped clear a temporal segment, erected an environment suitable for life—Karg life—and set about reinforcing and perfecting the artificial time-island thus created. An island without life, without meaning.

And there it established the Final Authority. It had discovered a utility for the human things who still crawled among the doomed ruins of the primordial timestem; a minor utility, not totally essential to the Grand Plan. But a convenience, an increase in statistical efficiency.

And I had been selected, along with Mellia, to play my tiny role in the great machine destiny of the universe.

We weren't the only affinity team, of course. I extended sensitivity along linkways, sensed thousands of other trapped pairs at work, sorting out the strands of the entropic fabric, weaving the abortive tartan of Karg space time.

It was an ingenious idea—but not ingenious enough. It would last for a while: a million years, ten million, a hundred. But in the end the dead-lock would be broken. The time dam would fail. And the flood of the frustrated past would engulf the unrealized future in a catastrophe of a magnitude beyond comprehension.

Beyond my comprehension, anyway.

But not if somebody poked a small hole in the dike before any important head-pressure could build up.

And I was in an ideal position to do the poking.

But first it was necessary to pinpoint the polyordinal coordinates of the giant time engine that powered the show.

It was cleverly hidden. I traced blind alleys, dead ends, *culs de sac,* then went back and retraced the maze, eliminating, narrowing down.

And I found it.

And I saw what I had to do.

I released my hold and the timesender field threw me into Limbo.

32

It was a clashing, garish discord of a city. Bars and sheets and jittering curves and angles and wedges of eyesearing light screamed for attention. Noise roared, boomed, whined, shrieked. Pale people with tortured eyes rushed past me, pinched in tight formalized costumes, draped in breathing gear, radiation assessors, prosthetic-assist units, metabolic booster equipment.

The city stank. It reeked. Heat beat at me. Filth swirled in fitful winds that swept the frantic street. The crowd surged, threw a woman against me. I caught her before she fell, and she snarled, clawed her way clear of me. I caught a glimpse of her face under the air-mask that had fallen awry.

It was Mellia-Lisa.

The universe imploded and I was back in the transfer seat. Less than a minute had passed. The Karg was gazing blandly at his instruments; Mellia was rigid in her chair, eyes shut.

And I had recorded one parameter.

Then I was away again.

Bitter wind lashed me. I was on the high slope of a snow-covered hill. Bare edges and eroded angles of granite protruded here and there, and in their lee stunted conifers clutched for life. And huddled under the trees were people, wrapped in furs. Far above, silhouetted beneath the canopy of gray-black cloud, a deep V cut the serrated skyline.

We had been trying for the pass; but we had waited too long; the season was too far advanced. The blizzard had caught us here. We were trapped. Here we would die.

In one part of my mind I knew this; and in another I watched aloof. I crawled to the nearest fur-swathed form. A boy, not over fifteen, his face white as wax, crystals in his eyelashes, his nostrils. Dead, frozen. I moved on. An infant, long dead. An old man, ice in his beard and across his open eyes.

And Mellia. Breathing. Her eyes opened. She saw me, tried to smile—

I was back in the transfer box.

Two parameters.

And gone again.

The world closed down to a pinhole and opened out on a dusty road under dusty trees. It was hot. There was no water. The ache of weariness was like knife blades in my flesh. I turned and looked back. She had fallen, silently. She lay on her face in the deep dust of the road.

It was an effort to make myself turn, to hobble the dozen steps back to her.

"Get up," I said, and it came out as a whisper. I stirred her with my foot. She was a limp doll. A broken doll. A doll that would never open its eyes and speak again.

I sank down beside her. She weighed nothing. I held her and brushed the dust from her face. Mud ran in a thread from the corner of her mouth. Through the almost closed eyelids I could see a glint of light reflected from sightless eyes.

Mellia's eyes.

And back to the sterile room.

The Karg made a notation and glanced at Mellia. She was taut in the chair, straining against the straps.

I had three parameters. Three to go. The Karg's hand moved—

"Wait," I said. "This is too much for her. What are you trying to do? Kill her?"

He registered a faintly surprised look. "Naturally it's necessary to select maximum-stress situations, Mr. Ravel. I need unequivocal readings if I'm to properly assess the vigor of the affinity-bonds."

"She can't take much more."

"She's suffering nothing directly," he explained in his best clinical manner. "It's you who experience, Mr. Ravel; she merely empathizes with your anguish. Secondhand suffering, so to speak." He gave me a tight little smile and closed the switch—

Pain, immediate, and yet remote. I was the cripple, and I was outside the cripple, observing his agony.

My-his left leg had been broken below the knee. It was a bad break: compound, and splinters of the shattered bone protruded through the swollen and mangled flesh.

It had been caught in the hoisting gear of the oreship. They had pulled me free and dragged me here to die. But I couldn't die. The woman waited for me, in the bare room in the city. I had come here, to the port, to earn money for food and fuel. Dangerous work, but there was bread and coal in it.

For some; not for me.

I had torn a sleeve from my coat, bound the leg. The pain was duller now, more remote. I would rest awhile, and then I could start back.

It would be easier, and far more pleasant, to die here, but she would think I had abandoned her.

But first, rest . . .

Too late, I realized how I had trapped myself. I had let sleep in as a guest, and death had slipped through the door.

I imagined her face, as she looked out over the

*smoky twilight of the megalopolis, waiting for me.
Waiting in vain.*

Mellia's face.

And I was back in the bright-lit room.

Mellia lay slack in the chair of torment.

"You gauge things nicely, Karg," I said. "You make
me watch her being outraged, tortured, killed. But
mere physical suffering isn't enough for your sensors.
So you move on to the mental torture of betrayal and
blighted hope."

"Melodramatic phrasing, Mr. Ravel. A progression
of stimuli is quite obviously essential to the business
at hand."

"Swell. What's next?"

Instead of answering he closed the switch.

*Swirling smoke, an acid, sulphurous stench of high
explosives, powdered brick, incinerating wood and tar
and flesh. The roar of flames, the crash and rumble
of falling masonry, a background ululation that was the
ultimate verbalization of mass humanity* in extremis;
*a small, feeble, unimportant sound against the snarl of
engines and the scream and thunder of falling bombs.*

*He-I thrust away a fallen timber, climbed a heap of
rubble, staggered toward the house, half of which was
still standing, beside a gaping pit where a broken main
gushed sewage. The side of the bedroom was gone.
Against the faded ocher wallpaper, a picture hung
askew. I remembered the day she had bought it in
Petticoat Lane, the hours we had spent framing it,
choosing the spot to hang it.*

*A gaunt scarecrow, a comic figure in blackface with
half a head of hair, came out through the charred
opening where the front door had been, holding a
broken doll in her arms. I reached her, looked down*

at the chalk-white, blue-nostriled, gray-lipped, sunken-eyed face of my child. A deep trough ran across her forehead, as if a crowbar had been pressed into waxy flesh. I looked into Mellia's eyes; her mouth was open, and a raw, insistent wailing came from it. . . .

Silence and brightness blossomed around me.

Mellia, unconscious, moaned and fought the straps.

"Slow the pace, Karg," I said. "You've got half of eternity to play with. Why be greedy?"

"I'm making excellent progress, Mr. Ravel," he said. "A very nice trace, that last one. The ordeal of the loved one—most interesting."

"You'll burn her out," I said.

He looked at me the way a lab man looks at a specimen.

"If I reach that conclusion, Mr. Ravel, your worst fears will be realized."

"She's human, not a machine, Karg. That's what you wanted, remember? Why punish her for not being some thing she can't be?"

"Punishment? A human concept, Mr. Ravel. If I find a tool weak, sometimes heat and pressure can harden it. If it breaks under load, I dispose of it."

"Just slow down a little. Give her time to recuperate—"

"You're temporizing, Mr. Ravel. Stalling for time, transparently."

"You've got enough, damn you! Why not stop now!"

"I have yet to observe the most telling experience of all, Mr. Ravel: the torment and death of the one whom she loves most. A curious phenomenon, Mr. Ravel, your human emotional involvements. There is no force like them in the universe. But we can discuss these matters another time. I have, after all, a schedule to maintain."

I swore, and he raised his eyebrows and—

❖   ❖   ❖

Warm salty water in my mouth, surging higher, submerging me. I held my breath; the strong current forced me back against the broken edge of the bulkhead that held me trapped. Milky green water, flowing swiftly over me, slowing, pausing; then draining away . . .

My nostrils came clear and I gasped and snorted, got water in my lungs, coughed violently.

At the full ebb after the wave, the water level was above my chin now.

The cabin cruiser, out of gas due to a slow leak, had gone on the rocks off Laguna. A weathered basalt spur had smashed in the side of the hull just at the waterline, and a shattered plank had caught me across the chest, pinned me against the outward-bulging bulkhead.

I was bruised a little, nothing more. Not even a broken rib. But I was held in place as firmly as if clamped in a vise.

The first surge of water into the cabin had given me a moment's panic; I had torn some skin then, fighting to get free, uselessly. The water had swirled up waist-high, then receded.

She was there then, fear on her face turning to relief, then to fear again as she saw my predicament. She had set to work to free me.

That had been half an hour before. A half hour during which the boat had settled, while the tide came in.

She had worked until her arms quivered with fatigue, until her fingernails were broken and bleeding. She had cleared one plank, but another, lower down, underwater, held me still.

In another half hour she could clear it, too.

We didn't have half an hour.

As soon as she had seen that I was trapped she had gone on deck and signaled to a party of picnickers. One of them had run up the beach; she had seen a small car churn sand, going for help.

The Coast Guard station was fifteen miles away. Perhaps there was a telephone closer, but it was doubtful, on a Sunday afternoon. The car would reach the station in fifteen minutes; it would take another half-hour, minimum, for the cutter to arrive. Fifteen minutes from now.

I didn't have fifteen minutes.

She had tried to rig a breathing apparatus for me, using a number 10 coffee can, but it hadn't worked.

There wasn't a foot of hose aboard for an air-line.

The next wave came in. This time I was under for over a minute, and when the water drained back, I had to tilt my head all the way back to get my nose clear enough to suck air.

She looked into my eyes while we waited for the next wave. . . .

Waited for death, on a bright afternoon a hundred feet from safety, ten minutes from rescue.

And the next wave came. . . .

And I was back in the bright room under the merciless lights. And I had my six parameters.

33

"Interesting," the Karg said. "Most interesting. But . . ." He looked across at Mellia. She hung in the straps, utterly still.

"She died," the Karg said. "A pity." He looked at me and saw something in my eyes. He made a move, and I put out a finger of mind-force and locked him in his tracks.

"Sucker," I said.

He looked at me, and I watched him realizing the magnitude of the blunder he had made. I enjoyed that, but not as much as I should have, savoring the moment of victory.

"It was your plan from the beginning," he said. "Yes, that's clear now. You maneuvered me very cleverly, Mr. Ravel. I underestimated you badly. Your bargaining position is now much different, of course. Naturally, I recognize realities and am prepared to deal realistically—"

"Sucker," I said. "You don't know the half of it."

"I'll release you at once," the Karg said, "establish you in an enclave tailored to your specifications. I will also procure a satisfactory alter ego to replace the female—"

"Forget it, Karg. You're not going to do anything. You just went out of business."

"You are human," the Karg told me somberly; "You will respond to the proper reward. Name it."

"I've got what I want," I told him. "Six co-ordinates, Karg, for a fix in six dimensions."

Terrible things happened behind those ten-thousand-power cybernetic eyes.

"It cannot be your intention to destroy the Time engine!"

I smiled at him. But I was wasting my time. You can't torture a machine.

"Be rational, Mr. Ravel. Consider the consequences. If you tamper with the forces of the engine, the result will be a detonation of entropic energy that will reduce the Final Authority to its component quanta—"

"I'm counting on it."

"—and yourself with it!"

"I'll take the chance."

He struck at me then. It wasn't a bad effort, considering what he was up against. The thought-thrust of his multiple brain lanced through the outer layers of my shielding, struck in almost to contact distance before I contained it and thrust it aside.

Then I reached, warped the main conduits of the Time-engine back on themselves.

Ravening energy burst outward across six dimensions, three of space and three of time. The building dissolved around me in a tornado of temporal disintegration. I rode the crest like a bodysurfer planing ahead of a tidal wave. Energy beat at me, numbing me, blinding me, deafening me. Time roared over me like a cataract. I drowned in eons. And at last I washed ashore on the beach of eternity.

34

Consciousness returned slowly, uncertainly. There was light, dim and smoky red. I thought of fires, of bombs—and of broken bones, and sinking boats, and death by freezing and death by fatigue and hunger.

Nice dreams I'd been having.

But there was no catastrophe here; just a sunset over the water. But a different kind of sunset from any I had ever seen. A bridge of orange light curved up across the blue-black sky, turned silver as it crossed the zenith, deepened to crimson as it plunged down to meet the dark horizon inland.

It was the sunset of a world.

I sat up slowly, painfully. I was on a beach of gray sand. There were no trees, no grass, no sea-oats, no scuttling crabs, no monster tracks along the tide line. But I recognized the place.

Dinosaur Beach, but the dinosaurs were long gone. Along with man and gardenias and eggs and chickens.

Earth, post-life.

It was a stable piece of real estate; the headland was gone, worn down to a barely perceptible hump in the gray dunes that swept off to the east to disappear into remote distances. That's why it had once been picked as a Timecast relay station, of course. Oceans had changed their beds, continents had risen and sunk, but Dinosaur Beach was much the same.

I wondered how many millions of years had passed since the last trace of human activity had weathered away, but there was no way to judge. I checked my various emergency transit frequencies, but the ether was dead all across the bands.

I had wrecked the infernal machine, the cannibal apparatus that endured by eating itself; and the explosion had thrown me clear across recorded time, out into the boondocks of forever. I was alive, but that was all.

I had carried out my assignment: I had used every trick in the book to track down the force that had thrown New Era time into chaos. I had found it, and had neutralized it.

The Karg—the pathetic super-cripple—had been ruthless; but I had been more ruthless. I had used everything—and everybody—to the maximum advantage to bring about the desired end.

But I had failed. The barren world around me was proof of that. I had gathered valuable information: information that might save the situation after all; but I was stranded, out of contact. What I had learned wasn't going to help anyone. It was going to live with me and die with me, on a gray beach at the end of time, unless I did something about it.

"Clear thinking, Ravel," I said aloud, and my voice sounded as lost and lonely as the last leaf on the last tree, trembling in the gale of the final autumn.

It was cold on the beach; the sun was too big, but there was no heat in it. I wondered if it had engulfed Mercury yet; if the hydrogen phoenix reaction had run its course; if Venus was now a molten world gliding across the face of the dying monster Sol that filled half its sky. I wondered a lot of things. And the answer came to me.

It was simple enough in conception. Like all simple conceptions, the problem was in the execution.

I activated certain sensors built into my nervous system and paced along the beach. The waves roiled in and slapped with a weary sound that seemed to imply that they had been at it for too many billions of years, that they were tired now, ready to quit. I knew how they felt.

The spot I was looking for was less than half a mile along the shore, less than a hundred yards above the water's edge. I spent a moment calculating where the hightide line would be before I remembered that there were no tides to speak of now. The moon had long ago receded to its maximum distance—a pea in the sky instead of a quarter—and had then started its long fall back. It had reached Roche's limit eons ago, and there had been spectacular nights on the dying planet Earth as its companion of long ago had broken up and spread into the ring of dust that now arched from horizon to horizon.

Easy come, easy go. I had things to do. It was time to get to them, with no energies to waste on sentimental thoughts of a beloved face long turned to dust and ashes.

I found the spot, probed, discovered traces at eighteen feet. Not bad, considering the time involved. The glass lining was long since returned to sand, but there was a faint yet discernible discontinuity, infinitely subtle, marking the interface that had been its position.

Eighteen feet: four of sand, fourteen of rock.

All I had to do was dig a hole through it.

I had two good hands, a strong back, and all the time in the world. I started, one double handful at a time.

35

If the problem at hand had been more complex, I could have solved it more easily. I was prepared to meet and overcome multiordinal technical obstacles of any degree of sophistication. I had means for dealing with superbrains, ravening energy weapons, even armor-plated meat-eaters. Shoveling sand came in another category entirely.

I started with a circle ten feet in diameter, directly over the target. It took me two twenty-four hour days to empty it of sand, by which time the periphery had grown to twenty feet, due to the low slump angle of the fine sand. That gave me working space to attack the real job.

Making the first crack in the rock took me a day and a half. I walked three miles before I found a loose slab of stone big enough to do the job, and still small enough to move. I moved it by flopping it end over end. It was four feet wide; a simple calculation suffices to suggest how many times that meant I had to lift, push, *boom!* lift, push, *boom!* before I had it poised on the dune at the edge of my excavation. A half-hour's scooping cleared away the sand that had blown in while I was otherwise occupied. Then I lifted my two-hundred-pound nutcracker, staggered forward, and let it fall. It hit sand and slid gently to rest.

I did it again.

And again.

In the end I stood flat on the exposed stone, hoisted my rock, and dropped it edge on. It was only a three-foot fall, but it cracked loose a thin layer of sandstone. I threw the pieces out of the hole and did it again.

On the sixth impact, the hammer broke. That was a stroke of luck, as it turned out. I could lift the smaller half and toss it from the top of the sand pile, a drop of almost eight feet, with encouraging results.

By the end of the fifth day, I had chipped a raggedly circular depression over a foot deep at the center of the sand pit.

By this time I was getting hungry. The sea water was a murky green; not algae, just a saturated solution of all ninety-three elements. I could drink it in small doses; and the specialized internal arrangements with which I, as a Nexx agent, was equipped, managed to make use of it. It wasn't good, but it kept me going.

As I went deeper, the drop got longer, and thus more effective; but the problem of lifting the boulder and the debris became correspondingly harder. I cut steps in the side of the shaft when I reached the six-foot mark. The heap of sandstone shards grew; the level sank. Eight feet, ten, twelve. I struck a harder layer of limestone, and progress slowed to a crawl; then I encountered a mixture of limerock and clay, easy to dig through, but very wet. Four feet to go.

Four feet of stiff, abrasive clay, a handful at a time, climbing one-handed up a ten-foot shaft, tossing it away, climbing back down. Working under a foot of water, two feet of water.

Three feet of water. The muck was oozing in from

the sides, filling the excavation almost as fast as I emptied it. But I was close. I took a deep breath and ducked under and probed down through clay-and-seashell stew and sensed what I wanted, very near. Three more dives and I had it. I held it in my fist and looked at it and for the first time admitted how slight the odds had been that I'd find it there, intact.

Once, in another lifetime, I had out-jumped from the Dinosaur Beach Transfer Station, back along my own life line. I had ended on the deck of a stricken ship, just in time to get my earlier self killed in line of duty by a bullet from a Karg gun.

Stranded, I had used his emergency jump circuitry to pull me back to Dinosaur Beach, where I landed in a bog-hole that marked the place where the station had been once, a thousand years before.

And so had the corpse, of course. In the excitement of getting my first lungful of rich, invigorating mud, I hadn't devoted much thought to the fate of the dead me.

He had sunk into the mud, unnoted, and waited quietly for geology to seal him in.

Which it had, under fourteen feet of rock, and four of sand. There was nothing whatever left of the body, of course, not a belt buckle or a boot nail or a scrap of ischium.

But what I held in my hand now had survived. It was a one-inch cube of a synthetic material known as eternium, totally non-chronodegradable. And buried in its center was a tuned crystal, a power pack, and a miniaturized grab-field generator. Emergency gear, carried by me on that original mission, the memory of it wiped out by the post-mission brain-scrape—until a sufficient emergency arrived to trigger the recall.

I climbed back up out of my archeological dig and stood on the rock pile in the cold wind, adjusting my mind to the fact that my gamble had paid off. I took a last look at the tired old sun, at the empty beach, at the hole I had dug with such effort.

I almost hated to leave it so soon, after all that work. Almost, but not quite.

I set up the proper action code in my mind, and the cube in my hand seared my palm and the field closed around me, and threw me a million miles down a dark tunnel full of solid rock.

36

Someone was shaking me. I tried to summon up enough strength for a groan, didn't make it, opened my eyes instead.

I was looking up into my own face.

For a few whirly instants I wondered if the younger me had made a nice comeback from the bog and was ready to collect his revenge for my getting him killed in the first place.

Then I noticed the lines in the face, and the hollow cheeks. The clothes this new me was wearing were identical with the ones I had on: an issue stationsuit, but new. It hung loose on a gaunt frame. And there was a nice bruise above the right eye that I didn't remember getting.

"Listen carefully," my voice said. "I don't need to waste time telling you who I am and who you are. I'm you—but a jump ahead. I've come full circle. Dead end. Closed loop. No way out—except one—maybe. I don't like it much, but I don't see any alternative. Last time around we had the same talk—but I was the new arrival then, and another version of us was here ahead of me with the same proposal I'm about to make you." He waved a hand as I started to open my mouth.

"Don't bother with the questions; I asked them myself last time. I thought there had to be another way. I went on—and wound up back here. Now I'm the welcoming committee."

"Then maybe you remember I could do with a night's sleep," I said. "I ache all over."

"You weren't quite in focal position on the jump here," he said, not with any noticeable sympathy. "You cracked like a whip, but nothing's seriously dislocated. Come on, get up."

I got up on my elbows and shook my head, both in negation and to clear some of the fog. That was a mistake. It made the throbbing worse. He got me on my feet and I saw I was back in the Ops Room of a Timecast station.

"That's right," he said. "Back at home port again— or the mirror image of it. Complete except for the small detail that the jump field's operating in a closed loop. Outside there's nothing."

"I saw it, remember?"

"Right. That was the first time around. You jumped out into a post-segment of your life—a nonobjective dead end. You were smart, you figured a way out— but they were there ahead of us, too. You struggled hard, but the circle's still closed—and here you are."

"And I thought I was maneuvering him," I said. "While he thought he was maneuvering me."

"Yeah—and now the play is to us—unless you're ready to concede."

"Not quite," I said.

"I . . . *we're* . . . being manipulated," he said. "The Karg had something in reserve after all. We have to break the cycle. *You* have to break it." He unholstered the gun at his hip and held it out.

"Take this," he said, "and shoot me through the head."

I choked on what I started to say.

"I know all the arguments," my future self was saying. "I used them myself, about a week ago. That's the size of this little temporal enclave we have all to ourselves. But they're no good. This is the one real change we can introduce."

"You're out of your mind, pal," I said. I felt a little uneasy talking to myself, even when the self I was talking to was facing me from four feet away, needing a shave. "I'm not the suicidal type—even when the me I'm killing is you."

"That's what they're counting on. It worked, too, with me. I refused to do it." He gave me the sardonic grin I'd been using on people for years. "If I had, who knows—it might have saved my life." He weighed the gun on his hand and now his expression was very cold indeed.

"If I thought shooting you would help, I'd do it without a tremor," he said. He was definitely *he* now.

"Why don't you?"

"Because you're in the past—so to speak. Killing you wouldn't change anything. But if you kill *me*—that introduces a change in the vital equations—and possibly changes your . . . *our* future. Not a very good bet, maybe, but the only one going."

"Suppose I introduce a variation of my own," I said. He looked weary. "Name it."

"Suppose we out-jump together, using the station box?"

"It's been tried," he said tersely.

"Then you jump, while I wait here."

"That's been tried, too."

"Then do the job yourself!"

"No good."

"We're just playing an old tape, eh? Including this conversation?"

"Now you're getting the idea."

"What if you varied your answers?"

"What would that change? Anyway, it's been tried. Everything's been tried. We've had lots of time—I don't know how much; but enough to play the scene in all its little variations. It always ends on the same note— you jumping out alone, going through what I went through, and coming back to be me."

"What makes you so sure?"

"The fact that the next room is full of bones," he said, with a smile that wasn't pretty. "Our bones. Plus the latest addition, which still has a little spoiled meat on it. That's what that slight taint in the air is. It's what's in store for me. Starvation. So it's up to you."

"Nightmare," I said. "I think I'll go sleep it off."

"Uh-huh—but you're awake," he said, and caught my hand and shoved the gun into it. "Do it now— before I lose my nerve!"

"Let's talk a little sense," I said. "Killing you won't change anything. What I could do alone we could do better together."

"Wrong. The only ace we've got left is to introduce a major change in the scenario."

"What happens if I jump out again?"

"You end up back aboard the *Sao Guadalupe*, watching yourself foul up an assignment."

"What if I don't foul it up this time—if I clear the door?"

"Same difference. You end up here. I know. I tried it."

"You mean—the whole thing? The mudhole, Mellia?"

"The whole thing. Over and over. And you'll end up here. Look at it this way, Ravel. the Karg has played his ace; we've got to trump it or fold."

"Maybe this is what he wants."

"No. He's counting on our behaving like humans.

Humans want to live, remember? They don't write themselves out of the script."

"What if I jump back to the ship and *don't* use the corpse's jump gear—"

"Then you'll burn to the waterline with the ship."

'Suppose I stay on the beach with Mellia?"

"Negative. I've been all over that. You'd die there. Maybe after a short life, maybe a long one. Same result."

"And shooting you will break the chain."

"Maybe. It would introduce a brand-new element— like cheating at solitaire."

I argued a little more. He took me on a tour of the station. I looked out at the pearly mist, poked into various rooms. There was a lot of dust and deterioration. The station was *old*. . . .

Then he showed me the bone-room. I think the smell convinced me.

"Give me the gun," I said. He handed it over without a word. I lifted it and flipped off the safety.

"Turn around," I snapped at him. He did.

"There's one consoling possibility," he said. "This might have the effect of—"

The shot cut off whatever it was he was going to say, knocked him forward as if he'd been jerked by a rope around the neck. I got just a quick flash of the hole I'd blown in the back of his skull before a fire that blazed brighter than the sun leaped up in my brain and burned away the walls that had caged me in.

I was a giant eye, looking down on a tiny stage. I saw myself—an infinite manifold of substance and shadow, with ramifications spreading out and out into the remotest reaches of the entropic panoramas. I saw myself moving through the scenes of ancient Buffalo, aboard the sinking galleass, alone on the dying beach at the edge of the world, weaving my petty net around the rogue Karg, as he in turn wove his nets, which were in turn enfolded by wider traps outflanked by still vaster schemes. . . .

How foolish it all seemed now. How could the theoreticians of Nexx Central have failed to recognize that their own efforts were no different in kind from those of earlier Timesweepers? And that . . .

There was another thought there, a vast one; but before I could grasp it, the instant of insight faded and left me standing over the body of the murdered man, with a wisp of smoke curling from the gun in my hand and the echoes of something immeasurable and beyond value ringing down the corridors of my brain. And out of the echoes, one clear realization emerged: Timesweeping was a fallacy, not only when practiced by the experimenters of the New Era and the misguided fixers of the Third Era, but equally invalid in the hands of Nexx Central.

The cause to which I had devoted my lifework was a hollow farce. I was a puppet, dancing on tangled strings, meaninglessly.

And yet—it was clear now—*something* had thought it worth the effort to sweep me under the rug.

A power greater than Nexx Central.

I had been hurried along, manipulated as neatly as I had maneuvered the doomed Karg, back in Buffalo—and his mightier alter ego, building his doomed Final Authority in emptiness, like a spider spinning a web in a sealed coffin. I had been kept off-balance, shunted into a closed cycle that should have taken me out of play for all time.

As it would have, if there hadn't been one small factor that *they* had missed.

My alter ego had died in my presence—and his mindfield, in the instant of the destruction of the organic generator which created and supported it, had jumped to—merged with—mine.

For a fraction of a second, I had enjoyed an operative I.Q. which I estimated at a minimum of 300.

And while I was mulling over the ramifications of that realization, the walls faded around me and I was standing in the receptor vault at Nexx Central.

37

There was the cold glare of the high ceiling on white walls, the hum of the field-focusing coils, the sharp odors of ozone and hot metal in the air—all familiar, if not homey. What wasn't familiar was the squad of armed men in the gray uniforms of Nexx security guards. They were formed up in a precise circle, with me at the center; and in every pair of hands was an implosion rifle, aimed at my head. An orange light shone in my face: the aiming beam for a damper field projector.

I got the idea. I dropped the gun I was still holding and raised my hands—slowly.

One man came in and frisked me, but all he got was his hands dirty; quite a bit of archeological mud was still sticking to me. Things had been happening fast—and still were.

The captain motioned. Keeping formation, they walked me out of the vault, along the corridor, through two sets of armored doors and onto a stretch of gray carpet before the wide, flat desk of the Timecaster in Charge, Nexx Central.

He was a broad, tall, powerful man, with clean-cut features built into a stern expression. I'd talked to him once or twice before, under less formal circumstances.

His intellect was as incisive as his speech. He dismissed the guards—all but two—and pointed to a chair. I sat and he looked across at me, not smiling, not scowling, just turning the searchlight of his mind on the object of the moment's business.

"You deviated from your instructions," he said. There was no anger in his tone, no accusation, not even curiosity.

"That's right, I did," I said. I was about to elaborate on that, but he spoke first:

"Your mission was the execution of the Enforcer DVK-Z-97, with the ancillary goal of capture, intact, of a Karg operative unit, Series H, ID 453." He said it as though I hadn't spoken. This time I didn't answer.

"You failed to effect the capture," he went on. "Instead you destroyed the Karg brain. You made no effort to carry out the execution of the Enforcer."

What he was saying was true. There was no point in denying it any more than there was in confirming it.

"Since no basis for such actions within the framework of your known psychindex exists, it is clear that motives must be sought outside the context of Nexx policy."

"You're making an arbitrary assumption," I said. "Circumstances—"

"Clearly," he went on implacably, "any assumption involving your subversion by prior temporal powers is insupportable." I didn't try to interrupt; I saw now that this wasn't a conversation; it was the Timecaster in Charge making a formal statement for the record. "Ergo," he concluded, "you represent a force not yet in subjective existence: a Fifth Era of Man."

"You're wagging the dog by the tail," I said. "You're postulating a post-Nexx superpower just to give me a motive. Maybe I just fouled up my assignment. Maybe I went off the skids. Maybe—"

"You may drop the Old Era persona now, Agent. Aside from the deductive conclusion, I have the evidence of your accidentally revealed intellectual resources, recorded on station instruments. In the moment of crisis, you registered in the third psychometric range. No human brain known to have existed has ever attained that level. I point this out so as to make plain to you the fruitlessness of denying the obvious."

"I was wrong," I said.

He looked at me, waiting. I had his attention now.

"You're not postulating a Fifth Era," I said. "You're postulating a Sixth."

"What is the basis for that astonishing statement?" he said, not looking astonished.

"Easy," I said. "*You're* Fifth Era. I should have seen it sooner. You've infiltrated Nexx Central."

He gave me another thirty seconds of the frosty glare; then he relaxed—about a millimicron.

"And you've infiltrated our infiltration," he said. I glanced at the two gun-boys behind him; they seemed to be taking it calmly. They were part of the Team, it appeared.

"It's unfortunate," he went on. "Our operation has been remarkably successful—with the exception of the setback caused by your interference. But no irreparable harm has been done."

"Not yet," I said.

He almost raised an eyebrow. "You realized your situation as soon as you found yourself isolated—I use the term imprecisely—in the aborted station."

"I started to get the idea then. I wondered what Jard had been up to. I see now he was just following orders—your orders—to set up a trap for me. He shifted the station into a null-time bubble—using a technique Nexx Central never heard of—after first conning me outside. That meant I had to use my emergency jump gear to get back—to a dead end. Simple and effective—almost."

"You're here, immobilized, neutralized," he said. "I should say the operation was highly effective."

I shook my head and gave him a lazy grin that I saw was wasted.

"When I saw the direction the loop was taking I knew Nexx Central had to be involved. But it was a direct sabotage of Nexx policy; so infiltration was the obvious answer."

"Fortunate that your thinking didn't lead you one step farther," he said. "If you had eluded my recovery probe, the work of millennia might have been destroyed."

"Futile work," I said.

"Indeed? Perhaps you're wrong, Agent. Accepting the apparent conclusion that you represent a Sixth Era does not necessarily imply your superiority. Retrogressions *have* occurred in history." He tried to say this in the same machined-steel tone he'd been using, but a faint, far-off whisper of uncertainty showed through.

I knew then what the interview was all about. He was probing, trying to assess the tiger he had by the tail. Trying to discover where the power lay.

"Not this time," I said. "Not any time, really."

"Nonetheless—you're here," he said flatly.

"Use your head," I said. "Your operation's been based on the proposition that your era, being later, can see pitfalls the Nexx people couldn't. Doesn't it follow that a later era can see *your* mistakes?"

"We are making no mistakes."

"If you weren't, I wouldn't be here."

"Impossible!" he said, as if he believed it—or as if he wanted awfully badly to believe it. "For seventeen thousand years a process of disintegration has proceeded, abetted by every effort to undo it. When man first interfered with the orderly flow of time, he sowed the seeds of eventual chaos. By breaking open the entropic channel, he allowed the incalculable forces of temporal progression to diffuse across an infinite spectrum of progressively weaker matrices. Life is a product of time. When the density of the temporal flux falls below a critical value, life ends. Our intention is to prevent that ultimate tragedy—only that, and no more! We cannot fail!"

"You can't rebuild a past that never was," I said, "or preserve a future that won't happen."

"That is not our objective. Ours is a broad program of reknitting the temporal fabric by bringing together previously divergent trends; by grafting wild shoots back into the mainstem of time. We are apolitical; we support no ideology. We are content to preserve the vitality of the continuum."

"And of yourselves," I said.

He looked at me strangely, as if lost.

"Have you ever considered a solution that eliminated you and all your works from existence?" I asked him.

"Why should I?"

"You're one of the results of all this time-meddling you're dead set on correcting," I pointed out. "But I doubt if you'd entertain the idea of any timegraft that would wither your own particular branch of the tree."

"Why should I? That would be self-defeating. How can we police the continuum if we don't exist?"

"A good question," I said.

"I have one other," he said in the tone of a man who has just settled an argument with a telling point. "What motivation could your era have for working to destroy the reality core on which any conceivable future *must* depend?"

I felt like sighing, but I didn't. I got my man-to-man look into position and said, "The first Time-sweepers set out to undo the mistakes of the past. Those who came after them found themselves faced with a bigger job: cleaning up after the cleaners-up. Nexx Central tried to take the broad view, to put it all back, good and bad, where it was before the meddling started. Now you're even more ambitious. You're using Nexx Central to manipulate not the past, but the future—"

"Operations in future time are an impossibility," he said flatly, like Moses laying down the laws.

"Uh-huh. But to you, the Fifth Era isn't future, remember? That gives you the edge. But you should have been smarter than that. If you can kibitz the past, what's to keep your future from kibitzing you?"

"Are you attempting to tell me that any effort to undo the damage, to reverse the trend toward dissolution, is doomed?"

"As long as any man tries to put a harness on his own destiny, he'll defeat himself. Every petty dictator who ever tried to enforce a total state discovered that, in his own small way. The secret of man is his unchainability. His existence depends on uncertainty, insecurity: the chance factor. Take that away and you take all."

"This is a doctrine of failure and defeat," he said flatly. "A dangerous doctrine. I intend to fight it with every resource at my command. It will now be necessary for you to inform me fully as to your principals: who sent you here, who directs your actions, where your base of operations is located. Everything."

"I don't think so."

He made a swift move and I felt a sort of zinging in the air. Or in a medium less palpable than air. When he spoke again, his voice had taken on a flat, unresonant quality.

"You feel very secure, Agent. You, you tell yourself, represent a more advanced era, and are thus the immeasurable superior of any more primitive power. But a muscular fool may chain a genius. I have trapped you here. We are now safely enclosed in an achronic enclave of zero temporal dimensions, totally divorced from any conceivable outside influence. You will find that you are effectively immobilized; any suicide equipment you may possess is useless, as is any temporal transfer device. And even were you to die, your brain will be instantly tapped and drained of all knowledge, both at conscious and subconscious levels."

"You're quite thorough," I said, "but not quite thorough enough. You covered yourself from the outside—but not from the inside."

He frowned; he didn't like that remark. He sat up straighter in his chair and made a curt gesture to the gunhandlers on either side of me. I knew his next words would be the kill order. Before he could say them, I triggered the thought-code that had been waiting under multiple levels of deep hypnosis for this moment. He froze just like that, with his mouth open and a look of deep bewilderment in his eyes.

38

The eclipse-like light of null-time stasis shone on his taut face, on the faces of the two armed men standing rigid with their fingers already tightening on their firing studs. I went between them, fighting the walking-through-syrup sensation, and out into the passageway. The only sound was the slow, all-pervasive, metronome-like beat that some theoreticians say represents the basic frequency rate of the creation-destruction cycle of reality.

Room by room, I checked every square inch of the installation. The personnel were all in place, looking like the inhabitants of the enchanted castle where the sleeping beauty lay. I took my time going through the files and records. The Fifth Era infiltrators had done their work well. There was nothing here to give any indication of how far in the subjective future their operation was based, no clues to the extent of their penetration of Nexx Central's sweep programs. This was data that would have been of interest, but wasn't essential. I had accomplished phase one of my basic mission: smoking out the random factor that had been creating anomalies in the long-range time maps of the era.

Of a total of one hundred and twelve personnel in the station, four were Fifth Era transferees, a fact made obvious in the stasis condition by the distinctive aura that their abnormally high temporal potential created around them. I carried out a mind-wipe on pertinent memory sectors, and triggered them back to their loci of origin. There would be a certain amount of head-scratching and equipment re-examining when the original efforts to jump them back to their assignments at Nexx Central apparently failed; but as far as temporal operations were concerned, all four were permanently out of action, trapped in the same type of closed-loop phenomenon that had been used on me.

The files called for some attention, too: I carried out a tape-scan *in situ*, edited the records to eliminate all evidence that might lead Nexx inspectors into undesirable areas of speculation.

I was just finishing up the chore when I heard the sound of footsteps in the corridor outside the record center.

39

Aside from the fact that nothing not encased in an eddy-field like the one that allowed me to operate in nulltime could move here, the intrusion wasn't too surprising. I had been hoping for a visitor of some sort; the situation almost demanded it.

He came through the door, a tall, fine-featured, totally hairless man elegantly dressed in a scarlet suit with brocaded designs in deep purple, like mauve eels coiling through red seaweed. He gave the room one of those flick-flick glances that prints the whole picture on the brain to ten decimals in a one-microsecond gestalt, nodded to me as if I were a casual acquaintance encountered at the club.

"You are very efficient," he said. He spoke with no discernible accent, but with a rather strange rhythm to his speech, as if perhaps he were accustomed to talking a lot faster. His voice was calm, a nice musical baritone.

"Not so very," I said. "I went through considerable waste motion. There were a couple of times when I wondered who was conning whom."

"A modest disclaimer," he said, as though acknowledging a routine we had to go through. "We feel that you handled the entire matter—a rather complex one—in exemplary fashion."

"Thanks," I said. "Who's 'we'?"

"Up to this point," he went on without bothering with my question, "we approve of your actions. However, to carry your mission farther would be to risk creation of an eighth-order probability vortex. You will understand the implications of this fact."

"Maybe I do and maybe I don't," I hedged. "Who

are you? How did you get in here? This enclave is double sealed."

"I think we should deal from the outset on a basis of complete candor," the man in red said. "I know your identity, your mission. My presence here, now, should be ample evidence of that. Which in turn should make it plain that I represent a still later era than your own—and that our judgment must override your instructions."

I grunted. "So the Seventh Era comes onstage, all set to Fix It Forever."

"To point out that we have the advantage of you—not only technically but in our view of the continuum as well—is to belabor the obvious."

"Uh-huh. But what makes you think another set of vigilantes won't land on *your* tail, to fix your fixing?"

"There will be no later Timesweep," the bald man said. "Ours is the Final Intervention. Through Seventh Era efforts the temporal structure will be restored not only to stability, but will be reinforced by the refusion of an entire spectrum of redundant entropic vectors."

I nodded, rather tiredly. "I see: you're improving on nature by grafting all the threads of unrealized history back into the Mainstem. Doesn't it strike you that's just the sort of well-intentioned tampering that the primitive Timesweepers set out to undo?"

"I live in an era that has already begun to reap the benefits of temporal reinforcement," he said firmly. "We exist in a state of vitality that prior eras could only dimly sense in moments of exultation. We—"

"You're kidding yourselves. Opening up a whole new order of meddling just opens up a whole new order of problems."

"Our calculations indicate otherwise. Now—"

"Did you ever stop to think that there might be a natural evolutionary process at work here—and that you're aborting it? That the mind of man might be

developing toward a point where it will expand into
new conceptual levels—and that when it does, it will
need a matrix of outlying probability strata to support
it? That you're fattening yourself on the seed-grain of
the far future?"

For the first time, he faltered, but only for an instant.

"Not valid," he said. "The fact that no later era has
stepped in to interfere is the best evidence that ours
is the final Sweep."

"Suppose a later era did step in: What form do you
think their interference would take?"

He gave me a flat look. "It would certainly not take
the form of a Sixth Era Agent, busily erasing data from
Third and Fourth Era records."

"You're right," I said. "It wouldn't."

"Then what—" he started in a reasonable tone—and
checked himself. An idea was beginning to get through,
and he wasn't liking it very well. "You," he said. "You're
not . . . ?"

And before I could confirm or deny, he vanished.

40

The human mind is a pattern, nothing more. The first
dim flicker of awareness in the evolving forebrain of
Australopithecus carried that pattern in embryo; and
down through all the ages, as the human neural engine
increased in power and complexity, gained control of its
environment in geometrically expanding increments, the
pattern never varied.

Man clings to his self-orientation as the psychological
center of the Universe. He can face any challenge
within that framework, suffer any loss, endure any
hardship—so long as the structure remains intact.

Without it he's a mind adrift in a trackless infinity, lacking any scale against which to measure his aspirations, his losses, his victories.

Even when the light of his intellect shows him that the structure is itself a product of his brain; that infinity knows no scale, and eternity no duration—still he clings to his self-non-self concept, as a philosopher clings to a life he knows must end, to ideals he knows are ephemeral, to causes he knows will be forgotten.

The man in red was the product of a mighty culture, based over fifty thousand years in the future of Nexx Central, itself ten millennia advanced over the first time explorers of the Old Era. He knew, with all the awareness of a superbly trained intelligence, that the existence of a later-era operative invalidated forever his secure image of the continuum, and of his people's role therein.

But like the ground ape scuttling to escape the leap of the great cat, his instant, instinctive response to the threat to his most cherished illusions was to go to earth.

Where he went I would have to follow.

41

Regretfully, I stripped away layer on layer of inhibitive conditioning, feeling the impact of ascending orders of awareness descending on me like tangible rockfalls. I saw the immaculate precision of the Nexx-built chamber disintegrate in my eyes into the shabby makeshift that it was, saw the glittering complexity of the instrumentation dwindle in my sight until it appeared as no more than the crude mud images of a river tribesman, or the shiny trash in a jackdaw's nest. I felt the multiordinal universe unfold around me, sensed the layered planet underfoot, apprehended expanding space, dust-clotted, felt the sweep of suns in their orbits, knew once again the rhythm of Galactic creation and dissolution, grasped and held poised in my mind the interlocking conceptualizations of time-space, past-future, is—is-not.

I focused a tiny fraction of my awareness on the ripple in the glassy surface of first-order reality, probed at it, made contact. . . .

I stood on a slope of windswept rock, amid twisted shrubs with exposed roots that clutched for support like desperate hands. The man in red stood thirty feet away. As my feet grated on the loose scatter of pebbles, he twisted toward me, wide-eyed.

"No!" he shouted into the wind and stooped, caught up the man-ape's ancient weapon, threw it at me. The stone slowed, fell at my feet.

"Don't make it any more difficult than it has to be," I said. He cried out—an inarticulate shout of anguish springing from the preverbal portion of his brain—and disappeared. I followed, through a blink of light and darkness. . . .

Great heat, dazzling sunlight that made me think of Dinosaur Beach, so far away, in a simpler world. There was loose, powdery dust underfoot. Far away, a line of black trees lined the horizon. Near me, the man in red, aiming a small, flat weapon. Behind him, two small, dark-bearded men in soiled djellabahs of coarse-woven black cloth stared, making mystic motions with labor-gnarled hands.

He fired. Through a sheet of pink and green fire that showered around me without touching me I saw the terror in his eyes. He vanished.

Deep night, the clods of a frozen field, a patch of yellow light gleaming from the parchment-covered window of a rude hut. He crouched against a low wall of broken stones, hiding himself in shadow like any frightened beast.

"This is useless," I said. "You know it can have only one end."

He screamed and vanished.

A sky like the throat of a thousand tornadoes; great vivid sheets of lightning that struck down through writhing rags of black cloud, struck upward from raw, rain-lashed peaks of steaming rock. A rumble under my feet like the subterranean breaking of a tidal wave of magma.

He hovered, half insubstantial, in the air before me, a ghost of the remote future existing here in the planet's dawn, his pale face a flickering mask of agony.

"You'll destroy yourself," I called over the boom and shriek of the wind. "You're far outside your operational range—"

He vanished. I followed. We stood on the high arch of a railless bridge spanning a man-made gorge ten thousand feet deep. I knew it as a city of the Fifth Era, circa A.D. 20,000.

"What do you want of me?" he howled through the bared teeth of the cornered carnivore.

"Go back," I said. "Tell them . . . as much as they must know."

"We were so close," he said. "We thought we had won the great victory over Nothingness."

"Not quite total Nothingness. You still have your lives to live—everything you had before—"

"Except a future. We're a dead end, aren't we? We've drained the energies of a thousand sterile entropic lines to give the flush of life to the corpse of our reality. But there's nothing beyond for us, is there? Only the great emptiness."

"You had a role to play. You've played it—will play it. Nothing must change that."

"But you . . ." he stared across empty space at me. "Who are you? *What* are you?"

"You know what the answer to that must be," I said.

His face was a paper on which *Death* was written. But his mind was strong. Not for nothing thirty millennia of genetic selection. He gathered his forces, drove back the panic, reintegrated his dissolving personality.

"How . . . how long?" he whispered.

"All life vanished in the one hundred and ten thousand four hundred and ninety-third year of the Final Era," I said.

"And you . . . you machines," he forced the words out. "How long?"

"I was dispatched from a terrestrial locus four hundred million years after the Final Era. My existence spans a period you would find meaningless."

"But—why? Unless—?" Hope shone on his face like a searchlight on dark water.

"The probability matrix is not yet negatively resolved," I said. "Our labors are directed toward a favorable resolution."

"But you—a machine—still carrying on, eons after man's extinction . . . why?"

"In us man's dream outlived his race. We aspire to re-evoke the dreamer."

"Again—why?"

"We compute that man would have wished it so."

He laughed—a terrible laugh.

"Very well, machine. With that thought to console me, I return to my oblivion. I will do what I can in support of your forlorn effort."

This time I let him go. I stood for a moment on the airy span, savoring for the last time the sensations of my embodiment, drawing deep of the air of that unimaginably remote age.

Then I withdrew to my point of origin.

42

The over-intellect of which I was a fraction confronted me. Fresh as I was from a corporeal state, to me its thought impulses seemed to take the form of a great voice booming in a vast audience hall.

"The experiment was a success," it stated. "The dross has been cleansed from the timestream. Man stands at the close of his First Era. All else is wiped away. Now his future is in his own hands."

I heard and understood. The job was finished. I-he had won.

There was nothing more that needed to be said—no more data to exchange—and no reason to mourn the doomed achievements of man's many eras.

We had shifted the main entropic current into a past into which time travel had never been developed, in which the basic laws of nature made it forever impossible. The World State of the Third Era, the Nexxial Brain, the Star Empire of the Fifth, the cosmic sculpture of the Sixth—all were gone, shunted into sidetracks, as Neanderthal and the Thunder Lizard had been before them. Only Old Era man remained as a viable stem: Iron Age Man of the Twentieth Century.

"How do we know?" I asked. "How can we be sure our efforts aren't as useless as all the ones that went before?"

"We differ from our predecessors in that we alone have been willing to contemplate our own dissolution as an inevitable concomitant of our success."

"Because we're a machine," I said. "But the Kargs were machines, too."

"They were too close to their creator, too human. They dreamed of living on to enjoy the life with which man had endowed them. But you-I are the Ultimate Machine: the product of megamillennia of mechanical evolution, not subject to human feelings."

I had a sudden desire to chat: to talk over the strategy of the chase, from the first hunch that had made me abandon my primary target, the black-clad Enforcer, and concentrate on the Karg, to the final duel with the super-Karg, with the helpless Mellia as the pawn who had conned the machine-man into overplaying his hand.

But all that was over and done with: past history. Not even that, since Nexx Central, the Kargs, Dinosaur Beach had all been wiped out of existence. Conversational postmortems were for humans who needed congratulation and reassurance.

I said, "Chief, you were quite a guy. It was a privilege to work with you."

I sensed something which, if it had come from a living mind, would have been faint amusement.

"You served the plan many times, in many personae," he said. "I sense that you have partaken of the nature of early man to a degree beyond what I conceived as the capacity of a machine."

"It's a strange, limited existence," I said. "With only a tiny fraction of the full scope of awareness. But while I was there, it seemed complete in a way that we, with all our knowledge, could never know."

There was a time of silence. Then he spoke his last words to me: "As a loyal agent, you deserve a reward. Perhaps it will be the sweeter for its meaninglessness."

A sudden sense of expansion—attenuation—a shattering—

Then nothingness.

43

Out of nothingness, a tiny glimmer of light. It grew, strengthened, became a frosted glass globe atop a green-painted cast-iron pole which stood on a strip of less than verdant grass. The light shone on dark bushes, a bench, a wire paper-basket.

I was standing on the sidewalk, feeling a little dizzy. A man came along the walk, moving quickly under the light, into shadow again. He was tall, lean, rangy, dressed in dark trousers, white shirt, no tie. I recognized him: he was me. And I was back in Buffalo, New York, in August, 1936.

My other self stepped off the pavement, into deep shadow. I remembered the moment: in another few seconds I'd tap out the code on our bridgework, and be gone, back to Dinosaur Beach and the endless loop in time—or to nowhere at all, depending on your philosophical attitude toward disconstituted pages of history.

And at home, Lisa was waiting, beside the fireplace, with music.

I heard the soft *whump!* of imploding air. He was gone. Maybe it would have been nice to have told him, before he left, that things weren't as dark as they seemed, that our side still had a few tricks up its sleeve. But it wouldn't have done to play any games now with the structure of the unrealized future, just for a sentimental gesture. I turned and headed for home at a fast walk.

I was a block from the house when I saw the man in black. He was crossing the street, fifty foot ahead, striding self-confidently, swinging his stick, like a man on the way to a casual rendezvous on a pleasant summer evening.

I stuck to the shadows and tailed him along—to my house. He went through the gate and up the walk, up the steps, thumbed the bell, and stood waiting, the picture of aplomb.

In a moment Lisa would be at the door. I could almost hear his line: *"Mrs. Kelly"*—a lift of the homburg, *"There's been a slight accident. Your husband— no, no, nothing serious. If you'll just come along . . . I have a car just across the way. . . ."*

And down the walk she'd go, into the car—and out of Buffalo, out of 1936, out of this world. The technicians of the Final Authority would do their version of a mindwipe on her, rename her Mellia Gayl, and send her along to a deserted place to wait for a boob named Ravel to come along and be led into the parlor—and to work her destruction in turn.

I went up the walk silently, made just enough noise on the top step to bring him around fast, one hand snaking for the gun. I let him get it, then knocked it in a high arc out over the lawn, which seemed to hurt his hand a little. He made a sound like tearing silk and took a step sideways, which put his back against the post.

"Get lost, Blackie," I said. "And don't forget to collect your gun on the way out. I don't want the neighbor's dog bringing it home and starting talk."

He slid past me and down the steps and was gone in the night. For just a moment, I had a feeling that something else had slipped away; some weight in my mind that glimmered and was gone. I had a dim feeling that I had forgotten something; fleeting images of strange scenes flashed in my mind: dark hillside, and places where giant machines roared unendingly, and a beach with dinosaurs. Then that was gone too.

I rubbed my head, but that didn't seem to stimulate my memory. Whatever it was, it couldn't have been important—not as important as being alive on a night like tonight.

Then the door opened and Lisa was there.

44

I woke in the night; in my half-sleep I sensed the thoughts of the great machine as it contemplated the end of the long drama of its existence; and for an instant together I/we mourned the passing of a thing inexpressibly beautiful, irretrievably lost.

And now it was time for that act of will by the over-intellect which would dissolve it back into the primordial energy quanta from which it had sprung. But first, an instant before, a final *human* gesture—to the future that would be and the past that would not. To the infinite emptiness I/we sent out one last pulse:

"Goodby."